The Power of Passionate Love

Shalada gasped as David Medway bent his head and kissed her breasts. "Has no man ever done this, Shalada?" he asked.

"No." She managed to spurt the word out.

"There is nothing to fear." His mouth moved on hers, his lips bruising, his tongue seeking. She heard his deepened, excited breathing as he trailed kisses down her face, her throat, her breasts, and then deliciously beyond. She felt each place where his lips had touched her burning flesh. She was wild with desire. . . .

And desperately, with all her strength and fury, Shalada began to fight before David Medway became the master of her body. For Shalada had sworn she would never allow herself to become an instrument of love. She would never give in—to him or herself. But as David pulled her closer to him, holding her tighter and tighter, she knew she was lost. She was melting in wave after wave of flaming delight. . . .

Woman of Fury

Big Bestsellers from SIGNET

If you wish to order these titles,

please see the coupon in

the back of this book.

Woman of Fury

By
Constance Gluyas

A SIGNET BOOK

NEW AMERICAN LIBRARY

TIMES MIRROR

NAL BOOKS ARE ALSO AVAILABLE AT DISCOUNTS IN BULK
QUANTITY FOR INDUSTRIAL OR SALES-PROMOTIONAL USE.
FOR DETAILS, WRITE TO PREMIUM MARKETING DIVISION,
NEW AMERICAN LIBRARY, INC., 1301 AVENUE OF THE
AMERICAS, NEW YORK, NEW YORK 10019.

SIGNET, SIGNET CLASSICS, MENTOR, PLUME AND MERIDIAN BOOKS
are published by The New American Library, Inc.,
1301 Avenue of the Americas, New York, New York 10019

FIRST SIGNET PRINTING, JUNE, 1978

    1 2 3 4 5 6 7 8 9

PRINTED IN THE UNITED STATES OF AMERICA

For my husband, Don,
my daughter, Diane,
my beautiful mother,
and likewise for Big Jim.
With all my love.

Woman of Fury

Part One

REBECCA

England, 1486

1

The staccato explosions of the huge mound of burning wood accompanied the roar of the fire. The flames, great orange and blue tongues trailed by streamers of sparks, reared so high that they seemed almost to touch the night sky with their fiery caress. Thick choking gusts of yellow smoke billowed out, obliterating the half-slice of moon and effectively strangling the laughter in the throats of the gesticulating people. But although laughter was gone, their faces were bright with smiles as they stared at the woman who was being consumed by the flames.

The young girl who had been pushed to the forefront of the crowd was the only one who was not smiling. Her eyes wild, her long brown hair wildly disheveled, she tried to shrink back. It was no use, the press of the people held her pinned to the spot. A bubbling cry broke from her pale lips, and she flung out her hands as though she was trying to thrust from her the horror of this moment. Her ears were filled with the high, inhuman screaming that issued from the burning woman. A smell filled her nostrils, the sweet heavy smell of roasting flesh. The smoke momentarily parted, showing her the face of the woman on the stone cross. A scream tore from the girl. "Mama, Mama!"

It was her own screaming that finally penetrated Rebecca West's nightmare and brought her back to reality. Sitting upright in the bed, she drew in a deep breath in an effort to calm the mad racing of her heart. The burning woman in the nightmare had been her mother. She put a hand to her trembling mouth. Why should her sleep present her with such a terrible image?

Her trembling gradually subsiding, Rebecca lay down again. Lying on her back on her low, straw-filled pallet, her face and her long brown hair silvered with moonlight, she continued to question the nightmare. She loved her mother dearly, and the vivid and dramatic imagination of which her mother was always complaining would hardly explain the nightmare. Shrugging, still vaguely uneasy, she forced herself to think of other things. There was happiness over her recent betrothal to Matthew Lorne, the witch-finder, but that happiness was mixed with sorrow for her mother, who was still mourning the death of little Mary Baxter. The three-year-old, the child of a neighbor, had been afflicted with the croup. Her mother had been treating Mary with her special infusion of herbs. It was not her mother's fault that the child had died. She had done her best to save her. If only she would not grieve so.

Restlessly Rebecca turned over on her side, the bright moonlight striking a gleam from her soft brown eyes as she did so. A faint breeze, filtering through the paneless window, did little to dispel the hot stuffy atmosphere of the June night. She touched her hand to her bed shift. It was plastered to her body with sweat, and her heavy fall of hair was dank against her neck. A slight smile curled her lips. Soon she would be leaving this three-room cottage where she had been born. As Matthew's wife she would become the mistress of his grand house. The house, set at the top of Briarly Rise, was, in its very grandeur, a source of wonder to all those who had known Matthew before he had become the rich and influential man he was today. Rebecca's smile deepened. But in the meantime, she was content with this tiny slice of a room that was set just below the eaves of the cottage. In the summertime she was compensated for the heat by the twittering and the rustling of the birds who had made their nests in the reed thatching. When it rained, she was lulled to sleep by the dripping of the water from the eaves. And in the wintertime, when the countryside was blanketed with snow, she would lie shivering beneath the quilts that had been woven by her mother's arthritic hands, pleasantly conscious of her privacy and of the white silent world that lay just beyond her window. But her mother did not approve of her sleeping beneath the eaves. She considered it unhealthy.

Rebecca moved restlessly. Nor did her mother approve of Matthew Lorne, or his profession. She loved Matthew, and her mother's dislike of him had always puzzled her. He was a very important man in the village of Waterford. As the only witch-finder for miles around, his power was even greater than that of Sir Richard Benjamin, the squire. In his search for witches, Matthew had traveled to many places, once even going as far as London. He had discovered and consigned to the flames many of these creatures who had wrought such misery with their evil powers. It seemed to her that her mother should be proud that such a great man, a man whose very presence awed most people, loved her daughter and wanted her for his wife. It was upsetting to know that she was so opposed to her pending marriage. Rebecca frowned. Sometimes it had even seemed to her that there was fear mingled with her mother's dislike of Matthew. Matthew, it was true, was known to be a hard and unyielding man when it came to the evils of witchcraft, but that was only one side of his nature. He could be kind and gentle too, and he had always been so with her widowed mother.

Diverted from her thoughts by a familiar creaking sound from below, Rebecca glanced toward her half-open door. Her mother was just settling in her bed. Was she still grieving over the death of the little girl, and the bitter knowledge that the father blamed her for

5

the death of his child? Rebecca shuddered as she recalled Timothy Baxter's red-rimmed eyes and his hate-twisted face. The threats and the violent abuse he had hurled at her mother had frightened her for a while, but gradually her fear had faded. The villagers would not let harm come to her mother, whom they both loved and revered. Margaret West, with her knowledge of herbs and their various healing properties, was always called upon to treat them for their ailments. The truth was that the fault for Mary Baxter's death lay with the parents. They had let too much time slip by before calling her mother to the bedside.

Rebecca turned on her back again. Tomorrow she would remind her mother of her many successful treatments. It would comfort her, and, in time, all would be well again. Closing her eyes, she conjured up Matthew's strong pale face with its square, rather pugnacious chin, his dark green eyes surrounded by thick pale lashes, the sandy hair which he wore in a smooth, immaculate bob that came to just below his ears. Many gentlemen wore their hair much longer, but he scorned this style. Dear Matthew, who had so amazingly fallen in love with an ignorant village girl. Smiling, her fears forgotten, she drifted off to sleep.

Standing before the huge fireplace in the Goose and Grapes Inn, Timothy Baxter fixed his gray eyes, fiery with passion, on his captive audience. "You've all heard my story," he shouted, brandishing his pewter mug of ale. "You've seen my baby girl lying dead on her bed. Margaret West could have saved her. But because she hates me, she let my Mary die. I say death! Death to the witch!"

"Why?" a man's voice shouted. "Why does she hate you?"

Timothy Baxter, his face dripping sweat, his complexion almost purple from the heat in the inn parlor, glared at him truculently. "We've had our differences in the past, and that's all you need to know." He brandished the mug again, and his glare went from face to face. "I saw her lips moving when she bent over my baby, I saw the look on her face, but by then it was too late to stop her. Mary was already dead." His voice cracked, then rose to a bellow. "She put a spell on my Mary, I tell you. She bewitched her to death. Are we going to let a witch live among us? I say burn her!"

In the silence that followed his words, the snap and crackle of the log fire was the only sound in the room. Then, as if pulled by the same string, all eyes turned to the gentleman who was seated at a table by the window.

Matthew Lorne was unruffled by their intense regard. Smiling inwardly, he placed his mug of ale carefully on the table. It was apparent to him that the drunken fools were so carried away by Timothy Baxter's eloquence that they had already forgotten Margaret West's many services to them and their families. Uncertain, frightened, they were looking to him to give them a lead. He nodded to them now, but he did not hasten to speak. The ruby ring on his long slender finger flashed as he touched the laced and pleated front of the fancy doublet he wore beneath a short gown of dark red velvet. With his pale brows drawn together, his eyes fixed on his outstretched legs smoothly encased in dark red hose, he appeared to be gravely considering the matter of Margaret West. It would take only a word from him, and these men, like stronger animals rending a doe, would turn on her.

He sat up straight in his chair. He would give that word, he decided calmly. Margaret West was not awed and flattered by his attentions to her daughter; instead, she had made it plain that she hated and despised him. He could not forgive her for that. Whenever he looked into the old woman's calm blue eyes, he felt that their expression was reminding him of his lowly origin, of the fact that he had climbed to his present position of eminence through the good offices of the squire. He had grown accustomed to the reverence of the villagers, and he wanted no reminders.

A shuffling of feet broke in upon Matthew Lorne's concentrated thought, reminding him that they awaited his decision. He looked up. Without a thought for Rebecca West, who was the only one who mattered to him in his cold, self-imposed solitary life, he spoke. "Death to the witch," he said quietly. The very lack of passion in his voice gave the words a frightening finality.

In the wave of almost hysterical excitement that followed, only one man raised his voice in protest. "Wait!" he shouted. "How do we know for sure that Margaret West is a witch? It seems to me that she ought to be tested."

A babble of angry and jeering voices was directed at the speaker. Matthew Lorne had spoken. It was enough for them. They were stirred by a hot primitive thrill, and they objected strongly to the voice of reason. Most of them there owed Margaret West a debt of gratitude, but they did not stop to think of that. She had become an object, someone on whom they could vent the violence that lies dormant in most men, needing only the right touch to bring it to the surface.

Matthew Lorne considered that he knew human nature, and he watched them with a secret amusement as they milled about. Rising to his feet, he lifted a commanding hand for silence. Obtaining it, he fixed his cold green eyes on the objector. "Listen to me, my friend," he said in his deep, soft voice. "When there is a reasonable question of doubt, a search of the suspected witch's person is most necessary. However, in the case of Margaret West, she is guilty beyond a question." He paused. "I have visited her home, I have studied her carefully. I have seen the black cloud of evil that hovers about her head. I know, from my experience, that she is a witch. What other proof must I offer to you?"

The man addressed could not look away from Matthew Lorne's eyes; their coldness repelled, and yet hypnotized. "It . . . it seems to me that the woman is good," he said in a stifled voice. "If it hadn't been for her, my Meg would have died of the childbed fever. She . . ." He broke off, confused and frightened by the roar that came from the other men.

Again Matthew Lorne called for silence. "Let the man speak," he said. "It is his right."

Wetting his dry lips, the man blurted out desperately, "Master Lorne, Margaret West is the mother of your betrothed. Have you forgotten that?"

"I have not forgotten." Matthew allowed the faintest touch of regret to tinge his voice. "But duty is duty; therefore I must put aside personal feelings. A witch must not be allowed to live."

The man's eyes shifted. How could he hold out against the powerful Matthew Lorne? If worse did not befall him, he and his family would be driven from the village. He thought of his farm, the crops growing and ripening, his children playing their carefree games, his wife singing as she moved between the house and the small stone dairy. It was a good life, and it was against nature to expect him to give it up for the sake of Margaret West. She was only one woman, and he had his family to think of.

"Well?" Matthew Lorne's soft voice prodded.

The man had a fleeting vision of Margaret West, with her familiar black cloak huddled about her frail figure. Her pale, kindly face, seen between the folds of her widow's headdress, was always smiling as she went about the village on her daily round of visiting the sick. Hastily he put the thought of her from him. Ashamed, he muttered, "You are right, Master Lorne, a witch must not be allowed to live."

Matthew Lorne regarded him for a long intent moment. Apart from himself, this man who had raised his futile objection was the only one in the room who was not muddled by drink. The other men, when they sobered, would regret this night's work, but by then it would be too late. "A witch is an offense in God's eyes," he said in a loud, ringing voice. Turning to the door, he beckoned to the others to follow him. "There is no time to waste. Let us get about our work of purification."

A loud cheer arose. Shouting, laughing, jostling each other, the men surged after him. The landlord of the inn watched them go, his eyes sober. Shaking his head, he picked up a rag and began to polish the pewter mugs. Let them get on with it. It was naught to do with him. All the same, it would be the first burning in the village since old Elizabeth Carter. As he remembered the part he had played in that burning, the landlord's eyes misted. God forgive him! He had known, even as they lit the faggots about old Elizabeth's feet, that the woman was not guilty of witchcraft. That knowledge had been a heavy burden on his conscience ever since. And now those fools, led on by Matthew Lorne, were about to assume a similar burden. Sighing, he put the rag down. Why fret himself? There was nothing he could do about it.

2

The rising and falling of voices, the tramping of many feet awakened Rebecca. Startled, she sat up in bed. The room was almost as bright as day, yet outside her window the moon and the clustering stars still patterned the dark sky. The mists of sleep clearing rapidly from her brain, she noted the odd flickering quality of the light that filled the room. Torchlight!

Her heart beating uncomfortably fast, she jumped out of the bed and ran over to the window. Really frightened now, she drew in her breath sharply as she saw the crowd of men who had turned into the lane. Carrying pitch-pine torches, they were headed straight for the cottage. The brightness enabled her to make out the tall form of Matthew Lorne, who was leading them.

"Matthew." Rebecca's long brown hair fell forward as she put her head out of the window. "Matthew, what . . .?" She broke off. Useless. He could not hear above the babble. She paled as voices lifted higher and words began to emerge clearly. "Death to Margaret West. Burn the witch!"

Rebecca drew in her head quickly. "No," she whispered. Those men, they were coming for her mother. They were calling her a witch and were going to burn her. She pressed a trembling hand to her pounding heart. Her Matthew was leading that rabble. It was her nightmare all over again, only this time it was real, and the reality was so much more terrible. Shaking, unable

11

to move from the spot, she stood there for a moment; then, with a wild scream, she rushed over to the door.

"Mama, Mama!" Stumbling down the steep, rickety flight of stairs, she forgot to lift her long nightgown out of the way. A stifled cry escaped her as her foot caught in the hem. Her body lurched outward, and her hands clawed for support. Unable to save herself, she fell heavily, landing with a jarring thump at the foot of the stairs.

"Becky!" Her mother was standing over her, a small wizened figure in a white linen bed shift. "Becky, child, what is happening?" Reaching down, she managed with some effort to drag the dazed girl to her feet. "There are men coming down the lane. They are shouting something. Can you hear what it is?"

Rebecca swayed. Recovering herself, she clutched at the newel post. She could feel warm blood trickling down the side of her face. She must have cut her head when she fell. Men coming, and Matthew leading them. "Witch!" they cried. Had Matthew, from the importance of his position as witch-finder, encouraged them in this madness? No, it was she who was mad. She must think. She put a hand to her throbbing head, and her terrified eyes turned to her mother. Her mother was more than a little deaf, so she would have heard only the roar of voices; she would not be able to distinguish words. Oh, God, save her! Let this not be true, let it be the nightmare again! Fear was beginning to dawn in her mother's eyes, and she wanted to say soothing words that would banish that look, but she could think of nothing. An idea came to her as her eyes fell on the window at the far side of the room. Perhaps if she could get her mother through that window, somehow hide her until tempers began to cool, all might yet be well. The men were drunk; she could tell that from their slurred tones. When they sobered, they would listen to reason. Her mother had always loved them and served them to the best of her ability. They could not really believe that she was a witch. And Matthew, was he drunk? But Matthew, the cool, the calm, would never allow himself to become intoxicated. Her heart twinged painfully. Quickly, unwilling to face the pain, she put the thought of him from her.

"Becky . . ." There was a quaver in Margaret's voice. "What is it, why are you staring at me like that?"

"Don't ask questions." She almost screamed the words. "There is no time. At any moment they will be at the door." She began to push the bewildered woman toward the window. "Go out the window, run. Hide in the woods until I come for you. The sheepherder's hut is empty just now. Go there."

A whimper broke from Margaret's trembling lips. She felt ill and confused and badly frightened. Something was happening that she did not understand. Those tramping, shouting men outside—did they want to hurt her, or perhaps Becky? She swallowed, trying to quiet her racing heart. Suddenly the stubborn courage that had been so much a part of her youthful character flooded through her. If there was danger, she would not run away and hide, leaving her daughter to face it alone. She stopped short, bracing her body to resist Becky's frantic thrusting hands. "No, Becky, stop! I will not run away and leave you here."

"You must. Please, Mama!"

Margaret shook her head. Turning, she looked closely at the girl. Torchlight flickered over her tear-streaked face and lit her terrified eyes. An inkling of the truth came to her then. Men outside her cottage, carrying flaring torches. Men shouting, sounding angry. Dear God, surely it could not be.

"Mama!" Rebecca was sobbing desperately, pleading with her. "There is so little time."

Margaret's hand touched Rebecca's shaking shoulder. So little time, her mind repeated. She thought of harmless Elizabeth Carter. "Lizzie Loon." the villagers had called her. Her only crime had been that she was born half-witted. In her later years, growing increasingly feebleminded, she would shamble about the village street, nodding and smiling and mumbling to herself. It was then that the dread word "witch" had been attached to her.

Margaret shuddered. She herself had been young at the time, but she still remembered vividly Simon Lorne, Matthew's father, pointing a condemning finger at poor Elizabeth. Simon, unlike his son, had not been a person of importance. He had been only a humble farmer, but he carried himself with arrogance, and spoke with an eloquent tongue that the townspeople listened to. So it was that men, carrying flaring torches, had come in the dead of night and taken Elizabeth from her home to the village square. There, after calling the villagers to witness, and without benefit of search or trial, they had burned her to death.

Margaret's shaking hand tightened on Rebecca's shoulder. When the men had come for her, Elizabeth Carter had not understood what was happening. There had been no need to drag her, for she had gone with them trustingly. She had been smiling when they bound her to the stone post. She believed that the men who handled her so roughly were playing some sort of game. Why should her childlike mind think otherwise? She had watched these men grow up. She had given them sweetmeats, and when they were hurt at play, she had often bound up their wounds. Her "childers," as she called them, would not hurt her. So she had called out to them brightly in her old, cracked voice, and her delighted smile did not diminish when they applied the torch to the faggots piled at her feet.

Margaret's hand tightened still more, bringing a faint cry from Rebecca. Yes, she had been young, just married to a man whom she adored, and with the anticipation of a happy married life stretching out before her, but she had never then, or ever, been able to forget Elizabeth's screams of agony when the flames had reached her. Poor feebleminded Elizabeth, who had loved her "childers" and who had believed she was one with them. The sight of the burning woman, the terrible animal sounds that had issued from her straining throat, had laid a cloud over her marriage. It had lived on in her memory, haunting her sleep at night.

Margaret's already pale face went paler still. Releasing Rebecca, she pushed back the lock of thin gray hair that had fallen over her sweating forehead. "Becky!" she breathed. Her head began a palsied shaking. "Becky, why?" Her hands, gnarled with hard work and arthritis, made helpless fluttering motions. "I . . . I have done nothing wrong."

"I know, Mama."

Margaret stared at Rebecca, and the look on the distraught face swept her last lingering doubt away. It was true, then. A little girl lay dead, strangled on her own phlegm, and for this she was to be accused of witchcraft. Her numerous cures were to be ignored, as though they had never been. "Oh, God!" she moaned. Her knees gave way beneath her, and it was only Rebecca's strong arms upholding her that kept her on her feet. "God have mercy upon me!" Her wild eyes turned to her daughter. "I tried to save Mary Baxter. You believe that, don't you, Becky?"

Rebecca's tears were blinding her; she felt as though her heart was breaking. "As if you needed to ask me that!" she cried out. Her eyes went to the door. The men were much nearer now, almost upon them. She had less than a minute to get her mother through the window. But once outside, she could lose herself in the darkness. Few ventured into the woods at night, for they were reputed to be haunted. As for Matthew and his followers, she would plead with them, say anything that came into her mind, and somehow she would manage to hold them off until sufficient time had elapsed.

"Becky, I—"

"No, Mama, don't say anything." Rebecca's voice was curt with the anxiety that drove her. She tugged desperately at Margaret's rigid arm. "Over to the win-

15

dow." She started violently as a thunderous rapping sounded on the door. She began to shake as she once more absorbed the shocking reality of Matthew's betrayal. Her mind cried out desperately, hoping to reach his. Matthew, this woman you hunt is my mother! If you do this thing, how can I ever believe in anything again?

Margaret fell back as the door bulged under the fists attacking it. The wood was old and worm-eaten; it could not withstand such an assault. Her face blanched as the door burst free from its flimsy catch and crashed back against the wall, dislodging a shower of plaster. Then, as Matthew Lorne, with an imperious gesture to the other men to remain where they were, strode into the room, her expression changed. It went as still and as lifeless as a death mask. Part of her, the part that was not consumed with terror, was aware of her daughter, but she could not look at her. She could not bear to see the suffering that would be reflected in her face. Hysteria rose inside her, and she pressed her lips tightly together to suppress it. Her brain, moving in fevered circles, hammered out words. Elizabeth Carter. Simon Lorne. Simon, Elizabeth's downfall. Matthew Lorne, Rebecca's betrothed, is mine. Oh, Becky, my dearest child! How will you be able to face the tragedy this man is about to bring into your life? Can you continue to love him, knowing what he has done, what he will do to many more innocents? Her mouth dry, Margaret stared at Matthew Lorne. She knew now why she had always hated and feared him. From being merely a humble tiller of the soil he had climbed high, so high that he had apparently forgotten the humanity owed to his fellow human beings. From a strange boy he had developed into a monstrous and terrifying man. Her eyes moved, traveling over his pale, haughty face, the cold green eyes, the fleshy sensuous mouth, which was, she knew, so at variance with his true nature. Those eyes of his, even when he had been a boy, had never held warmth. He had never been like the others. Quiet and withdrawn, he had never laughed. All he seemed to want was to be left alone to think his secret thoughts. Sometimes the other lads, not understanding, would attempt to draw him into their circle. He would rebuff them, attacking them with an unchildlike ferocity, driving them from him until once more he stood aloof. Like a tiger, lashing out, snarling, destroying, he had shown himself to be the true spawn of that evil man Simon Lorne.

Shuddering, Margaret looked away. Fate, in the form of the squire, Sir Richard Benjamin, had taken a hand in the forming of Matthew Lorne. Sir Richard, detecting what he believed to be a scholarly bent in the lad, had taken a keen interest in him. First he had taught him to read and write, and then he had turned the undiscipled mind in a new direction. He had set him upon the road to his present important position of witch-finder. When Matthrew returned from London, where Sir Richard had sent him for the purpose of thoroughly learning his profession, the lad had disappeared. Matthew came back to Waterford Village a man. Sir Richard, still interested, took up where he had left off. Now he taught Matthew how to dress with taste, how to talk without betraying his origins, and how to carry himself with the arrogance of one who had been born into the aristocracy. Matthew was an apt and eager pupil, grasping with both hands this unique opportunity to elevate himself. He cut himself off from his own family and concentrated on learning. In an amazingly short space of time one could not tell pupil from teacher. Matthew was ready.

Again the shudder shook Margaret. Soon after Sir Richard's polished creation had emerged, Matthew once more went to London. This time when he returned, he bore the title of witch-finder. It was then that his cold eyes had fallen on Rebecca. As much as he was capable of loving, he seemed to love her. But his love was mingled with impatience for her ignorance. Just as Sir Richard had done with him, he began to teach her. Rebecca, flattered by his attentions responded. Anxious to please him, she began to take more care with her dress. She, who had always been a clever mimic, almost immediately took on Matthew's own cultured tones. But Margaret, though she had tried, could not quite conceal her hatred of the man or her fear for her daughter's welfare. As for this moment that was upon her now, she had somehow known that it would come. It had been a disturbing but unacknowledged feeling deep inside her. Matthew Lorne despised her, she was a reminder of Rebecca's lowly origin, she represented everything he had grown away from, and therefore he wanted her out of his betrothed's life. He intended to climb high, and to take her daughter with him. Margaret's lips moved into a mirthless smile. How he must hate the tender feelings, the passion Rebecca stirred in him. She could imagine how he had fought against falling in love with a village girl. But even love would not deter him now. He had the power to order her death on some trumped-up excuse of witchcraft, and he would do so.

Despite her grim inner knowledge of his purpose, Margaret was swept by a wave of terror when, finally, he spoke. "Margaret West . . ." Matthew Lorne's lean jeweled finger pointed at her; his voice was deep and grave. "I, Matthew Lorne, in my official capacity, do hereby accuse you of wicked and unnatural practices. In contriving the death of the child Mary Baxter, you have exposed yourself as the witch I have long suspected you of being. Therefore, for the evil you have visited upon this innocent community, you will be punished unto death. You will be taken from here and—"

Rebecca's piercing scream cut him off. "No, Matthew, you can't do this thing. If my mother is suspected, there must be a search of her person. There must be a trial. That is the law."

Matthew's cold eyes did not warm as they turned on her. "In this village, my word is law. Because she is your mother, I searched my heart for excuses for her, and, in doing so, I all but failed in my duty to the people, the innocent ones. But no more. Beyond any doubt, this woman is a witch; therefore it is my decision that testing and trial are unnecessary."

"Liar!" Rebecca's strong young arms cradled Margaret, holding her close.

She dared to speak to him so, this humble girl whom he had honored by asking her to be his wife. Matthew's eyes grew yet more glacial. "I tell you that this woman is a witch."

"This woman. How can you refer to her so heartlessly?" Rebecca's trembling arms tightened hurtingly about Margaret. "You have made a mistake. We will prove it."

Prove it. Brave, useless words. Margaret looked at Matthew again. Now his face wore a closed expression, and his lips were folded into a tight, grim line. No appeal would reach him. He would not speak again. He would wait for the annoying commotion of fear and grief to subside before pursuing his chosen course.

"Becky, my darling"—Margaret's voice was low and soft, showing no trace of the fear riding her—"don't you know that it is much too late? Even if you could present Matthew Lorne with proof of my innocence, he would not consider it. He wants me dead, and he will not allow anything to interfere with that." She hesitated, and then brought out her inner thought. "I think I always knew that one day he would come for me."

Rebecca's tear-wet cheek pressed hard to hers. Rebecca, pleading silently, as she had done as a child, for her mother to make the hurt and the ugliness go away. Only this time, Margaret thought, she could not make it go away. She had tried desperately to hold on to her small store of courage, but now she found herself affected by the girl's trembling, the piteous sounds she was making. She could no longer pretend. She was a frightened, weak old woman. Death had stood at her elbow for some time now; therefore she knew that it was not dying that she minded so much. It was the pain that would come. It was the terrible memory of Elizabeth Carter's agonized face, her wild screaming. "Becky," Margaret's voice whimpered. "I am so afraid of the burning. I wish I could die here and now." Her eyes went to the men crowding the doorway. They were silent, waiting, and their faces were flushed with the sick excitement that possessed them.

Still Matthew Lorne spoke no word. He stood tall and straight, his hands planted upon his velvet-clad hips, apparently studying the woman and the girl, yet he did not really see them. His eyes were turned inward upon his own visions, his dreams of glory. He had closed his ears to what they were saying, and to the waiting expectant silence outside that spoke louder than any words. His brain moved, admitting thoughts of the present situation, reminding him that at first he had felt a fleeting pity for the terror that burned in Rebecca's brown eyes. Resolution came. He would not allow it to influence him. His hands moved from his hips, making a gesture that cast out pity. He was proud of that strength of character that enabled him to dismiss all emotions that disturbed him. He was dedicated to one thing only, the holy task of seeking out and destroying witches. He had no wish to hurt Rebecca. He had seen the look in her eyes that told him she looked upon his action as a betrayal.

Frowning, he absently twisted the ring on his finger, and in the bright glow of the torchlight filling the room, the big ruby winked a dark sultry fire. Matthew Lorne was a man who believed he was in complete command of himself, who knew himself thoroughly, but the truth was that he was not given to searching within himself. He rationalized everything in which he wished to believe, just as he was doing now, turning lie into truth. He wanted to believe that the trembling woman before him was guilty. Quickly his mind began to present him with reasons. The woman had not troubled to conceal her hatred of him. And then, too, he had noticed that more and more of late she was reluctant to meet his eyes. She would not, dared not meet his eyes, because she was afraid he would see the evil lurking in their depths.

He twisted the ring again, his brooding, unseeing eyes still fixed on Margaret's wincing face. By saving many from death, she had gained a reputation as a healer. But this had only been a cloak to hide her true intentions. In good time, she would have demanded the souls of those she had cured. Not only demanded, she would have taken them, whether or not it be with their will. Only a witch could possess such a terrible power, and Margaret West's case, brazen and flaunting as it was, needed neither search nor trial to proclaim her witch. Let the evil one go with all speed to her deserved fates. The burning cross awaited its victim.

Matthew blinked, breaking his intense stare. He looked at Rebecca, and for the first time since he had entered the room he saw her clearly. Her brown hair, usually so smooth, was wildly disheveled. Blood, seeping from a cut on her forehead, had left a trail down her white face and had spotted her thin linen bed shift. What if this burning should be remembered in later years, and the evil of Margaret West be held against Rebecca? Would it not be better for him, safer, if he broke off the relationship with Rebecca, if he eschewed all contact with one who bore the name of West? Even as he thought it, his mind closed, rejecting the idea. Recalling her slim young body, her pansy-soft eyes and the silky brown hair falling about her lovely face, he felt a fire burn inside him. She was the only genuine passion in his life. Though he burned in hell for it, he told himself, he would have her love, all of her. No other man should ever possess her. The terror in her big eyes and the trembling of her mouth moved him slightly, but not sufficiently to turn him from his purpose.

Rebecca was watching him, the granite face of this stranger who had said he loved her. She felt her mother's hot, trembling hand upon her shoulder, the pressure trying to restrain her. Her mother feared that the same fate would be hers. But she would not be stopped now. Rebecca fell back a step. "Liar!" she screamed at him, losing her head completely. "You devil!"

"It's you who lie, Becky West," a rough voice shouted from the doorway. "My girl was killed by that woman's witchcraft!"

Rebecca's eyes blazed with defiance as Timothy Baxter, red-faced, venomous in his drunken grief and hatred, thrust his way into the room. The torch wavered in his hand, its flame almost touching the low ceiling. "Damn you for the devil's whelp you are!"

There it was, the first accusation, Matthew Lorne thought. "Devil's whelp," Baxter had called her. Seeing Rebecca's mouth opening to speak, he turned swiftly on the man. "Later, when this is over, you shall answer to me for those words, Baxter. Get out of here! I alone will handle this."

Timothy Baxter was intimidated by the tone; it pierced his drunken belligerence. His previous feeling of comradeship with Matthew Lorne faded. In its glow he had been able to forget for a while that the man, though respected for his profession, was feared and hated as well. There was no man who could claim friendship with him. Some, having had dealings with that cold, driving personality, had given it as their opinion that he was scarcely human. In that moment, wilting before the narrowed green eyes, Baxter could well believe it. He did not look like a man, but more like one's image of Satan.

Impelled by that look, Baxter turned away. All the same, if Master Lorne had any thoughts of letting the old woman go, he and his mates would have something to say about that. He turned his head again, meaning to speak words of defiance, but he found that he could not bring them out. Defeated, despising himself for his cowardice, he directed a last malevolent look at Margaret West and then shuffled back to the door.

Liar, liar! The words whirled in Rebecca's head. How could she have ever believed she loved this terrible and implacable man? No appeal of hers would ever reach Matthew Lorne; he had armored himself against human feeling. He would enjoy watching her mother burn. The sufferings of others pleased and excited him. Thinking of his hands on her, his mouth touching hers, she shuddered. He repelled her. She had never loved him; she knew that now.

Watching her closely, Matthew Lorne guessed at the thoughts passing through Rebecca's mind. Shock had temporarily turned her love to hatred. But she would get over it; he would see to it that she did. When the shock and the grief had passed, when she could be brought to acknowledge that he, despite everything, would always put his duty to God first, then she would turn to him as eagerly as ever. He was not only famed in his profession, he was also wealthy. The things he would buy her would make up for anything she might be suffering now. She was beautiful, intelligent. Without the old woman to drag her down, she could be molded into a charming, gracious woman who was well-fitted to be the wife of the most important man in Waterford. He turned to the door, beckoning with his thin hand. "Take the witch." He issued the order in a loud commanding voice.

Her heart almost bursting with terror, Margaret stumbled blindly toward the girl. Rebecca caught her in her shaking arms. "I won't let them take you, Mama." Her eyes went wide with terror as the two men came toward them. "Don't you dare to touch her!"

Matthew Lorne watched her for a moment. She was fighting desperately with the two men who were attempting to drag her mother away. She looked demented, he thought. Her pale face was flushed to a brilliant color, and the sound of her screaming, a long, chilling, unending sound, pierced his ears. Her eyes were the eyes of a trapped and frantic animal. He went toward her. "Rebecca!" His hands clamped hard on her shoulders. "The death of this evil woman is inevitable, for all must pay for their sins. A witch must not be allowed to live."

"Murderer!" Rebecca struggled free of his hands and swung around to face him. With a sound like a snarl, she launched herself at him.

Matthew's face contorted as her nails tore a long furrow down his cheek. He lifted his hand and pushed her violently from him.

Rebecca stared at the blood dribbling down his face, and she began to laugh. Peals of hysterical laughter shook her slender body, and in the ears of the listening men, the sounds of her laughter was more terrible than her wild screaming. Exhausted, she stopped suddenly. "I hope you rot in hell, Matthew Lorne," she panted. "For what you have done this day, may you never know rest!"

For the first time in years, Matthew Lorne's icy control broke. "Get them both out of here," he shouted. "When you get to the market square, find the girl a place in the front. She is to watch the witch burn!"

Margaret was beyond crying out. As she was lifted from her feet and borne away, only the smallest whimper came from her throat. Before she went through the door, she focused her blurred eyes on her daughter's face, trying to impress each beloved feature firmly on her memory. It was all she had to take with her on this last journey. They were through the door now, and swinging down the lane. She tried to block her ears to the shouting and the laughter. She would not think of the waiting terror. She would think only of Becky. She closed her eyes tightly against the dazzling torchlight, and almost immediately Becky was gone. It was Elizabeth Carter's agonized face that floated on her mental vision. Once again she could hear the old woman's voice crying out words, words that rapidly changed to bubbling screams.

Margaret opened her eyes as they were lowering her to the ground in the market square. She could feel it cool and slightly damp beneath her scrabbling hands. Voices, milling bodies all about her. They were jeering at her and laughing. Looming above her was the blackened stone cross. Somebody began to scream, a high, terrible, frenzied sound that went on and on.

"Shut your mouth, witch!" Margaret shrank back as Timothy Baxter lunged toward her.

She pressed her hand to her mouth and stared up at him. It was she making that terrible sound, for now his hate-twisted mouth was snarling more words at her. "You save that racket for later. You'll have plenty to scream about then."

Rebecca looked down at her mother's sprawled figure. She was so frail, so old, so terribly frightened. Sobbing, she fell to her knees beside her and tried to lift her into her arms. "Mama! Mama, I love you!"

Rebecca's tears falling on her face, her long, soft hair touching her. Margaret stared at her. She saw the shadow of the stone cross striping the frantic tear-streaked face, and a terror greater than any that had gone before gripped her. Her Becky's face, shadowed by the burning cross! Was it an omen that they would burn her child too? Becky must not stay here beside her. Her fear for her would not subside until the shadow left her face. "Go away!" With all her feeble strength she resisted the girl. "I don't want you here." Her voice rose to a scream.

"Get her away from the witch." Matthew Lorne's voice rose above the tumult and the shouting. "Bring her over here."

Margaret watched as two men dragged her struggling, screaming daughter away. Thank God the shadow of the burning cross no longer lay across her face. Shivering with the aftermath of her superstitious terror, she closed her eyes again, shutting out the girl's look of heartbreak. Quite suddenly she felt terribly tired. Perhaps she would die before the flames could touch her. God would not let the innocent suffer. A thought came, driving the temporary comfort of the moment away. Had Becky understood why she had not wanted her near? Had she understood her fear for her? Suddenly certain that she had not, she opened her eyes. "Becky," she cried out frantically. "I love you!"

A clenched fist hit her. Moaning, she fell back, her head striking the base of the cross. Becky, she thought despairingly, can you hear me?

Hands touched her, lifted her to her feet. She did not try to resist them. Through her thin shift she could feel the cold rough stone of the cross pressing into her back. It would not be cold for much longer, she thought dully. Her searching eyes found her daughter's face. It leaped out at her, startlingly white. Through the tears and the terror, she thought she saw a shining response in Becky's eyes. Doubt struck her again.

There was a sudden bustle of movement. Margaret looked down, watching almost indifferently as men began to pile papers and faggots about her feet. The wave of terror that came to her then swept the indifference away. "I am afraid," she whispered, lifting her eyes to the star-studded sky. "I am so very afraid. If You love me, help me to bear the pain. Let me die quickly. I . . ." Her prayers frozen in her throat, she stared at the men moving toward her. "Please, God."

There were four men, each bearing a flaming torch. The flames of the torches loomed large before Margaret's eyes, larger than the world. Hypnotized, she watched them walk to their different positions. One man stood to the front of her; he held his torch high above his head as he waited for the signal. Another stood at her back, the other two men on either side.

"Light the fire."

Caught up in horror, Margaret saw the man at her front stoop down and apply his torch to the papers interspersing the faggots. The other three men did the same.

"So die all witches." Matthew Lorne's voice again.

Somebody began a prayer to guard them against evil. The responses to the prayer, and Rebecca's shrill screaming, rose above the crackling sound of the burning wood. Margaret stared at the ring of sluggish flames, the blood drumming in her ears. "Help me, my God!" she screamed aloud.

The ring of flames, gaining in strength, began to roar as they took firm hold upon the wood, licking in long streamers toward her cringing body. Margaret struggled to break free, her hands writhing against the bonds that held them. A gust of choking yellow smoke poured down her gaping mouth and put an end to her struggling. She was strangling on the smoke.

The flames touched her feet, licked hungrily up her legs, setting the edge of her shift alight. The searing agony was all over her body. Her eyes bulged madly, and a sound that was not human shrilled from her straining throat. Her head fell forward, her bleeding bitten lips opened, and her strangled voice spoke for the last time. "Becky, Becky!"

3

The hands that had been holding Rebecca captive, by order of Matthew Lorne, loosened and fell away. She swayed and her legs gave way beneath her as she sagged to the ground. There seemed to be no strength left in her; she had used it up in her frenzied efforts to break free and gain her mother's side as the flames from the cross died. Her nails dug into her palms as she listened to the callous remarks of the townspeople. A moan broke from her, and fresh hot tears jetted from her eyes. They had dared to call her gentle, harmless mother a witch and burned her frail body. She forced out words from a throat that was raw with screaming, "Christ, in Your mercy . . ." There was more to the prayer, but it eluded her staggering brain. She repeated the four words over and over again until they became only a senseless jangle in her head.

Matthew Lorne looked at Rebecca. Her eyes, surrounded by puffy skin, were staring straight ahead. They held a look of such profound horror that he found himself unwillingly moved. As though feeling his gaze upon her, Rebecca looked at him fully, and the look of horror changed into an expression of implacable hatred.

His softer feeling vanished. Coldly offended, he turned his head away and looked at the charred and smoking remains of the woman on the stone cross. Life had departed from her before the flames took real hold. He had seen her head fall forward when her shift caught fire, and after that there had been no more struggling or screaming. With her dying, the evil spirits that made their home in her body had vanished. The people of Waterford Village need no longer fear her spells. They could pursue their lives in true peace of mind, and they had Matthew Lorne to thank for their release from evil.

He moved uncomfortably, the memory of the hatred in Rebecca's eyes coming between him and the scene before him. Rationalizing as, unknowingly, he always did when he was determined to put an annoyance from his life, he had thoroughly convinced himself that the woman had been a witch. Armed in self-righteousness, he told himself that Rebecca had no right to hate him. Didn't she realize that, in ordering the death of the witch, he had been protecting her? His love and concern had reached out to her, and it would seem that her hatred was to be his reward. For a moment his self-confidence was shaken at this last thought, but almost instantly, as he shrugged the uncomfortable feeling away, it was restored. Later, he would go to her. He would take her in his arms and console her. He would explain that, where his duty to God was concerned, personal emotions must come last. She would understand that he had not really wished to order the woman's death. He was not an evil man, he had simply done his duty. If he and Rebecca were to be happy together, there was one other thing he must make her understand. She must stifle all feeling for the woman she had called her mother. Once she fully understood the wickedness of Margaret West, this should be easy for her to do. Matthew frowned thoughtfully. Yes, she must disown the woman, and without reservation of any kind. He would see to it that Rebecca made a public repudiation of the woman. With the spoken words, any lingering suspicion against Rebecca would gradually die. He nodded his head in satisfaction. It was a good plan.

Rebecca's hot, tear-blinded eyes stared at Matthew

Lorne's velvet-clad back. If only she had a knife she would creep up on him and plunge the blade deeply into his body. Bitterness overwhelmed her. People feared Matthew Lorne, and because of that fear, they would protect him. She looked away. Her mother was dead, and already the people's interest in the burning was waning. Soon attention would be focused on her, the daughter of Margaret West. Someday, she resolved, she would take revenge upon Matthew Lorne.

Get away. The words hammered in Rebecca's brain. She looked swiftly about her, thankful to see that no one was as yet looking her way. On hands and knees, like a wounded animal, she began to crawl away. Her mind and her heart agonized, she did not even notice the pain of the stones that grazed her flesh. A splinter from a dropped stick of wood drove sharply into her hand. Out of habit, she stopped her crawling, and, raising her hand to her lips, she sucked at the tiny puncture. Laughter and jesting remarks came from the milling crowd about the stone cross. Her head turned and she looked at them for a long, hate-filled moment; then, afraid that her departure might be noticed and challenged, she crawled hastily on. When she thought it safe, she rose slowly and painfully to her feet.

Walking past a row of small shops, dark and shuttered below, she saw that the windows above them were bright with candlelight. Women, even children, were leaning from the windows, looking toward the stone cross. Rebecca stopped before the shop of the fish vendor and looked upward. All of these people who were now staring at the charred remains of her mother had known her well and had called themselves her friends. Most of them had cause to thank her. Yet they had watched her die, she thought bitterly, and not one of them had voiced a protest. No one had lifted a hand to aid the woman who, in her own small way, had done so much for them. May God forgive them, for she never would!

A child, his eyes attracted to the silent figure below,

called out in a shrill, excited voice, "Look there at her standing 'neath our window, Ma. Ain't that the witch's daughter? Down there, see. Ain't that Becky West?"

There was a short silence; then the voice of Peggy Lipton, the fish vendor's wife, answered. "It's her, all right." The child started to say something else, but the mother hushed him.

The child was not to be subdued. "If her ma's a witch, don't that mean she's one too?"

"Didn't I tell you to hush, you young limb of Satan!" Mistress Lipton shouted. The sharp sound of a blow was instantly followed by the boy's aggrieved howling. "I never done nothing, Ma," he sobbed. "Why'd you have to go and clout me? All I . . . I said w-was, if her ma's a—"

Mistress Lipton appeared to have recovered her good humor, for she interrupted him in a half-laughing voice. "Asking for it, you are, Billy. If you don't shut that big mouth of yours, Becky West'll likely turn you into a toad. Do it as soon as look at you, she would, and serve you right."

"No, Ma, I don't want to be no toad. You ain't going to let Becky West do nothing to me, are you?"

"Shut up" the woman snapped, losing patience again, "or you'll be getting another clump round the ear. Try me patience good and proper, that you do."

The hinges of the window creaked as the woman pushed it wider and leaned out at a dangerous angle. In the light voice of one inviting another to share in a joke, she called to the girl below, "A real fool is my Billy, ain't he? What with the way he goes on at times, it's enough to drive a body mad, it is that. Thing to do is not to take no notice of him." There was a pause. Then, evidently feeling that she had been less than tactful, she added in a sobered voice, "You all right, are you, lass?"

Hating her, hating all these light and careless people, Becky stared up at the blur of her face without answering. "It's like I told you, lass," the woman resumed,

31

guilt sharpening her voice, "you don't want to go taking Billy seriously. Me neither. We all know you ain't no witch. Him and me was only having a little joke together, that's all. Why we don't for one minute believe . . ." She stopped speaking abruptly. When she spoke again, she sounded angry, almost frightened. "Anyway, Becky West, what you doing standing there staring up? Don't you stand idling about beneath honest folk's windows. Get along with you now!"

The woman's fear had been inspired by Matthew Lorne, who had come quietly up behind Rebecca. The girl did not sense his presence. "A joke!" she shouted at the woman, bitter anger breaking through her stunned grief. "My mother is dead. She was burned to death before your very eyes, and you make jokes. Peggy Lipton, how could you?"

"I'll tell you," Peggy Lipton answered sharply, her wary eyes on Matthew Lorne's still form. "Decent folk don't feel no grief when a witch burns. To put a witch to death is doing the Lord's work, and so I tell you to your face!"

Rebecca shook her head from side to side. Then, pressing her hand over her mouth to stifle the sound of her sobbing, she fled over the uneven cobbles. Once or twice, in her haste to reach the dark shelter of the surrounding woods, she almost fell.

Matthew Lorne stood perfectly still, looking after her. Then he turned his head and looked upward. He spoke no word, and Peggy Lipton could not see his expression, but she found herself suddenly chilled. "Is there . . . is there aught I can do for you, M-Master Lorne?" She faltered.

Matthew Lorne did not answer. Squaring his shoulders, he followed quickly after Rebecca. He lengthened his stride as he went, but he appeared to be making no real attempt to catch up with the girl's fleeing figure.

Shaking, Peggy Lipton drew in her head and slammed the window shut. "That Master Lorne," she said to no one in particular. "He gives me the creeps, he do!"

Rebecca blundered through the woods, her hands held out before her as she tried frantically to feel her way along. Brambles scratched at her face and her arms and tangled in her hair. She gasped as a thorny branch caught in her night shift, ripping the thin material and exposing her breasts. To her inflamed imagination the woods no longer seemed to be a safe hiding place. The trees were closing in on her, holding her prisoner. There is no place where I may hide in safety, she thought, shaken with blind panic. A rising wind caused the branches of the centuries-old trees to creak in loud protest. The sound added to her fear. Now and again the moonlight, managing to make a difficult passage through the tossing screens of foliage, lit a ground that was thickly carpeted with moss, dead branches, toadstools, and clumps of wildflowers clinging tenaciously to life despite the choking litter all about them.

"I must hide," Rebecca muttered feverishly. Her words broke off as she crashed into a tree. For a moment she stood there dazed; then, as the moonlight once more laced through the branches, she blundered on. Again the light abruptly disappeared, plunging her into darkness, leaving her to terror and to the menacing sound of the creaking, swaying trees. The wind had grown chill, and she shivered at the touch of it against her skin. She broke into sobs of fear and frustration as her way was impeded by a tall, unmoving object. She battered at it with frenzied fists. "God help me!" Matthew Lorne's face rose up in her mind. "Don't let him find me yet!"

The unmoving object took on life. Hands settled firmly on her quivering shoulders. A man's voice, soft, attractively accented, cut across her strangled scream. "Why do you run so blindly?" the voice inquired gently. "I saw your face in the moonlight, and it

33

showed me your fear. Tell me, little one, what is it that you fear?"

Rebecca stood very still. Had it not been for his grasp upon her shoulders, she would have fallen. A foreigner, her bruised mind automatically registered. Sometimes, when their great clumsy ships docked, foreign seamen would appear in Waterford. On those occasions, if one could judge by their expressions, their strange, quick speech, and the excited gesturing of their hands, it would appear that they had stumbled upon the village quite by accident. It may have been so, for the village was tucked away in a fold of the Essex hills, remote from the more general route. The quaint charm of Waterford seemed to make an appeal to these men from another land. Instead of departing for a more lively place, they would generally linger on. "Making nuisances of themselves" was the almost unanimous opinion of the disgruntled villagers. In a sense, it was true, for wherever they were, trouble always followed. The placid life was disrupted. Fights would break out between the villagers and the seamen. Tempers would flare to almost uncontrollable heights. For their own self-preservation, the seamen would be forced to travel in pairs.

Rebecca looked up at the man holding her, trying to make out his face. Was this man a seaman? And what was he doing walking alone through the woods? "Let me go." She struggled to break his hold. "Leave me alone."

The hands on her shoulders did not relax their grip. "You must not fear me," the attractive voice assured her. "I mean you no harm, *señorita*."

Señorita? A Spaniard. Of all the foreign seamen that came to Waterford, the Spaniards were the most hated and feared. Hot of temper, arrogant, they were quick to draw their knives for the most trifling offense.The fight went out of Rebecca. Perhaps this man would do the same to her. Let him. She would thank him for it.

"Who are you?" she said in a dull voice. "What are you doing here?"

He did not answer at once. The wind moaned through the trees, sounding strangely like a lament. "Why," he said at last, and he laughed softly, "may I not walk here? Do the woods belong to you?"

"No. I only mean . . ." She broke off, too tired and heartsick to attempt words of explanation.

"I know what you mean." His laughter sounded again. "You ask from natural curiosity, yes?"

He was wrong. There was no curiosity in her, no fear, there was nothing left but her aching grief.

He could not see her face in the gloom, but he seemed to sense that she was crying. His hand touched her wet face, and she could feel the smooth coldness of a ring against her flesh. "You wish to know who I am, *señorita*. I will tell you my name. It is Don Roberto Pérez."

With the agony stabbing with fresh force, she became eager to concentrate. Anything, so that she did not have to think of her mother's tortured, writhing body. Don. Wasn't that some kind of a title? Not a seaman, then, a Spanish nobleman.

"Why do you cry?" Through her fiercely concentrated thought, his voice came to her faintly.

She shook her head, afraid to trust her voice. At that moment the high-sailing moon poured a flood of silver through a break in the trees, and she saw him clearly. He was tall, slender of build. Young, dark-complexioned, handsome. The light showed her his faint smile, the sympathy in his dark eyes. That look broke through her defenses, shattering her self-control. Her immediate reaction was that of a heartbroken child seeking comfort. She swayed closer to him. Her arms clutched him tightly as she sobbed out her story.

Don Roberto's thin ringed hand gently stroked her tumbled hair. Appalled, his mouth tightening, he was shaken by a hot rage against the Matthew Lorne of her story. *Dios!* But these English were barbarians, and

35

Matthew Lorne, whom he had met briefly in the home of Sir Richard Benjamin, was surely the most barbaric of all. Such a man, who could put cold duty before the loved one, was beyond his understanding. He remembered that he had disliked the man on sight. His pale, austere face, his fleshy, sensuous mouth and his cold eyes, had repelled him. Sir Richard, his father's oldest friend, had noted his dislike, and he had laughed ruefully. "You are not the first to dislike Lorne, Roberto," he had said, "nor will you be the last. He is not a likable man."

"Then why have you taken such an interest in him?"

"I was impressed by his keen brain, I suppose," Sir Richard had answered him. "In his own field, Lorne is quite brilliant."

In his own field. Don Roberto shuddered. A witch-finder and murderer! He could swear that Sir Richard knew nothing about tonight's burning. He himself, isolated in the house, would have known nothing had he not decided to leave his sickbed and take a walk through the woods. Sir Richard was the squire; surely Lorne should have consulted with him first.

Rebecca, her body still racked with sobs, felt him shudder. She snuggled closer to him, loath to move from the shelter of the arms that held her so gently and comfortingly.

Her movement banished Lorne from Don Roberto's mind. Against his will, he became aware of the girl's scantily clad body, of the softness of her against him. His blood stirring, he tightened his arms about her. At the small movement she made, like a kitten snuggling closer, a flush of shame stung his cheeks as he realized the direction his thoughts had taken. Remembering the face he had glimpsed in the moonlight, he drew his dark brows together in a thoughtful frowning line. Her features had been so distorted by the tears she had shed that he could gain no conception of her true looks, but her pitifully trembling mouth had been lovely; so had the breasts exposed by the torn shift—

small, yet exquisitely formed. He imagined himself kissing them, and again he felt the prod of shame. It would be easy to take advantage of this tragic girl. She was so torn asunder by her grief, her mind reeling from the horror she had seen, that, he imagined, she scarcely knew what she was doing. She had felt the need of comfort, he had been conveniently there, and she had come into his arms easily and naturally. Yes, it would be easy, but he must not do it. Releasing her abruptly, he stepped back. "Come," he said, his soft voice grown harsh, "let us walk for a while."

Rebecca gave a moan of protest. The comforting arms that had upheld her were gone, and without that warmth and comfort she felt cold and bereft. "No, please!" the unthinking words of protest burst from her lips. "Let us stay here. Hold me just a little longer." She thrust out her hands, touching his shoulders in a blindly seeking movement. "Please!" she said again.

"No." Don Roberto brushed her hands away. "I have said we will walk."

Rebecca stiffened. He sounded angry now, where before his tone had been so gentle, so soothing. She clenched her teeth together to stifle a sob. She did not want him to be angry with her. Anger, hatred, cruelty—there had already been too much of it, and she could not bear more. Anxious to placate him, she said in a breaking voice, "I . . . I know that I am a great b-burden to you, but if you will just h-hold me again for a while, I proimise that I will go away and b-bother you no more."

Don Roberto's heart twinged painfully. She was a child begging for easement, and even knowing this, he was unable to suppress his desire. What manner of man was he? He must talk to her, he thought desperately, he must somehow try to make her understand. Despising himself, he said jerkily, "Listen to me, little one, I cannot hold you again. Unfortunately, I am all too human." He paused; then, driven on by her waiting stillness, he finished in a hard voice, "I am trying to tell you that it might be that I would forget myself."

Forget. Rebecca's tormented brain snatched eagerly at the word. Above all things, she wanted forgetfulness. "I don't want to remember," she babbled feverishly. "Don't you understand that?"

She had no notion of his meaning, he could tell. No doubt she was too stunned to take anything in. Don Roberto moved restlessly. Very well, then, he would put it into plain words. "It is you who do not understand," he said sternly. "I am a man, and I find you desirable. If I hold you again, I will want to make love to you. I am ashamed, but it is so."

Rebecca did not move or take her eyes from his dimly seen face. He wanted to make love to her. She felt a cold sense of shock. Make love. At a time like this! She gripped her trembling hands tightly together. No, it must not be. She would run from him. Hide herself among the trees. She could not let him desecrate the grief she felt.

"I see now that you understand, *señorita*."

Rebecca started as he took a step away. He would go away and leave her here alone. She began to cry quietly. A moment ago she had wanted to run from him, but now his movement had reversed the situation and brought panic in its wake. No man, not even Matthew, had touched her in that way, but rather than be alone with her thoughts, she would do anything, dare anything. What did it matter if he made love to her? Nothing would ever matter again. "Don't leave me," she cried. "Oh, please don't!"

As she stumbled toward him, the moonlight laced through the trees again. Its pale silver light lying directly across her face showed him the frantic pleading in the soft brown eyes. Don Roberto wondered if she really understand what she was saying. Still doubtful, he said in a strained voice, "*Señorita*, believe me when I say that I am very sorry for you, but I think it best if we say *adiós*."

"No!"

"You must not fear. I will see you safely to your home."

Rebecca shrank back. "I can't go back there, not yet. And if you leave me alone, I shall go mad."

Don Roberto drew in a sharp breath. "Are you saying that you want me to make love to you?"

No, her unwilling heart cried, but her dulled voice answered differently. "Yes, that is what I mean." She gripped his arm with tense fingers. "Help me to forget for a little while."

"*Señorita,* are you sure?"

Her hand dropped away. Then, suddenly fearful that he might misunderstand and leave her, she lifted arms that felt as heavy as lead. "If that is what you want," she mumbled.

Don Roberto's eyes sharpened. "I will not take an unwilling woman. It must be what you want too."

Anything. Her brain pounded out words. I will do anything you ask, so long as you do not leave me alone with the darkness and the terror. Aloud she said, "It is what I w-want."

"You are certain?"

What did he want from her? What more must she do or say to hold him to her? "Yes." Her voice came stifled from her throat.

"Do you realize that I do not even know your name, *señorita?*" Don Roberto gave a slightly distracted laugh.

Rebecca's arms dropped slowly to her sides. "My name is . . . is Rebecca."

"Rebecca." His laugh sounded again as he lifted her from her feet and crushed her close. "It is a lovely name."

She did not answer him. With a little sigh she closed her eyes and let her head rest against his chest. This man, this stranger, was to be her lover, she thought bitterly. Words mourned inside her. Forgive me my cowardice, Mama. Try to understand that I cannot, dare not let myself be alone.

Don Roberto's eyes were burning and intense on her still face. She had come to him willingly, he excused himself. He had not forced her. "Rebecca," he said in an uneven voice, "there is a place I have seen in my wanderings. There is a little stream, and the ground beside it is soft and green. It will make a nice resting place, yes, little one?"

Still she said nothing, but the nodding motion of her head answered him.

Don Roberto's arms tightened. He must give her one more chance; it was the decent thing to do under the circumstances. He said reluctantly, "You are quite sure, Rececca?"

Why did he persist, why did he not just take her? Fear of what she was about to do nibbled at her mind, trying to break through. She opened her eyes and looked at him. "Yes," she said, forcing a smile, "I am quite sure, Don Roberto."

He kissed the top of her head. "Then I will take you to this place I mentioned."

Rebecca lay very still in his arms. Now and again, in his haste, he stumbled over the dead branches that littered the ground, but he quickly recovered himself. Don Roberto smiled to himself. He had half thought that the exertion, after his two weeks of enforced rest, might reopen the wound in his side, but he felt not the slightest discomfort. The girl was so light in his arms that it was like carrying a child.

Matthew Lorne let them pass by; then he stepped out of the shadows and stared after them with malevolent eyes. Don Roberto and Rebecca. He drew in a deep unsteady breath. May God curse that tawdry little whore. And he had believed her to be so pure. Pure. She did not know the meaning of the word. He had followed her with the intention of reasoning with her, comforting her; he had been so sure, once she came into his arms, that all would be well between them. He

would have made her understand that he had only
done his duty. He would have shown her Margaret
West as she really was, an evil creature who cast her
spells against the innocent and the helpless. Instead of
finding her grief-stricken and in need of his comfort, he
had found her in the Spaniard's arms. He had heard
her agreeing that he should make love to her.

Matthew lifted a trembling hand and wiped the thick
beads of sweat from his forehead. He had met Don
Roberto Pérez in the home of Sir Richard Benjamin,
where, for the past two weeks, he had been confined to
bed. There had been trouble, Sir Richard told Matthew. While in his native Spain, Don Roberto had been
wounded in a duel with another Spaniard, a Don Sebastián Ramírez, whom he had killed. Fearing retribu-
tion, he had fled from Spain. Arriving in England, he
had bethought himself of his father's friend Sir Richard
Benjamin. His wound, which had not healed well under
the rough ministrations of the sailors on the ship that
had brought him to England, was still troubling him
when, sick and half delirious, he had presented himself
at Waterford Hall and the care of Sir Richard. It would
seem, Matthew thought viciously, that Don Roberto's
recovery had been little short of miraculous if he now
had the energy and desire to spill his seed into that
bitch's hot and willing body. He listened for a moment
to the sound of the Spaniard's retreating footsteps; then
he stepped from behind the tree. He knew where they
were going, he had heard the mention of the stream.
His mouth set in a tight ugly line of hatred, he followed swiftly after them.

Arriving breathless at Miller's Stream, Matthew
heard the low murmur of their voices. Careful to make
no sound, he chose a place of concealment. The moonlight, unimpeded here by trees, flooded the ground with
pale light. It silvered the water and Rebecca's naked
body, which, he had no doubt, was already panting for
her lover. His eyes glittering, his head pounding, he
watched Don Roberto remove his cloak and kneel

down beside the girl. Matthew's nails drove into his palms. As Christ was his witness, he would kill her for this betrayal, he would kill her mind and her heart first, and when she had suffered enough, her body. His first idea had been to step out and confront them, but now a better plan suggested itself. He would not stop them, he would watch and wait until the Spaniard had finished using Rebecca, and then he would follow after him. His fingers touched the leather sheath that held his knife, and he laughed soundlessly. He would have his revenge; first he would deal with the Spaniard, and then with her. She should live only as long as he willed.

Don Roberto smiled at the girl, placing the cloak beneath Rebecca's head. There was a look in his dark eyes that set her heart racing. They seemed to burn into hers, making her feel weak and slightly light-headed. She lay there naked, a stranger bending over her, and yet there was no room in her mind for modesty and embarrassment. There was still only the one driving emotion, the need to forget. She touched his face with a tentative finger as he bent his head over her, kissing first one breast, then the other. His tongue teased around the sensitive area of her nipples, his lips suckled.

Sensation shot through Rebecca; her whole body tingled with it. For a moment she stiffened, trying to resist the sensation, and then she relaxed, her arms reaching out to clasp him closer. Her fingers stroked the dark head resting against her breast. When he drew away from her, she gave a protesting cry, but smiling at her, he stood up.

She watched him through half-closed eyes as he undressed. He took off his coat and his scarlet doublet, flinging the garments carelessly to one side; his white frilled shirt was added to the pile, then his flat-soled buckled shoes of fine soft leather and his tightly fitting scarlet trunk hose. His naked body was slim-waisted, broad-shouldered, and powerful-looking, and there was a down of black hair on his chest. Her eyes traveled lower, and her mouth went dry. With fear knocking at her mind, she rose on her elbows, her expression wild. What was she doing here? Had she completely lost her mind?

Don Roberto stared at her. She was an enigma to him. In Spain, young girls, except for those of a certain type, did not thrust themselves at a man. They either waited for marriage, or, if they took a lover, the affair was conducted with the greatest of secrecy. He could not make up his mind about the trembling girl who lay before him. He had listened to her story, and he pitied her profoundly. Was it her need to forget that made her so bold? Was she virgin or whore? "Rebecca . . ." Once more he came to kneel beside her.

Her eyes flinched from his, going first to the round gold medal hanging from a fine chain that glittered against his swarthy skin, then to the ridged scar at the left side of his waist. His dark brows drew together in an impatient frown, and he touched her shoulder with caressing fingertips. When he spoke again, his voice was soft and questioning. "Rebecca?"

Her head rose and her eyes met his. He had made it plain that he would not force her. But now that she was free to go, the ugly memory of her mother's tortured death came sweeping back. Her ears were filled with the high-pitched agonized screaming. With a little sobbing desperate cry she put out seeking hands and touched his hard-muscled body. "Love me," she said in a thick voice. "Make me forget."

Rebecca jumped as his body settled over hers; then she was still. Her heart began to race as she felt the hard throbbing bulge of him against her slowly parting her thighs. He did not take her at once, as she had expected. His lips burned against hers with a fierce sweet pressure, leaving her half-suffocating. They traveled to her throat, her breasts, down her stomach with fiery shocks of delight that made her writhe and tremble. He was kissing the inside of her thighs, his tongue flicking lightly, going upward again, until his tongue entered her in the most intimate caress of all. With a choked cry she reared beneath him like a frightened animal. She wanted to shout to him to take his lips away, and yet at the same time she wanted the maddening, thrilling sensation to go on forever. She heard her own moaning, her voice begging him. "I w-want . . ." Her voice trailed away, unable to say the words.

His head rose. She saw the film of perspiration on his face, the bright glitter of his eyes; she felt his hands pushing her legs wider apart. He thrust his hard member inside her, and she screamed at the sudden agony.

The girl was a virgin. He stopped his hard thrusting, giving her time to get used to the feel of him inside her. He began kissing her body again, moving his lips slowly. "In a moment there will be no more pain," he whispered softly. "Soon there will be only delight."

The pain had gone, there was only a faint tingling sensation. As she remembered the kisses that made her body flame, her legs wrapped around his back of their own accord. Her fingers twined themselves in his hair, her hot trembling clutch telling him what her lips could not.

She felt the faint understanding nod of his head, and her fingers relaxed. She screamed as the hard thrusting began again, but this time it was a scream of delight as she pulled him farther into her. His strokes became faster; her nails bit into his shoulders as she urged him on with strangled cries, with the tight grip of her legs about him, as her sweat-slippery body moved with him in a violent, savage rhythm. One last explosion, and she felt the warmth of his release mingling with her own. He lay still for a while; then slowly, reluctantly, he withdrew. With his spent body resting heavily against hers, she heard his soft voice with a faint note of laughter in it. "*Querida,* you are so beautiful."

Still living in the dream that had temporarily vanquished nightmare, Rebecca touched his damp hair caressingly. "So tonight the little virgin has become a woman, eh," Don Roberto went on. He hesitated; then with an abrupt movement he raised his head and peered at her intently. "You are not sorry?"

Rebecca could not speak, but her eyes told him that she was not sorry. Don Roberto smiled. "We will meet again," he said. "Many times, I hope. I will not be returning to Spain for some months."

Spain. The pleasant lassitude left her. Pictures flashed into her mind. The stone cross, the burning woman, the twisted mouth that had screamed and screamed. Don Roberto had said that they would meet again, but she felt that his words were idly spoken. He did not mean them, he would leave her here, and she would never see him again. After tonight her neighbors would be unfriendly, fearing that if they showed sympathy, they too would be suspect. One did not befriend the daughter of a witch. She would be alone, her only company her mother's murderer and her searing terrible memories. "Please don't leave me alone tonight," she exclaimed in a choked voice.

Don Roberto sighed. He was very sorry for her, but for her own sake it would be best if she learned to live with the tragedy that had overtaken her. He winced as the wound in his side began to throb, bringing an unpleasant reminder that it was not yet fully healed. "The night is almost over, Rebecca," he said gently. "Soon it will be dawn."

She looked up quickly. The stars had faded; faint gray streaks were lightening the darkness. Soon the gray streaks would widen to project bands of flaming colors. "Stay with me," she begged. "I will take you to my home before it is full light." Her fingers touched his cheek in a brief caress. "I ask only a short time with you. I promise to make you very comfortable."

Pity almost overwhelming him, Don Roberto was certain now that she did not know what she was saying. With a wish to guide and protect her, he said quickly, "No, my little one, you must not dream of doing such a thing. Don't you know that your reputation would be quite ruined?"

She did know, but her need was stronger than her fear of the consequences. "I don't care." She flung her arms about him and clung desperately. "Don't leave me alone, not yet. Give me a few more hours."

"And when the few hours have gone, *señorita,* what then?" He tried to loosen her clinging arms. "Come, now, this will not do, you know."

Feeling his tight grip upon her wrists, Rebecca struggled to retain her hold. "If you are with me," she sobbed, "it will be better. I will be able to face what I must. But at this moment I am so lonely, so frightened. Say you will not leave me!"

Alarmed at the note of hysteria in her voice, he forced her arms down and held tightly to her wrists. "I have injured you enough." He looked earnestly into her tearstained face. "I took advantage of your grief, but I will not add to my crime."

"Please, Don Roberto," Rebecca whimpered, "I need you."

He looked at her for a long moment, and then, unable to bear her tears, he gave in. "Very well, little one, I will go with you, but first I must see my host. I have been ill, you see, and he will be alarmed at my absence. You know that I am staying with Sir Richard Benjamin at Waterford Hall?"

She had not known, but she nodded. "You w-will come back?"

"Yes, have I not said so?" He stroked her hair with gentle fingers. "You will wait here for me, will you not?"

She nodded her head. Smiling at her, Don Roberto drew her into his arms. "I need not go for a few minutes." His soft voice soothing, he began to tell her of his home in Spain, and of some of the traditions by which the Pérez family lived.

Matthew Lorne felt cold and cramped. He had been kneeling too long in one position. He tried to ease himself. Failing, he gave up, determined to remain until they made a movement. He listened intently to the

Spaniard's voice. "Shalada is the name that is always given by the eldest Pérez son to his first-born daughter," he was saying.

"Always?" Rebecca questioned. "You do not find it confusing?"

"This tradition of the naming is kept to my branch of the family alone, so it is not too confusing, you understand."

"I suppose not," Rebecca said uncertainly. "Shalada—it is pretty and unusual."

Don Roberto laughed. "Ah, I see that you are very impressed. It is a name of my family's own devising. All through our history there have been Shaladas. I am the eldest son, so when I marry, if the good God sees fit to give me a daughter, another Shalada will be added."

Matthew Lorne's lips stretched into a mirthless smile. There will be no wife, no daughter for you, my Spanish friend, he thought with cold enjoyment. For you there will be only the darkness.

Rebecca started as Don Roberto pulled away and rose to his feet. "You will come back?"

"I will come back, I promise." His eyes on her face, Don Roberto began to dress himself with fumbling fingers. He cursed softly beneath his breath as a button eluded him. *Dios*, he felt so tired, so ill. "Don't cry anymore, Rebecca," he urged. "You may trust me."

"I . . . I know." Rebecca rubbed impatiently at her brimming eyes. She must stop this senseless clinging to a stranger. Her tragedy was not his, and he owed her nothing. Perhaps it would be best if she told him not to come back. She opened her mouth to speak; then, as he picked up his cloak and swung it about his broad shoulders, her awakening common sense was swamped by her fear. "You will not be long?" she cried out.

That disturbing note was in her voice again, and he hastened to reassure her. "Never fear, the Hall is only a short distance from here. I will be back before you know it. *Adiós* for now, *señorita*." With a last smile, he turned away.

Rebecca watched until his tall cloaked figure was out of sight. Picking up her shift, she rose to her feet and pulled it over her head. Smoothing it about her, she tried, with an unconscious concession to modesty, to knot the torn pieces of the bodice together. The frayed material resisted her attempts. Shrugging, she gave up. She would be back in the cottage before it was light, and as for Don Roberto, he had seen all of her.

A rustle nearby halted her thoughts, causing her to start violently. Looking around apprehensively, she stared toward the dark undergrowth that began just beyond the stream. She listened intently, but the rustle was not repeated. Sighing, her eyes on the water, she tried to drag Don Roberto back into her mind, but he would not come. Instead she saw the hated face of Matthew Lorne, may he be forever accursed! She saw the slight smile on his lips as he watched the agony of the woman he had doomed to death. Now she could hear the crackling of the fire, the hungry roar. The jeers and comments, some laughing, some excited, of the villagers.

Trembling, Rebecca sank to her knees. Somehow she must find a way to drown out the pictures, the voices. As if to complete her anguish, her mother's voice came to her like a wistful loving echo. "Becky, I love you."

Don Roberto was uneasy. Ever since he had left the girl he had had the distinct feeling that he was being trailed. It was not that he had heard or seen anything to arouse suspicion, it was simply a strong impression. It was light enough to see now, and some of his apprehension faded. His wound was troubling him, and his nerves were rubbed raw, causing his imagination to work overtime. There was no other reason to account for this feeling of being followed. All the same, it would not hurt to make sure. He stopped walking and swung around abruptly, his eyes keenly alert. Nothing. He looked toward the trees bordering the narrow path that led upward to Waterford Hall. Again nothing, no one. He half-smiled at his own stupidity. No doubt it was the lingering effect of the fever he had contracted after being wounded in the duel with Don Sebastián. Shrugging impatiently, he walked on for a few more paces. The impression of eyes watching him became stronger than ever, and he stopped and swung around again. It was then that he saw his pursuer. "Lorne!" he shouted furiously, his anger immediately rising. "What do you mean by following me? Come out into the open."

"Certainly." Matthew Lorne's smooth, cold voice answered him. He walked from between the trees and stepped leisurely onto the path. "A very good morning to you, Señor Pérez," he said.

Looking into the pale smiling face, Don Roberto was conscious of a chill. He covered it with his anger. "You were following me, Lorne. Don't try to deny it."

His green eyes narrowing, Matthew Lorne placed his hands on his hips in his customary stance. There was no room for doubt in the great Spanish gentleman's mind, he thought with an inner sneer. Accustomed to command, Don Roberto, with his haughty manner, gave the impression that he was rebuking an insolent servant. He answered in a quiet, faintly amused voice, "Since you are so sure, *señor*, I would not dare to attempt a denial."

His face flushing with outrage, Don Roberto took a step toward him. "Be so good as to tell me why you were following me, witch-finder?"

"A pleasure, *señor*. I have something for you, and I wished to deliver it personally."

"Something for me?" Not even attempting to hide his dislike of the man, Don Roberto drew himself to his full height. "I do not understand."

"You will, *señor*. I promise you." Matthew's hand,

49

which had been resting nonchalantly on his belt, moved, jerked upward.

With a trembling along his nerves, Don Roberto stared with disbelief at the knife the man was holding poised. "I can only assume that you have a distorted sense of humor, Lorne," he said, forcing himself to speak coldly, "or else you have lost your wits." As he spoke the last word, his fingers were already fumbling for the hilt of his own weapon.

Matthew Lorne laughed softly. His arm rose higher. The knife streaked from his hand to bury itself in Don Roberto's throat.

Don Roberto staggered back, his eyes staring wildly. There was a great roaring in his head, but, strangely, he felt no pain. It seemed to him that the brightening sky was falling down to meet the earth, the landscape was tipping crazily, the trees falling inward. He tried to concentrate his already failing sight on Lorne, but the man was only a misty outline. Now everything was moving and swirling about him. Pain struck, a giant finger of blazing, jagged, unbearable agony. He clutched his hands to his throat. *Madre de Dios,* he was choking, dying, the giant finger was ripping his life away! How could he die, with his sins still heavy upon him? Forgive me my sins, his inner voice wailed. He screamed aloud as the pain drove deeper, but the wild despairing sound was only in his head. Choking on a gush of blood, he sagged heavily to his knees.

The perspiration beading Matthew Lorne's forehead ran down his face, spotting his clothes. Despite his enjoyment of the pain he had caused, he winced at the snarling, unintelligible sounds that came from the dying man. Blood frothed from Don Roberto's lips, staining his chin and dyeing his coat, but still he continued his useless struggle to pull the knife from his throat.

With the strength of madness that was born of pain, Don Roberto succeeded in wrenching the knife free. Blood poured from the wound, spewed from his mouth in a bright stream. With a last choked bubbling scream, he fell forward and lay still.

Matthew picked up the knife. He would not have believed it possible that Don Roberto would have had the strength to pull the knife from his throat. He looked at the dead man, then, ruefully, at the blood staining his hands.

Shrugging, he turned away, shutting out the sight. Stooping, he rubbed his hands over the tall, wild grass. Satisfied that they were clean, he next drew a fine linen square from his pocket. Wrapping the handkerchief about the hilt of his weapon, he plunged the blood-dulled blade several times into the soft earth beside the path before restoring it to the leather sheath. Straightening, he looked cautiously about him. Nodding with satisfaction, he stepped off the path and once more lost himself among the trees.

4

Rebecca was sleeping when Matthew Lorne returned to the clearing. She lay on her back, her arms flung wide, the ends of her hair floating upon the water. The orange light of dawn touched her swollen, tearstained face.

Trembling with the force of his hatred, Matthew stood over her, his eyes hard and glittering. In his mind, he began to recite her sins. Knowing full well that her mother was a witch, she had denied it. She had struck him, who was God's instrument. She had run from the holy, cleansing fire. And, finally, like the whore she must always have been, she had given herself to the Spaniard. She was soiled and filthy.

Rebecca stirred, and he got down on his knees and bent over her. When she awakened, his should be the face she should see. His face, with her judgment written upon it. He had believed her to be so pure. Crazy laughter rose up inside him. He clamped his lips tightly together, refusing to release the sound. Just as the Spaniard had done, and doubtless many others before him, he would possess her too. He would take her as often as he pleased, and in any manner he chose. She would know the very depths of degradation. Before he was finished with her, she should know hell. But first, because he was God's instrument, she must cleanse herself of the lust of others. He was in no hurry, he would give her ample time to prepare herself for his coming. Again he was forced to tighten his lips against the laughter. There would be little inclination left in the slut to have others push themselves inside her body; there would be no opportunity. Remembering his vow that no other man should have her, he relaxed his tight lips into a mirthless smile.

The dawn light glittered on the blade of his knife and he turned it this way and that as his thoughts roved on. It was obvious to him now that the blood of Margaret West ran strongly in Rebecca's veins. He had been blinded by love, and so he had not sensed the evil in her before. He struck the hilt of the knife sharply against the palm of his hand. He stared at Rebecca's bare breasts, and an impulse came to him to put his lips over those jutting nipples. With a great effort, he crushed the impulse. First she must be purified; in the meantime he would keep her locked in her cottage.

Rebecca's brows drew together uneasily as a small bug ran over her hand, but she did not open her eyes. He would supply the girl with the food needed to keep her alive; she would talk to no one, she would see no one but him, her jailer. He knew well that he had no need to fear the curiosity of the villagers. If they crossed him, they would be afraid that he might look too closely into the hidden part of their lives. Once they knew that Rebecca was his prisoner, they would not dare go near her. Fear was a wonderful thing; it pleased him to know that the villagers were afraid of him.

He frowned thoughtfully. He was uncertain of the length of time he would wish to keep the whore alive. He would ponder on that later. In the meanwhile, he would tell any who had the courage to inquire that he suspected her of witchcraft. That he needed time to observe her well before making his final judgment on her case.

He turned the knife over in his hand again, his breath quickening as he recalled the agonized look on Don Roberto's face. That arrogant fool! Even with the blade buried in his throat, he had still believed that he could save himself.

Rebecca moaned in her sleep. A quiver of nerves ran through her body, causing her to jump violently, but she did not awaken. He relaxed as her sleep-flushed face turned his way. She muttered something beneath her breath, and he stared at her with hot eyes. He would awaken her when he was ready, but for the moment he wanted to go on looking at her. Her slightly parted lips moved again, murmuring incomprehensible words. One hand came up to rest against her breast. Looking at her twitching fingers, which, to his mind, gave the appearance of fondling, he wondered if she were dreaming of her lover.

He sat back on his heels, his eyes narrowing, but never once leaving her. He could imagine her shocked reaction when she awakened to find him bending over her. But she would suffer more than shock once he had her safely locked away in her cottage. From that moment her mental torment would begin. She would never know when he intended to strike; that was the subtlety of his plan. Always hanging over her head would be the menace of that fiery death to which he would eventually consign her. Every day, with the terror gripping her, she would die a little. He would not even allow her the dignity of clothes. His face burned with the excitement produced by the thought of her naked form crawling to him on hands and knees. Rebecca's legs moved apart, and again Matthew had the impression that she was waiting for her lover to settle himself between her thighs. Tempted to accommodate her, he leaned over her, his breathing labored.

It was that labored rasping sound that finally penetrated through the veil of exhausted sleep. Rebecca's heavy lids lifted slowly, almost reluctantly, as though she fought the return to full, painful consciousness. Her eyes stared into his. "M-Matthew."

Smiling, he watched the blankness of sleep fade quickly to give way to terror. "Matthew!" She looked at the knife in his hand, and her body stiffened as she braced her muscles in preparation to spring up and run from him.

His smile faded. Run from him? No, never again! "You are going nowhere," he said, placing a restraining hand on her. "You will not move until I say you may."

Trembling, she stared down at the thin freckled hand that held her captive. "Let me get up." She said the words in a little rush, hoping to hide her fear.

His eyes dropping to her quivering breasts, he slowly shook his head. The blood drummed in his ears as he stared, fascinated. Her nipples had been prominent before, the aftermath of the Spaniard's touch, he had thought. But now, with the fear riding her, they appeared to him to be swollen to twice their size. His mouth dry with desire, his hands shaking, he tried to drag his eyes away, but he could not.

"Matthew, what—?"

He silenced her with an angry wave of his hand. His lips moving, he began to pray quietly and fervently: "O blessed Lord, put Your cleansing touch upon this woman." His prayer broke off as his mind presented him with a vivid picture of Rebecca's body beneath the Spaniard's. Her legs flung wide, her breath panting as she thrust and strained with the man to reach the peak of fulfillment. Matthew's face flushed with angry color as he thought of the Spaniard kissing her, his body atop hers. His lips tightened. He too would enter her. She would not remember the Spaniard then, for he would thrust higher than he had done, he would ride her longer. He was more of a man than that cursed foreigner could ever be. He would fondle her breasts, kiss them, as he had longed to do, and then he would . . . His thoughts broke off as he remembered his purpose. The prayer—he must finish it. Hastily he resumed: "Dear Lord, forgive me for my sinful thoughts. But the fault is not mine, for the woman has bewitched me. Even though it shames me in Your sight, I must

confess to the same weakness as that of lesser men."
The hand on Rebecca's body clenched into a tight fist.
"I have this terrible burning need for her.".

Rebecca stared at him in horror. It was obvious to
her that he believed he spoke directly to God, and that
his prayer, whatever might be its nature, had been answered and approved of by Him. Suddenly, as though
the strength had gone out of him, he fell against her.
Gasping, he lowered his head, and she felt his lips on
her flesh. It was not until he moved, his mouth blindly
seeking her breasts, that she came back to life. "Don't!"
she screamed. With a violent movement she pushed his
head away. "Don't ever touch me again!"

He straightened up, glaring at her. "You dare to say
that to me, you whore!"

She did not answer him. In a pathetic attempt at
defiance her hands fluttered upward, her fingers
spreading themselves over her breasts as she tried to
cover herself from his gaze.

His mouth shook uncontrollably for a moment. Re-
gaining mastery over himself, he struck her hands
away. "You did not cover yourself from the Spaniard"
he shouted, "and you will not cover yourself from me."
His anger mounting, he touched the tip of the knife to
her shrinking flesh. "Dear Rebecca, if you could only
see your white and frightened little face." His hand
moved. "Why, I can feel the pounding of your heart. I
have the feeling that it will soon burst through your
flesh. Tell me why you are so frightened, Rebecca." He
began to laugh, a low, soft, almost tittering sound that
added to her terror. "Come, love, have you nothing to
say to your betrothed?"

Suspicion grew into certainty. He was going to kill
her. She gave up thinking that Don Roberto would return; he would have been back long since.

"No, Rebecca, Don Roberto will not be returning,
so you must not count on him to rescue you." His terrifying laughter sounded again. "He is not, I fear, in a
position to rescue anyone." With brutal force he

slapped her across her wide-open screaming mouth. "What else did you expect, you vile bitch?" he shouted. His blow had split her lip. Slowly, painfully, the hysterical sobs shaking her, she touched the warm trickle of her blood. As she stared at her smeared fingers, her body suddenly convulsed. Retching, she spat the taste of blood from her mouth.

"Stand up straight," he screamed as she sagged beneath his loosened grasp. "You will not have to stand for long," he snarled. "Soon you will be lying down, in the position you favor, with your thighs stretched wide to receive your lover."

She stared at him. His own words had visibly affected him. He had begun to tremble again, and instinctively she knew that the sexual frenzy afflicting him sprang from his madness. He spun her about, slamming her roughly against the tree. "If your legs won't support you, harlot, you can hold onto the trunk."

"Don't hurt me, Matthew, please don't!"

"Hold on!" he roared.

Useless to appeal to him. Useless to run. She had not the strength. Fighting nausea and terror, she put her quivering arms about the slender trunk. The rough bark grazed her soft skin as she laced her fingers tightly together. Matthew laughed harshly. "That's much better. Obedience is perhaps the only virtue you have, eh, trollop?"

Rebecca tensed as he moved up behind her. Now he was standing so close that the hot gust of his breath fanned her face. His body began to jerk spasmodically against her own in those sickening movements that mimed the taking of a woman. His fingers quivered against her neck for a moment, then moved higher to grasp a hank of her hair. She bit back a cry as he tugged, forcing her head back. From the corner of her eyes she caught the glint of the knife blade, and then she knew what he was about to do. The sharp blade snagged in her hair, then it began to slice.

Unbelievingly she watched the thick strands of hair

falling about her feet. Her body sagged to the ground, and her mouth opened in a wild, wailing cry.

"You were always so vain about your hair, Rebecca," he panted. "Forever brushing and oiling and braiding it. Vanity, you know, is a sin in God's eyes."

Rebecca lay where he had let her fall for a moment, then she rose shakily to her feet. Bowing her roughly shorn head, she stared fixedly at the mossy ground. She was so afraid. So terribly tired that she could not seem to think properly.

"Witch!" He spat the word in her face. "May you be forever damned, you handmaiden of Satan!"

There was a choking sensation in her throat. She put a hand to it, trying to ease the pressure, her fingers digging painfully into her flesh. The fire! It was coming nearer. She could not breathe for the smoke. She was burning up. Witch! Witch! The words screamed in her head. She turned quickly, her eyes searching wildly, and then she saw it, the stone cross. It loomed high above her head. Mama! She plunged into the flames, trying to reach the figure bound to the cross. The flames were winning, they were beating her back. There was a searing pain in her head, and she knew that her hair had caught fire. She put her hands to her head, and she heard someone laughing and laughing.

Matthew watched her with amusement. She was so weak that she had difficulty in standing, let alone trying to get away from him. He laughed aloud, a high-pitched triumphant sound as she stumbled, almost falling.

"Murderer!"

His laughter died. She should pay dearly for that insult. He watched her with narrowed eyes. Her lips were moving again. But they were forming words without sound. Was it witchcraft? Had God punished her by striking her dumb? The flicker of fear left him as he became convinced it was the latter. He should never have doubted for a second, he thought with wild elation. He should have had faith. God would never allow

His chosen to be reviled and insulted. He felt humbled before the power of God, for certainly the Almighty was with him. His glory surrounded him, approving, guiding.

Rebecca put her hand to her uselessly working throat. Her voice! Why couldn't she hear the words her tongue formed, why couldn't she speak? Terrified, she stood still.

Matthew took a step toward her, then stopped again. His eyes dropped lower, and he was consumed by the burning heat of his desire. Crying out her name, he started forward.

Was she awake, or still dreaming? Uncertain, she looked at the agony in his face. She smiled at him compassionately. Perhaps he was ill. Little rivulets of sweat were running down his heavily flushed face, and he was trembling so violently that she was afraid he might fall. She put out a hand to aid him; then, seeing his start, she let it fall back to her side. When he reached out and ripped the shift roughly from her body, she made no protest, nor any effort to cover herself. It was a dream, after all. In that dream, the breeze swept over her hot flesh with a cool, caressing touch.

Matthew threw the torn shift from him. He wanted her to be afraid. He had preferred her that way. She was unreal to him at that moment, almost like someone that moved through a dream. Even her serene smile had a dreamlike quality. His light brows drew together uneasily. What had caused this abrupt change in her? Only moments before she had been screaming at him hysterically, calling him "murderer." Yet now, her smile seemed to be luring him on. Was she calling on the powers of witchcraft to aid her? For a moment he faltered; then his courage came rushing back. Whatever she planned, it would avail her nothing.

The pale early-morning sunlight filtered through the leaves of the tree, throwing a dappled shifting pattern over Rebecca's body. Matthew tensed as he felt the burning throbbing ache of his desire intensify. Striving for control, he passed his tongue over his dry lips. He stared at her slender waist, the graceful curving of her hips, the faint dark mysterious shadowing that shielded the place where the Spaniard had entered. Lastly, his eyes rose to her golden-skinned breasts. They seemed to him, with their thrusting dusky-pink nipples, to pulse with invitation.

Quite suddenly Rebecca became convinced that she was awake, and she flushed for her nakedness. She looked at the man. He must be her husband. If he were not, her modesty would be outraged, and certainly she could not stand so easily before him. Her brow wrinkled. But why couldn't she remember his name? Should she ask him what it was? She opened her mouth to speak, then closed it quickly. No, he would think her stupid. There was no need to worry. Obviously she had been sleeping, and, once the dullness cleared from her brain, her memory would return. She shivered, taking a step toward him. The breeze was no longer pleasant; she was feeling chilled inside and outside.

Watching his frenzied movements as he pulled off his clothes, Rebecca was disturbed. Also there was another thing puzzling her. When he had turned away, he had looked very angry. But why should he be angry? Had she, without realizing it, done something that displeased him? He came to stand before her, and the feeling vanished as her eyes appraised him. Without his clothes, he looked taller than ever, and almost painfully thin. His fair skin was blotched with freckles, and the hair on his body was sparse and sandy in color. He was not like . . . A memory came to her of a swarthy-skinned handsome face and a lean muscular body, of dark hair that fell curling over a broad forehead, and dark intense eyes that had seemed to burn into hers. No, this sandy-haired man was not like . . . She shook her head despairingly as she groped after the rapidly fading memory, and tears of frustration came into her eyes. She must remember. It was important.

Matthew pulled her to him. His hands grasped her

buttocks, pressing her so tightly against him that Rebecca had the feeling that he was trying to make them one body. She heard his gasping breathing, and she was frightened and struggled frantically.

Matthew gripped her tighter. Her struggling, the friction of her moving body against him, excited him to such a degree that he almost forgot the duty he owed to God. He held her a moment longer, feeling her flesh sear against his, fighting the temptation to throw her to the ground and plunge into her; then, with a groan, he pushed her from him. Falling to his knees, he bowed his head over his clasped hands.

Rebecca looked down at him. Her flesh tingled from his touch. She wished she could run away and hide from him. But that would be wrong, just as it was wrong to fear him. Obviously he was a good and devout man. Most people only prayed in church, or when they thought they were unobserved. They did not kneel beneath the blue sky, unashamed, as this man did.

Rebecca looked toward the faintly sun-sparked water of the little stream. Putting a hand to her head, she thought of the thick mists that sometimes came curling in from the sea, wreathing the hills and blanketing the countryside. Her brain felt like that, as though it was wrapped about by that ghostly sea mist. And her head. It felt so light that she had the feeling that at any moment it would fly from her body. Imagining her head floating in the air; she laughed softly. Despite the odd uneasy feelings that had assailed her a few moments before, she felt strangely carefree. And yet, she knew, she had been deeply troubled. She did not remember why, nor did she want to.

She started as the man's voice rose, then died again. Looking at him, she had the feeling that her previous troubled state had something to do with him. She clenched her hands together, willing the thought to go away. He would not harm her. Surely only good men knelt and prayed so humbly to God. Such a man would be kind. She drew in her breath sharply as, unbidden, a word jumped into her mind. "Hypocrite." Someone, at some time, had made such an accusation against this man. She rubbed her forehead. She could not remember who had called him so.

Rebecca heard the moaning sounds he made. She looked at him in dismay, wondering what she could do to help him. Poor man. He must be in great pain. A vague uneasy memory prodded at her mind, bringing with it a flashing recollection of a marriage that had been arranged between this man and herself. Again she could not hold on to it, but she felt that it must be true. The marriage must have taken place, for here they were in this quiet, secluded place, both of them naked. She put a clenched hand to her forehead. Stupid not to be able to remember. She looked down at him again and felt a shrinking all through her at the thought of touching him. But she must, she told herself sternly. He was her husband, and it was her duty to comfort him. Reluctantly she got down on her knees. "*Tell me what troubles you,*" she said, touching him timidly. "*Are you ill?*" She waited for him to answer, to move, but except for the jumping of his muscles beneath her hand, he was very still.

Matthew's hands dropped heavily. Fascinated, he watched her silently moving lips. So God had not yet thought fit to remove His seal. Perhaps He never would. It might be that He intended her to remain dumb until Matthew, His servant, consigned her to the flames. With a great surge of triumph, he looked up again. Her lips were moving again. Did she really believe that she spoke to him, was she totally unaware of the silence?

"*What is it,*" Rebecca said, "*why do you look at me so strangely?*"

With a desire to make her aware, he began to shout at her. "You fool! Why do you continue to try to make yourself heard? You are dumb, do you hear, dumb! God has set His seal upon your evil mouth."

Feeling a glimmer of the terror awakening, Rebecca

put her hands to her mouth. It was true, she was not able to speak, for no sound had emerged. The words were only in her head.

Now that he was no longer touching her, Rebecca's eyes looked back at him in total blankness. Staring at her, Matthew felt chilled. He was suddenly certain that the muscles of her face had frozen, and that the soul behind her eyes had fled. Only the tears that continued to roll down her cheeks gave any sign of life.

The few shreds of elusive memory that she had been trying to gather together and hold onto receded. There was nothing left but the pain, and the knowledge that she had no defense against this man. He would kill her if she did not answer him. He was mad. He was asking her if she could hear him; she could see the madness looking from his eyes. In desperation, she nodded, her lips forming a *yes*.

Rebecca forced herself to lie still as he caressed her breasts and pinched gently at her nipples. Useless to fight him; she had not sufficient strength. Let him do with her as he willed, and please God, it would soon be over. She stiffened as his finger entered her body, moving cunningly, conquering her pain and fear and bewilderment as it sent sensation coursing through her. Hating him, despising herself, she found herself helpless to control the instinctive arching of her traitorous body beneath his.

At this slight and unlooked-for pressure, Matthew lost all control. A violent shivering afflicted him as he collapsed against her. His tongue licked at her flesh. "Whore!" he shouted. Grabbing her breasts with rough hands, he kissed them savagely.

Her faint response vanished as he squeezed her breasts with cruel fingers. His sweating face, his slobbering kisses, the suction of his lips filled her with a sick revulsion. With a surge of strength she tried to push him away.

Matthew looked up. For a moment he stared at her blindly, almost as though he had forgotten who she was. Then, as she moved, recognition seemed to come back. Even while his face twisted with hatred, the hot desire glittered from his eyes. Vile words spilled from his loose mouth; his hands did things to her that made her wish passionately for death. Writhing in shame and agony, she screamed soundlessly.

Rebecca lay there. Even when he grasped her legs and jerked her upward, plunging deeper inside her, she still made no attempt to fight him. Resistance was useless. With her lips pressed tightly together, she listened to the grunting animal sounds he made and endured the painful battering of his furiously moving body.

As suddenly as it had begun, it was over. "Rebecca!" The change in him was sudden and almost ludicrous. Still on his knees, he looked at her with tear-filled eyes. "Rebecca!" Heaving with sobs, he fell against her. Like a child in need of comfort, his mouth sought her breast again. "Why," he kept demanding brokenly, "why did you turn whore, Rebecca? I trusted you, honored you. I thought you were so pure."

Rebecca watched him as he dressed himself. When he had finished clothing himself, she hoped he would go away and leave her there.

Fully clothed, Matthew returned to stand over her. "Get up," he said harshly. Seeing that she simply stared at him, without attempting to move, he stooped over her. The fingers of one hand hooked in her short hair, the other hand grasped her arm and dragged her upright.

Swaying before him, Rebecca did not see him draw his knife from the sheath. Her attention was on the stained and crumpled material of her shift, which lay a little distance away. She remembered him tearing it from her body and flinging it to one side. It would probably be of little use to her now, but at least it would serve to hide her partially from his eyes. Perhaps she could hold the two front pieces together. Without looking at him, she started forward. The prick of the knife in her back halted her.

Turning her head, she gestured with her hand toward the shift.

"You want to dress yourself. Is that what you are trying to tell me?" Matthew smiled as she nodded her head, a smile that did not reach his eyes. "But I can't allow that. The badge of a whore's trade is her body. You will walk naked before the people, so that they, too will know you for exactly what you are."

Tears that she could not seem to control leaked from her eyes as she felt the prick of the knife in her back again. Bowing her head, she stumbled before him. As she made her difficult passage through the woods, she heard his laughter.

Small groups of people had congregated together to stare at the unusual sight of the naked girl being driven along at the point of a knife before the witch-finder. Others leaned from their windows. Questions were in every mind. Rebecca West was his betrothed. Yet he drove her along like one who herded a wild beast to market. They stared at Rebecca's cropped hair, the blood on her chin, the bruises on her breasts, and the earth stains on her body. Eyes narrowed knowingly as they took in the crumpled condition of Matthew Lorne's usually impeccable clothing. But not one of them allowed the lewd thought to develop, lest it touch on the witch-finder's mind, and he find them guilty of sacrilege. It was said that he could see into one's mind. That he could pick up thoughts, and, even worse, had been known to punish an offender mercilessly.

They fell back as the two came on, forming a lane that allowed them to pass. The sight of Rebecca reminded most of them there of the case of Mary Frazer. The girl had been caught in a carnal act with the son of her employer. The young man, Giles Lawrence, had pleaded extraordinary seduction of his senses. He was, he said, helpless before the strong aura that came from the girl. Before he knew what he was doing, she had been lying unclothed beneath him, luring him on to sin.

Giles Lawrence was held to be blameless. Mary Frazer was quite another matter. She had been taken to the village square and placed in the stocks. There, in full view of her neighbors, her hair had been cropped to advertise her shame. Afterward she had been pelted with rubbish and other filth. For forty-eight hours the girl had remained in the stocks, the victim of adults and children alike. After her release, she had returned to her place of employment. At some time in the night, it was generally thought, she must have packed her few possessions and stolen away. She was never seen again. It was true, of course, that several days after her disappearance some children, returning to the village in a state of great excitement, had reported seeing Mary Frazer's body floating face downward in a lake. But the lake was some miles from the village of Waterford, and uneasy consciences were soothed by putting the story down to the exaggeration of children. It had never been investigated.

One of the onlookers, Sarah Lawrence, turned her eyes to her tall red-headed son, Giles, who was standing beside her. She looked once more at Rebecca West, and indignation rose in a hot tide. Here, creeping along, her cropped head hanging low, was just such another creature as Mary Frazer, who had led her poor innocent boy astray. No wonder she kept her eyes lowered, refusing to look at any of them. If she needed more proof of the girl's loose morals, which she certainly did not, it was there in the look of repugnance in Matthew Lorne's pale, austere face. The girl was no good. She was the true spawn of that evil witch Margret West.

Giles Lawrence's bright blue eyes rested uneasily on his mother as she made a choked sound. He started back in alarm as she stooped down and and gathered up a clod of earth. "Shameless!" Sarah screamed, flinging the earth at Rebecca. "Trollop, witch's daughter, whore!"

Matthew Lorne stopped dead, automatically bringing

Rebecca to a halt. His lips tight, he turned to the infuriated woman and fixed her with cold eyes. "There will be no more demonstrations, Mistress Lawrence, from you or anyone present." His voice rang out loudly in the silence that had fallen. He took a step nearer, looming over her, a tall, red-garbed, black-cloaked figure. "The punishment of this erring girl may be safely left to me. God is with me. He is inside me. If any here seek to impede me in the carrying out of His will, they will be punished." His voice rose, striking superstitious terror in the hearts of those who listened.

Nodding, Matthew Lorne stepped back. He raised his arms, the black cloak falling back from his shoulders. Tall, gaunt, awe-inspiring, he stood there in complete silence, his chilly eyes inspecting the apprehensive faces turned his way. Then once again his voice rang out, addressing the people at large. "If any here seek to dispute my right, through God, to punish this girl, let him or her step forward and speak."

No one moved or answered. Eyes avoided other eyes. Then, just as the silence was growing unbearably long, stretching tighter already taut nerves, it was broken by a short red-faced man, clad in a shabby coat and torn gray trunk hose. "Amen, Master Lorne!" he shouted fervently. Fierce blue eyes were turned contemptuously on Rebecca. Clearing his throat, he spat at her feet. "'Tis time our community was cleansed."

Inspired by his example, the people echoed him. Some there had known Rebecca from the moment of her birth. They had liked her serene smiling face, her graceful manners, and her pretty way of walking. She was like her mother, whom all had loved, always eager to help in times of trouble. Some had envied her her bethrothal to the most important man in Waterford, but in the main all had been fond of her. But now all these considerations were swept to one side. She had fallen beneath God's wrath. Because most of them feared Matthew Lorne more than they feared God, none dared to question him, or even to think for themselves. In any case, the girl's cropped head was mute evidence of the nature of her crime.

Matthew let his arms drop slowly to his sides. As clearly as if he could see into their minds, he knew their thoughts. There would be no interference from any here, no matter how long he chose to keep her imprisoned. He knew people. In time their curiosity to know what had become of her would abate to the point where she would be all but forgotten. From time to time they might give thought to the prisoner in the isolated cottage at the end of Ladyford Lane, but it would not be concentrated thought. After a while, it would be as if Rebecca West was dead. For a moment he was startled at the trend his thoughts had taken. How long, then, he asked himself, did he intend to keep her locked away? Weeks, months, years? His mind supplied the answer quickly: for as long as it might take to quench the fever she had created in him. He opened his mouth and let his voice roll out sonorously. "Remember this, good people, Rebecca West must await the judgment of God. Until that judgment comes, she is in my hands alone."

Heads were nodded. "No one will go near her," Matthew continued. "No one will speak to her. If any are found attempting to enter the cottage, or trying to communicate with her in any way, they will be punished." He drew himself to his full height. "And I, as God's instrument, will carry out that punishment."

Again the shabby man constituted himself spokesman. "Aye, sir, you need not fear. I speak for all when I say that we want naught to do with trash."

A roar of assent answered this pronouncement. Matthew let his eyes rove over them, and for the first time he allowed a hint of emotion to enter his voice. "All of you know that Rebecca West was my betrothed and she betrayed me. More than that, I cannot say, my heart is too full of grief."

Matthew smiled inwardly. These people were sheep, and he their leader. He knew his own power, he ruled through fear. He looked at Rebecca standing in the same position, her head bowed. He had the feeling that she had heard nothing, was aware of nothing. His eyes glistened as they went to her faintly quivering breasts. He had meant to hint to the people of witchcraft, but the time was not yet ripe. Later, when he had tired of her, he would put forth the first rumors. Becoming aware that his hands were shaking, he clenched them tightly together.

As though his eyes had pierced the fog of unreality that bound her, Rebecca moved for the first time. Her hands came up to cover her breasts, and her head lifted.

Matthew drew in a deep shaken breath as he saw her eyes, which were no longer blank. She had understood; could she also speak? Looking away from those wide, tormented eyes, he decided to gamble. "Do you wish to speak, woman?" he demanded. "Those who once respected you and were your friends are here. They await your confession." He put his hand on her shoulder.

Rebecca thrust his hand away and looked at the staring people. Her mouth opened, forming words that could not be heard. She put her hand to her useless throat; she could not denounce this murderer.

The red-faced man craned his head forward. "What's the matter with her?" he demanded. "Why can't she speak?"

"And the wicked shall be stricken dumb." Matthew smiled gently. "Is it not apparent to you, my friend, that God has set His seal upon her lips?"

Looking startled, the man backed away. "Aye, sir," he managed to mumble.

Talking excitedly among themselves, gesturing, they fell back as Matthew moved forward again. They watched until the naked girl and her guardian were out of sight; then, still talking, they left for their homes.

5

Pulling a three-legged stool up to the bed, the midwife sat down heavily. Her hazel eyes, which were usually so bright and twinkling in the brown, plump round of her face, were somber and watchful as she studied the occupant of the bed. The girl lay on her back. There was something rigid about her, Tabitha Owens thought. She reminded her of a small wary animal who was waiting for a blow to fall. At the best of times, since she was unable to talk, it was hard to tell what she thought or felt. But, judging from the expression that occasionally flickered across her still face, she could not help wondering if Mistress West's labor pains had started.

Frowning, Tabitha rose to her small plump feet. Drawing the bedclothes back, she examined the motionless figure with competent hands. Mistress West was at full term, and the child should be making an appearance very soon. If only the girl would move, make some attempt to cry out. As though the midwife's anxious thoughts had brought her back from wherever she wandered, Rebecca's eyes opened.

"So you're back with me, are you?" Tabitha said cheerfully. "And high time, too." She spoke loudly, like one who endeavored to make herself understood to a mentally deficient. "How are you feeling, are you in pain?"

Rebecca shook her head. Why did the woman always shout? She was not deaf. She closed her eyes. All she wanted was to be left alone. Words formed in her head. *"Leave me alone, please, let me die."* Her hand went to her throat, and then dropped heavily. She couldn't say the words. Was she to remain dumb for the rest of her miserable life? She closed her eyes, shutting out the sight of the cheerful face bent above her.

Tabitha studied her. Those wide brown eyes that were so resolutely screened against her, the heavy fringes of her lashes that lay against the pallid cheeks, were the only signs of youth she could discern in the pinched face. When she had learned that Rebecca West was not quite twenty years old, she had been taken aback. She would have believed her to be in her thirties, at the very least. But even at thirty, which was not old, of course, she should have looked more youthful than she did.

Sighing, Tabitha replaced the bedclothes. The girl was naked, as usual, poor creature. Master Lorne had ordered that she remain so at all times. She was a cousin of his, he had told her, but she was also a poor witless sinner. Sinners must be degraded and humbled. But if the girl was witless, as he said, then how did she know she was being punished? For the matter of that, did she even know that she had sinned? Not even a decent shift to put on. It was disgraceful and unnecessarily harsh. For all that Master Lorne was supposed to be so good and holy, the friend, as it were, of the Almighty, she did not like him. She was of the opinion that he kept the child naked, not for punishment and the proper humbling of her spirit, as he repeatedly said, but for his own private and twisted enjoyment. Though what enjoyment he could possibly find in the sight of a woman big with child, it was hard to say. Why, if she had not put her foot down, he would not have allowed the poor thing a sheet to cover herself with. He had been downright nasty when she had insisted that her patient be covered when she lay on the bed.

Tabitha shivered. How she detested this cold and supposedly holy man. For one dreadful moment, after she had defied him, she had thought he meant to strike her. Instead, he had inclined his head, muttered, "Good day to you, Mistress Owens," and stalked from the room, his head held high. Watching him walk down the lane, she had thought that for all his fine and fancy padded clothing, he looked as thin as a scarecrow, and as lifeless.

Tabitha pushed the stool to the wall. Sitting down, she rested her back against the roughly plastered surface. She had another opinion about Matthew Lorne. He was not quite right in the head. There was something nasty in those icy eyes of his when he watched the girl.

Sighing again, Tabitha fidgeted nervously, smoothing the folds of her white apron, lifting her hands to her head and straightening her white cap. Tucking a strand of graying brown hair more firmly beneath the cap, she glanced once more toward the bed. In the two weeks since she had come to Waterford to attend the girl, she had grown quite fond of the poor dumb creature. She often wondered what secrets lay hidden behind those terrified brown eyes. It was as though she was in hell, and was striving, with those expressive eyes, to tell her something. Strange, but then, wasn't the whole affair strange? The stern way that Master Lorne had advised her that her coming was to be kept secret. She was not to leave the cottage or to have any contact with the people living in Waterford. Why, he had almost smuggled her into the village. From the first moment she had set foot in the cottage, she had been uneasy and wishing herself back in London.

Tabitha folded her hands together and rested them on her ample stomach. She had first met Matthew Lorne in the home of her employer, Sir Sidney Lydon. She had delivered Sir Sidney's wife of three fine children. Later, when the children had begun to grow and thrive, Sir Sidney had remembered her. He had sought her out and offered her the post of nanny to his two handsome sons and his delicately pretty daughter. She had become tired of her arduous job of attending women in childbirth, and so she had accepted his offer with gratitude. In the course of her employment, she had caught glimpses of many famous people, but she had never thought she would see and actually meet the renowned Matthew Lorne.

Even in busy bustling London, Matthew Lorne's fame and profession was well-known. Because of his dedication in seeking out and destroying witches, he had become known in a certain circle, and to his friends, Sir Sidney Lydon in particular, as the "Holy Man." Therefore, when Sir Sidney had called her into the room, Tabitha had been quite excited at the prospect of meeting Matthew Lorne.

On first entering, she had been very nervous. With eyes downcast, she had stood in the center of the room. Sir Sidney, with that warm charm of his, had immediately put her at her ease. "Come forward, Tabitha," he had said.

"Yes, sir." Very conscious of her red and roughened hands, Tabitha had walked toward him, still keeping her eyes downcast. "Is there something you're needing, sir?"

"Tabitha, this is Master Matthew Lorne." Sir Sidney, who had always been a fervent admirer of Matthew Lorne's work, had spoken his name almost with reverence. "He has traveled to London to seek a favor from me."

"Yes, sir," Tabitha mumbled, not knowing what else to say.

"Well, woman, look up." There was a trace of irritability in Sir Sidney's voice. "Don't stand there gawking at the floor."

So she had looked up. For some reason, perhaps remembering the holy men she had seen going about the narrow London streets, she had expected the famed Matthew Lorne to be garbed in rusty black. Instead, he was clad in rich amber velvet. Above the high, gold-threaded velvet collar, his face had been very pale, and his green eyes had seemed to her to glow like the eyes of a cat. She has taken in the ring on his thin finger, his embroidered square-toed shoes, the elegant fit of his trunk hose, and the black velvet cloak flung back from his shoulders, and her first impression of him had been that he was very fine, almost a dandy. Her second impression was one of intense dislike. "Sirs . . ." Flustered, she had curtsied clumsily.

Matthew Lorne did not smile at her. His eyes looked through her as though she was of no importance. Then he had turned his pale austere face to Sir Sidney and had spoken abruptly. "I am, as I told you, Sidney, in search of a midwife, but not a carrier of infection," He gestured toward Tabitha. "I have heard that these creatures are not too particular in their habits."

Sir Sidney's eyes had turned away from her affronted face, and he had looked at Matthew Lorne in surprise, as though he had not expected to hear such words from him. "It is true that most of them are not particular. Matthew," he had answered quietly. Blue eyes looked into green. "Tabitha, however, is different. That is why I chose her to tend my children."

She had wanted to refuse. But Sir Sidney had been very kind to her, and now, in his own way, he was asking a favor. There was another consideration too. If she offended him, she might lose her comfortable post.

The next day, seated opposite Matthew Lorne in his varnished and gilded carriage, she had begun the long journey into Essex. In the dark stuffiness of the carriage, Matthew Lorne had issued his mysterious warnings. "You will not leave the cottage. Anything you require, I will bring to you. You will speak to no one, nor make any attempt to do so."

Nerving herself, she had asked, "Why?"

His only answer to this had been, "Because I say so." He had then gone on to describe the sins of his cousin Rebecca West. Her witlessness, the punishment he had decided upon. As he spoke of her, his voice had risen, and he had called the girl so many ugly names that her face had grown hot with embarrassment. When he had subsided into silence, she had nerved herself again. "Might I know, sir, if Mistress West is such a sinner, why you have gone to such lengths to arrange for her comfort?"

He had been silent for a moment; then he had said in his cold precise voice, a voice she was already coming to hate, "I think you forget yourself, woman. I have no need to explain to anyone. Least of all to you."

So he considered himself above other men. A law unto himself. Squeezing her hands together, she had tried not to look at him. Then he had said, "However, Mistress Owens, since she is to be your patient, I will tell you this much. I have plans for her."

The words were ordinary enough, but something about the way he uttered them had sent a chill through her. She had longed to ask him what those plans might be, but she had not dared.

She had been in such a state of nervous tension when they had finally arrived at the cottage that the driver of the carriage had been forced to get down from his high perch and assist her to alight. Seeing her looking at the man, Matthew Lorne had said calmly, "You are wondering about Sanders, I see. You need not worry, he will say nothing. He is privy to my secret, and he is completely loyal."

Indignation had banished some of her trepidation. The man was playing with her. Why should she worry—it was nothing to do with her. Still, she could not help wondering what his secret might be.

When she had entered the cottage, she had half-expected to see a vacant-eyed lunatic, for this was the impression she had gained from Matthew Lorne. Instead, she had seen a pale, quiet woman who was clutching a quilt tightly about her thin body. She had shortly cropped hair that was without sheen, a thin, lined face, and big, tragic eyes. She looked much older than the age Matthew Lorne had mentioned.

She had been about to speak to the girl when Matthew Lorne's next action had frozen her with shock. Going quickly to the girl's side, he had torn the quilt from her. "You have disobeyed me," he thundered. "You must be punished!" Lifting his hand, he smacked her sharply across the face.

Rebecca West swayed beneath the force of the blow, but she did not fall. Naked, her body heavy with the last stage of pregnancy, she stood there trembling.

Fury overcame Tabitha's fear. "Don't you ever do that again, Master Lorne!" She ran to the girl and put her arms about the bowed shoulders. "If I am any judge, Mistress West will soon go into labor. Do you want to kill her with your brutality?"

Matthew Lorne's green eyes glittered with anger. Raising his voice, he shouted, "Dorothy, come in here."

A door to the left opened at once, and a small dark-haired woman came scuttling into the room. "M-Matthew . . ." She raised frightened dark brown eyes to him. "I had not expected you so soon."

"So I imagine." An unpleasant smile touching his lips, Matthew gestured toward Rebecca. "I have told you that she is to go naked at all times. It is part of her punishment. Why have you disobeyed me?"

The woman looked at the quilt pooled about the girl's feet. "I didn't know, I only left her for a moment." She wrung her hands together. "It w-won't happen again."

"No," he agreed, "it won't, for you will not be here." Grasping her arm, he turned her to face Tabitha. "This is my betrothed, Mistress Dorothy Todd. She has been caring for my cousin. Now that you are here to take over her duties, her presence will no longer be required."

Tabitha had been so taken aback that her mouth had hung open for a moment. His betrothed, and treating her so scurvily. Catching the spiteful gleam in Dorothy Todd's eyes when she looked at Rebecca, she abruptly lost all sympathy for the woman. They were a fine pair, she thought, they deserved each other. Tightening her arm about Rebecca's shoulders, she had answered him in a colorless voice. "You need not worry, sir. I will take good care of Mistress West."

Matthew Lorne had been married to Mistress Dorothy Todd a few days later. The marriage had been performed at the bride's home, in the village of Adbury, lying sixty miles from Waterford.

Sanders, who had supplied Tabitha with the details, had remarked with gloomy relish, "He don't love her, and she's older'n him. Still, she's got plenty of money, and Master Lorne's always been partial to money. Another thing, I reckon he thought it was high time he got married and had some kids to carry on his name."

Tabitha disliked Sanders, considering him to be a toady, and mean-spirited, but his unusual loquaciousness encouraged her to sound him out about Rebecca West. In this ploy, however, she was to be disappointed. The man's habitual dour expression returned. "Don't know nothing about the wench. Don't want to know," was all Sanders would say.

True to her promise, Tabitha had taken as much care of her patient as the girl would allow. For although Rebecca was dumb and apparently terrified whenever Matthew Lorne came near, she had a certain quiet dignity that forbade a too excessive show of concern. Tabitha, when Matthew Lorne was not present, ignored his orders and allowed Rebecca to cover herself. For this, she was rewarded by a faint, tremulous smile. She had done other things too. Watching Rebecca carefully, she had deliberately unlocked the door of the cottage and left it standing wide. Rebecca had stared at the open door for a long moment; then she had turned her back on it. Perhaps she was afraid of a trap, Tabitha thought grimly, or, if she was in truth a prisoner, she was afraid to leave her prison and venture into freedom. What was it she

feared, what caused the violent trembling that sometimes afflicted her limbs?

Feeling sleepy, Tabitha settled herself more comfortably on the hard stool. Once or twice, noticing the
working of Rebecca's throat, she had encouraged her
to speak. "Try," she would insist, "just try, Mistress
West." It had been no use; whatever was inside the girl
remained firmly locked away. She thought of Rebecca's
eyes whenever Matthew Lorne came visiting, which he
did almost daily. Her eyes would come alive then,
flaming with hatred. As for Matthew Lorne, he would
remain for his usual length of time, saying nothing, but
his cold green gaze following her everywhere. In the
heavy silence, Tabitha would feel the perspiration
starting out on her face. So much hatred, so much terror, she felt stifled by it. For despite the hatred in the
girl's eyes, she had the feeling that terror was the more
powerful of the two emotions that seemed to ride her.
If, as she strongly suspected, Matthew Lorne was holding Rebecca against her will, a dumb girl could not
very well accuse him. Tabitha's head nodded sleepily.
As for herself, she was a nobody. Matthew Lorne was
a powerful man; even if she could get Rebecca's story
from her, nobody would believe her. Besides, if she
was a prisoner, why hadn't she taken the opportunity
presented by the conveniently opened door? It was all
very mystifying, she thought crossly, and perhaps the
truth of it all was that she was imagining things. It
might be, just as Matthew Lorne had said, that
Rebecca West was a witless sinner who was receiving
just punishment. Sinner she might be, but she was not
witless. Of that much, at least, she was certain. On this
last thought, Tabitha's head fell forward, and a soft
snore issued from her parted lips.

Rebecca opened her eyes and stole a look at the
elderly midwife. Seeing that the woman's head nodded
in sleep, she closed them again. She put her hands on
the mound of her stomach. Her pains, which had
started some time ago, were beginning to increase in

intensity. *Matthew Lorne's child, or Don Roberto's?* That was the question that constantly exercised her mind. *Oh God, let it not be Matthew Lorne's.* The plea welled up passionately inside her as she dug her fingers fiercely into her stomach. *please, God, I beg You, do not let it be the child of that murderer!*

The pain receded, and Rebecca allowed her taut body to relax. Perhaps she would die when the child was born. Sooner or later, when he had tired of his cruel sport, he would send her to the burning cross, just as he had sent her mother. She thought of the days, the weeks, the months of bodily and mental anguish she had endured. The brutal and degrading way he took her body. His insults, his threats, and his frequent blows. And lastly, his introduction of the stranger, that sneering, self-satisfied woman, Dorothy Todd, who was to be her new jailer. Where Matthew was cruel, Dorothy was petty and spiteful. While it was true that she did not strike her, as Matthew did, she nonetheless found innumerable ways to make her life a hell. The woman was the perfect complement to Matthew's hard ruthlessness. There had been times when she had longed to launch herself at Dorothy and batter her fists in that dark, sneering face, but she knew herself to be too weak. Dorothy was small, but she was strong; she would soon overpower her. Instead, Rebecca would retreat. Seating herself on her stool in the corner of the room she would avoid, as much as possible, looking at her tormentor

As in the case of the midwife, Tabitha Owens, Dorothy had been smuggled into the cottage, and her presence was not known to the villagers. Rebecca was aware of this, just as she was aware, with his constant repetition, of Matthew's true aim. Because she was unimportant to him now, except to satisfy the cravings of his body, he apparently did not mind stripping himself of all pretense and showing her the mean and shallow man he really was. In time, he told her, the people of Waterford would all but have forgotten her. Others, who might have thought of making inquires regarding her welfare, would not do so. Any lingering friendship felt for her would be lost in their fear of him. That was the time when he would bring her forth and she would be branded as a witch and publicly burned.

"*How long,*" Rebecca wanted to ask him, "*how long before I die?*"

He must have learned to read the expressions in her eyes, for often, taking pleasure in it, he would answer her unspoken question. "It will be when I am ready, dear Rebecca. It might be months, perhaps years before I denounce you. You must not be too impatient. You must wait and see, must you not?"

There had been the time when she found she was pregnant. Matthew had been very angry at first; his blow had sent her sprawling to the floor. He had stood over her for a long time, his hands clenched, his pale face red and congested. Then his rage had died, and she knew that his mind had taken another turn. He believed the child in her body to be his. She hoped and prayed that it was the child of Don Roberto. It was from that moment that she began to beseech God to let it be so.

It was in the seventh month of her pregnancy that he had brought Dorothy Todd to the cottage. Although they had never met before, Rebecca, encountering her look of spite, knew that she had found another enemy. How much of her story the woman knew, Rebecca did not know, but certainly she was aware of the betrothal that had once been between Matthew and herself. Her tongue spiked with jealousy, Dorothy would talk endlessly of her own coming marriage to Matthew. This was done to further torment her prisoner. She did not know that her babbling was received with stony indifference, or that the only emotion that animated the girl was her implacable enemiy and her burning hatred for Matthew Lorne.

At odd moments Rebecca had wondered where Dorothy had come from. It was Matthew himself who cleared up the mystery. Dorothy Todd came from the distant village of Adbury. She was the daughter of the squire, Bartholemew Todd.

Matthew had arrived unexpectedly at the cottage one night. With his eyes hard on Rebecca, he had abruptly dismissed Dorothy, telling her to wait outside in the carriage.

Dorothy listened for a moment to the wind howling down the chimney; then she looked at Matthew. Her mouth set in a sullen line, her unwillingness to leave them alone together apparent, she said sulkily, "It is cold outside. Why can I not wait in here? If you have something private to say to the girl, I promise you I will not listen."

Matthew's eyes were cold and scornful when he answered her. "You will not listen. My dear Dorothy, your second name should be 'curiosity.' "

She flushed. "I tell you that I will not listen!"

"Perhaps you didn't hear me. I told you to wait outside in the carriage."

Dorothy's eyes held his, and for a few moments it looked as though she might rebel. Then, her fear of him overcoming her indignation, she darted a last malignant look at Rebecca and departed.

No sooner had the door closed behind her that Matthew started toward Rebecca. Grasping her wrist, he dragged her over to the bed. throwing her down, he flung himself on top of her, keeping her pinioned there by the weight of his body. He did not take her, as, regardless of Dorothy's presence, he had done on a great many occasions. Instead, his face even paler than usual and his green eyes slitted, he began to talk. He told her of how he had first met Dorothy Todd. It had been in the home of Sir Richard Benjamin, two years ago. Dorothy's father, who had recently died, had left everything to his daughter, his only child. Motley Manor, his home in Adbury, a house in London, and a considerable fortune. At that time, Matthew went on, Sir Richard had hinted that a marriage between his protégé and Mistress Todd would not only be practical, but extremely desirable.

Rebecca listened to him dully. There was an expression in his eyes that seemed to anticipate her suffering. Bitter laughter welled up inside her; evidently his belief in the strength of his attraction was as strong as ever. He seemed to have entirely erased from his mind the murder of her mother, of Don Roberto, the rape of her own body, her imprisonment, and the degradations she was forced to endure at his hands.

She thought of the number of times he had taken her body in front of Dorothy's very eyes. Once, when she had put up a struggle, he had harshly commanded Dorothy to hold her down. The woman had obeyed, but Rebecca had felt the trembling of her hands when Matthew had lowered his head and begun to kiss her breasts lingeringly. She had heard her gasp when, without so much as a glance at her, he had thrust himself inside her body with a savage abandon to his movements that took no thought for the child soon to be born.

Dorothy's humiliation at that moment must have been as great as, if not greater than, her own, Rebecca had thought on the first time it had happened. She might have retained this feeling of pity for the woman who had been subjected to such an outrage, had not Dorothy herself killed the feeling. Despite everything, she continued to talk interminably to Matthew of their coming marriage. If his taking of another woman's body while she was forced to look on had hurt her, she did not allow it to show. So perhaps it was this outward compliance of hers, her obvious, if unexpressed, fear of losing him that had made Matthew think of himself as invincible.

Although her tongue remained silent, Rebecca had learned that her eyes spoke for her. Looking at him, she put into them all of her scorn and her utter indifference.

Matthew was silent for a moment, but she could feel the angry rigidity of his body against her own.

Rebecca's eyes closed against him. With a muffled exclamation of fury he pressed his thumbs against her eyes, forcing her lids upward. Still hoping to impress her and inspire in her those feelings he longed to see, he began to shout. "Dorothy is older than me, but no matter, she is still young enough to give me children, and I will have full control of her money." His eyes glimmered with an evil light. "But we will not live in Adbury. We will live here, in Waterford. You will like to know that I am near to you, will you not? Besides, I must be here. It would not do for a witch to escape, would it?"

Rebecca smiled, a derisive smile, and he lost his head completely. He had hit her repeatedly. Staring at the red stains his fingers had left across her pale cheeks, he had continued speaking in a low, heavy voice. "I could have married Dorothy a year ago, had I wished. She made it clear enough to me that she would be willing. But I, fool that I was, loved you. My Rebecca, so sweet, so pure. Oh, yes, a marriage for gain was very far from my thoughts then. But the sooner I marry her now, the better. As for you, when you have borne my child, perhaps I will begin thinking of ridding myself of you."

His words failed to fill her with the usual terror. She had no doubt that in time he would carry out his threat, but before that happened, a long road of suffering stretched ahead of her.

Misunderstanding her expression, Matthew had said triumphantly, "Yes, the burning cross awaits you. Always remember that." His anger died. His green eyes glazed, his hands began to wander. Tight-lipped, she endured. When he rose to take off his clothes, Rebecca saw the pale outline of Dorothy's face pressed to the window. If Matthew also saw her, he gave no sign. He flung himself upon her, his assault upon her body more ferocious, more degrading than ever before.

When he had finally withdrawn from her, her senses were beginning to darken. Nontheless she had managed to look at him directly and to force her pain-numbed lips into another smile. It was a pitiful weapon to use against his strength and brutality, but it was the only one she had to fight with.

Matthew continued to stare at her as he dressed himself. His dressing completed, he walked over to the bed, giving her a look that was full of menace. Her face remained still, her eyes unflinching. When he had turned away, and, without another word, walked over to the door, banging it shut behind him, she had had the feeling that she had gained a victory. Small though it was, she cherished it.

After that night, she lost all track of time. The dragging days merged one into another. As her body grew increasingly more uncomfortable and unwieldy, her every moment became haunted by the fear that she carried Matthew Lorne's child. Fear grew into conviction, and she began to seek some way of killing herself. Dorothy's brooding spiteful eyes were constantly upon her, making any independent move on her part impossible. It was only when physical discomfort forced the woman to seek the privy at the end of the small garden that she was able to conduct her desperate search for a weapon. It had all proved to be of no avail. Matthew had thought of everything. Any object with which she might conceivably harm herself had been removed.

During her frequent sleepless nights, Rebecca would lie huddled on the coverless bed, her arms tight about her for warmth, the sound of Dorothy's faint snoring in her ears. Sometimes, though not often, she would allow herself to think of Don Roberto. She had tried to shut him out altogether, when Matthew, taking a delight in the tears that fell from her eyes, had informed her that Don Roberto's body had been sent back to his native Spain, but she found she could not do it. His tragic death, Matthew told her, had been deeply mourned by Sir Richard Benjamin. As for his murderer, he had never been found. Matthew had laughed and put his face close to hers. "And he never will be found, will he, Rebecca? You can't tell what you know." Matthew was right. She was dumb, her voice silenced by shock. She could not even write what she knew. Matthew, when he had endeavored to elevate her to his lofty standards, had neglected one part of her education. She could not read or write. Unless her voice returned, there was no way she could betray him. And even if she could speak out against him, who would believe her, who would dare to take her seriously?

Those times when she did think of Don Roberto, her hard pillow would be wet with tears. She would see once again those intense eyes of his, feel the pressure of his tawny body covering hers. His darkly handsome image would move through her mind like a far-off dream of romance, and she would continue to weep like an abandoned child.

Rebecca's life took yet another turn when the door of her prison opened to admit the small, plump figure of Tabitha Owens. When the garrulous Tabitha informed her that Matthew, in his search for a suitable woman to preside at the birth, had traveled all the way to London, Rebecca's despair increased. Matthew would not have undertaken such a journey unless he sincerely believed that the child she carried was his. He would, if he had had any doubts, ignored the birth. He might even hope that the child would die.

With the removal of Dorothy Todd, Rebecca's life became a little easier. Tabitha was very kind, and her touch was gentle. She talked a great deal, her hazel eyes twinkling and her generous mouth smiling. But there was a firm, almost hard side to her nature; this was shown in her defiance of Matthew Lorne. In her zeal to make her patient comfortable, she would stand up to him, her ready smile gone. "Now, see here, Master Lorne," she had said to him on one occasion, "it's not for you to be telling me how to handle my patient. I've been aiding women in childbirth for more years than I care to count. As for your crack-brained notion of having the poor child lie uncovered on the bed, I'll not stand by and see it. No, 'tis not a bit of use glaring at me, I'll not, and that's that."

Shaking with fury, Matthew had shouted, "She is a sinner. It is part of her punishment. You will do as I tell you, woman!"

"Just yesterday you came in here and hacked off her pretty hair again. Is that part of her punishment, too?"

"Yes, I tell you she is evil, a vile sinner."

"Maybe she is," Tabitha retorted, "and then again, maybe she isn't. Looks a harmless enough wench to me."

Furious because she dared to question his judgment, and seemingly had no fear of his awesome person, he lost control again. "You will be silent, woman!"

"That I'll not, Master Lorne." Standing up to him, Tabitha had looked like an indignant pouter pigeon. "Why, the very idea! Sinner or not, Mistress West is going to have a child. That's all that concerns me."

Becoming aware that he had fallen woefully short of the standards a holy man should set, and convinced by the militant gleam in Tabitha's eyes that he had gone too far, Matthew sobered. Inclining his head stiffly, he marched over to the door. Opening it, he went out, banging it loudly behind him.

Tabitha's anger was not cooled by her victory. Sniffing indignantly, she glared at the door. "Him and his orders. Mad, that's what he is. And if he thinks I can't see into his nasty mind, then he's vastly mistaken. No doubt he's afraid that I'll tell Sir Sidney of his goings-on. Aye, I shouldn't wonder if that's why he gave in." Picking up the quilt, she wrapped it tenderly about Rebecca. "There, that's better. And folks actually look up to that weasel. Hah!"

On the day that Matthew Lorne was married to Dorothy Todd, it was Tabitha who informed Rebecca of the nuptials. "Sanders told me about it, she said. She winked broadly. "A pair of weasels taking their marriage vows, that's what they are. If you'll forgive me for saying so."

Rebecca's faint nod forgave her. "Married at noontime, they were," Tabitha went on. She leaned closer to Rebecca and said in a scandalized whisper, "And high time they were married, too. That Mistress Todd, or Mistress Lorne, as I suppose I should think of her now, has already got a little one beneath her belt."

Standing upright again, Tabitha caught Rebecca's startled questioning look. "Oh, aye, Mistress West, it's true, all right." Grinning, she straightened her cap and smoothed down her apron. Then, folding her hands over her stomach, she gave vent to her expressive sniff. "I knew it the first moment I set eyes on her, even though she was trying to hide it by pinching herself in tight. But I'm too old a hand to be fooled by tricks like that. She's been carrying on with our fine holy man, and so I tell you. About three months gone, she is. They should both think shame of themselves." She shook her head, the vigorous action once more dislodging the precariously perched cap. "Well," she went on with grim relish, "him and her are hitched up good and tight now, and much good may it do the nasty pair!"

Rebecca smiled, and for once her smile was warm and spontaneous. Delighted at this reaction, Tabitha reached out and patted the cropped head gently. "Serves her right, don't it, dearie? But you know, nasty though she is, I could almost feel sorry for her. Imagine being married to him."

Tabitha frowned as the shadows returned to Rebecca's eyes. Sitting down, she took the girl's hand in hers and held it firmly. "There, now, Mistress West, I'm an old fool. Don't you be paying no attention to me." She squeezed Rebecca's fingers. "Me and my babbling tongue, eh?" She sighed. "I'd give a lot to know what goes on in that head of yours." Excitement lit her features. "Can you write, Mistress West?"

Rebecca shook her head. Tabitha's face fell. "Not that I could read it, even if you could," she said in a subdued voice. "But if there was something fishy going on, and you could have written it down, I could have showed it to Sir Sidney. He admires Master Lorne, and more fool him for doing so, but he wouldn't stand for anything bad." She was silent for a moment; then she went on in a low voice, "But there's one thing I don't need telling. You don't like Master Lorne, do you?"

A flash lit Rebecca's eyes, and her face was momentarily contorted with an expression of such hatred that Tabitha was taken aback. Then, as Rebecca vehemently shook her head, she recovered herself somewhat. "Thought not," she said, giving her deep, comfortable chuckle. Because the girl's expression had chilled her, and not knowing what else to do, she sought to make light of it. "Can't say as I blame you," she rushed on breathlessly. "What's there about him to like? The man is naught but skin and bones, not that he can help that, of course, but he's a cold fish into the bargain. Not only that. He's a hypocrite too, or I miss my guess."

Thinking of that conversation, Rebecca moved in the bed. She stretched out her legs, which had cramped. The cramp easing, she went back to her thoughts. Tabitha's dislike of Matthew Lorne had grown. Whenever he was around, she seemed to bristle with hostility. It was obvious that she suspected that things were not as Matthew said they were.

Rebecca moved again, catching her breath as the grinding pain seized her. Soon it would be time to awaken Tabitha. The pain dulled a little. To take her mind off it, she thought of the occasion when Tabitha's suspicion of the "holy man," as she contemptuously called him, had flared higher than usual. The little incident had happened just after Matthew had taken his usual silent departure. Tabitha, without saying a word, had risen from her chair. Taking a key from her pocket, she had walked over to the door. Unlocking it, she had flung it wide in mute invitation. Then, turning her back, she had busied herself with some chores.

Rebecca's wide brown eyes went from Tabitha's averted back and traveled in fascination to the open door. Her legs trembling beneath her, she crept nearer. Now she could feel the cool wind playing over her flushed face. She had only to move forward. Tabitha would not stop her. The child within her moved, and the answer came quickly: she was heavy with pregnancy, and branded as witch and whore. Whom could she go to? Tears blinding her, sick with her longing to be free, she stumbled back to her stool, refusing to look again at the open door.

After some time had passed, Tabitha had closed and relocked the door. Seating herself opposite Rebecca, she had said, "Why, lass, I would have gone with you, don't you know that?"

"Too late." Rebecca's lips formed the words. Leaning forward, she laid her hand on Tabitha's knee, her eyes saying thank you.

She winced as her legs cramped again, and she stretched them out gingerly. As though the movement had caused something to break inside her, a wet gushing warmth burst forth, streamed down her legs, and soaked the sheet beneath her. Agony caught her, brutally rending her body apart. Sweat broke out thickly on her forehead. Her mouth opened wide in a scream for help, but only a grunting sound emerged from her straining throat. Her wild eyes went to Tabitha, begging her to awaken.

Soft though the sound that came from Rebecca had been, it penetrated through the mists of sleep. Tabitha's eyes flew open, the sleep clearing from them immediately. She looked with alert attention at the panting, writhing figure of Rebecca and the sweat-glazed agonized face. "It looks like it's time, dearie." She spoke in a soothing voice.

Rebecca's head turned to her, her distended eyes pleading for help. Tears ran down her face as her mouth opened once more in that pathetic soundless scream.

Her cap riding crookedly on her head, Tabitha approached the bed briskly. Throwing back the bedclothes, she made a hurried but careful examination. She took a square of clean linen from her capacious apron pocket and wiped the mingled tears and sweat from Rebecca's face. The grunting sound came from Rebecca's throat again as she reared upward. Tabitha caught her hand and held it until the spasm passed. Exhausted, but still clinging tightly to Tabitha's hand, Rebecca slumped back. Her eyes looked trustingly at the midwife.

"That right," Tabitha said, her voice gruff with emotion. "Just do everything I tell you, and it'll be over in no time." With an abrupt movement she leaned down and kissed the girl's damp cheek.

When Matthew Lorne entered the cottage some three hours later, Rebecca's travail was over. Soundly sleeping, she lay curled up in a clean, warm bed. Her lips were faintly smiling, as though her dreams were pleasant. But the dark shadows beneath her closed eyes showed the ordeal she had been through.

Tabitha Owens sat on a stool drawn up close to the bed. She was nursing a small bundle wrapped in a gray cloak.

Matthew stood there slapping his gloves against the palm of his left hand. For once he appeared to be at a loss. "The child is born, then?" he said in an uncertain voice.

Tabitha looked up at him with hostile hazel eyes. He was clad all in black. He looked, Tabitha thought, with the stark contrast of his pale face, and the long cloak falling from his shoulders, like a specter. Suppressing a shiver, she answered him curtly. "Aye, seems like, don't it?" Her mouth tightened. "T've had to wrap the little lass in my cloak. Without it, she'd likely freeze to death. 'Tis certain, Master Lorne, that you have made no provision for this child's coming."

Matthew did not answer her. With his eyes fixed on

the fluff of dark hair that showed above the cloak, he approached slowly. "Show me the child," he said harshly.

At his tone, Tabitha's arms tightened protectively about the small form. "You'll not be harming her," she blurted out defiantly. "I'll see to that!"

Matthew frowned. "Don't be a fool, woman," he snapped. "Show her to me."

Reluctantly, her eyes warning him, Tabitha drew the cloak to one side. Matthew stared hard at the perfect little body, the tightly clenched fists, and the tiny, crumpled red face surmounted by dark hair. Unusually thick hair. Except for that hair, she was like any other newborn child, and yet some instinct told Matthew that he was looking at the daughter of Don Roberto. His rage began to rise as Tabitha replaced the cloak, glad to hide the child from those penetrating green eyes.

He stared at the sleeping Rebecca. No doubt she thought she was going to keep her bastard. She would soon find out her mistake. In a few days, that interfering old hag Tabitha Owens would be on her way back to London. Once she had gone, he would take the child and she would be brought up as his daughter. When he judged the time to be right, he would tell her who her true mother was, only by that time it would be too late to claim kinship and too late for anything, except to look on while her mother burned.

An unpleasant smile touched Matthew's grim lips. He would allow Rebecca to see her daughter now and again. She could look, but never touch. As a further punishment to her, he would name the child Shalada. That name would be a constant reminder to the whore of her night of lechery, and of all she had lost by her lewd conduct.

Rocking the child gently, Tabitha stared at Matthew's straight, black-clad back. Quite suddenly she felt like crossing herself to ward off the evil he seemed to have brought into this place. The baby set up a thin, wailing cry, and Tabitha raised her and held her close to her breast. "Hush, my lovie, hush!"

The wailing cry brought Matthew's attention back to the baby. His rage and hatred were still apparent in his eyes when he turned to face Tabitha. He held out commanding arms. "Give me the child," he said.

Tabitha stared at him. Now he no longer looked like a specter to her, but like the Devil, who had come to earth in the form of a great black bat. She was being foolish, fanciful, and in her sensible mind she knew it. But in that cold moment of fear that assailed her, she could not seem to shake the notion. She shrank back. "No!" she said hoarsely.

Matthew's eyes narrowed. Enjoying the fear in the woman's face, he felt a sudden and overwhelming sense of power. "Give her to me," he repeated.

His arms were still outstretched. Tabitha's eyes went to his long pale hands with their faintly quivering fingers, and she could not control a shudder. *Go away*, she cried inwardly, *leave us alone*.

"Did you hear me, Mistress Owens?"

It was no use, Tabitha thought despairingly, his will was stronger than her own. She must deliver the child into the arms of the Devil.

Matthew came closer and leaned over her. Tabitha could feel the warm gust of his breath against her face. "You know, Mistress Owens," he said in a soft voice, "if I am forced to struggle with you, the child will surely fall." He straightened up. "Do as I tell you, please."

That soft voice, so unlike his usual harsh tones, had a devastating effect upon Tabitha. There was nothing she could do to oppose him. If she refused to give him the child, he would wrench it from her arms. In the short time she had been in attendance, she had learned that he was capable of anything. He had never actually struck Rebecca in her presence, yet she knew that he did abuse her.

"Well?" Matthew's voice broke into Tabitha's whirling thoughts. "Do you intend to just sit there staring into space, old woman?"

Tabitha looked up. His eyes glowed a bright green. The eyes of a cat watching a helpless mouse. Rising shakily to her feet, she tried to laugh at herself. She was just full of fancies today. She hesitated a moment longer, then placed the small, warm bundle in his arms. "You'll be careful with the little mite, Master Lorne?" Her voice was shaken with pleading.

A violent impulse seized Matthew. He would have liked to smash his fist against that wrinkled, pleading face, but his emotion did not show in the cold expression with which he regarded her. He would be glad when she returned to London. The woman had, from the very first, defied him. Composing his inner turmoil with some difficulty, he said in a level voice, "You will wait outside, if you please, Mistress Owens."

Her agitation growing, Tabitha's hands plucked at her apron. "I must stay with my patient, Master Lorne. She may awaken and need me."

He was amused by her distress. "If she does have need of you, I will call you."

Drawing in a deep breath, Tabitha tried again. "If you have no objection, I . . . I think it is best that I stay."

"I do not agree." Holding the child awkwardly in the crook of his arm, Matthew advanced upon Tabitha. "I will not tell you again, Mistress Owens. If you do not go now, at once, I will put you out."

Tabitha stared at him like a hypnotized rabbit. Cold voice, icy eyes, a tall, gaunt figure garbed in funereal black. She was swept with a sense of horror. She knew, if she resisted him, that he would make good his threat. "Very well, Master Lorne."

Her steps dragging, Tabitha went over to the door. Opening it, she paused there a moment, turning her head toward the bed. Her heart plunged; Rebecca was awake. The girl's wide brown eyes were fixed on her, eloquent eyes that seemed to be begging her to stay, to help her. Defeated, despising herself for her cowardice, Tabitha went out, closing the door softly behind her.

Leaning against the wall, shivering in the wind, Tabitha looked up at the sky. The threatening storm clouds had been driven away by the blustering wind. A full golden moon rode high, surrounded by stars. The stars, pinned like diamonds to black velvet, reminded her of a gown her mistress, Lady Lydon, often wore. She opened her eyes and straightened up. She could open that door now and go back inside. But then again, if she openly defied Matthew Lorne, he might make arrangements to send her back to London immediately. She must stay. She owed it to the babe and to that poor speechless girl. Tabitha shuddered; she did not care to think of what would happen after she was gone.

Matthew looked down at the peacefully sleeping child. The only sounds in the room were the crackling of the fire and Rebecca's quick, agitated breathing. She was afraid; he did not need to look at her to know that. Afraid for herself, but mostly, he guessed, for this brat he held in his arms.

Dragging out the suspense, Matthew turned around slowly to face her. He walked over to the bed and seated himself on the side. Without looking at Rebecca, he remarked in a light, conversational tone, "You have given me a fine healthy daughter."

He looked up as Rebecca's hot fingers touched his hand in mute pleading. "You want to hold the child?" he asked her. When she nodded, he said abruptly, "No!"

He saw the bright terror dawning in her eyes, and he was satisfied that she was beginning to understand. Later, he would tell her in detail his plans for the child. Plans that would not include her. "I have never told you this," he went on in the same light voice, "but I once had a sister. Unfortunately, she died a few days after her birth. I was very young at the time, but I remember her well. Her name was Matilda. This child greatly resembles her."

Rebecca's hands clenched as she saw his sardonic smile. He lied. He knew, even as she had known when she had first held her daughter, that it was Don Roberto's child.

"My sister's name was Matilda, Rebecca. A hard name. I have never cared for it. My daughter shall bear an old and traditional and musical name. I shall call her Shalada." He paused. "You will like that, I know." Rebecca shook her head in wild protest. Matthew watched her narrowly. "You seem upset, Rebecca," he said softly. "The name should please you. It should remind you of a pleasant interlude in your life. Come, now, confess. You do like it, don't you?"

Her eyes were begging him for mercy, for compassion. Placing the baby on the bed, he reached out and patted Rebecca's hand. "You are afraid for Shalada," he said in a low voice, "and I quite understand that. But there is really no need to fear. Is she not my own beloved daughter?" His smile turned into a sneer. "And as my beloved daughter, I shall teach her to love and respect the Lord, and to shun the Devil. When she is old enough to understand the meaning and the reason for prayer, she shall spend her mornings and her evenings on her knees. She shall be told of her mother's sins, and I have no doubt she will wish to ask the Lord's pardon for that poor misguided woman. Don't you think so?"

Matthew broke off. "But, dear Rebecca," he went on smoothly, "if you look at me like that, I shall think you are not grateful. You would not wish me to think that, would you?" He patted her hand again. "Shalada will have a good life, as long as she obeys me. In bringing up a child, discipline is, unfortunately, most necessary. You agree? Shalada shall be God-fearing, meek, and obedient, everything that I would wish my daughter to be."

She is not your daughter. The words sounded in Rebecca's throbbing head. *She is mine.* Madness seized her, and she saw Matthew's sneering face through a red haze. She jerked upright in the bed. A sound came from her throat, inarticulate, yet unmistakably threatening. She launched herself forward, knocking him off balance. *Mine, my baby!* The words went on, and inside her head they were like the tolling of a great bell. Her hand flashed out, her nails tore savagely at his face.

Mopping the blood from his face, he was stunned by the unexpected ferocious attack. Behind him, the door opened and closed. He did not turn his head. Let the old woman came in, he thought. Let her tend the child and her lunatic mother. He would not return to the cottage until Tabitha Owens was safely on her way to London. Then it would be his turn. When he did not return, Rebecca would think that she and her child were safe, that he had thought better of his threat to take Shalada. Her mind would be occupied with thoughts of escape, of going to some village where she was not known. Dumb though she was, perhaps she would be hoping to find work so that she could support herself and her bastard. He would enjoy telling her that she was still a prisoner. That her daughter was to be taken from her, and that her imprisonment would end only when she drew her last breath.

With a last look at the oblivious Rebecca, he turned on his heel and went over to the door. The wind snatched at his cloak as he stepped outside, billowing it out behind him. Without troubling to close the door, he strode away.

Part Two

❧

SHALADA

1505

6

Matthew Lorne frowned as he watched the girl run the last few yards to the top of Ladyford Hill. She was slim and graceful in her dark blue gown with the crisp white apron covering it, and even in her clumsy wooden clogs, worn today as a preventive against the mud, as surefooted as a mountain goat. Fitful sunlight touched the long, thick black hair that fell in a bright sheen from beneath a little white winged cap.

Sighing heavily, Matthew shook his head. Tomorrow, March 6, Shalada would be eighteen. Every day, so it seemed to him, she grew in beauty. A radiant golden-skinned beauty that reminded him too forcefully of the many years that lay between them, and of the barrier of fatherhood that he himself had erected. A barrier that he had now determined to tumble.

"Father . . ." Her voice drifted down to him. "Are you coming?" Even the wind, thinning her voice, could not disguise the coldness of her tone, or that faintly imperious note that had always maddened him.

He was not her father. She would know it soon. But he must be careful how he revealed the truth. Deciding to ignore her for the moment, Matthew seated himself with deliberation upon a sparsely grassed hummock. In an effort to quieten the excited racing of his heart, he forced himself to dwell on the faults in Shalada's character. She was everything he found occasion to sternly rebuke in others, as, before this fever of desire for her had come upon him, he had daily done with her. She was altogether too pert, overbold, lacking in patience, and irreverent to her God, and to himself. She was a creature of strong and stormy emotions, and she was not civilized enough to hide them. Although, in the beginning, he had looked with cold dislike upon the child, seeing in her too strong a resemblance to her Spanish father, he had nonetheless tried to train her in the way he thought she should go. Dorothy, his wife, had tried too. It was, he had often thought, like trying to train a tigress. Shalada was full of fire and spirit. Except in the early days, when she had been too young and frightened to strike back, she could not be cowed or subdued, and she could no longer be frightened into submission. She was the stormy petrel in the household, and every day saw a fresh battle of wills. Dorothy's hatred of the girl, which had always been there, had grown with the years. But for himself, though he had not realized it, love had grown that was not the love of a father for a daughter.

Matthew looked up. Shalada was standing very still on the crest of the hill, her dark blue skirts blowing in the wind. Today, because he had said that she could visit Rebecca West, the mute whom she had befriended, Shalada's hatred of him, always simmering just below the surface, and sometimes erupting into displays of violence, was not so much in evidence.

Rebecca West. Matthew's mouth tightened into the hard, familiar line as he thought of her. For eighteen years he had kept the woman alive, living on his bounty, supplying her with food, fuel, and clothing. While it was true that he still held the threat of burning over her head, she was no longer a prisoner. Since the day he had forcefully taken Shalada from her frantic arms, he had not troubled her again. He was satisfied that, with the removal of the child, he had his revenge. It was Rebecca, hungry for the occasional glimpses he allowed her of her daughter, who had elected to stay. That hunger had even overcome her fear of the burning cross. As for Shalada, she had no idea that

Rebecca West was her mother. There had been times, when Shalada had defied him and he was particularly angry with her, when he had been tempted to tell her that the mute, shriveled-up little woman with the yellowed and deeply lined face, on whom, on those rare visits, she expended such affection, was her mother. He might have done so had he not thought that the news would have gladdened rather than horrified her. He knew that Shalada's hatred of Dorothy ran only second to her hatred of him. She would be overjoyed to find that Dorothy was not her mother.

Matthew glanced again at Shalada. She was still standing in the same position. From the very beginning the girl had been a disrupting influence. She had maddened him and bewildered him and set all his strict rules at naught. He had beaten her, and, knowing that she could not bear to be enclosed in a small space, he had quite often locked her away in the dark cupboard beneath the stairs. He had even deprived her of food. The punishments seemed to make no difference to Shalada; if she suffered, she refused to show it. She would appear to be quite unchastened. Her mouth would be set as obstinately as ever, her dark eyes regarding him with a mixture of hatred and defiance. He sometimes had the feeling that she would rather die than allow him, or any other member of the household, a glimpse into her secret mind.

His frown deepening, Matthew poked the stick he was carrying into the earth. The intense feeling he now had for Shalada had come about just after she had turned sixteen. That was when he had begun to feel such a trembling excitement, such a bewildering joy in her presence. The feeling had intensified to the point where he could no longer ignore it or pretend that it did not exist. When he finally acknowledged the feeling for what it was, he did not think of the carnal thoughts that possessed his mind as sinful. After all, Shalada was not his daughter. She was clearly the feminine edition of Don Roberto Pérez. He wanted so much to touch

Shalada that sometimes, passing her, he would allow his hand to brush against her. Once, when she had been seated in a chair by the window, her dark eyes far away, he had leaned over her and asked her what she was thinking about. Casually, he had placed his hand on her breast, allowing it to linger there. "Come, tell me your thoughts," he had repeated.

Shalada's reaction had been immediate. With an expression of loathing, she pushed his hand away. Jumping up from her chair, she faced him. "If you ever touch me like that again, I shall kill you!" With her eyes flashing dark fire, daring him to come closer, she had been like an angry, spitting cat.

Almost choking on his rage, he had shouted at her, "I do not understand you. And how dare you speak to me like that? I am your father!"

"You understand only too well," Shalada had answered, her lip curling. "As for being my father, to my shame I must admit the truth of this. However, perhaps it would be as well if you reminded yourself of that fact now and again." Brushing past him, she had left the room, her head held high.

Vixen! With the memory of his anger strong upon him, Matthew poked the stick deeper, turning over a clod of earth. Without interest, he watched a line of ants break formation and scurry for cover. His thoughts gentling after a moment, he told himself that perhaps he could not altogether blame Shalada for her attitude. Before this change in his feelings had come about, he had indeed been harsh with her. He had punished her for her mother's betrayal, for the blood of the foreigner which ran so strongly in her veins. In comparison, his treatment of Robert, his son, and Tasmin, his daughter, had been almost gentle. It was easy to reduce Tasmin to a quivering jelly of fear, for she, with her vacant blond looks and empty blue eyes, had no spirit. But the fact that he could not break Shalada had made him all the more determined to do so. Then had come the unexpected change. Frightened, completely unprepared for this abrupt reversal, he did not know what he felt for Shalada, would not dare to name it. But he knew now it was lust.

He had spent many a sleepless night dreaming of her naked golden-skinned body in his arms, as, he vowed, it would be one day. He could see her breasts pulsating, her thighs parting to accommodate him, and he had heard her moans of passion mingling with his own. So vivid had his imagination been that he had found himself trembling and sweating. In desperation he would light a candle and look at the sleeping Dorothy lying on her side. Her body had grown slack-muscled and stout, and he had not desired her in years, but he could expend himself inside her and gain a measure of relief. Turning her over on her back, he pushed up her night shift. Ignoring her sleepy protesting cry, he roughly thrust her legs apart; then, his face grim, he plunged inside her. As he rode her, he thought only of Shalada, and his movements became so frantic that Dorothy had screamed out that he was hurting her. He had cared nothing for her pain; he burned with his need for Shalada. In his mind he had cried out her name. Seeing the expression in Dorothy's eyes the following morning, he wondered if his tongue as well as his mind had cried out.

One morning he had gone to Shalada's room, hoping to catch her unaware. He had not troubled to knock as he lifted the latch and pushed the door open. To his disappointment, Shalada had been fully dressed. She turned at his entrance. "I have been expecting you," she said.

"Get your shawl," he bade her. "We are going on a journey."

At once her eyes became hard and suspicious, and he sensed that she was wondering if this was to be some new form of punishment. "Where do we journey?" she asked.

He smiled. "You will see. It is to be a surprise."

"A surprise?" Her arched dark brows lifted. "I

would imagine, knowing you, Father, that it is bound to be an unpleasant one."

He refused to be ruffled by the faint mockery in her tone and ignored the insult. Shalada had seemed to lay undue stress on the word "Father." But then, since he was sensitive on that particular point, perhaps it was his imagination. In any case, he told himself, it did not matter. On her eighteenth birthday, he would tell her the truth. "My dear," he would say, "you wrong me when you accuse me of abnormal desires toward you. You see, I am not your father." Then he would tell her of his true feelings. He could see the hard suspicious look leaving her eyes, her radiant smile as she allowed him to caress her.

Matthew knew that Shalada had not wanted to go with him. As he took her arm with an unfamiliar gallantry and escorted her downstairs, he could feel the tensing of her muscles. So the little wildcat was prepared to fight him, he thought with an inner amusement. But she would shortly find out how loving and generous and kind he could be. Leading her through the hall, he saw Robert and Tasmin standing by the kitchen door. Robert looked faintly startled when he saw them, but Tasmin's normally vacuous face wore a smirk. No doubt she, too, believed that he had thought up a new form of punishment.

He had taken Shalada to the nearest town. The town was not large, but it did boast a seamstress who had achieved a fair measure of fame locally through the imaginative and stylish gowns she created for various well-connected ladies. Without consulting Shalada's taste, he had ordered that a gown be made for her. It was to be cream, piped with red, and of the finest material. The thought of Shalada's dark beauty set off by the cream gown excited him.

The seamstress, her face flushed, her gray hair untidy beneath a lace cap, had betrayed agitation. "I am indeed honored by your patronage, Master Lorne," she said in a high, rather shaky voice. Her faded blue eyes turned to the silent Shalada. "It will be a pleasure to dress such a beautiful young lady."

Impatient with this small talk and annoyed by something he sensed in her attitude, Matthew had asked her abruptly when the gown would be ready.

Intimidated by the cold gleam in his eyes, the seamstress dropped him a curtsy. "There is a small problem, Master Lorne. I cannot have the gown ready in under two weeks. I have so much work, and I—"

"Nonsense!" Matthew cut her off rudely. "If you would care to keep my patronage, you will have the gown ready in three days."

The flush deepening in her thin, lined cheeks, the seamstress wrung her hands together. "Sir, much as I would like to oblige you, I cannot. I must have more time."

"You cannot? You say that to me!" Matthew drew himself up, wondering if the woman, for all her previous gushing, was really aware of who and what he was. Deciding that she must be aware, for who had not heard of Matthew Lorne, he was at his most intimidating when he spoke again. "You can and you will." He eyed the flustered woman frostily. "But as a matter of interest, what is this problem of which you speak?"

"I am Mistress Hart's problem," a deep, amused voice said.

Startled, Matthew swung around. The owner of the voice was just then emerging from behind some stacked-up bolts of cloth. The man who stood facing Matthew, a smile on his deeply tanned, ruggedly handsome face and amusement glimmering in his intensely dark eyes, was very tall. The short black velvet robe he wore, trimmed at the hem and at the cuffs of the elaborately slashed sleeves with a rich black fur, proclaimed him to be a man of wealth and position. As did the black cloak clasped with silver that swung carelessly from his broad shoulders. A silver chain from which depended an embroidered dagger pouch encircled his lean waist. His long powerful legs were encased in black hose, and his black silver-buckled shoes were extravagantly pointed in the latest fashion. Thick, dark, curling hair showed beneath a black velvet hat adorned with a curling white feather.

Matthew flushed as the amusement in the dark eyes deepened. "You spoke to me?" he said haughtily.

"I did indeed." The deep voice took on a faintly drawling note. "I dislike to see a woman bullied. I therefore thought it best to intervene."

"Bullied!" Matthew exclaimed in outrage.

The tall man shrugged aside the outburst as though it were of little consequence. "Mistress Hart has agreed to make some gowns for my mother," he went on calmly. "The order I have given her is quite large. Naturally, since she has already begun the work, this is the reason for the delay in the execution of your own order. I am sure you will understand."

The words were pleasantly said, but Matthew caught the mocking undertone. Flushing, he stole a quick look at Shalada. She was staring in wide-eyed fascination at the stranger. Looking away from her, he said coldly, "Sir, I have not seen you before. I take it you are a stranger to these parts."

"You take it correctly. My name, sir, if it is of interest to you, is David Medway." He bowed.

With a renewed surge of fury, Matthew found that the small obeisance was every bit as mocking as his tone. He inclined his own head stiffly in answer. Then, watching the man narrowly for any reaction, he said, "I am Matthew Lorne. Perhaps you have heard of me."

There was no perceptible change in David Medway's face. "To be sure I have heard of you, Master Lorne. You are known as the Holy Man, are you not? The terror of witches and other evildoers. Even in Cornwall, where I make my home, your name is known."

Matthew took a quick step forward. "I find your tone insulting, sir."

"How strange, I meant only to be pleasant." David

Medway shook his head. "It is sad indeed when one is misunderstood. Don't you agree, Master Lorne?"

Nervously, Mistress Hart intervened. "Sir David is not quite a stranger to me, Master Lorne. Though, to be sure, he was a babe when I last saw him." Her tongue stumbled over the last word, and she went on hurriedly. "Many years ago, when I lived in Cornwall, I made gowns for his mother. Sir David, who had business in London, was kind enough to remember me, and to make a journey that was out of his way. He will shortly be returning to Cornwall. That is why I wish to complete the work."

"Explanations have already been made, Mistress Hart," David said easily. As he spoke, his eyes were on Shalada, boldly appraising her. "I see no need to labor the point."

"No, Sir David, of course not. It is just that I wished to make quite sure that Master Lorne understood."

"But of course he understands," David said. "Anyone with perception must realize that Master Lorne is a very understanding and generous-hearted man. However, Mistress Hart, I have this very moment discovered a reason to delay my return to Cornwall. You may make the gown Master Lorne requires." David took a step toward Shalada. "The gown is for you, my pretty?" he asked in a soft voice.

Beneath his regard, the color flared into Shalada's face. "It is," she answered him curtly, "and I will thank you not to address me in such a fashion."

"You do not think you are pretty?" David's smile revealed even teeth that were very white against the brown of his face. "Perhaps you are right; you are more than pretty. You are beautiful."

Shalada's eyes flashed. "I suppose I should thank you for the compliment, sir."

"But you do not. Is that what you would say?"

"Exactly." Shalada's head rose haughtily. "No doubt you mean to be kind, but you are a stranger, and I am not interested in your opinion of my looks, or, for that matter, in anything else you might have to say."

"Unkind! But we are not strangers, for I have seen you many times."

"You have?" Shalada said, surprised. "Where have you seen me?"

"In my dreams, of course."

"You are foolish and impudent."

"Impudent, I grant you. But never foolish."

"Anyway, I knew you were lying. If I had seen you, I would not have forgotten you." No sooner were the words out of Shalada's mouth than she could have bitten her tongue, for the look in his eyes grew warmer and even more intimate.

"Thank you," David said. "It makes me happy to know that."

"Oh, you! I did not mean . . ." Shalada broke off. Glaring at him, she said coldly, "You are a conceited popinjay!"

"Call me what you will, my pretty. You and I will meet again."

"Not if I can avoid it."

"Ah, but you have no choice in the matter. I have made up my mind." David laughed as her mouth opened to make a furious reply. Cutting her off, he went on smoothly, "Such fire and fury! I must remember that there are claws beneath that velvet skin."

Listening to them, Matthew was outraged. Unable to control his emotions, he felt his jealousy mounting. How dare this stranger talk to Shalada so. And as for Shalada, for all her coldly rebuking tones, it was obvious to him that she was enjoying the little encounter. Matthew asked himself why he hadn't stepped forward and put an end to Medway's infernal impudence. Was it because of the expression he momentarily glimpsed in the man's dark eyes when they had met his, an expression so bleak, so almost threatening that it had seemed to hold him at arm's length, jolting him, and rending asunder his normally complacent attitude? To the best of his knowledge, he and Medway had never met before. Still he did not move, even though Medway's deep, intimate glance seemed to be devouring the girl, mentally stripping her of her clothes, seeing her naked, as he himself so longed to do.

Perhaps Mistress Hart had sensed his feelings, Matthew thought, for suddenly she was beside him, her face flushed with her earnest desire to please, her nervous fingers twisting a strand of her gray hair. "Master Lorne"—she spoke to him in a soothing undertone such as one might employ with a child—"it is wrong of Sir David to be so bold with your daughter, but I am sure he means no harm." Having said this, she beamed upon him. "But there, I suppose we can't expect young gentlemen to be as they were in our day, can we?"

Much of the deep inner disquiet Matthew was experiencing in regard to Sir David Medway was blown away by the rage her words aroused. He turned his glare upon her, and he was gratified to see her face crumple into lines of dismay. How dare she speak of "our day," as though he were her contemporary. He must be fifteen years her junior, perhaps more. Mastering his rage, he snapped, "You will take Mistress Lorne's measurements, if you please, and hurry. We have much to do this morning."

"Yes, sir, at once." Like a startled rabbit, Mistress Hart scurried away.

Shalada, her cheeks still brightly flushed, consulted with Mistress Hart. Matthew made a pretense of examining some materials so that he need not be forced into further conversation with the stranger. He was startled when David Medway's deep, drawling voice said from behind him. "You know, Master Lorne, as I have already told your daughter, we will meet again."

"I doubt that." Matthew did not turn; he continued to finger a bolt of rose-pink silk.

"Ah, but one should never doubt a certainty. But you seem nervous, Master Lorne, your hands are trembling. Is something the matter?"

Matthew swung around to face him. "I have no reason to be nervous, Sir David, and I find your attitude very strange indeed."

"Do you?" Matthew saw David Medway's eyes widen as though in genuine perplexity. "Is it possible," he went on, "that I have given you cause for offense?"

Something of the icy control Matthew employed when speaking with strangers slipped. "Everything about you offends me." Despite himself, his voice rose on the last word, and he noticed the seamstress's startled glance in his direction. Forcing himself to speak quietly, he added, "Have we met before?"

"Now, I wonder why you should think that." David Medway seemed amused, and the menace had disappeared from his dark eyes. "I am vain enough to hope, if we had met before, that you would have remembered me."

Matthew looked at him, his eyes narrowing as something prodded at his mind, something, he felt, that he should remember. Angry because he could not capture the elusive memory, he said in an icy forbidding voice, "If you should appear in Waterford and continue your unwelcome attentions to my . . ." He stopped. In his mind he had already thrust the false relationship between himself and Shalada aside, and he could not bring himself to say "my daughter." Instead, as a compromise, he went on, ". . . to Mistress Lorne, then I warn you that it will be the worse for you. I am not without influence."

David Medway seemed not to notice his hesitation. "I know," he said, and the mockery in his voice was very apparent. "You do have considerable influence in many parts of the country, and you do not fail to use it."

"What do you mean?"

David Medway shrugged his broad shoulders. "My meaning for the moment is unimportant." He smiled, adding thoughtfully, "Waterford, eh?"

Matthew drew himself up. Did the fellow actually

think he had trapped him? "Yes, Waterford. That is where I live. Anyone could have told you that."

David nodded. "Quite. Matthew Lorne is, after all, very well known."

Matthew stared at him. He was sure now that there was something he should remember. He said hesitantly, "Are you certain we have not met before? There is something in your attitude that leads me to believe we have."

David shook his head. "I am sorry if my attitude disturbs you. It was quite unintentional on my part. It might be, of course, that I bear a resemblance to some-one who once crossed your path. Could that be it, do you think?"

It was Shalada, returning quietly to his side, who cut through the growing tension. Without looking at the other man, she said with unaccustomed meekness, "I am ready, Father."

"Very well." Again Matthew was forced to control his anger as David Medway, sweeping off his hat, bade them a smiling farewell. Matthew acknowledged this with a curt inclination of his head, and hastily ushered Shalada from the little shop.

On the way home, Shalada had sat quietly in a corner of the carriage. She did not look at him, and she made no attempt at conversation. As a consequence, Matthew found his thoughts revolving about the dark stranger. Medway. He had heard the name before. He thought of the tone of the man's voice, the underlying mockery, the disturbing look he had seen in his eyes. At the end of the journey he had come to no conclusion save one. The man represented danger, and he himself, in some inexplicable way, was his target. He must find out more about him, for he had the sudden urgent feeling that it was vital that he know everything about Sir David Medway.

Banishing the memory of that day with some difficulty, Matthew looked up again. Shalada stood in the same position on the crest of the hill. From beneath the cap, her hair streamed in the wind, and her skirts were plastered against her, outlining her slender hips. Behind her, the sky had grown increasingly dark. Only a thin streamer of sunlight showed between the fast-encroaching clouds.

Shivering, Matthew drew his cloak about him. Perhaps the rain would hold off for a while. In any case, it would not matter. He was used to being out in all sorts of weather. Shalada had not called to him again, so obviously her impatience to be with Rebecca had subsided. He was aware of weariness. There was really no need for him to go to the top of the hill, he reflected, since Ladyford Lane, their destination lay below. He had an impulse to call to her, to beckon her down. He raised his hand, then let it drop again. No, in a little while he would get to his feet and complete the climb. He would show Shalada that, at forty-seven, he was as agile as any young man. Once she knew the real truth about their relationship, she might still fight him. But he was prepared for that. Willingly or unwillingly, he intended to have her. Once he had subdued her, she would find that the twenty-nine years that lay between them made little difference, for he would be a virile and tireless lover. In a way, he would prefer her to be unwilling; it would make her conquest the more exciting. He thought of himself inside that golden body, moving slowly at first, then faster and faster. Shalada! Her round breasts, pink-tipped, soft and inviting. Her long shapely legs opening to receive him! With a stifled moan he closed his eyes. Crouching forward, he clasped his arms tightly about his knees to still his trembling.

As though to cool his fever, David Medway entered his mind again. Medway, young, dark, and handsome, so unbearably arrogant. Matthew's mouth tightened. Curse him! Why should he think of him now? Why should his sensuous thoughts of Shalada bring Medway in their train? He tightened his clasp about his knees. He had been wrong to think of Medway as a danger to himself, or, if it came to that, to Shalada. Danger, bah! His thinking had been upside down because he had read Medway's desire for Shalada in his eyes, and he had put the wrong construction upon it. The man was obviously a profligate, but, if he were not mistaken in him, he would be too careless and lazy to pursue a chance acquaintance.

Trying to ignore his physical discomfort, Matthew thought of how slight an impression Medway had made upon Shalada. After that encounter with the man, he had watched her carefully. There had been no change in her demeanor, and not once had she mentioned Medway's name. Because her indifference had pleased him, he had begun to think of other things he planned to buy for her. A fan, a bracelet to adorn her slender wrist, a ring, a gold net for her hair, some bright ribbons to tie it. Maybe several pairs of those newfangled perfumed gloves that he had heard were so much favored by the ladies of the English court. With Dorothy's fortune added to his, he had become a very wealthy man. He had always been careful with his money, but he would delight in spending it on Shalada.

Shalada contemplated the steep downward incline that lay before her. At the foot of the hill, looking from her vantage point like a muddy thread, was the winding rutted track used mainly for the lumbering farm carts. This track, after many devious turns, would eventually lead her to the home of Rebecca West. The low, thatched cottage at the end of Ladyford Lane. She had climbed the hill chiefly to escape the distasteful company of her father, whose labored breathing had told her that he was tiring. But she must move soon. Rebecca was not expecting her today, but she would be delighted to see her. She always was.

Her eyes softening, Shalada tucked a flying strand of hair beneath her cap. Dear Rebecca, how she loved her. And she knew from the expression in Rebecca's eyes, her tremulous eager smile, and the soft little pats she always gave her, that she was loved in return. Poor Rebecca, she was the nearest thing to a mother she had ever known. From her own mother she had never known love, but only harshness and blows.

Shalada's eyes looked downward at the huddled form of her father. He had made her life a misery. Only by fighting him, by taking the continual punishments in silence, had she been able to survive. There were times when she had wanted to kill him. Once she had even gone so far as to hide a knife in her apron pocket. So great was her hatred and her resentment of him that she had been fully prepared to use the knife. Not even the sobering thought of hanging for her crime, or perhaps being burned to death, would have prevented her from plunging it into his back. And then, suddenly, bewilderingly, he had changed. His harsh voice was gentled when he spoke to her. There were no more angry tirades. Blows were exchanged for small, furtive caresses. His fingers would brush against her as if by accident, his hand would rest upon her breast. At first she had told herself that she was imagining things, and then she had seen the look in his eyes. The same look that was always present in Robert's eyes, forever seeking a chance to make love to her. She remembered the time when her brother had come to her room. She had been prepared for bed, and she had asked him what he wanted.

Robert had stood by the closed door for a moment, then crossed quickly to her side. She could still see that look in his eyes, still hear his stammering voice. "Shalada, I . . . I want to make love to you."

"You what!" Stunned, she had drawn back. "Either you are insane or you can't know what you are saying."

"I know what I am saying. I watch you all the time. The way your hips sway when you walk, the beautiful outline of your breasts. You're so beautiful, so perfect!"

"You are mad. Have you forgotten that I am your sister?"

"I don't care about that. I don't care about anything but you. If I am mad, it is you who have driven me into madness." Before she could move, his hand reached out and his strong fingers ripped away the front of her night shift. "Let me, Shalada!" He was almost sobbing.

Holding the torn pieces of her shift together, trying to fight her sickness and panic, she had struck out with her other hand. "Get out!"

His face reddening from her blow, his eyes fixed on her body, Robert had just stood there, his clenched hands hanging at his sides.

There was nothing Robert could do. His face sullen, he had left. She had said nothing about the incident. Even had she done so, she would not have been believed. Robert was her mother's favorite child. She would not hear a word against him. But after that, Shalada carefully bolted her door every night. Lying rigid in her bed, she ignored Robert's faint tapping, his soft voice calling to her. Would she now have to bolt her door against both father and brother?

It was an evil and unnatural situation in which she found herself. Her mother appeared to be blind to the tension in the house, but sometimes she wondered if Tasmin knew what was going on. She would often find the girl's blue eyes fixed on her with a strange expression. And lately Tasmin had grown very insolent. Twice she had boxed the girl's ears. It was useless to attempt an explanation of her actions to her mother, for though Robert was the favorite child, Tasmin came a close second. It was she who was and had always been the outcast. In her more thoughtful moments she had thought that perhaps she could not altogether blame her mother for favoring the other two. She was different in every way from Robert and Tasmin, in looks, in temperament. They were industrious and sober, while she, in her work about the house and the dairy, was careless and impatient. They were even-tempered, but she was fiery. They were practical, but she was a dreamer. They were everything that she was not. As a child, this difference had troubled her, and she had made spasmodic efforts to be more like them. But now she was glad to be different, for though she could be vengeful, she was not mean and petty by nature, as Robert and Tasmin had proved themselves to be. If that was a virtue, then she had one other, the ability to recognize her own shortcomings, of which she had plenty. But virtue fell short then, for hating every member of her family as she did, she did nothing to correct these faults in herself.

She looked down at her father again. Perhaps out of all of them she hated him the most. In her heart, she feared him too, but she would die before she would let him know of that secret fear. To hide this fear she had always stood up to him boldly. Where Tasmin would cower and whimper, she would ignore her own pain. Standing as erect as possible, she would spit out defiant words. In the days before he had begun to change toward her, this would always bring extra and savage punishment. With his face contorted with rage, he would stand over her, and with every swish of the cane he would call her "bastard." For all his anger, she had thought that the uttering of the word seemed to give him a special pleasure. But since the change, her defiance seemed to excite rather than anger. It would bring that look to his eyes that made her skin crawl with loathing, and the furtive caresses would become more frequent.

Matthew Lorne, her father. His shadow stretched far, touching everyone in the village. He had once been mixed up in Rebecca West's life. Was it he who had set the shadows in her eyes and had reduced her to her present pitiful condition? Once, so the village gossips said, Rebecca had been beautiful and bright, and she had not always been dumb. It was the shock and terror of her mother's death that had taken her voice. By listening when she was unobserved, for the gossips did not speak freely in front of the witch-finder's daughter, Shalada had learned that Rebecca's mother had been a witch, and for her many crimes, she had been burned. She heard, too, that Rebecca had once been betrothed to Matthew Lorne. He had loved her dearly, it was said, but she had betrayed him with another man, a foreigner. It was true that Margaret West had been burned, for Shalada had seen her neglected and unhallowed grave. In the spring and summer a drooping tree hid Margaret West's grave from sight, protecting it with a fragile green beauty. In the autumn, a litter of leaves and twigs disfigured the mound, and then in winter it was again hidden by a blanket of snow.

Shalada had no difficulty in accepting the fact that her father was responsible for Margaret West's death, just as she believed that the unfortunate woman, like so many of his victims, was innocent. But surely, she would argue, the rest of the gossip was nonsense. She truly believed that her father did not have it in him to love, so how could anyone as sweet and gentle as Rebecca have been betrothed to such a man? Bewildered, she once questioned Rebecca on the subject. She asked her outright, "Is it true what the people say, Rebecca, were you once betrothed to my father?"

She expected Rebecca to answer her question with a nod or a shake of her head, and was unprepared for the expression of pure terror. The fragile little woman had shrunk back as though from a blow. Then, the tears running down her lined cheeks, she had hidden her face in shaking hands.

Full of remorse, Shalada gently stroked the gray-streaked hair, then took the trembling form into her arms and held her closely. "It's all right, there is nothing to fear."

Rebecca, though she appeared to have recovered from the first shock, was still afraid. When Shalada made her infrequent visits, her fear was plain in her expressive eyes. Shalada's visits were necessarily infrequent; her father had forbidden her to visit more than once a month, and then only if he accompanied her. He himself never entered the cottage. Shalada had the feeling that he could not bear the sight of Rebecca. Since she knew that he never did anything without a purpose, she wondered what his purpose might be in permitting the visits at all. At the back of her mind she was suspicious and vaguely troubled. Then, with her father stationed right outside the front door, she would forget everything but her pleasure in seeing the little woman again.

Shalada smiled. It was Rebecca's fear and her own continually seething rebellion that now enabled them to share a wonderful secret. Because she wanted to cheer Rebecca, she had begun sneaking away to the cottage whenever her father was absent. With the result that she was now visiting every week. The regular visits had begun three months ago, and that was when she had begun urging Rebecca to speak. "I know you can speak if you really want to," she had urged. "Won't you try?"

At first Rebecca had resisted. Pointing to her throat, she had shaken her head violently. Kneeling beside her, Shalada had stroked her hand. "Please try, do it for me."

Rebecca's eyes had lit up, and her lips had silently formed words. *"For you."*

Excited because she had managed to decipher the moving lips, Shalada had hugged her. "Yes, yes, that's right, do it for me. I love you, Rebecca, and I want to hear your voice. I know you can do it."

Rebecca nodded, and there was such a shining look in her eyes that Shalada had found herself almost unbearably moved. Intuition told her that it was the words "I love you" that had put the shining look there. From now on, she had vowed then, since it seemed to mean so much to Rebecca, she would make a point of speaking her affection aloud.

And so the struggle for speech had begun. It had

proved so painful to watch that Shalada, after a while, had tried to call a halt to the experiment. It was Rebecca, however, who had persisted. She would pat Shalada's worried face in reassurance, and her lips would form the words *"For you."*

Touched, Shalada had answered her quickly. "I know. You want to go on trying. But please don't try too hard."

Two weeks ago, just as Shalada was about to take her leave, Rebecca, looking very excited, hurried to her side, placing her hand against Shalada's cheek. Her throat began the painful process of talking again. Shalada waited patiently without much hope, and then, like a miracle, a single word jerked out. "Pretty." The word was rusty and uncertain, but intelligible. Rebecca's thin fingers stroked Shalada's cheek lovingly. "Pretty," she said again.

Overcome, Shalada cried out, "That's wonderful, Rebecca, wonderful!"

Rebecca had been almost shy, so great was her pleasure in this praise. But after that valiant try, she had not spoken again for several days. And then, just when Shalada was beginning to despair, she had managed, with a struggle, to produce two more words. "Love y-you."

Shalada had kissed her cheek. "And I love you, Rebecca. You are like a mother to me."

The joy in Rebecca's face had been so vivid that Shalada, who rarely cried, had wanted to do so then. But after the emotional moment was over, she felt that she had drawn even closer to the lonely little woman. On an impulse, she told Rebecca about the man she had met in Mistress Hart's dressmaking shop. "He was so handsome," she said, "so exciting. He was so . . . so alive."

Smiling, Rebecca had stroked her hand. With her soft, anxious eyes fixed on Shalada's face, she had asked, "Love?"

Taken aback by the question, Shalada had stared at

her with her mouth agape. "Love, good gracious no, Rebecca." She laughed. "He is a stranger, and an arrogant one at that. I meant that I admired his looks and that certain quality about him that made him seem so different."

Remembering her enthusiastic words, Shalada blushed for her foolishness. Small wonder, when she had gushed so about him, that Rebecca had believed there was more to it than a chance encounter. Since she had looked into David Medway's dark eyes and had heard him say in his deep voice, "You and I will meet again," she had done little else but think about him. It was time she stopped, for of course his words had meant nothing. She must not continue to dream. She must stop looking for him whenever her mother sent her into the village to shop. Sir David Medway. His name lingered pleasantly in her mind. But what a fool she was to think he could have any real interest in her. He was from a different world from her own, a different level of society.

On this last thought, the arrogance in Shalada's own nature asserted itself. Whatever David Medway might think, she was not an ignorant village girl. Her father was a cruel, heedless man, but he had a great deal of pride. In deference to that pride he had seen to it that his three children were well-educated. He imported a tutor from London, who after several months had returned thankfully to London. But her father continued to tutor them in the social graces. After one such lesson, when her father left the room, Tasmin had remarked to Robert, "It is all well and good, but what is the use of all this education if we are going to be forced to spend the rest of our lives in this miserable village?"

For once Robert was good-natured. Rumpling her pale hair, he had laughed at her petulant outburst. "Who says we have to remain here?"

"What else can we do?" Tasmin had cast a fearful look at the closed door. "I would like to go to London.

But our father keeps us in rags. He is too close-fisted to buy Mother a gown, let alone provide any of us with the new clothes which would be required for such an expedition."

"Are you calling our father close-fisted?" Robert inquired in a loud voice.

"Oh, hush!" Tasmin said in an agony of apprehension.

"Don't worry, I won't give you away." Robert smiled lazily at Tasmin. "Anyway, I daresay you'll get yourself a husband. And then, I have no doubt, you'll move up in life."

"A husband!" Forgetting her fear of being overheard, Tasmin had flung the word at him with unusual passion. "And where, pray, am I to find this husband? If you think I'd marry any of the oafs about here, you are much mistaken." Her blue eyes darted spitefully at Shalada. "The gypsy might settle for one of them, but I certainly shall not."

The good-natured smile left Robert's face. "I have told you before about calling Shalada a gypsy. If you do it again, I will box your ears."

Tasmin backed from him. "Why shouldn't I say it, she is as dark as a gypsy. She is not at all like me, or you either."

Robert's eyes turned to the silent Shalada. Seeing the scorn in her expression as she regarded Tasmin, he said softly, "You are quite right, Tasmin, Shalada is not like you. Shalada is beautiful. So beautiful that she could marry a king."

"Shalada, always Shalada!" Tasmin had cried out in a shrill voice. "I'm sick of the way you're always fawning over her. One would think you were in love with her."

"Shut your stupid mouth," Robert growled.

"I won't. I'm not the only one who's noticed it. The other day I heard Mother telling Father that she wouldn't stand for the way you went on with Shalada."

Robert's eyes narrowed. "I see. And what did Father say?"

"He said that she wouldn't have to worry much longer." Tasmin's eyes looked with a faint bewilderment from Shalada to Robert. "Mother cried," she went on. "She said that she knew, from the first moment she laid eyes on Shalada, she would bring nothing but trouble." Tasmin hesitated. "What do you suppose she meant, Robert?"

"How should I know?"

Tasmin smiled. As though Shalada was not in the room, she said cheerfully, "Oh, well, it doesn't matter. But Mother's quite right about Shalada being trouble. She's got such a nasty temper. Last week, when we were working in the dairy, she hit me. And I'd hardly said anything to her."

Again Robert glanced at Shalada. "And she's likely to hit you again, Tasmin, if you don't shut up."

Tasmin darted a quick look at Shalada. Then, deciding to get back into Robert's good graces, she said in a wheedling voice, "What about me, Robert, don't you think I could marry a king?"

Robert's laughter burst forth. "You, by Christ! Tasmin, surely you would not dream of comparing yourself to Shalada?"

Tasmin's face flushed a dull red. Her eyes brimming with tears, she shrieked at him, "I hate Shalada, and I hate you. Just wait until I tell Mother what you said."

Robert shrugged. "Tell away, you pudding-faced little idiot, and much good may it do you. She won't believe a word you say."

"She will!"

"Not when I deny it. And of course I shall."

"Then I'll tell Father."

"No you won't," Robert answered, giving her a look of scorn. "You're much too frightened of him to open that rabbit mouth of yours, and you know it."

Bursting into tears, Tasmin had run from the room.

As soon as she had gone, Shalada rose to her feet. "Where are you going?" Robert queried.

"As far away from you as I can possibly get," she had answered him in a cool voice.

"You're an ungrateful bitch," Robert said, strolling toward her. "Didn't you hear me defending you?"

Shalada tried to control herself. "I don't need your defense," she said coldly. "You are despicable."

"Shalada." His arms went around her. "Kiss me, my beauty."

"Leave me alone!" Instinct guided her next step, and her knee jerked upward. As the moaning Robert stumbled over to a chair, she ran for the door.

Shalada hastily dismissed the distasteful memory of Robert from her mind. Almost immediately she found her thoughts reverting to David Medway. Once more she saw the bold dark eyes in the handsome swarthy face. She felt the same tingle she had felt then, the same weakness in her limbs. What would it be like, she wondered, to be loved by a man like that?

Frowning, she tried to dismiss David Medway as she had done Robert, but he would not be dismissed. Curse him! Why couldn't she stop thinking about him? While it was true that she was not unlettered, he would no doubt see her as such. So, even if she were to meet with him again, her pride demanded that she ignore him. Her father, on the only time he had referred to David Medway, had had one word to say about him. "Lecher." Though she hated to agree with her father on any point, she was mentally obliged to concede that this might well be so.

Shalada looked down at her dropped cloak. Picking it up, she swung it about her shoulders. She had let it fall into the mud, and she would be in for a fine lecture from her mother on the sin of ruining good clothes. Shalada's mouth tightened. What did it matter? She could not do right in her mother's eyes, and she had long since ceased to try.

"Shalada. I'm coming." Her father's voice scattered thought.

"No. Wait there, please. I'll save you the trouble." If he came up, she would be forced to endure his company until he cared to move again. Her ambition, these days, was to avoid being alone with her father or her brother. Firmly she tied the strings of the cloak beneath her chin, and began the descent.

Matthew's annoyance that she had deprived him of the chance to prove his agility faded as she came closer. How lovely she was with her shining hair, her creamy skin, and her exotic dark eyes with their slight intriguing tilt at the outer corners. Her features were finely cut, her firm chin clefted. Her mouth was full, but beautifully formed. That mouth of hers, so red, so lush. How he longed to feel it crushed beneath his own!

"Shalada." As she stopped beside him, he put a trembling arm about her shoulders. "Come, child, we have wasted enough time."

"Yes." She ducked from beneath his arm. For the sake of something to do, she straightened her cap, and then summoned a smile. She was uncomfortably aware that the smile must look forced. A mere grimace that covered hatred. But she had no wish to fight with him at this moment, for he might forbid her visit to Rebecca. "Then, if you feel we have wasted time, let's hurry." Even to her own ears, her voice sounded hard.

"Very well," Matthew said curtly. He could wait, he thought, as he watched her hurry ahead of him. His time would come.

Why? Shalada asked herself. Surely it was wrong to feel so much hatred for this man who was her father? Her soft mouth hardened. But then of course she came from an unnatural family. The behavior of Robert, and more recently of her father, was proof of that. Why should she be different?

7

Rebecca West watched from the tiny window of her cottage as Matthew Lorne and Shalada came slowly down the lane. She had been watching for some time now, and she had begun to think that Shalada would never come. Her eyes studied Matthew Lorne, who was walking very slowly. He was looking old these days, she thought, far older than his forty-seven years. His sandy hair had whitened, and his shoulders were stooped. Perhaps it was the evil in his nature that had graven the deep lines into his sallow face and had turned him into an old man.

Rebecca drew back a little as the two came closer. She must be careful not to let the man see her. It might be that the sight of her would cause him to stop Shalada's visits altogether. For if her hatred of him was undying, his was equally so for her. Although Matthew Lorne had never put it into words, it was not hard to guess that he had taken a vow to look upon her as little as possible. That was why he never entered the cottage, stationing himself instead outside the door until Shalada emerged. If Shalada overstayed the time he had allotted to her, he would begin a soft persistent knocking that both she and Shalada found impossible to ignore. Rebecca had learned to dread that sound that signaled the parting from her child. But one day Matthew Lorne would enter the cottage. When that day came, she would know that he was about to complete his revenge. In the meantime, she would not allow his threatening presence outside her door to spoil the visits with her daughter. Not even the presence of Satan himself could have clouded her joy in those cherished moments.

Rebecca's hand clenched tightly upon the curtain. For eighteen years he had let her live, not out of compassion, she had no delusions about that, but out of a desire to hurt her still more. In watching her daughter grow from little girl to beautiful young woman, he wanted her to suffer the full torment of knowing she could never claim Shalada as her own. To intensify her suffering, he permitted her to see her child. She knew that in time this punishment would no longer be enough for him. He would never be done with her until she was dead and beyond his malignant reach. He might pretend to himself that she was free to leave the cottage, free to leave the village, but in his heart he knew that she was not free. She was bound as helplessly as any prisoner by her love for her daughter. And so he went on providing for her, and he was careful to let it be known that he did so. He did not, of course, concern himself directly in this matter, but he saw to it that it was done by others. How could she denounce him? She was mute, could not read or write. Matthew left nothing to chance. To suit his own purposes, he had not yet spread the story of her supposed witchcraft. But he had taken care to indicate that Margaret West's tragic though well-deserved death had left Rebecca feebleminded. The first she had heard of this lying story was on the day when a small boy had come to her door to deliver a basket of groceries. The boy had seemed ill at ease. Smiling at him, she had signed to him to enter the cottage. She was fond of children, and she had wanted to give him a small reward for his trouble. The boy, his round blue eyes going rounder still, had drawn back in obvious fear. Shaking his head, he had shoved the basket so roughly into her arms that much of the contents had spilled to the ground; then he had scuttled rapidly down the path. With distance between them, he paused for a moment and shouted loudly, "I ain't coming no further. Your ma was a witch. Master Lorne told us you ain't got no brains left 'cause you're still grieving over her."

Trembling with the shock of his words, Rebecca watched him till he was out of sight. Matthew Lorne had scored another victory; those people who might have visited her would now take pains to avoid her. And so it had been all through the long and aching years. If it had not been for Shalada, her lovely girl, she would have died of loneliness.

Rebecca closed her eyes for a moment. Shalada's name no longer troubled her, for she had grown used to it, but there were times when it was still capable of bringing back a poignant memory of that long-ago day in the woods. She could still remember clearly the ecstasy of that moment when Don Roberto entered her body. Sometimes, when she lay in her lonely bed, she would deliberately conjure up the memory of those moments when Shalada had been created. She could almost feel him moving inside her, the sweetness and thrill of his lips against her breasts. Then another memory would come, effectively driving out the first. Matthew Lorne, Don Roberto's murderer, her mother's murderer, shuddering and sobbing as he drove himself into her body. Then she would see the leaping flames again. She would hear her mother screaming, and she was back at the scene of the murder, with the noise, the jeers, the laughter of the crowd in her ears, the dreadful stench of roasting flesh in her nostrils. She would know that there was only one way to obtain relief from the violence of her memories. Rising from her bed, she would fall to her knees in prayer. Gradually a calm would come over her and she would go back to her bed and sleep.

Opening her eyes, she put her hand to her throat. Matthew must not know she was no longer dumb; she would warn Shalada to keep silent. Shalada would not understand why she wanted to keep it from him, but she knew that she would respect her wishes. She could not help thinking that if Matthew knew, her position, and perhaps Shalada's too, would become very dangerous. Matthew would not want Shalada to know the truth about her birth.

Perseverance had paid. It was still difficult for her to bring out words, but each day it became easier. Shalada had wrought the miracle. She had said to her, "For me. I love you. You are like a mother to me." It was those magic words from Shalada's lips that had poured life into her, had forced her to fight the silence of years, and to win.

Rebecca pressed her face closer to the window. Shalada was coming up the path now, with Matthew close behind her. Rebecca's gaze sharpened suddenly. It seemed to her that Shalada was looking troubled, almost frightened. Had Matthew threatened her in some way?

As a rule, Rebecca avoided looking directly at Matthew, but now, when he put his arm about Shalada's shoulders and drew her close against him, her eyes were drawn to his face. What she saw in his expression caused her heart to hammer with terror. She knew that look. His mouth looked loose and wet, as though he had continually run his tongue over his lips. She could not see his eyes, but she knew they would be searching and avid. He no longer saw Shalada as a daughter, but as a desirable woman.

Rebecca's head began to throb as a great surge of rage banished terror. Shalada must not stay in his house a moment longer. She would warn her, tell her that she must go far from this place. For a weak, fleeting moment she thought of how lonely she would be without the girl, and then she put the thought firmly from her. She didn't matter. Only Shalada mattered. Once she knew that her daughter was safe from Matthew Lorne, she could find the courage to bear anything. Shalada's young life must not be ruined, as hers had been.

"Shalada"—Matthew's voice came clearly to Rebecca's straining ears—"why do you look at me in that way? Do you think I mean you harm? You cannot be afraid of your own father."

"You disgust me." Abruptly Shalada broke free from his hold. "If you think I am ignorant of what goes on in your mind, you are mistaken."

Rebecca put a hand to her trembling mouth. Oh, my child, she thought, you have courage. Much more than I had. But in dealing with a man like Matthew Lorne, too much courage and spirit might well be foolish.

Matthew looked at Shalada with malevolent eyes. One day she would go too far.

"Well?"—Shalada looked at him boldly—"may I go in now?"

"In a moment," he answered. "You have insulted me, and I should be very angry with you, but instead I am only grieved."

Hypocrite! Rebecca's legs trembled so much that she had a fear she would fall. She clutched at the back of a chair for support. He spoke to Shalada with difficulty, as though he was hanging on tightly to his control, but there had been a smooth hypocrisy in his voice when he had condemned her mother to death. She listened again.

"Tomorrow is your birthday, Shalada," Matthew said, "and I have a very nice surprise for you. I think, from that moment on, that you will begin to see me in a different light."

Uneasily, Shalada put her hand on the doorlatch. He terrified her, but she was not going to let him see her fear. "What do you mean?"

Matthew shook his head. "If you understood, then it would not be a surprise. Just remember that pleasant surprises always come on birthdays."

"I want nothing from you," Shalada answered him coldly. "Unless, of course, you can arrange it that I be as far away from you as possible."

Matthew forced his lips to smile. "Be careful,

Shalada. In a moment you will find yourself becoming quite distraught. I have learned to recognize the signs."

Shalada stiffened. "You are mistaken."

Matthew's eyes narrowed. "Sometimes I am not sure if you are entirely sane."

Shalada's fingers tightened on the doorlatch. What cruel game was he playing now? "I think, Father," she said in a clear voice, "that it is not my sanity which should be questioned."

Matthew's eyes glittered coldly. "You must not distress yourself, Shalada. It is natural that you should defend yourself against such a charge. After tomorrow, I think I can promise a change in your mental attitude." He shrugged. Then, out of a desire to frighten her, he added, "If there is no change, there is always Lammington Manor." His eyes pierced into hers. "You have heard of Lammington?"

Rebecca fought the scream that was struggling to emerge. He was threatening her baby with Lammington. Her hands crooked into claws, and the expression on her face would have chilled Matthew Lorne if he could have seen it.

Trying to subdue the fear his words had inspired, Shalada drew in a deep steadying breath. "Yes, I . . . I have heard of Lammington," she answered. "It is a place for the insane."

"Exactly." For the moment Matthew was satisfied. His words had caused the color to drain from her cheeks, and though she was making a great effort to speak calmly, he could see the fear in her eyes. His smile returned. "Behave yourself, and Lammington need not concern us." His eyes lingered meaningfully on her face. "However, should you continue to behave like a wild thing, as you have done in the past, I will have to give the matter more serious thought."

Looking at him, Shalada found that she was not convinced he would not do such a thing. He would lock her away, if it suited him to do so. She felt an overwhelming sense of despair, but still something in her refused to surrender. "I understand that you are threatening me," she said, trying to keep her voice even. "But I doubt that the Lammington authorities could be persuaded to take in a sane person."

She could not disguise her fear. He would let her worry tonight. Tomorrow she would know everything, but the burden of what he had just said would still be on her mind. It would make her more amenable when he took her to his bed. Amenable, and so much more loving. Deliberately taunting her, he said, "Don't worry about the Lammington authorities, Shalada. I assure you that the word of Matthew Lorne will carry great weight with them."

Her eyes looked enormous in her pale face. There was something about their haunted expression that reminded him of Rebecca's eyes. Rebecca had looked at him in just that way when she had realized that Don Roberto was dead and she was completely at his mercy. She was so frightened she temporarily lost her wits and her power of speech. His thoughts swung to Dorothy, his wife. She would suffer too when he put her out of their bedchamber and installed Shalada in her place. But she would have to put up with it. He knew that she would never leave him, for she loved him still, and she had no pride. He had never loved Dorothy, and he had made no secret of it. On their wedding night he had told her plainly just why he had married her, for her money and possessions. Once she had been reasonably pretty, but all traces of it had vanished. He despised her ugliness, her thick, flabby body, her coy and pathetic attempts to seduce him into making love to her. He despised the children she had borne him. Robert, who turned out to be a weakling, and Tasmin, who had always been quick to whine.

Matthew started out of his thoughts as Shalada's voice came to him. He looked at her vacantly for a moment. Then, his eyes clearing of their abstraction, he said curtly, "Did you say something?"

Shalada nodded. "I did. I said, if you have no objection, I will go inside and see Rebecca."

Matthew smiled his thin smile. "By all means. Run along and see your old woman."

He watched as Shalada fumbled with the latch. "Old woman" was a true description of Rebecca, he reflected. Though she was younger than he, she looked many years older. He thought of her trembling behind the door as she listened to the conversation between himself and Shalada, and he smiled inwardly. She would be terrified but helpless at this threat against her beloved daughter.

Rebecca drew back as the door opened and Shalada burst into the room. "Rebecca!" Shalada's voice was low, but it seemed to Rebecca to hold a cry for help. "Were you listening, did you hear what my father said?"

Rebecca stumbled toward her, her arms outstretched. Tears of sorrow and anger coursed down her lined face as she caught the girl to her in a fierce embrace. "He . . . he is not your father," she said quite clearly.

Shalada was very still for a moment; then, gently, she released herself from the clinging arms. "Not my father." Her bewildered eyes searched Rebecca's face. "Do you know what you are saying?"

Rebecca stroked Shalada's cheek. "You are m-my child." She said it with the pent-up love of years. Struggling to convince, she did not stop to think of how she could form her words, and they came out shakily but freely. "That man t-took you from me!" Her voice rose. "He is not your father."

Shalada clutched the thin shoulders with trembling hands.

"M-M-Matthew Lorne burned my m-mother, and murdered your father."

Shaken and frightened, but convinced by the look of shining truth on Rebecca's face, Shalada backed away from her. "All those years with him, and he is not . . ."

Overcome, she hid her face in her hands. "Oh, my God!"

"You must go away, Sh-Shalada. He must n-n-not be allowed to . . ." Rebecca broke off as the door crashed open. She stared at Matthew Lorne with terror in her fever-bright eyes. "Go, my darling," she said hoarsely.

Shalada started across the room. Her head was reeling with shock, and she was blind to Matthew's murderous expression and Rebecca's obvious terror. She only knew that she had to get away. "I will come back," she mumbled.

"You will stay here, Shalada," Matthew Lorne commanded sharply.

With a sudden movement that took him by surprise, Shalada pushed him roughly to one side, catching him off balance, and seized the chance to rush out the door.

A fine rain had started, but Shalada was not even aware of it as she ran down the lane. The wind, which had risen to a new strength, whipped the cap from her head so that it dangled by its strings down her back; it gusted the rain against her face and blew her hair across her eyes, momentarily blinding her. She pushed the hair back with quivering fingers and ran on. Rebecca's words roared in her head. "He is not your father, he burned my mother, he murdered your father."

Lightning forked the sullen sky, dazzling her; thunder rumbled heavily on its heels. "He is not my father." Shalada shouted the words to an uncaring sky. Joy pierced through the confusion in her mind. She turned her head and looked at the tall, thin figure of Matthew Lorne silhouetted against the doorway of the cottage. "Thank God that you are not my father!" she cried. Then, afraid that he might come after her, she ran on.

Shalada disappeared from Matthew Lorne's view. He turned about slowly and fixed his eyes on Rebecca. "So the witch has been keeping secrets from me," he said quietly. His soft voice held far more menace and violence than if he had shouted the words. "The witch can speak. She can raise her voice and accuse Matthew Lorne of murder. She can do that, can't she?"

Rebecca fell back against the bed as he advanced upon her. "I saw your f-face," she stammered. "I heard wh-what you said to her. You desire Shalada."

Matthew stood over her, his hands clenching and unclenching. Rebecca saw the glitter of his eyes, the flush that stained his pale face. "And I will have her."

"No!" Rebecca cried out desperately. "It is wrong, unnatural."

"Unnatural." Matthew's lips twisted into a mirthless smile. "You forget that I am not her father, so how can it be unnatural? I was going to tell her the truth about our relationship, but you have saved me the trouble. My thanks, Rebecca."

"If she did not come to you willingly, you were going to put her in L-Lammington. I heard you."

"You will fight for your daughter until the end. But what good will it do you or Shalada? Who will believe the accusations of a witch? Poor Rebecca." Above the rapid beating of her heart she heard his soft taunting voice again. His fingers twined in her hair and jerked her to her feet. "Poor crazy old woman. No one will believe a word you say. What a pity."

Rebecca screamed as his fingers twisted viciously, forcing her to look at him. Through tears of pain she saw that his flush had faded. His face was so white that it had the appearance of a mask. His eyes were dark holes in that mask, his mouth a hard gash of hatred. Her limbs began to tremble so violently that only his grip on her hair upheld her. "You are h-hurting me." Her voice quavered piteously. Foolish words, when he had already condemned her to death. There was no way out for her. No way out for Shalada.

Matthew laughed. "This is but a little hurt, Rebecca. Very soon I will be forced to hurt you still more. You know what must happen. You can take comfort in that thought. There is only one way to destroy a witch, and I must take that way. It will grieve me, but if I should falter, I know that strength will be provided."

The flames were leaping high, they were licking greedily at the woman bound to the stone cross. Rebecca could see them plainly, she could feel the intense heat. The terrible smell of death was again strong in her nostrils. And Matthew Lorne had decreed this fate for her.

Rebecca's head shook in a nervous spasm, and then she began to scream. Matthew tensed as the high, shrill sounds went on and on, assaulting his nerves. A muscle beside his mouth began to jump, and a pulse throbbed heavily in his temple. Taking her by the shoulders, he shook her hard.

Rebecca's head lolled helplessly. Then, as he stopped shaking her, it snapped back. Her glazed eyes stared at a point just beyond him. The cords in her throat strained as she continued to scream.

Matthew's mouth began to shake uncontrollably. Quite suddenly it seemed to him that Rebecca's twisted and agonized face symbolized the faces of all those women whom he had sent to a flaming death. The faces he always saw when the choking, billowing smoke momentarily parted. Her screaming was their screaming, and it made an insufferable din in his ears. She was all of those women in one. Looking at her, he found himself remembering his recurring nightmare, when he would find himself led into the same hell he had created for his victims. Choking on the smoke, struggling madly against his bonds, he would experience to the full the creeping terror of the flames. The fire would begin to roar, he would feel the searing, unbearable pain. Only then would he awaken. Lying there, sweating and trembling in the aftermath of his nightmare, he would remember that he had thought of those women as victims. He had been right to condemn them. In every action he took, he was right. "Be quiet!" he shouted. "And take your gibbering ghosts with you!" He doubled up his right hand and drove his fist into her face. The screaming died as she slid to the floor.

Matthew got down on his knees beside her. The silence hummed in his ears as he looked into her unconscious face. His blow had pulped her nose and split her lip. There was blood smeared over her face, blood splashes on the front of her gray gown. Suddenly afraid that she had cheated him, he crouched lower and put his ear against her chest. She must not die; this was not the death he had planned for her. He heard the faint beat of her heart, and he straightened up, smiling. The burning cross awaited Rebecca West.

8

Emerging from the Goose and Grapes Inn, David Medway shut the door on the warmth and the babble of conversation from within. Oblivious of the rain, which, in the past five minutes, had turned into a soaking downpour, he casually pulled on his gloves and fastened the clasp of his dark red cloak. His movements brought him an unpleasant reminder of his stiff neck and aching back, and he silently cursed the jovial landlord of the Goose and Grapes, who had declared his beds to be the best to be found in the length and breadth of England. David pulled off one of his gloves. Raising his hand, he looked ruefully at the raised red lumps on the surface of the skin. As far as he was concerned, he thought, replacing the glove, their only claim to fame lay in an abundance of bedbugs. As for the naive belief of the landlord, he could never have been outside Waterford Village, he decided.

He turned his head as a mournful clucking came to his ears, and watched with a faint, amused smile as two chickens, their feathers wet and bedraggled and their small eyes blinking rapidly, went scuttling past him. The birds were stalked by a morose-looking man in a brown smock and manure-caked boots who looked curiously at David, half-pausing, as though he would speak. Then, as the grandly dressed stranger calmly returned his look, he muttered, "Afternoon, sir," and made a leap after his quarry.

David grinned as the clucking of the birds rose to

a crescendo. The man, missing his footing, went sprawling. The birds, further alarmed, rose partway from the muddy cobbles, leaving several feathers behind them, and then resumed their frantic scuttling. With an oath, the man picked himself up, and the trio disappeared around a corner of the inn.

His smile lingering, David turned his attention to the two bills nailed to the wall of the inn. His eyes scanned them with idle interest. One bill told of a fair that was to be held at Waterford Village on the twenty-ninth day of the month of April. Various amusements were set forth. Listed prominently among them was the fitting of a scold's bridle to one Mary Garrett. "Mistress Mary Garrett," the bill read, "having grievously injured the peace of mind of her spouse, Thomas Garrett, by her ceaselessly prattling tongue, shall be fitted with this contraption of silence, and shall afterward be ducked several times in the village pond." The bill then went on to state that Thomas Garrett, who had earnestly requested the fitting of the bridle, hoped that the ceremony would not only provide the onlookers with amusement, but would serve as a lesson to other goodwives who might, unwittingly, by the length of their tongues, have done similar injury to their spouses. David's dark brows rose. "A formidable man, this Thomas," he murmured.

David looked at the second bill. This one dealt with witchcraft, and the punishments thereof. His amusement vanished as he read on. He had seen many bills on witchcraft, but none as severe as this one. For every offense listed, first or second, the punishment was death. Usually, for a first offense, the offender might serve a year or two in prison, where it was hoped that he or she might repent of evil ways and shun the practice of witchcraft. Or perhaps the punishment would be the forfeiture of goods and property, or some hours spent in the pillory. For a second offense, it was believed that the person in question was incorrigible, and the sentence of death usually followed. But this bill,

signed by Matthew Lorne, made no distinction whatever.

David's eyes were suddenly bleak. The name of
Matthew Lorne had always been anathema to him. He
had grown from childhood to manhood with a burning
desire for vengeance against Lorne, the man who had
killed his father. It was only his mother's frantic pleading, her fear for his safety, that had prevented him
from carrying out his desire.

David's gloved hands clenched tightly together as he
tried to block out memory. But he found that memory
would not be denied. It transported him back to Cornwall and that warm July night sixteen years ago. A full
moon rode a clear, star-spattered sky, and the night air
was fragrant with the perfume of flowers. The four-
teen-year-old David, lying restlessly in his bed, could
hear the sighing of the sea and the curling of the waves
at the foot of the cliffs. His feelings were mixed. He
felt resentful and hurt because his father had not only
banished him to his bed, but had said things that had
frightened him. When he had begged to be allowed to
stay up later so that he could meet their distinguished
visitor, Matthew Lorne, the renowned witch-finder, his
father had abruptly refused his request. Marcus Medway's voice had been stern, and the customary twinkle
had been absent from his dark blue eyes.

Still hopeful, David had persisted. "Just an extra ten
minutes. Please, Father."

"I said no, David. If it means so much to you to
meet this . . . er . . . this witch-finder, then tomorrow
morning will do just as well."

David knew what his father's hesitation meant. He
said curiously, "You don't like him, do you?"

"No." Marcus Medway spoke the word abruptly.

"Why not?"

Marcus Medway hesitated. "It doesn't matter why,
my son. In any case, you are too young to understand."

David stared at him indignantly. "I am not," he
burst out. "I am fourteen."

His father reached out a hand and ruffled his dark hair. "So you are. I do tend to forget your advanced age, don't I?"

David knew that his father was teasing, but he said solemnly, "Yes, sir, you do. If you please, sir, I would like to know why you dislike Matthew Lorne."

Marcus Medway's face changed. Looking at him, David was frightened. His father suddenly seemed much older than his forty years. "I'm sorry, Father . . ." He faltered. "You don't have to tell me."

Without speaking a word, his father took his arm and led him up the stairs. When he was tucked into bed, his father sat down on the side and looked at him for a long moment. "I will answer your question, David," he said at last. "I dislike Matthew Lorne because, to me, he is the personification of evil."

"Evil?" David stared at him in bewilderment. "But I thought he was your friend."

"No, my son, he is not my friend."

"Then why have you invited him to our home?"

"I did not invite him, David. Master Lorne has business in this part of the country. I happen to be part of that business."

Again David felt frightened. Because he did not like the feeling, he decided to change the subject. He said crossly, "When I came back from play this afternoon, Mother was sitting on the couch, and she was crying. She wouldn't tell me why."

He looked at his father expectantly. Marcus Medway did not answer. David knew then that he had not managed to change the subject at all. In some way, his father's strange expression and his mother's tears were all bound up in this Matthew Lorne. "Anyway," he added lamely, "I don't like Mother to cry. I hope she won't do so again."

"So do I." Marcus Medway placed his hand on David's arm. "Listen to me, David. If anything happens to me, you must promise to take care of your mother." He smiled. "You know how helpless she is."

David was not warmed by the smile. He swallowed hard in an effort to calm his fluttering heart. Then, out of his fear, he burst out almost rudely, "I don't want you to talk like that. Nothing is going to happen to you."

His father did not rebuke him. "Perhaps not. But if something should happen, you will take care of her?"

"Of course, Father," David answered miserably.

"And you will obey her in everything?"

"I will do my best." Struck by a sudden thought, David sat up in bed. "Father, you are not ill, are you?"

Marcus Medway shook his head. "No, I am not ill."

"Then everything's all right, isn't it?"

"I hope so, David."

David had another thought. "You said Matthew Lorne had business here, and that you are part of it. But his business is finding witches, isn't it?"

"Yes."

"Oh, I see now." Sure that he understood, David laughed. With a desire to trap his father into an admission, he said cunningly, "You have been teasing me all along, haven't you?" Without waiting for an answer, he rushed on. "You thought I would make a fuss about going to bed. But I think I have it worked out. Everybody knows that witches are women, so Matthew Lorne could not possibly have business with you. Isn't that right?" He waited for his father to smile. When he did not, he said fearfully, "It . . . it isn't Mother is it? N-nothing is going to happen to her?"

"Your mother is quite safe." Marcus Medway stood up abruptly. "It is true that witches are generally thought to be women," he said in a heavy voice, "but you need have no fears for your mother."

Still feeling the coldness of his last thought, David shivered. "You are sure?" he whispered. "About Mother, I mean?"

"Quite sure." Walking over to the door, Marcus Medway paused there a moment, as though he might have more to say. The candlelight from the corridor shone on his curling dark blond hair, picking out the distinctive touches of silver that threaded it here and there. Then, apparently deciding against further conversation, he nodded and said, "Sleep well, son." The door closed firmly behind him.

After the tragic affair was over, David was always to remember his father that way. Standing tall and straight by the door, with the candlelight shining on his hair. But on that July night, with the curtains blowing softly in the warm, salt-laden breeze, he had no idea that his safe, comfortable world was about to be turned upside down. Lying in his bed, he no longer felt like laughing. He had been teased and sent to bed like a small child, and so he nursed his resentment. Yet, at the bottom of his resentment, he was uncomfortably aware that the uneasiness still stirred. Frowning, he tried to work the matter out. It was not like his father to be so grave and unsmiling, or to make remarks that were sure to make him unhappy. And certainly it was not like his gay and lovely little Spanish mother to cry. Naturally he understood that no one could be laughing and happy all the time, but all the same it was very disturbing. Something must be wrong.

A sound came to David's ears. He jerked upright in the bed, his head inclined in a strained listening attitude. It had sounded to him almost like a stifled scream. Undecided, he remembered the peacock. His father kept the flaunting bird for the amusement of his mother, who spent much time admiring the iridescent spots on the proudly spread tail. The peacock's cry, which both he and his father found irritating, sounded like a screaming woman. David bit his lip. But the peacock made a high, shrill sound, and the sound he had heard had been stifled. He must find out if anything was wrong. His heart beating unpleasantly fast, he threw back the covers. Sliding out of the bed, he ran over to the door.

In the corridor, David moved as quietly as possible over the scented rushes his mother used to sweeten the house. The rushes seemed to him to crackle very loudly beneath his feet, giving out a series of small, sharp explosions which he felt sure would give him away. Telling himself that it was his imagination that had enlarged the sounds, he reached the stairs, and went down them without further hesitation. Voices came from the partially open door of the room where his parents always entertained guests. He moved as silently as he could toward the door. Peering into the room, he saw his mother. She was standing between two men. Her face looked white and strained and her big dark eyes held an expresssion that he had never thought to see in them. Something, or someone, had frightened her very badly. Was it the two strange men who had frightened her? Had they said something, done something to insult her? It might well be so, for his mother was still looked upon as a foreigner, and foreigners, as David had cause to know, were not popular in this part of Cornwall. She had been a sixteen-year-old girl when she had sailed from her native Spain to become the bride of Sir Marcus Medway, and from the moment she had set foot on Cornish soil, she had been made to feel the dislike and distrust given to foreigners. The years that had passed had not gentled their suspicion of "that Spanish woman," as they invariably referred to her.

Thinking of this, David stiffened with outrage. He was quite sure now that the men had insulted his mother, and he was prepared to charge into the room and defend her. He would have done so, but at that moment the two men moved away, and his father and another man come into his line of view. David studied the man intently. Dressed all in gray, he was very tall and thin, with a pale face and smooth sandy hair that just barely touched the shoulders of his gray gown. Was this unsmiling man Matthew Lorne? he wondered. For no reason that he could think of, he experienced a shiver of dislike.

"Master Lorne," David heard his father say in a

hard and unfamiliar voice, "for some reason known only to yourself, you have seen fit to accuse me of witchcraft."

David's eyes widened, and there was a great fear all through him as he waited for the witch-finder to answer. "I do so accuse you, Sir Marcus." Matthew Lorne's answering voice was soft and deadly. "As for my reasons, they are based on the testimony of several persons."

"You lie!"

"Do I, Sir Marcus? We shall see."

Marcus Medway looked him up and down contemptuously. "And it is on the testimony of these probably fictitious people that you have based your absurd accusations."

"I must ask you to be very careful, Sir Marcus. The accusations made against you are by no means absurd, nor are the people who made them fictitious."

Marcus Medway laughed, and his laughter was as contemptuous as his look had been. "We have not met in many years, you and I, Lorne, but you have not changed, more's the pity. You are a fool if you think you can come here to Tregurrion and immediately point the finger of suspicion at me. Did you really think you could get away with something like that?"

His pale face flushing, Matthew Lorne looked at the other man with malignant green eyes. "I arrived in Tregurrion several days ago," he answered in a tight voice. "My reason for coming to this remote spot was to test a suspected witch. At the time of my arrival, I had no thought in my mind of you."

"I know exactly when you arrived, Lorne. But you had forgotten, of course, that I make my home in Tregurrion."

At this sarcasm, Matthew Lorne's angry flush deepened. "No, I was aware of it. Our last meeting, however, was not friendly, and I had no intention of calling on you. I—"

"No, Lorne, indeed it was not friendly," Marcus

Medway interrupted. "As I remember, you arrived at my home in London, expecting to be received as an honored guest. A man like you, who has been responsible for so much suffering."

Matthew Lorne's green eyes glittered, but he answered calmly enough. "Say, rather, Sir Marcus, a man like me who has endeavored to do God's work. Yet you turned me away from your door, you insulted me in front of your guests. I have not forgotten."

"I turned you away like the dog you are. I did not expect you to forget, for I have heard that your memory is unpleasantly long where an insult or a suspected insult is concerned. I am only surprised that you have taken this long to avenge yourself on me."

"You may call it vengeance if it pleases you to do so, Sir Marcus. I call it justice, which is a very different thing. But whatever you choose to think, when these people came to me and accused you, I was forced to take notice."

"But of course."

Matthew Lorne ignored the jeering interruption. "Under the circumstances, I could do nothing else. I have spent some time going over these people's stories, in the course of which I unearthed further evidence against you."

"You have been a very busy lad. Should I commend you?"

"I will always endeavor to do my duty, Sir Marcus. First and foremost to God, whose servant I am, and then to the people."

Marcus Medway moved impatiently. "You might at least spare me your hypocrisy, Lorne. And I warn you again, you will not get away with it."

"But I will, as you put it, Sir Marcus, get away with it. I have proof that you have dabbled in witchcraft." Matthew Lorne's hand tightened over his silver-handled cane. "Believe me, I quite understand that you are a wealthy and influential man," he went on, not troubling to disguise the sneer in his voice, "but even

the wealthy and influential are as one with the poor
and the lowly in God's sight. So it will avail you nothing once the case is proven against you. And it will be,
Sir Marcus. It will be."

"I am sure you will do your best to prove your
trumped-up case. But there seems to be no end to the
surprises you have in store for me. I have heard that
you do not usually bother with a trial. Your victims
burn, screaming and protesting their innocence to the
last. I wonder how it feels to die, knowing that you
have been condemned not by a court of law but by a
man who has come to believe he is God, a man so
swollen with a sense of his own importance that he has
usurped the duties of God."

Matthew Lorne's smile was slow and unpleasant.
"Your insults fall on barren ground, Sir Marcus. I take
comfort in the knowledge that God sees into my heart.
He knows my intent."

"Aye, He does indeed. I trust this will trouble you
severely when you are on your deathbed."

"I understand that you are afraid, Sir Marcus. But
you need not be. You will have a fair trial."

"By Christ!" As though he suddenly found it too
tight, Marcus Medway pulled at the collar of his green
robe. "It would take more than a little maggot like you
to frighten me, Lorne."

David gasped as he saw Matthew Lorne half raise
his stick. For one terrible moment he thought the man
intended to strike his father. The stick was lowered,
and he breathed a sigh of relief. He felt fear, and yet
he was not too much concerned. His father had always been able to handle any situation. Before he was
through, he would make this Matthew Lorne eat dirt.
Witchcraft and his father was ridiculous. David's comfortable belief that all would come out right was badly
jolted when he stole a quick glance at his mother. In
contrast to the crimson of her gown, her face was
deathly white. Looking at her, David felt the fear becoming terribly real. Suppose he was wrong and his fa-

ther could not handle the situation? He took a deep breath, suppressing the impulse to cry. At his age, he thought, tears would be considered unmanly. Besides, there was no point in losing his head. He must wait and see what would happen.

"Marcus . . ." David heard his mother's trembling voice. "Marcus, please."

For the first time that David could remember, his father spoke to her angrily. "What do you expect from me, Sybilla, should I crawl to this little worm?"

"No, my darling. But perhaps a little discretion."

Marcus stared at her. "Sybilla, why should I be discreet? I am not guilty, therefore I have nothing to hide. Surely you are not telling me that you believe this prating fool?"

Sybilla Medway looked stricken. "*Dios*! How can you even ask me such a thing, Marcus? Of course I do not believe, not for an instant." She laid her slim white hand on his arm, and David saw the sparkle of her ring as her fingers squeezed warningly. "But, my husband, lies are sometimes believed. I have much concern for you."

"And so you should have, *señora*." Matthew Lorne's voice was very cold. "I have irrefutable proof of your husband's guilt."

Goaded, Marcus Medway turned on him. "You have irrefutable proof, do you, Lorne? So what happens now, do we dispense with the trial?"

"By no means. You will have your trial. I give you my word."

"Your word means nothing to me, Lorne. But I will tell you something, in case it should have slipped your mind. I am not without friends. Your irrefutable proof will be shown up for the pack of lies it is, and you will find yourself an object of ridicule in that courtroom. I advise you to think well on what I have just said."

"We will see, will we not?" Matthew Lorne bowed stiffly. "There is no point in continuing with this discussion, Sir Marcus. I will take my leave of you now. I must be in London as soon as possible." He pointed with his cane. "Those two gentlemen will remain until you have packed a few necessities. After that, they will see you safely lodged in the prison."

"What!"

Matthew Lorne inclined his head. "Just until I return, of course."

Sybilla, with a choked cry, threw herself into her husband's arms.

"Hush, Sybilla." Marcus stroked her dark hair with gentle fingers. "Let him play his little game until the end. It means nothing."

"But, Marcus, what will we do without you?" Sybilla's large dark eyes were wet with tears. "I am so terribly afraid."

"There is nothing to fear, my love." Marcus kissed her smooth forehead and her trembling lips. "Trust me, for the first time in Matthew Lorne's infamous career, he is about to be proved a fool, a liar, and a charlatan. I will see to it that he is shown up for what he is."

"I do trust you. But I am still afraid."

"You must not be, for I tell you again that there is nothing to fear." Over Sybilla's head, Marcus' eyes met Matthew Lorne's. "Nothing at all," he repeated softly.

"But you look outraged, Sir Marcus." Matthew Lorne's voice was as smooth as cream. "You must know that it is customary procedure to confine a suspect until such time as he can be dealt with. If, as you say, you are innocent, then you have nothing more to fear than a few uncomfortable days."

Marcus put Sybilla gently from him. "I will go with your men, Lorne. But after my name is cleared and I am freed, as I will be, I will come after you. That is a promise."

Matthew Lorne smiled as he turned toward the door. "If you are freed, Sir Marcus, I will look forward to our meeting."

David backed away from the door. Hidden from view in the darkest corner of the hall, he watched Matthew Lorne leave the house. Hardly daring to breathe, confused and frightened, he remained still as his father, accompanied by the two men, mounted the stairs. After what seemed to David like a very long time, his father came down again, the two men still dogging his footsteps. "Wait here." Marcus Medway's voice was cool as he addressed them. "I wish to take farewell of my wife."

The men hesitated, looking at each other. Then one of them said in a loud blustering voice, "Ain't got no objection as long as you hurry. We got our duty to do, and we ain't got all day to do it in, either."

"Good of you." Shrugging, Marcus turned on his heel and entered the room where his wife waited.

"Sarcastic bastard," David heard the taller of the two men say. "Still, he'll be singing a different tune very soon." His voice turned serious. "Now, about this job that devil give us. It's got to be done quick and neat. No fumbling, if you know what I mean. He wouldn't like it if anything went wrong."

The other man laughed. "The devil'll give us the devil. That what you mean, Brody? Anyway, I never fumble. I know what I'm doing, take my word for it." He paused, then went on reflectively, "Wonder why he hates him so? Seems like a lot of hate for an insult, don't it?"

"Maybe so." Brody sounded nervous. "But you got to remember that he's different. He ain't like you and me, or anyone else for that matter. Devil's a good name for him. He's that full of spite and evil that he gives me the cold shudders."

"He got something on you, is that why you does what he says?"

"That, and the good money he pays. Speaking for meself, I wouldn't like to get on his wrong side like what this Sir Marcus has done."

"Nor would I," the other man answered, "and that's a bloody fact! The real truth about him, Brody, is that he's mad." He touched his forehead with a grimy finger. "He just keeps it hid better'n most madmen, that's all."

"No, Conners, he ain't mad," Brody said quickly. "It don't pay to say things like that."

"What's the matter with you?" Conners said lightly. "You afraid I'll tell on you? Go on with you, we both know he ain't all there."

"Maybe so. But I still say it's safer to keep a still tongue."

Laughing, Conners slapped his leg. "You'll be the death of me yet, Brody. Still tongue or not, that fiend'll do you dirt at any time he's a mind."

Brody shuddered. "Shut up, Conners, or I'll land you a bash on the beak that'll put you out for hours."

"No you won't," Conners answered with undiminished cheerfulness. "You want to know why you won't? You need me, that's why. I'm the one what's had a deal of practice with rope."

David's confusion and fear grew. He stood there, his body rigid, the words the men had spoken whirling in his head. What were they planning to do to his father?

"Don't say no more, Conners." Brody's abrupt voice caused David to jump. "Best if you keep your big mouth shut, 'cause here he comes."

David heard the sound of his mother's sobbing as Sir Marcus rejoined the two men. *"Qué debo hacer?"* her voice cried despairingly after him.

"Nothing, Sybilla," Sir Marcus answered her. "Tell David I have had to take a little journey. I will be back with you both before you know it."

Watching his father disappear, a man on either side of him, David automatically translated his mother's words: "What must I do?" He wavered for a moment, undecided what he himself should do. Should he stay behind and comfort his mother, or should he follow after his father? The fear for his father was the stronger. Barefoot, clad only in his thin nightshirt, he slipped out of the house.

Managing to keep out of sight, David followed the

three men to the stables. There, his heart thumping unpleasantly fast, he waited as calmly as he could while his father saddled a horse. At last, the three of them rode away, and David ran into the stable to get his own mount. His mare, recognizing him, gave a plaintive whinny as he approached. "It's all right, Betsy," David reassured her as she began butting his shoulder with her soft nose. "There's nothing to worry about, we're just going for a little ride."

Anxious to lose no time, David decided not to saddle the mare. Vaulting onto her back, he gripped the dark mane for support, urging the nervous animal to move.

What followed was to stay with David in continual sweating nightmares. Night after night he would be transported back, and the grim scene would replay itself. He would see the three men pull up and then dismount. He would hear the raised voices, the prelude to the violent fight that followed. His father slumping to his knees beneath a barrage of vicious blows, falling over on his face to lie terribly still. Then he himself would enter the nightmare. He could feel his heels digging into the animal's sides, the rush of wind in his face as he went forward at full gallop, his frantic voice crying out to the prone man. Hard hands seized him and dragged him from his horse. The last thing he remembered was a blow on the back of his head, and then a long sliding into darkness. Then would come the painful return to consciousness.

David found, when his senses came back to him, that he was lying on his back. For a moment he was bewildered. What was he doing out here in the open, why wasn't he in his bed? The bright moonlight that flooded the countryside made it almost as bright as day, and he narrowed his eyes against the silvery light. The first thing he saw was his mare, peacefully cropping grass at the side of the road. Beside her was Valkyrie, his father's big black stallion. From somewhere an owl set up a mournful lonely hooting, and with the sound David's memory came rushing back. What had those men done to his father? He pressed shaking fingers to his head in an effort to subdue the bursting pain, and then he got shakily to his feet. The second thing he saw was his father, with a rope cutting deeply into his neck, hanging from the stout branch of an oak tree. Backward and forward the body swung, a grisly object silvered by the moonlight. With each successive swing the branch from which the body was suspended gave a loud protesting creak, bending just a little more, until, finally, David knew, it would snap beneath the weight.

Paralyzed, unbelieving, David stared at the strange angle of his father's neck, at the contorted face, the wide-open bulging eyes, and the hideously lolling tongue. The truth came to him like a great scalding shock. Matthew Lorne had had his father murdered. Now he knew the meaning of the words he had overheard; they beat into his brain like hammer blows: "About this job that devil give us. It's got to be done quick and neat. No fumbling. He wouldn't like it if anything went wrong." Then another voice: "You need me . . . I'm the one what's had a deal of practice with rope."

David put both hands to his head, clutching at his hair as he tried to block out words. With a wild cry he threw himself forward and clutched at the dangling feet. The devil to whom those men had referred was Matthew Lorne. It had to be him. He had ordered those men to hang his father. "Matthew Lorne," David muttered, "I'll get even with you, with all of you. Before God, I swear it to you. You shall pay for what you have done!" He began to cry, his body convulsing with his grief, his hot bitter tears falling on the soft leather of his father's shoes.

David came back to himself as a blustering wind drove rain into his face. He was no longer the four-teen-year-old boy who had held his father's feet to him in an agony of grief, whose young voice, broken by sobs, had sworn vengeance on the men who had killed his father, and on Matthew Lorne in particular. He was a man just past his thirtieth birthday, but the hatred inside him burned no less intensely. Yet, because of a promise he had made in a moment of weakness and compassion, he had had to forswear the revenge he had planned. His mother, broken with grief over the fate of her husband, and deathly afraid that the same fate would befall her son, had forced from him a promise that he would not seek out Matthew Lorne or attempt in any way to avenge his father. "Listen to me, my son." Sybilla Medway had clutched at him with frantic fingers. "Matthew Lorne is powerful. He has proved to the satisfaction of the authorities that he was, not in Tregurrion when the hanging took place. He was in a public coach, on his way to London. He swears that the two men whom he brought to the house were unknown to him until that day. They asked for work, and he hired them on an impulse."

"I don't believe it," David had answered her stubbornly. "He killed my father. I know it, *Madre*, even if you do not."

"I believe as you do, my son." Tears ran down her face as she continued to plead. "But what can we do? The two men have disappeared. Matthew Lorne tells his story, and such is his influence that he is believed without question."

"I will do something, *Madre*. You may be sure of that."

His mother's tears were cold against David's cheek. "You are only a little boy. There is nothing you can do."

"I am fourteen years old," he reminded her. "Soon I shall be fifteen. Old enough to bring the murderers of my father to an accounting of their sins, don't you think?"

Sybilla shook her head despairingly. "No, I do not think this. To me you are a little boy." With an impulsive movement she knelt before him and took his face between her slender, ringed hands. "My David, your years are so few, and you are very precious to me, even more so now, for you are all I have left of Papa."

David looked at her as her hands dropped away from his face. Her full red lips were trembling; her dark eyes, usually so bright, were dimmed with the many tears she had shed. Her black hair, escaping from the confines of her widow's bonnet, hung heavily about her shoulders, and little tendrils wisped against her drawn white cheeks. His eyes traveled over her face, seeing the lines of suffering that were grooved deeply on either side of her mouth, and the puffy skin beneath her eyes; yet, oddly, in that moment, she struck him as being very young and vulnerable and infinitely pathetic. In an effort to harden himself against the appeal she made to his senses, he spoke harshly. "That may very well be, *Madre*. But you cannot expect me to sit here and do nothing about my father's murder."

"Forget your ideas of revenge, I cannot lose you also."

Sybilla looked at him for a long moment, and there was something in her eyes that made him flush uncomfortably. Temporarily, he knew himself to be defeated. "I will do nothing now, I promise," he said reluctantly.

"Now, or ever," Sybilla insisted. "Promise me."

David turned his face away. "You ask too much of me, *Madre*."

Sybilla smiled at him tenderly. "I know I do." Her fingertips stroked his rigid hand in a gentle caress. "David, humor your foolish mother. Promise me this one thing, and I will never ask anything of you again."

He took no joy in her begging him, and he knew then that she had defeated him.

As he grew older, his bitterness and frustration seemed to grow in proportion, and he found it increasingly necessary to keep busy. He tended his estates, saw to the wants of those who depended upon him for their livelihood, and made sure that the cottages of his tenant farmers were always comfortable and weather-proofed. He tried, in short, to turn himself into a model landlord. He indulged, too, in a few love affairs, but since he had never yet met a girl who could mean anything to him, these affairs were without meaning. He had, in fact, done everything he could to block out the memory of that night when he had found the body of his father. But sometimes, when he had fallen into a deep exhausted sleep, he would find himself back in the toils of the nightmare, and he would relive the tragedy all over again. Even his relationship with his mother was not the same. Something had been taken from it, and both of them knew it. The promise she had forced him to make all those years ago made him bitter toward her. He tried to be kind to her, but he knew that he was often brusque, and he knew, too, that the deep resentment he felt colored his every word and action. The years had not cooled his hatred of Matthew Lorne, it had only added to it.

Rain spangled David's lashes, and he blinked his eyes to clear his vision. And now, because of a trick of fate, he was here in Waterford Village, a scant four miles from Matthew Lorne's house. The trick of fate had been the girl whom he had met in the seamstress's tiny shop, Lorne's daughter. She had looked at him, had touched his senses in some subtle way, and because he could not stop thinking about her, he had come to Waterford in pursuit.

David's black brows met in a frown, and the hot blood of shame stung his cheeks. What sort of man was he, if he could nurture thoughts of revenge for all these years, and then find himself so moved by the daughter of his father's murderer? He stirred uneasily, willing himself to forget about her, but he found that he could not keep his thoughts from straying to that encounter in Mistress Hart's shop. The girl, with her great dark, thickly lashed eyes, her exquisite features, and her long waterfall of shining raven-black hair, had reminded him of a woman of his mother's country. Her golden skin had had a glow to it, and her haunting eyes had seemed to beckon him on, even while her haughty manner had held him at arm's length. All through the long night, lying in the lumpy uncomfortable bed so much extolled by the landlord of the Goose and Grapes Inn, he had thought of her, and cursed himself for his folly. He had pictured himself taking her into his arms, the feel of her breasts crushed against him, the softness of her lips beneath his. He imagined himself stripping the clothes from her body, exploring every inch of her with his lips, until, finally, he entered her.

This last thought had brought him upright in the bed, the sweat beading his forehead. What was the matter with him if the mere sight of her could reduce him to such a state? There had been many women in his life, and most of them willing to be bedded, so what was so special about this one?

David pulled up the sodden collar of his red cloak. He must have lost his wits to be standing here in the rain thinking of a girl in whom he could have no possible interest. She was beautiful, yes, but what lay beneath that quite remarkable beauty of hers? She was, after all, Lorne's daughter, and it would be as well if he kept that in mind. No doubt she was fully as cold and as calculating as the man who had sired her, perhaps even as murderously inclined as he. Did Lorne have other children? he wondered. "Devil's brood." The words leaped into his mind. Yes, the children of Matthew Lorne might well be called that. He would put nothing past a member of the Lorne family.

The man who had been chasing the chickens reappeared around the corner of the inn. His ginger beard and straggling mustache were darkened with rain, and he looked more morose than ever. This time, when he passed David, his look was more suspicious than curious.

"Did you catch the birds?" David called after him.

The man paused. "No, sir," he answered, his work-stained fingernails scratching nervously at his beard. "But I'll catch up with them perishers. When I do, I'll be wringing their scrawny necks. Due for the stewpot are them two." He hesitated. "Seeing you standing in the rain, I was wondering if you be waiting for someone? If you'll pardon my curiosity."

"No, I'm alone." David smiled at him. "Just taking a look around, that's all."

The man's eyes flickered uneasily. "You must not be minding the wet, sir."

"I don't mind it a bit."

"Aye, well . . ." The man abandoned his scratching. He shifted from one foot to the other, then wheeled around abruptly. "I'll be getting along, sir."

David laughed inwardly. The man probably thinks I'm a lunatic, he thought. And I can't say that I blame him. His eyes wandered over the tightly closed windows of the living quarters above the shops that surrounded the village square. He wondered if the people behind those windows were as curious about him as the ginger-bearded man had been. No matter, he would be leaving Waterford tomorrow. He would forget about the girl he had seen in Mistress Hart's shop. Matthew Lorne's daughter was not and never could be for him. He was a fool to have given her a thought. And certainly he must be in a mood to waste his time, for he was doing just that by lingering in Waterford. Now he had decided that in his mind, he was impatient to be on his way. The lowering sky, however, promised more rain, and he was in no mood to push for Tregurrion until the morning.

David glanced about him again. The square was deserted except for the young woman imprisoned in the stocks. When he had first come out of the inn, he had glanced only casually at the prisoner, for such sights were common. But now, in view of her increasingly miserable condition, he observed her more closely. His lips tightened and the old fury against senseless cruelty rose inside him. The custom of stocking a prisoner had always seemed to him to be barbaric. He knew himself well enough to know that if the occasion demanded it he could and had been quite ruthless, but in that part of Tregurrion of which he was the overlord, he had forbidden stocking, ducking in the pond, and other such activities which did not, in his opinion, serve the purposes of justice. His edict had at first been resented, for his people liked to make a public holiday of such punishments, but now it was accepted in good spirit, and he was even respected for the stand he had made.

The girl in the stocks made a faint moaning sound. David wondered what crime the poor wretched creature had committed. His dark eyes softened with pity. It seemed to him that she must have been in the stocks a long time, for her bruised face, her dangling hands, and her bare feet were mauve with cold. Her long unbound brown hair was plastered to her head and neck, and her soaked clothing clung to her thin, shivering body. Scattered around her were the remnants of the ammunition with which she had been pelted—cabbage stalks, potatoes, pieces of rotting fruit, stones, the contents of eggshells mixing their slime with fish bones and all manner of rubbish.

The girl moaned again. Moved to pity, David removed his cloak and started toward her. As he stopped before the girl, the windows above the shops began to show signs of life. Curtains were drawn to one side, faces peered out. He did not notice; his attention was on the shivering victim.

The girl cringed as David stooped and placed his cloak about her bowed shoulders, her manner that of one expecting a blow. "What you doing, mister?" Her voice was high and reedy with fear. She looked at him with wide-open pale blue eyes that held a curiously blank expression. It was as though the fear expressed in her voice was unable to mount to her eyes. She began to gasp and moan. "What do you want of me?"

"Nothing," David said gently. He patted her quivering shoulder. "The cloak is wet, and it won't be much protection, but it might help a little."

The girl did not seem to be reassured. The lids over the blank eyes began to flicker rapidly. "Ain't done nothing, mister," she whined. "Don't hurt me no more."

"I won't," David said. "You mustn't be afraid of me."

She sagged suddenly. "The babe was starving, mister, him and me mum, that's why I stole that milk." Realizing she had said too much, she caught her breath sharply. "No, that ain't true," she rushed on. "Never stole no milk. Ain't done nothing."

So she had stolen milk to feed her child. "Where is your baby now?" David asked her.

Tears welled up in her eyes and slid down her bruised cheeks. "What you want to know for, you ain't going to hurt the babe, are you, he's only a little scrap of a thing."

"Of course I won't hurt him." David hid his pity with impatience. "What the devil do you take me for? Now, then, where is your child?"

"He's . . . he's with me ma."

"And where is she?"

The girl stared at him unhappily. "Cottage at the other end of the village," she muttered. "Maybe they's both dead now. Both of 'em was as weak as kittens."

David adjusted the cloak more comfortably about her shoulders. "Be easy in your mind. I'll take care of the boy and your mother."

Her blank eyes filled with sudden hope.

David smiled at her. "I'll help them."

The girl's face took on a sullen cast, as though she forced herself to deny hope. "Don't seem likely you'd be wanting to help," she muttered, "grand gent like you."

"Nevertheless, I will help." David touched one of her cold hands. "I repeat, be easy in your mind."

"Mean it, don't you?"

A faint smile dispelled the sullen look. "Then may God bless you, mister." Her head lifted in a pathetic attempt at pride. "Ain't got no job, or wouldn't be needing no one's help." She glanced at him. "I had me a job once. Used to work for Master Lorne up at the big house. Couldn't please him, though. He's that finicky, and so's Mistress Lorne. She beat me once. Said I never swept the floors good enough, nor put down no clean rushes."

David, who had stiffened, said abruptly, "So you worked for Lorne. Tell me, what manner of man is he?"

The girl's eyes went to the blackened stone cross to her left, and she shivered.

David's lips folded grimly as he followed her gaze. He understood from her silence that she was afraid to speak. Without knowing why he persisted, he asked another question. "He has a daughter, I believe?"

"Aye." The girl nodded. "He's got two of 'em. Got a son too. Robert is his son's name."

"And the names of his two daughters?"

The girl gave him a look that was a blending of curiosity and suspicion. "Miss Tasmin and Miss Shalada," she answered. "What you want to know for?"

David shrugged. "Just talking for the sake of talking."

"One of the daughters is a real bitch," the girl suddenly volunteered. "Don't know much about the other one, she sort of kept herself to herself, if you know what I mean. But if she's anything like her sister, she's a bitch too. I . . ." She stopped short and looked fearfully at David. "You won't tell no one I said that, will you?"

"No one," David assured her gravely. "You may believe me."

Emboldened, the girl went on. "I did hear that somebody tried to kidnap Miss Shalada a year back. That was before I worked for the Lornes. I hear tell that Miss Shalada hit the kidnapper on the head with a stone and got clean away."

"Kidnap, eh?" David murmured. "This Lorne must be very rich."

"Aye, he's rich enough. There's some, though, that think the kidnapper didn't want no money. They think maybe he just wanted Miss Shalada, 'cause she's so beautiful. Got all the looks, has Miss Shalada. Miss Tasmin is sort of small and fair and ordinary-looking."

So now he knew the name of the dark haughty beauty. Shalada. It suited her.

"Seems like Master Lorne can't forget about that kidnapping attempt," the girl went on. "Folks say they ain't never seen him so upset. I did hear that Miss Shalada's the only one who he really loves." Her eyes lit with a sudden vindictive fire. "If he's got a heart, I reckon it would break if anything happened to that girl."

Looking into the man's dark, handsome face, the girl sensed something that was beyond her understanding, and she became frightened again. He looked so peculiar all of a sudden. What was he thinking about so deeply? And, if it came to that, he was a stranger who had appeared out of nowhere. How did she know she could really trust him? "You promised you wouldn't say nothing to no one," she said in a faltering voice.

David came back to himself with a start. He was reluctant to leave the idea that was flickering at the back of his mind, but he could return to it later. He smiled at the frightened girl. "I give you my word, Mistress . . ." He looked at her questioningly.

"Carter," the girl supplied. "Polly Carter."

David nodded. "I give you my word, Polly." He paused, then added with a touch of bitterness, "If I can be said to have any virtue at all, it is that I have never yet broken my word."

Polly looked at him curiously. "Why'd you say it like that, mister? It's a good thing to keep your word, ain't it?"

"Yes, as a general rule, Polly. But there are times when the keeping of it can grow irksome beyond belief. I gave my word to someone once, and I have had to fight the temptation to break it ever since."

"Yet you never did break it."

"No, I never did," David answered. He looked deeply into Polly's eyes. "Tell me, are you really so afraid of the Lorne family?"

Polly blinked at this abrupt change of subject. She let him hold her gaze for a moment; then her eyes shifted uneasily. "Everybody is," she muttered uneasily, "and especially of him. Matthew Lorne, well, he's . . . he's . . ." She broke off, her mouth trembling and her eyes going once more to the stone cross. "If you don't mind, mister," she went on in a low voice, "I'd rather not say nothing more about 'em. It don't pay to talk about the Lornes. Everybody's got their ear to the ground and they report what they hear to Matthew Lorne." Her lips twisted cynically. "They think it might help 'em if trouble comes. But if he's got his eye on you, it don't help none at all."

"And you, Polly, have you ever reported to Matthew Lorne?"

Polly's head rose and a flash of spirit showed in her eyes. "No, I ain't never done that, and I ain't likely to start in now. I'm not one for crawling to the likes of him."

"You hate him, Polly?"

"Never said that, mister." The fear was back in her eyes. "Never meant nothing like that. You're mixing me up. It's like I just told you, it don't pay to talk about the Lornes."

"I understand."

"Don't pay to live, neither," Polly went on, as if talking to herself. Her head turned. "Them people what's watching us from the windows, they'll be hurting me again come time the rain stops."

"I wish I could help you." Knowing that he was powerless to interfere in village affairs, David turned away. "But I won't forget about the child. I promise you that, Polly."

"You're good, mister, and I thank you. I'll be remembering your kindness." She started as he nodded and began to walk away. "Wait!" she called after him.

David came back and looked at her inquiringly.

"You'd best take your cloak," she mumbled. "You spoke to me kindly, and that's enough to make them people angry. They won't be liking it none at all if you give me your cloak."

David's dark brows rose. "Your comfort is of more importance to me than any injury to their feelings." He touched her shoulder briefly. "You keep the cloak, Polly, and try not to be afraid."

"I'll try, mister." Polly broke into noisy sobs as he turned and left her. More for the benefit of her audience than for him, David guessed, she began to wail out words: "I'm cold. I'm freezing, and I ache all over. Ain't there a soul among you who cares what becomes of me?" Her sobs became harsher. "Ain't fair. Ain't done nothing. Don't want to be hurt no more."

"You shut up that row, Polly Carter, bloody thief that you are," a loud voice answered her.

David heard other voices joining in the verbal abuse, but he did not look around. Other than seeing to it that her child and her mother were fed, there was nothing he could do to help her. Deciding to brave the rain, he made his way toward the stables. He would see Polly Carter's mother first, and then he would go for a long ride. Shalada. The name sang in his brain as he walked.

9

Holding the horse's reins loosely in his hand, David propped his back against a tree. Rain dripped from the young foliage above his head, splashing large drops on his already saturated hat and trailing coldly down his neck. He did not move from his position. He was already so wet, he thought ruefully, that an extra showering would make no difference to his condition. He looked at his drooping horse with some amusement. "Sam, old friend," he said, patting the animal's head, "I fear you have grown sadly spoiled, and I would have you know I stopped solely on your account, to give you a breather. Ah, now, don't you toss your head at me, you know it's true. Look at you, you're blowing like an old plow horse."

Sam's ears pricked eagerly as he attempted to nuzzle the caressing hand. Failing, he gave a resigned snort, followed by a whinny, and hung his head. David laughed. "Do I hear reproach, you old fraud? I know I've pushed you, but things are not as bad as all that." He patted the animal again. "Wet you certainly are, Sam, but then so am I, so stop your complaining." He looked up at the sky. "It's stopped raining, and the clouds are breaking up."

Sam whinnied again, as though in reply, and walked past the man as far as the hold on his reins would allow. Reaching the bank, the animal lowered his head and began lipping the wet grass. "Another hint, eh, Sam?" David said, laughing. "Trying to tell me you're hungry, aren't you? All right, you win. We'll head back to the inn." Turning the animal about, he mounted. Sam pulled away with long easy strides, giving no sign now of his apparent exhaustion. "Fraud!" David shouted, setting the horse to a full gallop. "With oats on your mind and some warm straw to bed yourself in, you've got plenty of life."

The rush of wind stung David's eyes, forcing out moisture and blurring his vision. They had almost reached the inn when he glimpsed what he took to be a bundle of cloth lying at the foot of a steep bank. Someone had dropped the bundle, he supposed, or simply thrown it away. The inn was in sight when it registered on his mind that it might not have been an object he had seen, but a person. Uncertain, impatient with himself, he knew that he would not be satisfied until he had investigated. Sawing on the reins, he checked Sam's headlong pace. Turning him about, he headed back.

Thoroughly disgruntled, Sam blew a gusty breath through his flaring nostrils as he was brought to a standstill and his rider dismounted. So it wasn't a bundle of cloth, David thought, his hand resting against Sam's rain-darkened chestnut neck, it was a girl. He stared at the slight figure. She was lying face downward. She had lost her bonnet, and her long rain-tangled black hair fell on either side of her, pieces of it clinging to the back of her dark blue gown. David's heartbeat increased as he went forward and knelt beside her. Even before he turned her over, he somehow knew who it would be. Shalada Lorne. On the way back to the inn, just before the object had caught his eyes, he had been thinking of her again, and now here she was. He had pictured her in many ways, usually sensual in nature, he was forced to admit, but he had never thought to see her like this, soaked, mud-caked, and unconscious.

Shalada came back to her senses as strong hands touched her and turned her over on her back. She made no attempt to open her eyes, for her lids felt weighted and her head ached abominably. With the shadow of her rescuer across her closed eyes, she remembered she had been running, her purpose to put as much distance as possible between herself and Matthew Lorne. She had been attempting to clamber up the bank and get into the field beyond, when she had slipped and fallen. She had felt a searing pain in her head; then she had known nothing more until the hands touched her. She frowned faintly. In the field was a wooden hut that seemed to belong to no one. She had taken it for her own. She went there whenever she wanted to be alone or to think out a problem. She wanted to be alone now, but Matthew Lorne had found her. With a picture of his pale face rising in her mind, she said in a strangled voice, "Leave me alone. I . . . I hate you!"

A prey to conflicting emotions, David looked down into the mud-smeared face. Here she lay, the daughter of his enemy, the girl who had inflamed his imagination to such a degree that he had temporarily forgotten the hatred that must extend not only to Matthew Lorne but also to the whole clan. She is a Lorne, remember. Despite himself, his heart softened. There was a large bump on the left side of her head, her trembling lips were colorless, and tears were sliding from beneath her long black lashes and making pale tracks down her cheeks. Her tears unmanned him. Brushing the wet hair gently away from her face, he said in a light rallying voice, "I must say, my pretty, that you look a mess. So you hate me, do you? Well, I can't say that I'm particularly fond of you either. But with a little encouragement, I could learn to be."

Shalada tensed. She had heard that deep, drawling voice before. Her eyes flew open. Intense dark eyes, a faint smile in their depths, were looking into hers. Thick, curling black hair dripped water onto her face, and his smile, just as it had been that first time, was startlingly white against the brown of his face. Her heart began to thump at such an alarming rate that she actually felt sick. It was the man she had met in Mistress Hart's shop, the tall, handsome giant who had occupied so many of her thoughts. His hair, she thought, experiencing a sudden urge to touch it—the rain had only caused it to curl more vigorously than ever. Then, because he appealed so strongly to her senses, she wondered what appearance she must present in his eyes. Almost immediately she recalled his words, and she stiffened in resentful anger. "A mess," that was the way he had so gallantly described her. Her winged black brows drew together in a formidable frown as she said in an icy voice, "So it is you again."

David nodded. "It is indeed. I told you we would meet again. Are you pleased to see me, my pretty?"

"I am not. And since I am a mess, why do you bother to call me pretty?"

"Ah, so that stung." David stooped lower, putting his face close to hers. "Well, so you are a mess. But once the mud has been washed away, I imagine that you will be fairly tolerable again."

His face was too close. So close that she could feel his warm breath against her lips. Her brain whirled in confusion at the thought that came to her then. She was cold, wet through, and her head hurt, but despite these physical discomforts she had a burning wish to feel his lips against hers. Either she was mad or else she was completely wanton.

As though he sensed her turmoil, David drew back a little. "What is it?" he asked.

"I wonder," Shalada snapped, resorting to sarcasm. "I like lying here on the cold ground with an impudent stranger looming over me. I could stay here forever."

"Oh, good." David grinned at her. "I am glad you are resting comfortably."

"Oh, you . . . you . . ."

David looked at her inquiringly. "You were about to say . . .?" he said in an amiable voice.

Shalada looked down at the lean brown hand that was resting so lightly and so disturbingly on her body. Guilty color flared into her face. What manner of creature was she, she asked herself in disgust, if even under these circumstances he had only to touch her to make her feel this pulsing excitement? "Take your hand away," she said abruptly. "There is no need to touch me. What are you doing here anyway?"

Shrugging, David withdrew his hand. "I was passing by when I saw what I took to be a bundle of cloth. I almost didn't stop, then it occurred to me that I had best make sure of what I had seen." His smile widened. "So here I am."

She wondered if he had been looking for her. She must stop this foolishness at once. She was too aware of him. "You might just as well have saved yourself the trouble, sir." Hiding her emotion behind a barrier of anger, she spoke in an overloud voice. "I do not need your assistance."

Now it was he who showed anger. "You have suffered a bump on the head, you ungracious chit, and damned if I'm not tempted to give you another one to match."

"You are a fine one to talk of graciousness, are you not?" Shalada's lip curled into what she hoped was a scornful smile. "I saw nothing of that quality in you when last we met. I thought then, just as I think now, that you have the manners of a hog."

His fury mounted. "And you, my sweetheart, have the manners and the disposition of your father. As for myself, I would rather be called hog than Lorne." He gave her a long, considering look. "It is a pity, with such an angel face, that you could not escape the Lorne taint."

Shalada winced inwardly. She wanted to cry out against the unfair accusation: No, you are mistaken— thanks be to God, I am not a Lorne. Instead, because he had put her on the defensive and she recognized the impossibility of pouring out her story to this hostile stranger with the hatred in his eyes, she said coldly, "Why do you dislike the Lornes so much?"

" 'Hatred' rather than 'dislike' would be more accurate description of my feelings toward your father, Mistress Lorne. As for the rest of his brood"—his eyes swept over her with something like contempt—"it would not surprise me to find that they are fully as evil and treacherous as he."

Flushing beneath that look, Shalada suppressed the temptation to agree with him. "A sweeping statement, surely, Sir David," she said in the same cold voice. "What did Matthew Lorne do to you?"

David did not answer her. Briefly he wondered why she did not say "my father," or, if she must refer to the man by his full name, why she did not invest the two words with more warmth. He shrugged the thought aside. It was not important. As he looked into Shalada's eyes, Polly Carter's voice sounded in his ears again: "I did hear that Miss Shalada's the only one he truly loves. If he's got a heart, I reckon it would break if anything happened to that girl. . . ."

Looking at his expression, Shalada felt a tremor of fear. Sir David Medway looked a very different man now from the bold smiling stranger she had met in the seamstress's shop. His handsome face seemed to have taken on a satanic cast and his dark eyes looked dangerous. She had the feeling that the hatred he felt for Matthew Lorne had now been extended to her. Refusing to let him see her fear, she repeated the question. "What did he do to you?"

"You don't know?"

"No, how could I?"

David nodded. "Foolish of me. How could you know, when Matthew Lorne himself seems to have forgotten the existence of the Medways? No doubt the misery he has brought to others has blotted them from his mind."

Again Shalada felt a tremor at the savagery in his voice. "Tell me, please."

"He took everything that was loved and valued." David spoke slowly, spacing the words. "He was responsible for the murder of my father. He broke my mother's heart, and he destroyed all happiness." He took a deep shaken breath. His eyes were still dangerous, but now there was a bleakness to them. "I was fourteen years old when Matthew Lorne first came into my life."

Burning blood swept into Shalada's face. David Medway's hands were clenching and unclenching, giving her the impression that he felt the neck of his enemy between them; a vein throbbed heavily in his temple. She shuddered. Was there no end to Matthew Lorne's infamy? It did not occur to her to disbelieve his story—the ring of truth was in his voice—but now she no longer wanted to hear. Her own pain and bewilderment were too raw and new; she did not want David Medway's pain added to it. Shrinking, she was nontheless forced to listen as his voice went on. "It was I who discovered my father's body. The two men hired by Matthew Lorne had hanged him. Naturally," he added bitterly, "nothing could be proved against your father. He was much too clever for that."

"And . . . and the two men?"

David was looking at her, but it was as though he did not really see her. "The two men could not be found. No, Mistress Lorne, there was no proof. But as sure as I am breathing, I know that Matthew Lorne ordered the murder of my father."

Shalada wanted to say something comforting, but intuitively she knew that words of comfort from her would be rejected and disbelieved. In the face of his pain, they would be an insult. Suddenly overcome by the horror she felt, her complete and utter loathing of Matthew Lorne, she cried out wildly, "If the story you have told me is true, why have you not avenged yourself? You said you were fourteen at the time it happened, so why have you waited so long?"

"I gave my word that I would not kill Matthew Lorne."

"To whom?"

"To my mother."

His mother, surely the very one who should have urged him on. "I don't believe you." Shalada's voice trembled with the force of her emotion. "You were a boy then. I can understand the boy refraining, but not the man. Word or no word, had Matthew Lorne brought such suffering to me, I would have found him and killed him."

Wondering at the blaze in her eyes, David said curtly, "Obviously the word of a Lorne would not be sacred. I imagine it would be adaptable, depending on the circumstances."

"You think so, do you? At least I am not lily-livered."

"Implying that I am?"

"Yes." Shalada sat up with a jerk. Remembering all that Rebecca West, her real mother, had endured at the hands of Matthew Lorne, her own sick disgust with him, his threats, the beatings and the abuse she had endured all through her childhood, she was overcome with frenzy. Without realizing or caring how her words would seem to David Medway, who thought of her as a Lorne, she sobbed out hysterically, "You should have killed him. Why didn't you?"

Shalada had doubled her fists as though to strike. With an exclamation of disgust, David caught her wrists and held them tightly. "So you turn on your own, do you, my woman of fury?" There was such biting contempt in his voice that she understood how he was thinking, and she was momentarily dismayed. "It would seem that one Lorne now desires the death of another," he went on.

She cried out desperately, "No, you don't understand. Let me explain."

"I have no wish to hear anything from you." Forcing her down on the wet ground, David held her there with a hand on each shoulder. "I feel sure your explanation would be just as ugly as your sudden display of violence."

Shalada glared at him. Damn him, then. He didn't want to hear, so let him think as he pleased. "You are a coward," she shouted. "If you are not, why don't you prove it by seeking Matthew Lorne out?" Her body bucked as she struggled to free herself from his grip.

Dark blood surged into David's face and he was consumed with a desire to slap her hard. God curse the traitorous bitch, she was well worthy of the Lorne blood that ran in her veins. You don't understand, she had said. But what was there to understand other than the fact that she, for some dark reason of her own, wanted her father dead? Controlling himself, he looked into her stormy eyes. "My killing him would make it very safe and convenient for you, would it not, Mistress Lorne?" he said coldly. "And what follows after that—has he left you all his wealth? For your own sake, perhaps you should wait until he dies a natural death, or until one of his many enemies kills him."

There was a look in her eyes that puzzled him. Had he not known better, in that unguarded moment he would have thought that his words had stricken her. "Well," he went on tauntingly, "don't you think that waiting for him to die a natural death would serve you better than hanging by the neck for your crime against him?" He paused, his eyes searching her face. "I have every reason myself to wish him dead, but patricide is a very ugly thing."

Shalada made a muffled sound, and for a moment David thought she was about to answer him. Then he saw her full lips fold tightly together, refusing him an answer. Again he had to fight the urge to slap her. At first, his pride stung by her calling him coward, he had been tempted to explain the real reason why he had not set out to avenge his father's death. He was glad now that his pride had not led him into that particular temptation. His mother's driving fear for him, which had forced the promise from him in the first place, seemed to have grown stronger with the years. The few conversations he had had with her on the painful subject of his father's murder had convinced him of this. And he had actually thought to explain his mother's fear to Shalada Lorne, he thought with a flicker of bitter humor. Her own words had incriminated her, proving her to be a cold-blooded little monster who would be utterly incapable of understanding love and tenderness and driving anxiety for a parent. She would laugh in his face.

"Am I to lie here all day?" Shalada's loud imperious voice broke in on his thoughts. She glared at him. "Let me up at once, it will be raining again in a few moments."

David's hands tightened on her shoulders. "That is not the way to ask, Mistress Lorne. Try for a little humbleness."

"Swine." Her eyes flashed hatred at him. "If you expect me to humble myself to you, then you will wait a very long time."

David ignored her retort, Shalada felt herself flushing beneath the hard critical look in his eyes. "You wanted me to be your pawn in a game of murder, Mistress Lorne," he said in a harsh voice. "But you must find someone else to do your killing for you, for I have no intention of accommodating you." The critical look in his eyes deepened, and she felt herself to be judged and condemned. "You should not find it too hard to arrange for the murder of your father," he went on. "You are beautiful enough, I suppose, to prevail upon some fool of a man to do your bidding."

He was mad, Shalada thought. How dare he speak to her so, how dare he judge her? It was true that she would shed no tears if she heard of Matthew Lorne's death, but she was no murderess, and he had no right to have such thoughts of her. And even if she were murderously inclined, she would have the courage to do her own killing. She would not employ some skulk-behind-the-hedge to do the deed for her. Staring into David Medway's dark, arrogant face, she unconsciously echoed his own thoughts in regard to her. No explanation. She would tell him nothing now. Her only desire at this moment was to wound and outrage him with words, as he had wounded and outraged her. Deliberately fostering his impression, she answered him in the same taunting voice he had used upon her. "Yes, I have no doubt I could prevail upon a man to murder Matthew Lorne, if such was my desire. But obviously you are not a man, therefore it was a mistake to ask it of you."

"Be quiet." Driven, David pulled her up and shook her violently. "Throw one more insult at me, and I'll break your damned neck!"

Shalada's heart jumped as he released her so abruptly that she fell back. He looked capable of murder. "So you can insult me all you please," she answered him in a furious voice, "but I must not say one word to you." She struggled to get up, only to fall back again. "If you believe you can cow me, you are very much mistaken. Another thing. I suppose you think, because this road is deserted, that you can do as you please with me. Someone will come by, take my word for it."

David smiled grimly. Though he despised her for what she had proved herself to be, he still could not help but admire her courage and spirit. "This road, as you are pleased to call this muddy track," he said, "is usually deserted. Brief though my time in Waterford has been, I have taken note of that. No, Mistress Lorne, I doubt that anyone will come by."

Shalada looked at him defiantly, but she could not control the agitated fluttering of her heart. It would seem that he was deliberately trying to frighten her; but she would not play his game. "What is it you want of me?" she said coldly.

David did not answer at once. After a moment he

said in a slow, significant voice, "For the time being, Mistress Lorne, I require nothing from you."

"For the time being—what does that mean?"

"I gave my word not to kill your father, but there are other ways of exacting vengeance. As he took from me, so I will one day take from him." Rising to his feet, he looked down at her. "Get up!" he snapped.

If his object had truly been to frighten her, Shalada thought, he had succeeded, but she would die before she would let him know it. "I am happy to oblige you," she said in an even voice. With an air, she held out her hand to him. "You will help me up, if you please."

David looked at the small extended hand. "But I do not please, you damned arrogant little bitch." He put his hands on his hips. "No, be cursed if I will, Mistress Lorne. You must help yourself up."

"I had hoped you had some gentlemanly instincts, but it would seem that I was wrong." Despite her determination to show no emotion, Shalada's voice shook slightly.

"Gentlemanly instincts from a hog?" David said in a mocking voice, turning her own words against her. "Surely that is asking too much."

"Yes, it is, isn't it!" Shalada's calm vanished. "I should have known better." She almost screamed the words at him. Feeling the trembling of her hands, she gripped them tightly together.

"You should indeed." David regarded her flushed face with sardonic amusement. "I regret if I have disappointed you. With the dazzling example of your saintly father always before your eyes, we lesser men must show up in a very poor light. Is it not so, Mistress Lorne?"

"Shut up!" Shalada shrieked. He kept prodding at her, driving her mad with his cold eyes and his hateful drawling sarcasm. Losing her head, she scooped up a handful of mud and flung it at him. "Don't you keep calling me Mistress Lorne. You just shut up, or I'll ... I'll ..." Her voice died.

David looked down at his mud-spattered hose. "Charming, Mistress Lorne. Just what I might have expected of you."

He was doing it again. "Then you are not disappointed, are you?" Becoming aware that she was on the edge of hysteria, Shalada struggled to control herself. "I don't need your help, you beast." As she tried to rise, her wet skirts caught in her shoe, and cursing, she fell back into the mud again.

David turned his head to hide his laughter, enjoying her discomfort. "You are wasting my time. I had hoped you would be more graceful. I think, after all, that I will help you up. We'll be here forever if I don't." Reaching down, he grasped her hand and jerked her roughly to her feet. "Get over to the horse." He gave her a little push.

Stung by his jeering tone, Shalada stared at him with wide eyes. "I am going nowhere with you."

David returned her stare calmly. "I said get over to the horse."

Shalada looked quickly at the drooping animal. Afraid that he would seize her, she began to back away. Her foot slipped on a patch of mud, but it was too late to catch herself. She gave a stifled scream as she went sprawling. She lay there for a second; then, shakily, she managed to get to her hands and knees. Finding further effort beyond her, she remained where she was, her muddied hair concealing her face, awaiting his sarcasm.

This time David couldn't hide his laughter. "Fool girl." With feigned impatience he strode forward and hauled her to her feet again. He held her firmly by the shoulders, steadying her. "There, now, do you think you can manage to keep on your legs, or must I carry you? Speak up. Don't gape at me like a loon!"

"My God, but I hate you!" Shalada's teeth came together with a distinct click. "I can manage on my own."

"I think not. You are scarcely in a condition to go wandering about by yourself."

With a trembling hand Shalada swept her hair away from her eyes. "And why should you care?" she challenged him. "You have made it plain enough that you despise me."

"I don't particularly care, Mistress Lorne."

"Then why?"

David shrugged. "Perhaps because it seems the humane thing to do."

His words were delivered with such biting sarcasm that Shalada lost her head again. "Curse you, I want nothing from you!" With a swift movement she lashed out with her foot, catching him on the shin. She laughed hysterically as she heard his grunt of pain. "There," she panted. "Perhaps that will teach you a lesson, you unmannerly boor."

"Bloody little bitch. Laugh, will you?" Pulling her against him, David clamped his arms tightly about her struggling body. "Try that again, Madam Spitfire," he said in a grim voice, "and I'll use my hand on your behind. A thrashing would do you all the good in the world. It might take some of the fight out of you."

Shalada opened her mouth to make a furious reply, then, thinking better of it, closed her mouth again. There were other ways to defeat him. She sagged against him. "I can't fight you anymore," she said in a weak voice. "You must do with me as you please."

David frowned uneasily. He had expected further resistance from her, and he had been prepared to deal with it. Though he scarcely knew her, it seemed to him that her sudden surrender was uncharacteristic. He loosened his arms a little. "What game are you playing now?" he demanded.

Shalada looked steadily into his watchful, suspicious eyes. It was absurd, she thought angrily. She was no business of his. Why should she have to resort to tricks to gain her freedom from this bullying oaf? Hot words came to her lips, but she suppressed them. Instead, she sighed heavily. "No game, I assure you," she said in a low voice. "I'm cold and tired and my head hurts."

"And so it should," he answered her in a hard, unsympathetic voice. "I have no doubt that it is the rasping of your confounded tongue that has caused the ache, rather than the bump you took on your head." His arms dropped. "All right," he said curtly, nodding toward his horse. "The sooner you mount Sam, the sooner I can get you home."

Hating him, Shalada stiffened. She had no intention of returning home until she was ready. Even then, it would only be to pack her boxes. She would not spend another night under Matthew Lorne's roof. She would live with Rebecca. She would be welcome to share the cottage, she knew. This interfering David Medway was watching her, the suspicion in his eyes deepening. "Yes," she said, nodding her head meekly. "Perhaps that would be best." She turned from him as though to walk toward the animal. "Anything you say, sir," she said in a louder voice as she drove her elbow forcefully into his stomach.

For all the force she had employed, there was not enough strength behind the jab to catch David completely off guard. He staggered back a pace, then, recovering himself, caught at her arm and swung her around to face him. "Oh, no, you don't," he said from between gritted teeth. "That was a clever move, but not quite clever enough."

Shalada saw the fury in his eyes, and her own rose up to meet it. "Let me go!" Her voice was a shriek of pure rage. Her face grim and determined, she began to fight him in earnest. "Take your hands off me, you swine. I am none of your damned business."

"I am making you my business now," David shouted. He cursed as her sharp fingernails raked across his hand, and then aimed for his face. "If only to teach you that you can't have things all your own way." He jerked his head back, trying to evade her clawing fingers. Unable to use his full strength on her, he was getting the worst of the encounter. It was like trying to grapple with a spitting, infuriated wildcat. Small though she was, she seemed to be everywhere at once. Breathing heavily, his face smarting from her punishing nails, he tried to pinion her flailing arms. "If you were a man," he snarled, "I'd clout you into the middle of next week."

"Try it, then." Shalada's fingernails tore at him again, bringing a yell from him. "Go on, you've done everything else."

"Be still, I am taking you home."

"You're not. Curse you for an interfering swine!" Breathless and panting, she continued with her attack, fighting him in silence now, save for the sobbing breaths she drew.

Sam gave an agitated whinny and reared slightly as the two struggling humans crashed heavily to the ground, sending a fine spray of mud over his hocks. The muscles quivering beneath his hide, the animal turned his great head to survey them as they rolled over and over the muddy ground. His nostrils flaring, he blew out a snorting breath as rain began to fall from the lowering sky, splashing down in heavy drops. He pawed the ground with a nervous hoof, his ears drooping miserably.

Shalada's skirt ripped as she dragged it free of David's clutching hands. "Get away from me!" she shrieked. Kicking out at him, she rolled clear. She managed to regain her feet, only to feel his grasp on her ankles, endeavoring to drag her down again. Screaming wildly, she fell backward, landing with a jarring thump behind a screen of thick bushes growing by the side of the road. The breath knocked out of her, she lay there, her breasts rising and falling rapidly from the force of her exertion.

David made no attempt to get to his feet. In battling with that little fury, he felt far more exhausted than if he had taken on a full-grown man. He glanced at Shalada, and for the first time, seeing her lying so still, he experienced a touch of irritated anxiety. He began crawling toward her. He had not really meant to hurt her, he thought guiltily, but only to teach her a lesson. As it was, in being forced to restrain himself, he had taken most of the punishment. To his relief, he saw that her eyes were open. "Had enough?" he asked.

Her eyes glared at him in hatred. "Never!" She raised her hand to strike.

He knocked her hand aside. "Well, I have, curse your obstinate hide." Spreading himself across her body, he grasped her wrists and forced her arms down. "Let us have done with this nonsense. By God, but I pity the man you marry. If he is to survive and be master in his own home, he must be sure to give you a good trouncing every week."

Speechless, she glared at him. His curling hair was plastered flat, and his eyes gleamed at her mockingly through a mask of mud. At any other time she would have found his sorry state amusing, but at the moment she was too angry to find any humor in the situation. With thoughts of her own appearance haunting her, her fury rose in a hot tide. "If you had minded your own business, none of this would have occurred." She wriggled frantically beneath him. "You are hurting me, you damned bully. Get off, you are crushing me."

David did not move. The feel of her struggling body beneath his had made him intensely aware of her. His eyes dropped lower, and a surge of heat went through him. Her renewed struggled had been too much for the already tattered bodice, and the golden skin of her pink-tipped breasts was fully exposed. He felt the swelling of his desire; and his anger, his hatred of this girl's father, were temporarily forgotten. He wanted Shalada Lorne, wanted her with all the strength of this passion that had come upon him so unexpectedly. He put his hands on her soft breasts, and it seemed to him that her chilled skin warmed and pulsed beneath his touch. "Shalada"—his deep voice was hoarse and shaken—"there is mud on your breasts." His fingers moved to wipe the mud away, and his touch became a gentle lingering caress.

Shocked, embarrassed by her exposure to his eyes, she tried to push his hands away. She succeeded, but almost instantly his hands returned. She gasped, panic mingling with her anger.

"I won't hurt you, Shalada." His fingers resumed their gentle stroking, sending the oddest feeling through her. She gasped as he bent his head and kissed her breasts. Feeling her stiffen, he looked up again. "Has no man ever kissed you in this way, Shalada?"

She did not answer; she could not find the words. She felt drugged by his touch, his deep voice, the dark intensity of his eyes that seemed to her to burn with feeling. "No." She managed to jerk the word out. The panic was overwhelming her, it was drowning out the new, strangely sweet feeling inspired by his touch.

"Hush," he said softly, "there is nothing to fear."

She stared at him in horrified fascination as his face came closer. His mouth covered hers, his lips bruising, his tongue seeking. "Beautiful Shalada!" He said the words against her lips.

For a moment she felt herself responding to his long, hungry kiss. Ashamed, her body resisted violently. His hands were still on her breasts, and she drove her fingernails into his wrists. For all the effect it had upon him, she might never have resisted at all, for he seemed to be impervious to pain. His lips left hers. She heard his deepened excited breathing as he trailed kisses down her face, her throat, until, finally, his lips were once more against her breasts.

She could feel each place where his lips had touched her burning flesh. Desperately resisting the thrill that raced through her, she renewed her onslaught. She pounded at his back with her clenched fists, she twined her fingers in his thick muddied hair and pulled savagely. She must find a way to stop him, or he would take her here and now. Trying to shut out the insidious thought that came to her—telling her that surrender to this man who, from the first moment she had set eyes on him, had seemed to hold her in some strange bondage, would be sweet indeed—her mouth hardened at her own weakness. She must fight him. She would never let him take her as though she were a whore to be had for the asking. How dare he touch her so intimately, how dare he regard her so cheaply. Damn him, she would play strumpet to no man.

"Hush!" His voice again, the tone that of one who spoke to a frightened child.

His lips left her breasts. She felt his hands touch her legs as his fingers fumbled for the hem of her skirt. She cried out to him, using the only weapon at her command. "You have forgotten, have you not, that I am Shalada Lorne?" It hurt her to call herself a Lorne, but it had to be done. Her voice went on, hard, urgent, compelling. "Shalada Lorne, the daughter of your father's murderer."

Her words were like freezing water, cooling his desire. A shudder shook David. He had forgotten that fact in the moments of his mad passion, because he had wanted to forget. He would not, could not continue now, she had pricked his conscience too harshly. She had conjured up that horrifying picture of sixteen years ago. A moonlit night, the hungry sound of the sea in his ears, and his murdered father hanging from the stout branch of a tree.

Shalada started as he raised himself and looked at her. His dark eyes still burned, but with anger rather than passion. "You have ruined the moment," he said coldly, "which, of course, was your intention."

"It was indeed." Shalada looked at him defiantly. Behind the coldness in his voice, she could swear there was accusation. Accusation from him, who had intended to rape her. Or had she only imagined it? It was impossible to tell. He bewildered her, this tall, handsome man, who was unlike anyone she had known before. Fascinated, and frightened, she went on. "And why shouldn't it be my intention? I am no whore, and I will not be treated like one."

"There are worse things than being a whore, Shalada Lorne." David smiled grimly. "There is, for instance, cruelty, cold calculation, treachery planned against one's own. But I have no need to tell you that, for you know all about it, do you not?"

If she were not feeling so weak and tired, she would hit him.

"Shall we pass by the maidenly indignation? It sits ill upon you, you know." He leaned closer to her. "I will tell you something, Mistress Lorne. Willing or unwilling, I intend to finish what you so coldly put an end to."

Trembling with reaction, she still had to taunt him. "Then my name, who I am, makes no difference to you?"

"Only for this moment, which, as I have already said, you managed to ruin. You are a bitch, Shalada Lorne, but you are also a beautiful and desirable woman. The reminder has served you this time, but it will not always do so."

"You do not live here. You . . . you will go away and I will never see you again." Shalada blinked in surprise. What had been meant to sound triumphant had emerged in a forlorn voice. Why had she spoken in that way? Flushing at the look in his eyes, she would have given much to be able to recall her words. Now the great conceited fool would believe he meant something to her.

David smiled. "If I did not know better, I might believe that you want me to stay. What lies behind your change of tone—is it the sugar to catch a fly?" He shook his head in mock reproof. "You waste your time. I will not do your killing for you."

She felt the shock of his words all through her. How could he be so cruel? She found her voice. "If you really believe that of me, then may the devil fly away with you!"

"Such indignant heat." David clicked his tongue admiringly. "Have you ever thought of joining a troupe of strolling players? You would do well, for you apparently have excellent acting ability."

She could bear no more. Her hand lashed out to strike him.

David caught her hand easily. Rising to his feet, he pulled her up with him. "No more scenes," he warned. "I'm going to take you home now." His eyes examined her. "Your pretty breasts are showing." He laughed as she tried to cover herself. "You need not fear to shock your family. I have a dry cloak in my saddlebags. You may have it."

"I don't want it!"

"Nevertheless, it is there, and you will wear it." With a quick movement his arms went around her, and his lips pressed hard on hers. "Something to remember me by, spitfire."

Her limbs trembled beneath her as he drew her along and helped her on the horse. She was numb now, and without resistance. Her lips burned from the pressure of his hard, almost brutal kiss, and she dared not look at him or even speak, so divided was her mood between laughter and weeping.

Afterward, Shalada could never remember how long it took them to reach the place she could no longer call home; she was too conscious of the masculine warmth of the body pressed close to hers. But she did remember the house looming up, and Matthew Lorne's pale, startled face when he opened the door. Most of all, she remembered being dropped ignominiously at Matthew Lorne's feet, as though she were a bundle of dirty washing, and David Medway's voice saying lightly, "Your daughter, sir. Good day to you." And for that, she vowed, she would never forgive him. Somehow, in some way, she would be revenged for the insult.

10

Matthew Lorne stared after David Medway's retreating figure with dazed eyes. An odd feeling held him in its grip. The feeling robbed him of anything he might have said to the impudent stranger who had entered their lives so dramatically and unexpectedly. He was unable even to summon anger at the calculated insult implicit in Medway's action; it was past bearing. He couldn't help thinking that Medway had taken Shalada's body, and then returned to the house to drop her at his feet as though she were a person of little account.

Matthew watched Medway, the man he believed to be his enemy, mount his horse and ride away. Frozen, he still did not move from his position in the doorway. Medway, in his bedraggled state, looked very different from the elegantly dressed stranger he had encountered in Mistress Hart's dressmaking shop, but all the same he had had no difficulty in recognizing him. There was no mistaking that tall, broad-shouldered figure, the arrogant bearing and the proud lift of the head, or the eyes that had gazed at him only a moment ago with the same contempt and hatred as on that first meeting. Matthew was unable to repress a shiver. There was a sickness inside him that always came whenever he felt uneasy and at a loss. His sickness was compounded by these feelings, and of a sense of approaching doom. Who was David Medway, what part had he once played in his life? If only his memory would take hold, then perhaps he would be able to counter the threat he had twice felt in Medway's presence. Since first he had seen the man, he had brooded on the matter a great deal. Lying in his bed, unable to sleep, he would attempt to chain elusive thoughts. There were times when he saw a sandy beach and waves curling at the feet of great brooding cliffs. Then, just as he thought he had it, it would dissolve and leave him once more in angry confusion. He brooded too much on Medway, he would think, taking refuge in that anger. A sandy beach, cliffs, sea birds wheeling and crying, moonlight shining on turbulent water, making a tossed silvery track to . . . to where? That was the unanswered problem. In his long career he had been to many places, so many that they all tended to merge in his mind, one having no difference from the other.

The small sound that came from Shalada penetrated Matthew's dazed state and brought the first stirring of anger in its train. He slammed the door violently, as though with the action he chased out memory, and then he turned about slowly and looked down at her.

Robert, standing with his mother and sister at the end of the dimly lit hall, shuddered in horror at the look on his father's face. He glanced at his mother and then at Tasmin. With a sinking heart he saw that Tasmin's expression was a faithful copy of their mother's. Both of them looked alert and eager as they waited without compassion for the punishment that would surely come to Shalada. They were like dogs on a scent, Robert thought with a flash of anger. And yet what of himself, what did he want? Did he want to see harm come to Shalada? Uncertain, he bit down hard on his lip, but the small stinging pain did nothing to clarify his thoughts. At this moment he could not tell what he wanted in regard to her. He was so confused and miserable. Shalada defied him, repulsed him, treated him with a mixture of withering contempt and hatred. Robert glanced at his mother again. She had not taken her eyes away from the girl on the floor. She was watchful where he was concerned, and he feared that his thoughts would be evident to his mother's sharp eyes, and that she, with that sometimes uncanny intuition of hers, would read his mind.

Robert, feeling a flush creep over his face, looked away from his absorbed mother. He shook his head in an effort to clear it. He saw the little tableau before him through a mist. The girl on the floor, her breasts showing through the tattered remnants of her bodice, his father looming over her, murder in his eyes. Jealousy burned suddenly, drowning out his fear for Shalada. From her deplorable condition it was obvious to him that she had given herself to the tall, insolent fellow who had brought her to the door and dumped her so unceremoniously at their father's feet, and a black rage came to mingle with the jealousy.

"Look at Shalada's tits showing." Tasmin's low-pitched gleeful voice struck against Robert's ears. "You always said she was a strumpet, Mother, and you were quite right."

Dorothy Lorne turned hard dark eyes on Tasmin's flushed face. Yes, Shalada was that, she thought, the implacable hatred she had always felt toward the girl bubbling hot and strong within her. Had she not turned her husband's thoughts away from her? She could not help wishing her dead. Beside her, Tasmin moved restlessly. Controlling herself with an effort, she said in a tight voice, "Tasmin, you must not use such language, I am ashamed of you."

Matthew was unaware of the presence of his wife and children. Their whispering, their restless little movements, had not impinged on his conscious mind; he was aware only of the girl at his feet. When Medway had dropped her so contemptuously to the floor, his attitude had seemed to say: Here is your daughter, I have used her, and now you can have her back. Looking at her now, Matthew saw that her head was turned away. If she was aware of his anger, he thought, she appeared indifferent to it. Likewise she seemed to be unaware of her surroundings and her seminudity, or indeed of anything except the man who had just left. His eyes went to her boldly thrusting breasts. Her nipples were dark red, swollen, fully aroused, as though her flesh still felt and responded to the touch of her lover's lips. Her long luxuriant hair, plastered with mud, fell about her shoulders in limp strands. Mud smeared her face and her neck and her torn and soaked gown. Further evidence that Medway had taken her. The sight of her told him all he needed to know.

He pictured her panting beneath Medway, her long slim legs tightly clasped about his body as she gave him back thrust for thrust; he could almost hear the guttural sounds of passion that emerged from her throat. And Medway, his dark eyes would be hot upon her naked writhing body, her pulsating breasts. He could see him kissing those breasts. Shalada's legs parting to receive him, her cry of joy as he made his forceful entry deep into the recesses of her warm and willing body. Passing his hand across his sweating forehead, he looked blindly at his wet palm before wiping it dry on his sleeve. He felt ill with his savage jealousy and rage, and she was the cause of it.

Shalada turned her head sharply at the groan that burst from Matthew's lips. Her eyes widened as she saw his face. He looked like a man in torment. His skin seemed bleached, and yet the ghastly pallor held a faint greenish cast. His mouth was a tight straight line, and his eyes were narrow with accusation. The tightly held lips opened. "Get up, you filthy slut!"

His harsh voice flicked across Shalada's taut nerves like a whiplash. She stared at him. For the first time since she had left her childhood behind she felt the touch of cold fear. Lowering her eyes lest he read the fear in them, she got slowly to her feet and faced him. "Why do you call me slut?" She brought out the words with a boldness she was far from feeling. "I have done nothing wrong."

Matthew felt as if he were choking on her brazenness. He put a clutching hand to his throat, digging his fingers into the flesh as he fought for control. She would pay for her lies and her deceit, for all the torment that her very presence had put him through since she had become a woman. He would make her scream for mercy, beg him on her knees to stop. And afterward, if she did not surrender to him, he would burn her with her accursed mother.

Matthew was not aware that he had put his angry chaotic thoughts into words. He did not see the change in his wife's face, or hear the gasp that came from Robert. Robert, standing perfectly still, felt as though his heart had momentarily stopped, so great was the shock of his father's words. If Shalada did not surrender to him, he would burn her with her mother. Was his father mad? Searching for understanding, he turned his eyes to his mother's set face. "Mother," he said in a hoarse whisper, "he has said he will burn you with Shalada. What does he mean?"

Dorothy Lorne did not answer him. Her heart felt as though a giant hand had squeezed it. His filthy desire for the girl was out in the open; there was to be no more pretense. This morning, when Matthew had returned alone from his outing with Shalada, he had been very angry. She had not questioned him, knowing from past experience the uselessness of this. She had been surprised when, without prompting, he had informed her that Rebecca West was to be lodged in the village prison on the following morning, there to await burning for her sins. Now, it seemed, he was ready to burn Shalada with Rebecca, if the girl did not give in to his lust. A great bitterness welled up in Dorothy. She did not care if Rebecca West burned with her daughter. As far as she was concerned, it would be good riddance to both of them. Each had contrived to make her life empty. But she did care that Matthew had shamed her in front of her children. She was that pitiful thing, an unwanted wife. His actions in the past, his sneering references to her lack of charm and grace, his constant allusions to Rebecca West, had made her position in his life abundantly clear. He had now put his feelings into words that could never be recalled. After all her years of devotion, she was to be thrust aside for Rebecca West's bastard. Tears of self-pity filled Dorothy's eyes. She had been pretty once, she had had beaux. Why had she chosen Matthew Lorne to marry? A frown creased her brow on this last thought. Chosen Matthew? Nay, he had chosen her. It was the money she had inherited that had influenced him, for certainly he had never loved her.

Dorothy brushed a hand across her wet eyes. Wrapped in her bitterness and humiliation, it did not occur to Dorothy that her children were far from understanding the true relationship between themselves and Shalada. She could hear Robert's rapid distressed breathing and Tasmin's frightened whimpering, but these signs of mental confusion meant nothing to her.

Matthew took a step toward Shalada. There was a heavy pounding in his ears, and his brain seemed to be on fire. He took another step, his green eyes opening wide to reveal their glittering menace. Shalada did not see. Her fear had grown, but still she kept her eyes obstinately lowered. He must not know that at last he had succeeded to frightening her.

Matthew snarled at her. "You filthy wanton bitch!" His hand lashed across her face, the force of the blow sending her staggering back against the wall. "I'll kill you."

Shalada's head rang with pain and she had the frightened feeling that his vicious blow had dislocated her jaw. She touched her jaw with trembling fingers, and relief washed over her when she found she was wrong. Turning her head, she saw Robert standing at the end of the hall, his mother and sister beside him. The stark horror of Robert's expression brought no comfort to Shalada. She knew that she could expect no help from him, from any of them. She had always had to fight her own battles, and this time would prove to be no exception. She turned her head again and looked fully at Matthew. Her eyes widened with horror as he got closer to her, his fists clenched to strike. "Stop!" the word came out rusty and uncertain from her swollen lips. "Have you gone mad?"

Matthew halted his advance. The blow he had given her would have reduced most girls to whimpering bundles of fear. But not Shalada, she had to show him that she was unafraid. His eyes watched her as she sidled along the wall. The mark of his hand was imprinted in a flaming brand across her cheek, and through her tears he could glimpse her hatred and defiance. As he stared at her, his eyes played tricks. For an instant he could swear that he had seen Rebecca standing beside Shalada. Rebecca, young and beautiful as she had once been, who had deceived him, made a mockery of his deep feelings, as this girl, her bastard, had done. He blinked his eyes rapidly, the vision of Rebecca fading slowly. With an inarticulate sound Matthew sprang toward Shalada, crowding her back against the wall. His hard fists pummeled at her face, her head, her body.

Robert started forward as he saw Shalada fall beneath the rain of blows. Instantly Dorothy Lorne's restraining hand was on his arm. "I hope he kills her. That brat has been the bane of my life, a constant thorn in my flesh. And now she is getting what's due her."

This last was said with such savagery that Tasmin gave a stifled scream and shrank from her mother. Robert felt a cold horror as he met his mother's eyes. "How can you?" he reproached her. "Shalada is your own daughter."

Dorothy gave a shriek of hysterical laughter. "Shalada is not my child, I have no love for Rebecca West's bastard!"

Her high-pitched words reached Matthew, sundering his insane fury. Stepping away from Shalada's crumpled body, he swung around on Dorothy. His gaze traveled over her dumpy figure clad in a faded housedress, lifted to examine her lined face, her gray-threaded brown hair caught back in an untidy knot. The look of him, calm now, where before had been a raging fury, his sneer, the expression in his cold eyes that told her as plainly as if he had spoken the words aloud that she was old, worn-out, and distasteful to him, caused something long dammed up to break inside Dorothy Lorne. Her head jerked toward Shalada. "You brought Rebecca West's bastard to me. You put her in my arms and forced me to tend her." Dorothy paused to sweep back her hair from her flushed face. "As she reached adulthood I saw the leacherous look in your eyes. To you she was Rebecca and Shalada in one. Well, from the look of her, you waited too long, another man entered her before you, just as the Spaniard entered Rebecca."

Matthew Lorne stood like one turned to stone. Only the flame in his eyes gave signs of life. "I have always hated you, my dear, dear wife. Only the money and the property you brought to the marriage made you in any way endurable. Your children are like you, whiners, cowards, And now—"

"No, you are wrong." Upheld by the courage of anger, Dorothy rushed on. "Tasmin is like me, but Robert is like you, sly and lecherous. Haven't you seen the way he looks at Shalada? Yes, old man, he is like you."

As if she had not spoken, Matthew went on with that icy calm: "And now, dear wife, I am about to put you out of your misery." He began to walk toward her, his hands outstretched.

Dorothy shrank back, wild frightened sobs shaking her body. Her heart gave a great leap as Matthew drew nearer, and then it began to hammer so rapidly that she could not get her breath. Pain clawed up her arm and across her chest. "Robert!" she screamed as Matthew's hands touched her, "help me, R-Robert!"

Ignoring her, Robert walked toward Shalada. He heard his mother's body fall to the floor, but he did not look around. Tasmin's frantic voice sounded in Robert's ears as he bent over Shalada, but the sense of her words did not register. Lifting Shalada into his arms, he felt his heart fill with a wild joy. She was not his sister. It was like a miracle, a reprieve from mental torment. Her hair streamed over his arm as he carried her toward the stairs, and he was filled with unusual tenderness. Her face, though bruised and battered and smeared with blood, was beautiful to him. Shalada would be his.

"Robert!" Tasmin's cry came again, and this time he heard the despair and terror in her voice. Frowning, Shalada held tight against his chest, he turned. His mother lay on the floor, her face distorted with agony. She was sometimes subject to attacks of severe pain, and would get over this one just as she had the other attacks. His father stood still and straight, as though the woman on the floor had nothing to do with him. Tasmin was crouched low over the body; it was like her to make a dramatic outcry over nothing. His mind dismissed them. There was Shalada to think of. He turned away and began to mount the stairs.

Matthew Lorne turned his head, his narrowed eyes observing his son's progress up the stairs. Robert disappeared with his burden, but Matthew did not move. There was something terrifying about his immobility, Tasmin thought. Craning forward, she saw the look on his face, and her heart gave a lurch of fear. This man, her father, was unmoved and could look calmly upon his wife lying there. She began to weep again and wring her hands.

Turning, Matthew looked at the woman on the floor, then back at Tasmin, surveying her with some distaste. Her white embroidered cap was askew, revealing the light untidy hair, which, he had no doubt, had not been groomed in days. Her nose was running and her eyes were red. She was, he thought in severe criticism, an altogether unattractive child. "There is no need for staring, Tasmin," he said in a cutting voice. "I assure you she is quiet dead."

Matthew looked at her contemptuously. She had no spine, no spirit, she was her mother all over again. He thought of Robert, and his mood darkened yet more. "What do you suppose is to be done, Tasmin?" His voice was harsh with impatience and anger. The impatience for Tasmin, and the anger for Robert, with whom he intended to deal in a short while. Collecting himself, he made an effort to observe propriety and conceal his real feelings. "Your mother is dead," he went on, "and although we may wish it, we cannot bring her back to life. However," he went on in a toneless voice, "we are but poor mortals, therefore we must make arrangements to dispose of the body."

Dispose of the body. Tasmin felt as though he had struck her in the face. How could he be so cruel and unfeeling? He was speaking again, but she closed her ears against him. When she was forced to be with her father, it was a form of self-protection she often indulged in. In the past it had brought harsh punishment, but she could not think of that now. If there was something you could do, Father, to bring Mother back to life, you would not do it, she thought in desolation. You are glad she is dead. You hated her. You hate me and Robert, everybody, except Shalada. And now Mother's death has cleared your way to Shalada. Tasmin drew in a deep quivering breath as her mind turned with venom to the girl upstairs.

"It would please me, Tasmin," Matthew said in a low voice, "if you would stop that sniveling. It will not help your mother, and it offends me."

Tasmin took her kerchief from the pocket of her green gown and dabbed at her swollen eyes.

"That is better," Matthew said, trying to gentle his harsh voice. "Now, then, I wish you to go and find the Reverend Baxter. You will tell him that he is to attend me at once."

Attend him at once. Tasmin felt a flash of rebellion

as she got to her feet. He behaved as though he were a king, able to command anybody. She could not look at him, and she dreaded looking at her mother's stiffening body. Staring miserably at the floor, she nodded her untidy head.

"After that, you will go to Jack Windsor and bring him back to the house."

Tasmin's whole body trembled with nerves. Jack Windsor, the coffin maker. Her father intended to lose no time.

Reading her thoughts, Matthew smiled grimly. "You object to visiting the coffin maker, Tasmin?"

Her eyes flinched away from him. "I wish your mother to have the finest of coffins to house her remains."

He was playing with her like a cat with a mouse. Words clogged in her throat, and she could not answer him. Her head bowed, Tasmin crept toward the door. There were to be no gentle words, no tenderness, no clinging together in mutual grief. There was only her father's crisp unemotional voice issuing his orders, and his macabre comments that held no love for her mother, but only the wish to torture his daughter in her stead.

Outside, the rain stung Tasmin's face, and a boisterous wind blew strands of her fine hair across her face. She began to weep again, and, strangely, with the flowing of her tears, some of her foreboding left her. Going toward the reverend's house, she even felt a faint pleasure in her emotion. She, at least, was paying her mother the tribute of tears.

Turning a corner Tasmin gasped as the wind hit her full blast and fluttered her white apron over her head. Catching at the apron, she drew it down and held it firmly. Blinking water from her smarting eyes, she found her thoughts reverting to the man who had brought Shalada home. She had been standing by the side wall of the house when he had arrived, and she had had a good glimpse of him. He had seen her too, but his eyes had rested on her only briefly. She had watched in openmouthed amazement as he lifted Shalada from the horse and carried her to the door. Taller than her father the man had been, slim-waisted and broad-shouldered, and there had been something about him, something powerful and masterful that had reached out to her and excited her imagination. She had not been able to see his features clearly through the mud that smeared his face, but she rather thought that he would be handsome. When he had thundered on the door, she had fled to the back door of the house, fearful of missing something. Entering, she had seen her mother and brother standing at the back of the hall, and she had joined them. Tasmin giggled, her woes temporarily forgotten as she recalled the stranger's deep drawling voice as he faced her father. "Your daughter, sir," he had said, dropping Shalada to the floor. And then: "Good day to you." She could not help admiring the cool outrageous nerve of him. To bring Shalada back in such a state, covered in mud, her breasts naked, to be in such a state himself, and yet to attempt no explanation. She only wished she could have seen her father's face. Tasmin sighed, and then, thinking of Shalada, the storm center, lying in the stranger's arms, she drew her mouth into a tight line. It wasn't fair, she thought venomously. Besides Shalada's undoubted beauty of face and figure, things always seemed to happen for her. She had everything, while she herself had nothing. Excitement never came her way, and she had the dismal feeling that it never would. If only something bad would happen to Shalada. Perhaps, she thought with a flicker of hope, she could help it along.

David Medway saw the girl coming along the cobbled street. Recognizing her as the pale rabbit of a girl whom he had seen standing by the wall of Lorne's house, he drew back into the shadow of a shop doorway the better to observe her. He looked after her as Tasmin, without a glance in his direction, passed the herbalist's shop. She would be the other Lorne daughter, he thought, remembering that Polly Carter had informed him that Matthew Lorne had two daughters.

The rabbity girl, David thought, had a distinct look of Matthew Lorne. Shalada, on the other hand, most fortunately for herself, bore no resemblance to him at all. Neither did she resemble her mother, if the worn-faced woman he had glimpsed at the end of the hall was indeed Mistress Lorne.

David pulled up his collar against the penetrating wind. He had no need to wonder which of the two girls might be the one Polly described as a bitch. Shalada, obviously. Tasmin would be the quiet one who kept to herself. Certainly she looked meek enough. She had the appearance of one who would be frightened of her own shadow. Smiling, he let his thoughts return to Shalada. He remembered with pleasure the furious struggling of her body against his, how she had fought him. She had proved herself to be cold-blooded enough when hoping to promote the murder of her father, but for all that she was fiery by nature. The woman of fury, as he had aptly named her. David's smile faded as he thought over the sequence of events that had brought them together in such a clash of temperament, and he was surprised at the sadness and the sense of loss that gripped him. In that revealing moment it seemed to him that Shalada was everything he had ever wanted in a woman, but she had one fatal flaw. She was a Lorne, and murderous-minded at that. Yet he knew from the strong appeal she made to his senses that, if only circumstances had been different, he might have loved her.

Frowning, David emerged from the shop doorway. In the distance he saw the short slight figure of Tasmin, the flutter of her apron strings as she rounded a corner and was lost to his sight. Remembering the girl's puffy red eyes and the look of strain on her pallid, somewhat sly face, he felt a fleeting curiosity. Instantly he dismissed it. What did it matter to him why she had looked so? Doubtless there was always trouble in that nest of vipers. Shrugging, annoyed that he had allowed his mind to dwell so much on the Lorne family, he made his way back to the Goose and Grapes Inn.

Outside the inn, David glanced toward Polly Carter. Polly was still huddled in the stocks, his sodden cloak draped about her thin bowed shoulders, but she no longer looked dejected. She was staring toward a party of men who were coming in her direction, and her face wore a look of bright interest. The men were busily engaged in scattering the damp ground with what looked to David to be a mixture of ashes and stones.

Polly turned her head as David came toward her. Smiling, she nodded at the approaching men. "Witch's trail," she said.

"Witch's trail?" David's dark brows drew together. "What do you mean?"

"Ain't you never seen one, then?" Polly said in an amazed voice. "Where'd you come from?"

"Cornwall," David answered abruptly.

"But ain't there no witches in Cornwall?"

"There are reputed to be, Polly. What is this witch's trail?"

Polly stared at him. "Seems funny to me that you don't know. Still, maybe they treats witches different in Cornwall." Catching David's look of impatience, she added hastily, "They always lay down a stone-and-cinder track. It's for the witch to walk over on the way to the prison."

In his mind's eye David saw Matthew Lorne's pale face, the tightly held lips and the merciless eyes. "Burning is not enough," he said in a voice charged with bitterness. "There must be an added torture to satisfy the witch-finder. How typical."

Polly shivered at this mention of Matthew Lorne. Wondering at the hatred she glimpsed in David's eyes, she said uncertainly, "Why'd you mind so much about them witches? They don't feel nothing, you know."

Forgetting that he was battling ignorance and superstition, he said impatiently, "Don't be absurd, of course they feel. They are human beings."

"That they ain't," Polly said indignantly. "They ain't nothing like you and me. Oh, they suffer at the end, when the flames get to 'em, but that's God's will. He's forcing the evil ones out of their bodies. God's beat Satan, see, and I reckon He feels it right that they should suffer. You understand that, sir, don't you?"

David did not answer. He glanced at the small squat building that was the village prison. There were slits set high in the stained walls, the only source of air provided as far as he could see. With an inner shudder he thought of the miserable prisoners and the wretched conditions that must prevail. He said compassionately, "Was it very bad in the prison, Polly?"

Polly seemed to grow smaller before his eyes, and her face took on a pinched look. "Aye, it's bad, sir." She gasped out the words. "I was there two days afore they brought me to the stocks. I'd rather be dead than go back in there."

"I'm sorry." David placed a soothing hand on her suddering shoulder. "I didn't mean to upset you."

"It's all right, sir. It ain't none of your fault."

"But I should not have reminded you."

"It don't make no difference," Polly assured him. "I'll always see that place in me mind. I ain't never going to forget. Not to me dying day." She sniffed back tears. Then, hesitantly, she fixed her misted eyes on David's face. "Sir, did . . . did you see me mum and the babe?"

"I did." David gave her a warm smile. "There is nothing I can do about your situation, but at least you need not worry about your mother and the child. I have seen to it that they have a warm fire and plenty of food."

For a moment Polly seemed at a loss for words; then she burst out in hoarse gratitude, "God'll bless you for that, you see if He don't. You're a good man, you are!"

"Not so very good, Polly," David answered her gravely.

Polly folded her lips tightly, as though daring him to argue. She looked at the men who were passing by on their way to the scarred door of the prison; then her eyes turned back to David. She studied his tall elegant figure. His short tunic was of deep blue velvet, his hose and his soft leather boots of a matching color. A black fur-lined cloak swung from his broad shoulders, and a black velvet brimmed cap embellished with a curling blue plume was pulled rakishly forward on his head, the brim casting the upper part of his face into shadow. "My but you're a handsome gent!" Polly said, giving him a wavering smile. "Still, though you look grand enough now," she went on with a hint of mischief, "you wasn't looking near so grand when you went into the Goose and Grapes a while ago. All covered with mud, you was. Looked to me like you'd been in a fight with the Devil himself."

Thinking of that fight with Shalada, the fiery stabbing of her nails tearing his flesh, the viscous mud weighting clothes, chilling the skin, and oozing into eyes and ears as they rolled over and over on the ground, David could not forbear a smile. Seeing Polly's curious eyes on him, he said lightly, "Well, so I had been in a fight. And devils may come in many forms, as I'm sure you know."

"Me, I don't know but the one." Polly shivered with the cold, but she managed a laugh at the end of the spasm. "If it wasn't the Devil, then, who was it?"

"One of his assistants."

Polly's dull eyes rounded, and behind them was a shade of apprehension. "Not . . . not Matthew Lorne?"

David considered her for a moment. "Ah, then you do know two devils."

Caught out, Polly looked faintly sullen, which expression was, David knew, a cover-up for fear. "Never said nothing like that," she muttered, "and you ain't to go saying I did."

"I won't," David assured her. "Have no fear."

Polly brightened, the apprehension fading from her eyes. "I won't, sir. I knows I can trust you. You proved that, ain't you?"

"I hope so, Polly."

" 'Course you did, looking after me mum and the babe the way you done." She hesitated. "Who was you fighting with, then, if I may make so bold as to ask?"

David saw Shalada's blazing eyes, he heard once again the harsh words she had flung at him, and then another memory came, stirring him and bringing a flush of heat to his face, the momentary yeilding of her body, as though against her will she had been attracted to her aggressor. It had lasted but a moment, but it had been there. Again the smile touched his lips. "Let us say, Polly," he answered, "that the fight was with one of the devil's female assistants."

"It was?" Polly breathed, awed by this statement. "And would I be knowing her, sir?"

"You would indeed. A bitch, I believe you called her."

Polly appeared to be thinking this one over. When she looked up at David again, her eyes wore a look of disappointment. "I remembers what I said, sir. You must be meaning Miss Tasmin?"

David stared at her. "Miss Tasmin? Now, what makes you say a thing like that?"

"Well, she's the bitch, ain't she?"

"Tasmin?" David looked thoroughly astonished. "Don't you mean Shalada?"

"No indeed, sir. Miss Shalada's the quiet one. The one what keeps herself to herself. Never give me a cross word, not Miss Shalada. Oh, she was spirited enough, but she wasn't never unkind. 'Twas the other un, that Tasmin, what I couldn't stomach."

David was about to challenge this surprising statement when his attention was arrested by the men. They had cut a wide swath to the prison door and were now busily engaged in sprinkling the last of the ashes and stones in the area before it. As he watched, a man detached himself from the group. Unlike the others, he was a splendid personage, and obviously of some importance. The man, dressed in a heavily padded red coat over a short green gown, his stout legs tightly encased in green hose that disappeared into short, square-toed red boots, his gray locks topped with a round red cap fronted by a green feather, was an impressive and colorful sight. In one meaty hand embellished with several sparkling rings he carried a rolled parchment scroll. He paused for a moment to say something to the group of workers, who, pausing in their task, nodded their heads in reply; then he came strutting forward to take up his stand near the stocks.

A nauseating combination of colors, David thought eyeing the short, stout man.

Polly just had time to say to David, "That's Simon Loft, the village crier," before the rustling of the parchment followed by the man's booming voice silenced her.

"Good people," Simon Loft began, and his voice was as fully rounded as his person. His light brown eyes glanced at the now unrolled parchment, and a suggestion of a smile touched his lips, as though he was enjoying what he was about to say. Almost immediately, as windows opened to disclose attentive faces, and still others began to emerge from doorways to crowd about him, his fleshy mouth hardened to a grim expression and the eyes flickering over the parchment became hard. Clearing his throat, he began again. "Good people, it is my terrible and sorrowful duty to inform you that evil, in the form of witchcraft, has once more come among us. And the evil—"

His voice was drowned out by shouting voices. "Witchcraft?" a woman's voice shrilled in apprehension touched by anger. "Are we never to be free of witches?

Are we never to sleep safe in our beds without having to dread the spells of the evil ones?"

Simon Loft's face reddened with anger at the interruption. The parchment trembled in his hand and the green feather on his cap quivered. "Silence!" he bellowed. "If you would hear the words of our revered Matthew Lorne, you will hear me out in silence!"

A hush fell. Simon Loft looked sternly about him, evidently determined not to continue until he had made certain that the hush was to be permanent in nature. A stifled cough from a man brought a black frown from the village crier.

David felt a rush of anger as he saw the change in the faces about him. There was fear in all their expressions, even in the faces of the children. It seemed to him that their fear hung over the village square like a smothering black pall. Even Polly had responded to the general feeling. Her hands, mauve with cold, were trembling in the holes that held them fast, and her eyes were distended. Matthew Lorne must indeed have great power if the mere utterance of his name could strike terror into their hearts. No man should have such power over people, David raged silently, not even the king. His frown deepened as he thought of Henry VII, whom he had met on several formal occasions. Henry Tudor, a mean and avaricious king who believed in piling his treasure house high through unfair taxation of his people, while he himself went about in shabby doublet and hose, earning the resentment and anger of his people, was nonetheless not as feared as this Matthew Lorne, may God curse his evil soul. But if the king's mind was centered on all he could accumulate before death closed his eyes, it would be a vastly different story when that young golden lion of a son of his came to power. Henry VIII, as he would be then, would be quite unlike his tight-fisted father, and in more ways than one. Even now the young prince's extravagant nature was all too evident, as was his belief in the absolute and unquestioned power of a monarch. He liked to be popular, and to this end he would always be in close accord with his people. The evil that Matthew Lorne represented would be cut down and never allowed to flourish again. With his deeply rooted views on the power of monarchy, such as Matthew Lorne would be most unpopular with young Henry, who would allow no one other than himself a sway over the minds and the hearts of the people.

Apparently satisfied that he had recaptured the full and undivided attention of the people, Simon Loft began again, taking up from where he had left off: ". . . and that evil is embodied in the person of Rebecca West, the daughter of the accursed and condemned witch Margaret West. I regret that, after these many years spent in hiding from the eyes of respectable and God-fearing people, the inherited evil in Rebecca West has sprung forth to create havoc among the innocent. To destroy, if we do not at once put a stop to her power. Therefore, on the morrow, by the order of Matthew Lorne, Rebecca West will walk the witch's trail. Afterward she will be lodged in this prison, there to await the burning of the evil spirits from her body."

Simon Loft paused, his light brown eyes going from one face to another, as though inviting them to speak, yet not really expecting it. David deliberately sent his voice into the throbbing silence. "Has this witch, Rebecca West, been examined by a magistrate?"

With the gasps of the people in his ears, Simon Loft seemed momentarily at a loss. Then, his light brown eyes blinking rapidly at the speaker, he pulled himself together. "Who are you, sir?" he thundered. "It seemes to me that you are a stranger here."

David smiled. "My name, if it matters, is David Medway. I am a stranger to Waterford, but that has no bearing on the matter. Has this so-called witch been examined by a magistrate?"

Simon Loft passed his tongue over his lips. "Young man"—his tone was one of rebuke—"one does not question Matthew Lorne."

"Has she?" David insisted.

"To . . . er . . . to the best of my knowledge, yes."

"But you do not really know."

Simon Loft cast David a look of smoldering dislike. "I was not present, if that is what you mean."

"I see." David drew himself up to his full height. "I take it that you are aware if she has been pricked or scratched? Tell me, has this Rebecca West confessed to witchcraft? Has her property been burned, has she been ducked, and did she fail to sink when immersed in water? All of these things are the sign of the true witch, you know." He paused. "Naturally you will tell me that these things have been done."

Simon Loft raised his hand, quelling the uproar that David's words had aroused. "Listen to me, young man. Matthew Lorne does not need such tricks. God has given him the power to detect a witch, however hard the creature may seek to hide her evil. That is my answer to you."

David's eyes flashed angrily. "And here is mine to you, village crier. You and your master would condemn without trial. Therefore your words can mean only one thing to me. Matthew Lorne believes himself to be above the laws of this land. And no man may be allowed to think in such a way."

"Be silent!" With an angry flourish, Simon Loft rolled up the parchment. "Be silent, I say, lest you too find yourself lodged in the village prison. Matthew Lorne does not go by the laws of man, but of God." Without giving David a chance to reply, he lifted his voice to a shout, "A witch must not be allowed to live!"

As Loft turned away, a babble of voices broke out and several angry and resentful glances were directed at David. Several times he caught the name of Rebecca West, and he had the strangest impression that though their anger was reserved for him, the stranger in their midst, their emotions in regard to Rebecca West were more of surprise than of anger or alarm.

Polly, visibly trembling, was looking at David with wide, horrified eyes. "Oh, sir, how could you speak out against Matthew Lorne? 'Tis not safe to do so. I am greatly afeared that harm will come to you."

David gave her an impatient look. "Waste not your fears on me, Polly. I am well able to protect myself."

"You do not know him, sir."

"You are wrong." David's smile was grim. "If, as you seem to fear, he should attack me, then I will be forced to defend myself, will I not?" He was silent for a moment. "It will not be an act of revenge, nor yet planned murder, it will be self-defense. Under those circumstances, I will be breaking no vow."

Polly stared at him. "I don't understand you, sir."

"You were not meant to, Polly." David took a step nearer to her. "These people, unless I am mistaken, seem surprised to find that Rebecca West is the one accused."

"They are, sir." Polly's eyes skimmed the excited chattering people. "And so am I. When I saw those men laying a trail, I knew that a witch had come among us, but I never thought it would be Rebecca West."

"Why not?" David bent over her, his silent eyes urging her to speak. "Who is this woman? What is so different about her?"

Polly sucked in her breath, as though considering how to answer him. "I ain't never seen Rebecca West meself," she began slowly. "I thought she was dead, I did truly." She nodded toward the people. "I reckon they thought the same an' all. The older folk have seen her, of course, but not for years."

David's black brows met in a frown as he considered this. "What happened that they should think of her as dead? Where has she been?"

"Locked up in her cottage, I reckon. The one at the end of Ladyford Lane. I wouldn't have known nothing 'bout the Wests except for me mum. It was her what told me 'bout Margaret and Rebecca West." Polly hesitated, as though undecided whether to go on; then, encouraged by David's obvious interest, she began to recount the story of the two unfortunate women.

Listening intently, David understood from Polly's breathlessly told story that Rebecca West had once been beautiful and desirable, and that she had been the betrothed of Matthew Lorne. Then, according to Polly, whose story was a little vague at this point, Rebecca, driven mad by the burning of her mother, had betrayed Matthew with another man. It was not known by Polly or her mother just where this betrayal had occured, or to whom Rebecca had given her body. But that she had betrayed him was certain, for had not Matthew Lorne hacked off all her beautiful brown hair? And then, to further advertise her shame, he had driven her naked through the village. Polly, who obviously relished this part of the story, went on enthusiastically, "I always believed that that was a dirty shame. Anyway, after he had her safely locked away in her cottage, it seems like some little boys seen her from time to time. Used to take her food, something like that. She couldn't talk, so the boys said. She could only grimace at 'em and make funny sounds. Frightened 'em so much that they never went there no more. That's how come she weren't never seen again."

"If she is alive, someone must have seen her," David said impatiently. "She would have to be fed, clothed."

Polly flushed. "That's as may be, sir. I'm only telling you what I heard."

"I know," David said gently, deciding to appease her. "I'm sorry."

Polly relented at once. "Oh, well," she said, "I daresay it's a surprising story, one what's a bit hard to swallow, if you take me meaning, and especially with you being a stranger to these parts." She gave him a sideways look, not quite sure how he would take her next words. "There's a couple of things I did hear, but they's only rumors, you understand."

David nodded. "Tell me anyway."

"Well, one of them rumors is that Rebecca had a child from that affair with the stranger."

David's expression did not change. "That particular rumor is to be expected, I suppose." He shrugged. "We all know that there are those who like to add embroidery to a story."

Polly bridled and said defensively, "I ain't one of 'em, I'd have you to know. And anyway, never said it was true, did I? I'm just telling you what's been said in the past."

"Yes, I know." David's gloved hand pressed her damp shivering shoulder reassuringly. "What's the other rumor?"

"Ain't much, sir, though 'tis surprising. " 'Tis said that Shalada Lorne's been seen going into that cottage."

"Shalada Lorne!"

Polly jumped at the explosive sound with which he brought out the two words. "Why, yes, sir," she said, giving him a quick, almost furtive look. "But how true it is, I can't say. It do seem to me that if I was one of them Lornes I'd not have the bare-faced nerve to go visiting that poor woman. Not after they went and locked her up like a wild animal."

The "they" filled David with a sudden sharp resentment. Shalada could not have been born, or just barely, at the time of Rebecca West's incarceration. The resentment, surprising even to himself, showed in his voice when he spoke. "Why do you say 'they'?" he asked sternly. "Shalada cannot . . . I . . . I mean that the other members of the family cannot be held responsible for Matthew Lorne's action."

Polly had noticed the "Shalada," and then the quick reversal. Hiding a smile, she answered quickly, "Well, now, take that Robert, for instance, he's the son. He's a bad lot if ever I saw one. And as for that Tasmin, she ain't much better. Real cat, is Tasmin."

David moved impatiently. "And Shalada, what of her?"

Polly peered into David's frowning face. She remembered the earlier conversation, when she had questioned him about his muddied appearance. Quite suddenly she knew that it was Shalada with whom he had been fighting, Shalada in whom he was interested. She would have given a lot to know how he had happened to meet up with her, and what had occurred between him and the high-and-mighty Shalada Lorne, but, with a pang, she managed to suppress her natural curiosity. He was a closemouthed gentleman, for all that he was so kind, she decided, and she'd get nothing out of him by prodding. She said in a sighing voice, "Well, now, it's been me experience that Miss Shalada's not as bad as them others. At any rate, she was kinder to me than Mistress Lorne or that Miss Tasmin." Afraid of offending him, she hesitated, then brought out what she considered to be the truth. "But still an' all, Miss Shalada's a Lorne, ain't she, and they do say blood'll tell."

Yes, Shalada was a Lorne, David thought with a spasm of bitterness, but did blood necessarily have to tell? He could have laughed at his own foolishness, his tendency to make excuses for Shalada Lorne, for had he not, and only a few hours ago, believed exactly that, that blood would tell? Now, fool that he was, he knew not what to believe. He thought of her lovely face, her great dark eyes, and he again felt that his insides were melting. So Shalada had gone to the cottage to visit her father's prisoner, for how else could the unfortunate Rebecca West be described? The question of why she went teased his brain. Had she some tenderness, some pity for the imprisoned woman, or were her visits made to annoy her father, whom, she had made it clear, she hated? Another possibility presented itself to David, and he frowned uneasily. Did she perhaps go to the cottage in order to further bedevil the wretched woman? Almost violently he found himself rejecting the thought. Whatever else Shalada might be, a cold-blooded little bitch when her hatred was aroused, a fiery fighting tigress, he'd not believe such spite of her.

It occurred to Polly, alarmed by his sudden savage expression, that he would be a bad man to cross. She said hastily, but with an underlying note of timidity. "Ain't no need to glare at me like that, sir. 'Tis like I said, they's only rumors."

David did not hear her. Scowling down at the ground, he was busily turning over in his mind the various significant points of the story Polly had related. Why, for instance, had Lorne, a vicious and vengeful man, waited so long to take revenge against Rebecca West? David had not the slightest doubt that this charge of witchcraft against the woman was Lorne's long-delayed revenge. Faces swam into his mind. Matthew Lorne's merciless face. Rebecca West, the unknown quantity, who came to him as a blur. Rebecca, who had been beautiful. In that moment he found himself endowing her with the figure and the face of Shalada Lorne. Shalada, whom he saw walking that torturous path to the prison. Rebecca West, Shalada Lorne—the two met and merged, and he found he could not bear the picture.

"Sir . . ." Polly's frightened voice came to him faintly. "What is it, why do you look so?"

David looked up and met Polly's wide-eyed stare. "Merely my foolish imagination." Nodding an absent good-bye, he went on his way. And Shalada walked by his side. Savage, fighting, glorious Shalada, why couldn't he get her out of his mind? She was the daughter of his enemy, curse her beautiful hide. He had almost reached the door of the inn when he heard Polly's tremulous voice calling him back.

Frowning, almost resentful of the interruption, he made his way back.

Polly glanced nervously about her. "It's them people," she said in a whisper. "I been noticing the way they're looking at you. It's true that they ain't got no love for Matthew Lorne, 'cause they're mostly frightened of him, so they ain't about to cross him. But you're a stranger to 'em, see. They don't like you asking all them questions about Rebecca West. They's maybe thinking you'll interfere with the way of things, and likely get 'em into trouble with him. Matthew Lorne, I mean."

"There is no need to worry about me."

"All the same, sir," Polly insisted, "I am worried. You been good to us, me and Mum and the babe. I don't want no trouble to come to you."

David casually turned his head. Seeing the whispering groups looking in his direction, their lowering expressions, he shrugged. "If trouble does come," he said to Polly, smiling, "I'll handle it."

"You ain't going to start nothing, are you, sir?"

"That depends, Polly."

"On what, sir?"

Still smiling, David dug his silver-handled cane into the earth between the cracks in the cobbles. "On whether *they* do, of course. If so, I would be forced to finish it."

Polly gulped. "Don't reckon they will, sir. Not 'less they's provoked."

"Provoked." David considered this. "By Matthew Lorne, you mean?"

Polly's eyes flickered nervously. In encouraging this conversation, she was inviting danger to herself, but she didn't care. "He . . . he don't like strangers neither."

David's dark eyes considered her seriously, and beneath the look Polly's nervous flush deepened. She went on desperately, "If he was to take a dislike to you, he might encourage them others to attack you."

Polly found his smile strange and unsettling.

"He has already taken a dislike to me. As, I might add, I have to him. But that began long ago."

Frowning her bewilderment, Polly looked about her again. Meeting hostile eyes, she turned back to David and said with a burst of courage, "There might be a lot of things I don't understand, sir, but there's one thing I do know. Should I ever be freed of this thing, and I could see a way to help you against them, I'd do it. I would, sir, true as me name's Polly Carter."

David could not carry her imprisoned hand to his lips, as had been his first intention. Instead he covered her chilled fingers with his hand and pressed them warmly and comfortingly. "Take heart, Mistress Carter, you will be freed soon enough."

"And do you believe I'd help you?"

David's eyes laughed into hers. "I do indeed, sweetheart."

Polly flushed again, but this time with pleasure at the look in his eyes and the little endearment.

Standing a few yards away, on the corner where Paisley and Stream streets met, Tasmin Lorne saw the small exhange between the tall stranger and the prisoner in the stocks. He had changed his clothing, and his appearance was altogether different, but Tasmin had no difficulty in recognizing him as the man who had created such a furor, the man with whom Shalada had lain. A bitter envy shook her. He was dressed like a grand lord, and she found him quite magnificent, such a one as she had always dreamed of. She was near enough to put out a hand to touch him, but as he turned away, to her chagrin, he did not even notice her. She saw the flash of his deep dark eyes, the crisp curling of his black hair against his shoulders. She drew back a little, her swollen eyes watching him yearningly as he crossed the muddy cobbles and disappeared inside the inn.

Sighing, Tasmin wiped a dribble from her reddened nose with the corner of her apron and tucked a lock of blond hair beneath her cap; then, signing to the tall, gray-haired reverend, who waited patiently behind her, she walked forward to mingle with the crowd. Her mind registered their excitement, but it was full of the exciting stranger, so full indeed that the news that the witch

Rebecca West was to walk the witch's trail on the morrow only vaguely interested her.

Brought to order by the reverend's shocked and pitying exclamations as to the fate of Rebecca West, Tasmin belatedly remembered to impart the news of her mother's death. She received the commiserations of the people gracefully, but with ill-concealed impatience before shouldering her way through the crowd and wending her way home. The reverend, a thin-figured, mournful-faced, black-garbed shadow, his hands clasped over a prayer book, trailed reluctantly behind her. He did not like the Lornes. In his opinion they were a godless family. Even less did he like the glow on Tasmin Lorne's usually sullen face. It seemed to indicate that she was not thinking of her dead mother, and certainly not of the fate of the unfortunate Rebecca West. He would have preferred tears and sighs. It would surely have been more natural. Shalada Lorne's face rose in his confused mind, but it brought him no comfort. Black-browed, black-haired, almost sinfully beautiful was Shalada Lorne. Perhaps she was not quite like the others, but she was nonetheless an enigma. He sighed deeply. He was a simple man. He loathed sin, and he disliked enigmas.

Polly Carter turned her head and looked after Tasmin Lorne. What a shameful creature; she had just told the people of her mother's death, and there she was, skipping along the path like a lamb in the springtime. But that was the Lornes; one should expect nothing better from that heartless heathen lot. Polly's eyes rested briefly on the reverend. From the look on his face, he agreed with her thoughts on the Lornes. But he'd not speak aloud his shock, or level his reproaches. Reverend he might be, but though he was a servant of God, he was all too human. Like most people, he was afraid of Matthew Lorne.

Polly wriggled her chapped hands, purple with the cold, hoping to bring some life back into them. Her movements reminded her of her other discomforts, and her body squirmed. Shivering violently, she tried to distract herself from her misery by thinking of the burning. Likely, if Matthew Lorne had his way, and he always did, it would take place within a few days. But in the meantime Rebecca West, after walking the witch's trail, would have to spend time in that terrible prison with its lice and rats, its bone-shattering cold, its filthy vermin-infested straw, the all-prevading stink, and its brutal warders. May God help this woman whom she had never seen but whom she had heard of all her life. Her eyes tightly closed, Polly was attacked by shivering again, and she shook as one in the grip of an ague. In the wild confusion of her mind and her consuming despair at the circumstances in which she was forced to live, she was sure of only one thing. She would like to take her mother and her babe and go someplace far away. To a magic land, if such a place existed, where cruelty was unknown. Where witchcraft would be unknown, a foreign word that meant nothing. In her magic land the people would be smiling and happy and loving. In that atmosphere her babe would thrive. He would become tall and strong. Perhaps he would grow into just such a man as David Medway.

11

Tasmin lingered in the upper hall, her eyes on Shalada's bedchamber door. Robert was in that room with Shalada. Downstairs, she could hear her father's crisp voice issuing his orders. "Tomorrow," he was saying, "do you understand me, Windsor, tomorrow Rebecca West will walk the witch's trail, and following immediately behind her will come my wife's funeral cortege."

There was a silence; then Jack Windsor's cringing voice answered. "But Master Lorne, sir, 'twill not give me sufficient time to finish the coffin for your good wife."

"We are simple-living people, Windsor," Matthew Lorne said impatiently. "In her lifetime my wife despised folderols. I have no reason to believe that death has changed her views. If you cannot finish the coffin, then you must have one in your stock that will adequately house her remains. That is all that is required."

"A cheap coffin for Mistress Lorne." Windsor's voice was shaken. "Sir, you cannot mean it."

"Have you ever known me not to mean what I say? A plain coffin." Matthew Lorne's voice was emphatic. "Also, there will be no flowers. My wife did not care for them. On your way home, you will inform Treadwell that he need not expect to make money from me by the sale of his flowers, which, doubtless, he has snatched from the cottage gardens for that very purpose."

"I have never known a woman not to care for flowers, Master Lorne." The Reverend Baxter, conquering his natural awe and timidity of the man before him, spoke with a hint of stern censure. "A flower or two to mark her passing would not be out of place. Also, sir, why this indecent haste? Mistress Lorne, as your respected wife, held a place of some importance in this community. Has it occurred to you that the people will wish to file past her body and pay their last respects?"

"No flowers." Lorne snapped off the words. "And are you accusing me of disrespect, Reverend?" Lorne's voice became low and dangerous, causing the reverend to blanch. " 'Indecent haste,' I think you said. Does that mean that you think I have something to hide?"

"I . . . I . . ." Reverend Baxter's courage faded before the flat glare in Lorne's eyes. Fingering his worn prayer book nervously, he stammered, "You h-have mistaken my meaning."

"For your sake, Reverend, I hope that I have." Mathew Lorne sat down. Ignoring the trembling coffin maker, he crossed one leg over the other. Then, looking into the reverend's scarlet-tinged face, he said calmly, "But I see, my good man, that I must make my holy purpose clear to you, for it is apparent to me that naught else will satisfy that uneasy conscience of yours." He waited, inviting comment, his bleak satirical eyes going from one confused face to the other. Then, in the studiedly patient tone of one instructing backward children, he went on. "In allowing my wife's cortege to follow the witch, I am paying my wife the greatest respect. Good is following after evil, and maybe weakening that evil. Can you not see that, Reverend?"

The Reverend Baxter lowered his eyes. Never before had he been guilty of the sin of hatred, but he hated this evil man before him. The knowledge that he was afraid to give voice to that hatred completed his humiliation. He was not a man of God. He was the tool of

Matthew Lorne. "Yes, sir," he mumbled, all but consumed by his shame and his self-contempt. "Now that you have pointed it out, I do see."

Lorne smiled, fully aware of the reverend's emotions. "I am glad you see," he said in a purring voice. "The burial of a pure woman together with the penance trail of a witch."

The Reverend Baxter lifted his shamed eyes.

"I thought you would agree." Matthew turned his head. "And you, Windsor, do you agree?"

Jack Windsor clasped his big red-knuckled hands together. "Yes, sir, anything you say."

Tasmin peered over the banister. Her mother lay stretched out on the wooden table that had been cleared to accommodate her body. Her eyes had been closed, her lower limbs composed decently, and her hands were crossed on her still bosom. Tasmin shuddered as she saw her face. No preparation could erase that contorted look of agony which death had frozen into her face. Seated on a chair by the table was her father. The earlier violent scene between himself and Shalada might never have been, for he looked as composed as ever. He even appeared to be faintly amused by the obvious agitation of the other two men. The Reverend Baxter, his eyes closed and his lips moving silently in prayer, was trembling. Jack Windsor, his red hair wildly rumpled, his striped apron stained with the chemicals he used for his work, hovered over the body. His pale blue eyes fixed on Matthew Lorne as though seeking guidance, he reached out a hand and laid it on the stiff shoulder of the dead woman.

As though sensing Tasmin's presence, Matthew Lorne looked up at that moment. Tasmin gasped at the sudden blaze in his eyes. Shaking, she drew back. She knew what that look meant. His thoughts were with Shalada and on what was going on behind that bedchamber door. He could not wait to get rid of the two men. He could not wait to mount the stairs and fling open that door.

Her hands clasped together to still their trembling, Tasmin crept on noiseless feet to Shalada's door. She pressed her ear to the panel. She heard a low moaning that she recognized came from Shalada. Above the moaning Robert's low, cajoling voice could be heard. "Come, Shalada," he was saying, "do not pretend, I know well that you are not that injured." Tasmin's heart began to beat faster as the cajoling voice blurred with the first edge of anger. "Come, now, my darling, this is foolish of you. You know that I will win in the end. We were meant for each other, you and I. Open up your legs and let me into your body, or I will force them apart. Do you hear me, Shalada?"

As though her moaning had been a ruse to disarm him, Shalada's voice rose clear and strong and furious. "If you dare to touch me, you evil swine, I will find a way to make you regret it!"

"Shalada, listen to me. There is no shame. I am not your brother."

"I know it, and I thank God for it. And I tell you now that I would as soon mate with a worm!"

Tasmin gasped with excitement. Not for the world would she miss this. She knew from Robert's tone that he would not give in, and that Shalada, that arrogant bastard of the witch woman, was about to get what she had long had coming to her. Her mind turned to the handsome stranger as she silently entered the room. Unheard, unseen by the others, she stood there staring at the scene before her.

Robert had obviously removed Shalada's clothes when she was unconscious, for they were scattered about the floor. Naked, her long black hair wildly disheveled, she lay on her back on the bed, pinned there by Robert's hand. Her legs were pressed tightly together, refusing him the entrance he craved. Her breasts were rising and falling rapidly with the violence of her emotion and the fight she had obviously been putting up. Her bruised and bloody face, which appeared to have taken on more marks in the combat that had been raging, was twisted into a mask of rage, and her dark eyes blazed with murderous defiance. Tasmin's heart skipped a beat. Shalada would kill Robert if she could. The dark evil blood of the West women ran in her veins, and it was very evident at this moment. Murder, witchcraft, it was all there in her nature. Tasmin pressed a hand over her mouth to smother the burst of hysterical laughter that sought to escape. Perhaps she would even put a spell over Robert. But at this moment, fight though Shalada may—and, if Tasmin knew her, she would to the end—she had been too weakened by the blows of their father to prevail for too long against Robert's determination to possess her. He would rape that uppity bitch, and she, who had always loathed Shalada, was here to witness her humiliation.

Tasmin looked at Robert. Naked too, he was stooping over Shalada, his hard fingers pressing into the soft flesh of her rigidly held legs. He looked like a demented stranger, his face a dusky red and his expression a combination of anger and passion. Sweat dripped from his face, great droplets falling from his forehead and splashing onto Shalada's body, running down her flesh like oily streaks. There was a change in Robert's voice, a note that sounded almost like a sob. "I must have you, Shalada." Flinching before the hatred and the utter revulsion he read in those great blazing eyes, he cried out desperately, "I have waited so long!"

"You filth!" Shalada spat the words at him. Her fist lashed out and caught him a hard blow on the side of the head. Her voice rose to a scream of pure rage and hatred.

Robert appeared deaf to her words; he did not even seem to feel the blow. With a gasping cry he fell forward and burrowed his hot sweaty face between her legs. His tongue licked and caressed her.

For a moment Shalada was rigid with horror, her eyes looking almost blind. "My God!" The frenzied cry was torn from Shalada. Life came back to her, and the vivid color of fury flooded her face. At this added violation of her person, Shalada seemed to go completely mad. Like a snarling tigress she fought him with hard blows, with viciously slashing nails. Tasmin heard the breath laboring in her lungs, she saw the snarl on her face change to a hard mask of implacable hatred. Now her body reared up so violently that Robert fell back. Her triumph was fleeting, however, for now she was unguarded. Yelling, spittle spraying from his mouth, Robert seized his opportunity. Flinging himself upon her, he grabbed at her loosened legs and forced them farther apart. A wild cry came from Shalada's throat as he plunged inside her.

Smiling, Tasmin watched the rise and fall of his body. She heard his sobbing breaths, the battering of flesh against flesh as he rode her like a man demented. She saw the bloody lacerations appearing on his neck and his back as Shalada continued to fight him with all her strength.

Tasmin did not hear the soft opening of the door behind her. She did not sense her father's presence. Her starting eyes were on the tangle of thrashing limbs, her ears were filled with Shalada's wild cursing, the filthy words that came from Robert's lips as he sought to subdue the tigress to his will. Only when Matthew Lorne's hard hand seized her shoulder and hurled her to one side did Tasmin become aware of him. She crashed against the wall, striking her head. Whimpering, she slid to the floor, her terrified eyes staring up at her father. There was a look on his face such as she had never seen before, and she went cold with dread. She wanted to crawl away and hide, but she could not summon the strength to move. She put a shaking hand to the trickle of blood at the side of her head, and waited for what she knew must happen.

Long after the event, Tasmin was to wonder if it was the blow on her head that slowed up her reactions, for everything after that seemed to her to happen in slow motion. She was to ask herself if, had she been more aware, she could have stopped the terrible thing that happened. If she had had more courage, could she have saved Robert? But at this time she could only lie there, her terror-distended eyes watching. There was Shalada's struggling violated body, that murderous look still on her face, her wide-open mouth resembling a round black hole as it emitted scream after scream. Even in her dazed and frightened state Tasmin still clung to her hatred of the other girl. She told herself now that there was more fury than fear in those ear-piercing screams. Her lip curled. Shalada, the exotic, with her strange, high-cheekboned foreign-looking face, was made up of wickedness and fury.

Tasmin looked at Robert. He was unconscious of anyone but Shalada. Sweating, shuddering, moaning low in his throat, his body thrusting feverishly in passion's mad rhythm, he did not know that he rode the daughter of the Devil, or that because of that ride he was to meet his death. For she knew that it was Robert's death she had seen in her father's eyes.

Like one hypnotized, Tasmin swiveled her head to regard her father. A scream welled in her throat, but it remained unuttered. Frozen, she saw the movement of his hand toward his pocket. Light glittered dully on the blade of the knife he drew out. It occurred to her that she should say something, anything, that would appease her father's deadly, insane rage, but it was as if her lips were sealed.

Matthew Lorne's hand rose, the hilt of the knife clutched tightly. "If thy right eye offends thee, pluck it out!" his voice boomed through the room. "If thy son desecrates thy house, kill him!"

Robert's shuddering movements stopped abruptly. Afraid to turn his head, he stared for a moment at Shalada. She was looking beyond him, lying so still that she might have been composed of stone rather than flesh and blood. He saw the horror in her eyes, and the freckles stood out starkly on his paling face. Like a small terrified boy Robert began to whimper.

"Turn and face me, my son!" Matthew Lorne's voice was hard and dangerous.

Shalada's head turned as Robert's tears fell on her body, and her eyes softened to something that was almost pity. This terrible house, she thought, how could it have come to this? Robert Lorne had attacked her like a ravening wolf, and though she hated him, he did not deserve to die. At least not like this, at the hands of his own father. She looked at Matthew Lorne, and the words she addressed to him, though urgent, were tinged with hopelessness. He would not listen to any pleas, least of all to one that came from her. He wanted her himself, and he believed that she had already been violated by David Medway, and now, for the second time, by his own son. The fury and hatred he was feeling was Robert's death warrant. "You must not harm him. Whatever he has done, he is your son."

Her words had fallen on deaf ears; Matthew did not even look at her as he repeated in a deadly monotone, "Turn and face me, my son."

Robert put his hands on Shalada's shoulders, his fingers digging painfully into her soft flesh. "Help me, Shalada. Please."

"There is nothing she can do for you." Matthew's whispering voice struck terror into Robert's heart. He wanted to cover his face with the sweaty tangled sheet. Anything rather than face the man of whom he had always been terrified. His father, he thought bitterly, he had never been a father to him, but only a hated grim specter who stalked the house impregnating it with fear. Who spouted always of the wrath of God, while he himself was so evil, so corrupt. "There is nothing she can do for you."

Robert's silent prayer resounded deep inside him, but he knew that it would not help him now.

"Get up and face me!"

Cold and trembling, his heart beating suffocatingly,

Robert rose from the bed. Turning slowly, he faced the implacable man who was his father. His eyes widened as he saw the knife in Matthew Lorne's hand. Whatever he had expected, it was not this. A thrashing, perhaps, a further sample of Matthew Lorne's own brand of brutal sadistic punishment, but not this. His voice rose to a scream of pure animal terror. "Dear Christ!" He thrust out trembling hands of appeal. "You would not kill me, not for something like this. Not for a creature like her."

Matthew nodded, a smile stretching his fleshy mouth, giving him a silent answer.

Robert's eyes, distended with terror, flew to Shalada. She was his only hope, the only one who might perhaps be able to manage this madman. But she merely lay there, her face expressionless. Again Robert was reminded of a carving in stone. Robert did not know it, but Shalada was afraid to move. She believed that any word, any movement of hers would send the knife streaking from Matthew's hand. There was a reluctant pity in her for this youth who had raped her, but even greater was her horror of seeing murder done.

Robert saw only her expressionless face, which gave no hint of human feeling. He turned on her viciously, hoping even now to save himself. "Look at her," he cried, pointing a shaking finger in Shalada's direction. "See how shamelessly she lies there. Even now her thighs are spread wide to receive a lover. She is naught but a trollop, she has been begging me these many weeks to mount her. You cannot blame me."

"Yet I do blame you." There was a flame in Matthew's dark-green eyes. "You took what was mine, and no man, no sniveling cub like you does that to me."

"Yours!" Robert's voice rose to a shriek. A spurt of courage came to him. His pale face flushed purple and distorted with passion, he cried out, "Do you tell me that you, a man supposedly dedicated to God's work, wishes to crawl between her thighs? Do you . . . ?" Robert's voice wavered and died before the look in his father's eyes. His courage dissolved into harsh racking sobs. "I beg you to forgive me. She tempted me, bewitched me. When she opened up her legs to me, I was still under her evil spell, and I could not resist."

"Liar, you have always been after her. Even when you believed her to be your sister, you could not keep your lascivious eyes from her breasts, your hands from fumbling at her skirts."

Matthew's hard bitter eyes went to Tasmin. She was slumped forward, moaning, her perspiration-darkened blond hair hiding the hands that covered her face. "There is your true sister," he said in a biting contemptuous voice. "That creature who crouches there moaning and whimpering. Why did you not pursue her with your unsavory intentions? Why did you not raise her skirts above her head and plunge yourself between her skinny thighs?"

The purple hue faded from Robert's face, leaving his complexion a sickly yellowish white.

Matthew went on. "How lucky I have been in my children," he said in the same contemptuous voice. "Tasmin, my daughter, who is too cowardly to look upon her brother's death, or to raise one hand in his defense—is she not admirable?"

Matthew looked at Robert's blanched face, his staring eyes, and his naked shuddering form. But it was not his son's face he saw. He saw instead Don Roberto. Tall, darkly handsome, arrogant, haughty. Unable even then to believe that his death was about to be delivered at the hand of one whom he considered his social inferior. How contemptuous his dark eyes had been, how coldly sarcastic his voice when he had said, "I can only assume that you have a distorted sense of humor, or else you have lost your senses."

Words, Matthew thought, words that had availed him nothing. Contempt and sarcasm from a man who was about to die. It was not Don Roberto who faced him now, it was David Medway. Medway, as handsome in his own way as the Spaniard. It was he who would take Rebecca from him. Now he must kill Medway.

Robert's eyes measured the short distance from the bed to the door. If only he could slip past, he could yet save his life. He took a step forward.

"Get back, Medway," Matthew made a menacing move with the knife toward Robert. "I know you now. I have remembered at last. I hanged your father. I will kill you too. I will not let you have Rebecca!"

"I am not Medway!" Robert shouted. "Rebecca is not here. She is no longer the girl you loved. She is a crazy old woman who has been locked away in her cottage these many years. Her sin against you happened long ago, before you married my mother, before Tasmin and I were born."

Matthew's head swung to Robert. "Try to die like a man, Medway, I detest a coward."

Just as when he had killed Don Roberto, great beads of perspiration formed on Matthew's forehead, ran down his face, and splashed on his clothes. For a moment he regarded the star-shaped splotches darkening his buff-colored tunic; then he raised his eyes to Robert's terrified face. "The men who hanged your father tell me that he died like a man," he said in a low voice. "Try to do the same, Medway. You would not want to disgrace your father's memory."

"For Christ's sake, look at me," Robert sobbed. "I am Robert, your son."

Matthew's expression changed. "Robert, my son," he repeated. His eyes cleared, and his expression went stony with purpose. It was indeed Robert. And behind him, like gibbering ghosts, were the tall figures of David Medway and Don Roberto. Sons, lovers, what did it matter? Evil was evil, and it must be punished. Not a muscle of his face moved as the knife flew from his hand into Robert's chest.

Robert sank to his knees, a gurgling sound coming from his throat. Feebly he lifted his hands and tried to pluck out the deeply buried knife. His eyes filmed over.

His writhing lips made one last unintelligible sound. Then, blood spewing from his mouth, he pitched forward onto his face. The last sound he heard before he died was his father's soft laughter, and rising above it, Tasmin's terrified screaming.

Matthew saw Shalada jump from the bed and reached her in one bound. Dragging her by the hair, he pulled her back and thrust her down on the bed.

Shalada's eyes blazed up at him. "You killed my father, and now you have killed your own son. Who is next?"

Matthew's hand gripped her by the throat, his fingers pressing painfuly into her flesh. The eyes with which he regarded her painful struggle for breath were cold but sane. It was almost as if, with the death of Robert, the madness had left him. "It will be your mother." His fingers pressed deeper. "As for you, you will live as long as you appeal to me. Once you have lost your appeal, it will be the same for you."

Great stars of lurid colors were bursting in Shalada's tortured head. She could not breathe. Her heart was beating so rapidly that she feared at any moment it would burst. Downstairs, the woman who had tormented and beaten her lay dead and unmourned. Robert too was dead, his life's blood staining the bare wooden boards. Tasmin was huddled in a corner, her screams having died to whimpering moans. As for herself, a madman stood over her, his hand gripping her throat, squeezing her life away. Soon now she would be dead, for she could not keep up this desperate struggle for life.

A croak of sound came from Shalada's throat as Matthew's fingers loosened slightly, then tightened again. The colors were beginning to fade, giving way to blackness. In the center of the blackness she saw David Medway. The deep intense eyes in the dark, hawkishly handsome face, the ironical lift of his brows. How strange that she should think of him in her dying moments. David, who had fought her to a standstill, who had made her treacherous body feel things it had never felt before. But even in the midst of that attack that had turned out to be almost a rape, he could not wholly hide the tenderness that lay beneath his savagery. Now, in this moment of truth, she could admit that she had wanted to give in. She had wanted to feel him inside her, body crushed to body, his lips sealing hers. She knew now that David Medway was just such a man as she could have loved. Who could have loved her, had things been different. Too late now; she was going to die. She would never have the chance to show him her own tenderness, or warm him with that fire within her, that fire that she had cherished for the coming of the right man. Even as she thought it, something inside her refused to give up. Her silent voice cried out to him urgently if hopelessly, but it was with all the force her fainting spirit could muster.

Matthew looked down at Shalada. She did not look so beautiful now with her dark eyes starting out of her head, her engorged face, and the mute agony in these eyes that seemed to him to be asking for mercy.

His laughter began again as he slowly took his hand away from her throat. He heard the wheezing sound her breath made as it rushed back to fill her tortured lungs. Looming over her, he waited until her breathing became easier and a faint color stole into her blue-tinged face; then he said in a coaxing voice. "Stop fighting me, Shalada. Will you never learn?" He put his face close to hers. "Say that you will love me and be true to me, and you will have nothing to fear from me ever."

Shalada's brain began to work rapidly. She could not be certain if she were dealing with a madman or merely with an evil and cold-hearted man who could kill his own son without a tremor of conscience and then assume the guise of madness to excuse himself to others for what he had done. If he were really mad and she continued to hurl her hatred and defiance at him, he would surely kill her. But if she relented, or pretended to do so, there might be a way to catch him off guard. She knew only one thing. As soon as she could, she must escape from this terrible house. Her breasts rose in a sigh. "I . . . I cannot be any man's mistress, Father."

"Matthew," he thundered. "Call me, Matthew."

"Matthew, then. I cannot by your mistress."

He captured her hand, his fingers pressing it warmly. "Have I asked you to be my mistress? No, Shalada, you shall be my wife. We will be married immediately. Tomorrow, the next day, it you wish it. Think of it, Shalada, the wife of Matthew Lorne! You will like that, won't you, my darling?"

With difficulty she repressed a shudder. "Yes, Matthew," she lied desperately, "I would like that. But there are too many things in the way."

His light brows met in a frown. "What are these things?"

"How can you even ask? Your wife has just died. Even now she lies below. How will it look to others if you were immediately to take another wife?"

"I care nothing for the opinions of others." He bent his head and covered her hand with hot moist kisses. "I will marry whom I choose and when I choose. I love you, Rebecca."

He had called her Rebecca. Why was it that even now she could not bring herself to believe in his madness? It was a cloak with which he might conveniently hide from a world that otherwise might have condemned him. But she had no choice at this moment other than to play out the farce to its end. He was looking at her intently. She said faintly, "And then there is Tasmin. She hates me. She will never become reconciled to our marriage."

"Tasmin?" He said the name questioningly, as though he did not understand to whom she referred.

Then slowly his eyes began to clear.

What an actor he would have made, Shalada thought scornfully, certain now that she was on the right track. It was a clever trick to cover his own viciousness with the guise of madness. All the same, she was fighting for her life, and she could not afford to take chances. Let him call her Rebecca, let him play his little game. Mad or sane, he would still kill her if the spirit moved him. "Tasmin," she prompted gently.

He took the cue almost eagerly. "But you have no need to worry about her. I intend to rid myself of her."

She heard Tasmin's loud gasp and risked looking in her direction. The girl was still on the floor, but she was sitting bolt upright, her thin arms clasped about her knees. Her blond hair was untidy about her tear-streaked face, and the eyes fixed on her father were filled with glowing hatred. Her eyes reminded Shalada uncomfortably of Matthew's. Tasmin could be used, she thought. She could foster the girl's hatred for her father to such a pitch that it would far outweigh the hatred that Tasmin now bore toward her. Shalada looked at Matthew again. "You say you have ways of ridding yourself of Tasmin," she said softly. "I would be most interested to hear them."

"I can see to it that Tasmin is accused of her brother's murder." Certain of Shalada's pleasure and approval, he smiled at her. "You see how clever I am. It will be easy, my darling."

Tasmin's face was livid, her trembling lips colorless, and in her distended eyes was a belief in her father's insanity. Seeing it, Shalada felt a qualm of doubt. For all that her clear-thinking mind had indicated to her the cruel game he was playing, yet she still found herself balanced on the edge of uncertainty. Quickly she closed her mind against the possibility. It was not insanity that she and Tasmin were seeing and experiencing, it was the inherent evil in the man. As for Tasmin, it would take but a little more to push her over the edge and send her running in her direction for protection. "You must not do that, Matthew," Shalada said in a loud shocked voice that she knew would reach the girl's stunned ears. "You could not stand by and see

229

them hang your own daughter for a crime she has not committed."

"And why not?" Matthew's eyes narrowed to glittering green slits. "You are bold in your defense of that bitch. Have you forgotten that she has helped to make your life a misery?"

Tasmin's eyes, full of wild pleading, were fixed on Shalada's face. Help me, her eyes seemed to be saying.

Shalada's slight nod in the direction of the girl was one of reassurance.

Tasmin burst into wild sobs. "I will change, Sh-Shalada. I p-p-promise."

Turning back to Shalada, Matthew said, "I do not care if Tasmin turns into a saint. The fact of the matter is that I will not have that woman's child in this house. We will chase out the unpleasant memories and start all over again." He looked at her with frowning brows. Then, as Shalada stared back at him she saw his lips begin to twitch. "A saint." He chuckled. "Tasmin shall become a saint. I will send her to a convent, and she shall become one those long-faced prating nuns."

Tasmin's tear-swollen eyes watched her father as he walked over to the body of his son. He stood there looking down at the pathetically sprawled figure, as though not quite certain of what he must do. Then, grunting, he stooped down and gathered the body into his arms. Robert's blood stained his clothing as he carried him over to the door, but he did not seem to notice or care, for there was no emotion in his face.

Tasmin shuddered as he paused by the door, still tightly clasping his gruesome burden. She was afraid that he would turn his head and pierce her with those chill eyes of his. But when he spoke, he did not even bother to look at her. "It will be a double funeral tomorrow, Tasmin," he said harshly. "Your brother, most unfortunately, has met with an accident."

Tasmin closed her eyes. So he did not mean to accuse her of the murder of Robert. Perhaps he would relent still further and allow her to stay in her home.

Dimly she realized that he was speaking again, and she concentrated with painful attention, ready and eager to thank him should he show mercy.

Then her eyes flew wide with shock. "As for you, Tasmin," he continued, "you will go to your room and pack your boxes. You will not require much, for I understand that the holy sisters shun material possessions."

He ignored her anguished outcry. "The day after your mother and your brother have been buried, I will be taking you to the Ursuline Convent."

He would lock her away behind the grim stone walls of the convent? She, who had never experienced life, who had never known the touch of a man's lips on hers. The nuns would shave her head, taking away what was her only claim to beauty. She heard the ruthless snip of the shears, her blond locks falling about her feet. She felt the coldness of soap and water on her head as the last of her hair was shaved away. In that convent she would grow old and shriveled. She would never be a wife, never hold a child in her arms. Instead, she would become the bride of Christ. A barren marriage in which the bridegroom never appeared. She could not bear it. "I will tell," she cried out in a choked voice, "I will tell everybody that you killed your own son and drove my mother to her death by your cruelty."

Now Matthew turned. His icy eyes looked her over from her disheveled hair beneath the crumpled white cap, the swollen eyes and the reddened nose in the twitching tear-blotched face, the thin curveless figure, and the bony trembling hands. "A pretty sight," he sneered, "but tell me again, Tasmin"—his voice dropped to a low, almost caressing note—"just what it is you will tell."

Tasmin's head drooped; she was beaten.

"Well, shall it be the convent?"

"Yes, Father," she whispered.

"You have chosen wisely, my daughter."

Matthew left to make funeral arrangements for Robert. Hearing the door slam, followed by brisk footsteps going down the path, Tasmin rose shakily to her feet. Weaving like someone under the influence of strong drink, she made her way toward Shalada.

Shalada was strong, a rock of strength. There were no circumstances that could subdue her fighting spirit. Tasmin could lean on Shalada, rely on her. Shalada had saved her life. All her previous animosity and jealousy forgotten, she was filled with admiration and a surge of emotion that might almost be described as love. Yet still a question came to trouble her. "Perhaps we will be safe for the night, but what of tomorrow?"

Watching her, Shalada guessed at the thoughts passing through her mind. Tasmin was very transparent. At the moment Tasmin admired her, perhaps even believed that she loved her, but the feeling would pass. Once she knew herself to be safe, Tasmin would revert to her true nature. Forcing herself to speak as gently as possible, she said, "We will let tomorrow take care of itself. I will think of something."

Tasmin's eyes showed a trust that had never been there before. "You will think of something, I know you will. You won't let anyone hurt me, will you, Shalada?"

That was the true Tasmin speaking, Shalada thought wryly. She was concerned only with her own precious skin. "No, Tasmin, I won't let anyone hurt you." Despite the tight control she had imposed on herself, her impatience mounted. "I am not sure, but I think there may be someone in the village who will help us."

Shalada's thoughts were with David Medway. She wondered why her thoughts turned to him so hopefully, and she asked herself why he should help them. He hated her, he had made that very plain. And yet, when he had looked at her with that watchful and intent expression in his dark eyes, it occurred to her to wonder if, after all, his hatred for her was so very deep-rooted. Her woman's intuition told her it was not.

It told her that she appealed strongly to his senses even as he appealed to hers. It was her name he hated, not herself. After what had happened between them, she had no right to ask his help, but ask it she would. Perhaps if she begged him. The thought of herself begging David Medway, or indeed any man, brought a slight smile to her lips. But there was one thing she could do. She could tell him the truth, about her father.

Shalada's brow wrinkled in a thoughtful frown; she would make him believe, enough so that he would help to get her and Tasmin away from Waterford and beyond Matthew Lorne's vengence. Perhaps the spice of adventure in flight and possible pursuit would appeal to him. He was that kind of man, she was suddenly sure, who would love danger for its own sake. She thought of herself calling him a coward, and her face flushed hotly. She might know little of him as yet, but if she had her way, she would know a great deal more, but whatever else he might be called—rogue, devil, evil-tempered, as he had proved—he was certainly no coward.

Shalada turned her head on the pillow, thinking of escape. Her mind touched on Rebecca. Her eyes misted with tears as she thought of the fate that awaited the fragile little woman. She bit down hard on her swollen lower lip. Rebecca, she thought in agaony, who had been so very young at the time she had been forced to watch her own mother die in flaming agony. Half-deranged by the sight, was it any wonder that she had allowed a stranger like Don Roberto to comfort her, to kiss her, and to enter her body? Perhaps she had even wanted him to do so, anything so that she might not have to think. But after that incident, her life had become one long nightmare. With the stranger's child growing in her body, she had been ill-treated and savagely abused by Matthew Lorne. And, finally, the greatest blow of all, she had been robbed of her child. Dear Rebecca, Shalada thought with a spasm of pain. Wrapped in her silence, she had been unable to speak aloud her love for her daughter, but she had tried in many small and pathetic ways to show it.

Shalada's tears overflowed the corners of her eyes and ran down into her hair. She had always loved and been drawn to Rebecca, but if only she had known that she was her mother, how very much more would she have loved and cherished her. In every way that she could think of, she would have tried to make up to her for all that she had suffered.

Shalada's tears flowed faster. If was her fault; if only she had let Rebecca continue on in her silence, she would be safe today. She had to interfere, had to urge and prod until, wanting only to please her, the long-dammed-up stream of words had finally burst from Rebecca's throat. It was because of her that Rebecca must now pay such a high price. She had spoken out against Matthew Lorne, and he feared that she would speak out against him publicly. Because of this, he would force Rebecca to die as her mother before her. She would suffer for a while in the stinking prison, and then, chained like a helpless animal to the blackened stone post, she would end her life in fiery agony.

A sudden thought came to Shalada, drying her tears and causing her heart to beat faster. Her eyes flared wide and bright with hope. David Medway wanted revenge for the death of his father. He had given his vow to his mother not to seek that revenge or to attempt to kill Matthew Lorne. But if he were to kill him in a fair fight, in defense of a helpless woman, that would be different.

Shalada's thoughts raced excitedly. What it David were to attempt to rescue her and spirit her away? Enraged, Matthew Lorne would fight to keep his victim. And David, to defend both himself and Rebecca, would be forced to fight back. It would be self-defense, not murder. But what if it should be David who was killed? Not for a moment did she doubt his ability, but Matthew Lorne was known to be quick and vicious with both dagger and sword. Besides which, Lorne would have the population with him. They did not love him, but they did fear him, and it was that fear that would cause them to range themselves on his side.

The bright hope faded from Shalada's eyes as she faced a truth she had been avoiding. Angry with David though she might have been, fighting him, scratching and spitting like a wildcat, she could not deny the warm glow that always sprang up inside her whenever she thought of him. In the eyes of most people they would be called strangers to each other, and yet, from the very first glance they had exchanged, they had known each other. They were alike, and like always called to like. Despite the animosity that had marked their first two meetings, the recognition had been there. Angry though David had been when he fought to subdue her, she had seen that same recognition in his eyes. Without understanding or even attempting to analyze the feeling, she knew now that they were meant for each other. She could so easily love that dark, swaggering pirate of a man who had used her so roughly and without regard to her sex, and she felt that he could love her in return.

The sound of sobbing broke her thoughts. Tasmin, that sniveling little fool. "Tasmin," she called sharply, "get yourself in here!"

After a few moments of silence, Tasmin came slowly through the door. If she had been pale and disheveled before, she was even more so now. Tasmin's voice rose high and thin with hysteria. "They are dead," she said, staring at Shalada with wild eyes.

Shalada had no time to be gentle; she only knew that she must quell the girl's rising hysteria before it reached its peak. "I know that," she shouted. "Why do you think we have to get away? Your father has killed more than once; he will not hestitate to kill again."

Sobbing, but still submissive to the voice of authority, Tasmin stumbled forward.

"Go over to the clothes press and get me something to wear." Ignoring the pain that movement brought,

Shalada swung her legs to the floor. It was agony to dress in the gown that Tasmin handed her, but she managed it. Smoothing the burgundy-colored folds over her hips, she picked up a gray cloak and swung it about her shoulders. Pulling the hood well forward, she announced that she was ready to go.

Tasmin stared at her stupidly. "But you have no shoes on. I . . . I will get you a pair."

When Tasmin brought her the shoes, one green and one brown, though, fortunately, fitting the right and the left foot, Shalada found it impossible to bend. Her attempt to do so brought on a whirling in her head and a feeling of nausea. Her impatience to be gone mounted almost to a fever as she was forced to submit to Tasmin's fumbling attempts to fit the shoes onto her feet.

"I must go to my room and fetch a cloak," Tasmin said, rising to her feet.

"You will do nothing of the sort," Shalada said, pushing her toward the clothes press. "Wear one of mine."

Picking out a black cloak, Tasmin emulated Shalada by pulling the hood well forward to hide her face. With hoplessness and despair in her heart, she followed the other girl to the door.

Downstairs, some of Shalada's frantic hurry to be gone seemed to leave her. Moving over to Dorothy Lorne, she stared solemnly into her dead face. She waited to feel something, wanted to, but she could not. Like a demon chorus, the sound of her own childish terrified screams were loud in her ears as she recalled Dorothy Lorne, her eyes glaring from a round face that was red with the passion of hatred. She saw her hand clenched about a stout stick. The hand rose and fell as it belabored her small victim until she could no longer stand.

Closing her ears to the terrified screams of the child she had once been, and to the loud voices of hatred that had pursued her through the years, Shalada laid her fingers lightly on Dorothy Lorne's cold hand. "I'm sorry you hated me," she said in a soft voice. "I'm sorry that I hated you, and that I still do. It is wrong to hate, but I do hate you, and I always will."

"Shalada, let us go," Tasmin's tearful voice pleaded.

"Yes, Tasmin." Shalada looked at Robert. Sly and mean and lecherous, he was not even worth her hatred. Averting her eyes, she led the way to the door. Opening it, she stepped outside, closely followed by Tasmin. The door closed behind them with a loud bang, shutting them out of that house of horror. Taking Tasmin's trembling arm in a firm grip, Shalada led her down the path.

12

Holding the fair-haired listless-looking child in arms
that already trembled beneath his slight weight, Polly
Carter stood beside her mother. Jane Carter, Polly's
mother, was a tall gaunt woman. Her iron-gray hair
was drawn tightly back from a severe face that was
deeply etched with lines of suffering. She had brown
eyes framed by surprisingly heavy lashes. In her youth
her eyes had been quite beautiful, but they squinted
now. The diminishing of their size had somehow given
her a perpetually frightened look. Even at this moment
their brown was clouded by a look of dread as they
darted quickly from the face of her daughter, to the
child, and then to the solemn faces ringed about the
open graves. They lingered longest on Matthew Lorne,
who was standing stiffly erect, his black feathered cap
crushed in his hands. Jane saw the tears streaking his
face as he watched the two coffins being lowered. He
had lost both wife and son, the son having been foully
murdered by persons unknown, and yet somehow Jane
found that she could not quite believe in those tears.
She was astute enough to know that he was angered
rather than grief-stricken. She knew it from the constant tensing of his hands about the cap, the whitening
of his knuckles, and the way his eyes would wander
from time to time—hot, angry, searching eyes behind
the glimmer of tears. For whom did he search? she
wondered.

Jane was suddenly terribly afraid. Polly had been released from the stocks so that the way might be cleared for the witch's walk. But an angry Matthew Lorne, she reasoned, might well order Polly to be restored to the stocks after the witch, Rebecca West, had been safely lodged in the prison.

Jane's tired heart lurched and her thin lips trembled. She was old. She had been widowed for a long time, so long that it took an effort of memory to recall her man's face. This time, when her daughter had been snatched from her, it had been the kindness of the grand stranger who had saved them from starvation. But what would happen if her daughter was taken from her a second time? She could scarcely fend for herself, let alone cope with the care of a two-year-old child who was beyond her strength to control.

The child in Polly's arms, contrary to his grandmother's foreboding thoughts, seemed to have no strength at all. Unlike his mother, whose nose and cheeks were nipped to a bright red by the cold, the complexion of the child remained a waxen white. There were faint blue circles beneath his lightless pale amber eyes and a bluish tinge about his small slack mouth.

The child began to whimper, a faint mewing sound that had no strength behind it. Anxiously Polly tucked the now dry cloak that David Medway had given to her about the small shivering form and cuddled him closer to her breast. The child gave a small sneeze as the fur lining tickled his nostrils; then, sighing, comforted by the closer pressure and the added warmth, he closed his eyes.

Overhead, the trees with their burden of tightly furled bright green buds soughed, their branches rustling and rattling in the wind and occasionally sending down small driblets of rain, the residue of yesterday's deluge.

Satisfied that the child slept, Polly tenderly wiped some drops of rain from his pale forehead. She did not once look at Matthew Lorne or at the men that were now laboring to fill in the graves. Shivering, she heard the dull thud of earth falling on the coffins and the sharp scraping of the spades. Seeking comfort, she turned her eyes on David Medway. He was not looking at her, but the reassuring sight of him sent a faint warmth through her. David Medway, through her grateful and somewhat muddled reasoning, had come to seem to her like a savior. Tall, dark, and, to her, handsomer than a god, he had come striding into her miserable little world bringing aid and comfort. Jamie, her son, though still very weak, was much stronger than he had been. David Medway had saved both Jamie and her mother. He had fed them, he had seen that the child had milk, and he had caused fires to be kindled to soothe their shivering bodies. And still his kindness went on. This morning, before first light, another load of firewood had arrived at the cottage. An hour later, a sour-faced grumbling cowman had delivered a churn of milk. This had been followed by a huge carton of groceries, packed not only with essentials but also with every conceivable delicacy. There had been no message with any of the deliveries, but she knew whom she had to thank. Was it any wonder that she loved him. There was nothing in this world that she would not do for him; her son lived, and for that she would lie down and let him walk over her, if he so desired.

Her heart in her eyes, Polly continued to stare at David Medway's tall figure. Today, as though in defiance of the mournful occasion that had brought them all together, he was garbed in red and white, almost as though the two funerals were gala occasions. His short sleeveless red robe was edged with white fur, but beneath the robe he wore a fine white shirt. The sleeves ballooning from the robe were excessively full, in the latest fashion, and gathered at his wrists with a triple layer of white lace that fell over his hands. A red cloak lined with white fur was slung about his broad shoulders and fastened at the neck with a great silver clasp. Red-and white-striped hose disappeared into red leather boots that came to his knees, and his face was shadowed by the brim of a red hat that was embellished with a curling white feather.

Polly could not help wondering why he had decided to attend the funerals. Matthew Lorne was nothing to him. Or was he? He was an outstanding and arresting figure, a bright note of color in the crowd of soberly dressed people. Had he dressed to attract the attention of the people? That did not seem like him at all. Then perhaps the attention of one person in particular. The name of Matthew Lorne leaped into Polly's mind as she found herself remembering the bleak look in David's eyes whenever the man's name was mentioned. Somewhere, at some time, Matthew Lorne must have done him an injury, and Polly was suddenly sure that he had attended this funeral to mock rather than to mourn. His bright clothing was meant to be a subtle insult.

With shrinking facination, Polly let her eyes stray to Matthew Lorne. Dressed entirely in black, his high collar unrelieved by even the slightest hint of lace, he was staring hard at David Medway. Polly felt a quivering inside her as she saw the dangerous blaze in his eyes. Looking at David for reassurance, she found none. A slight smile on his lips, he was calmly returning Lorne's gaze. His smile was not pleasant. In its own way it was as dangerous and as naked with hatred as the blaze in Lorne's eyes.

He knows, David thought. At last he has made the connection between me and the man he caused to be so cold-bloodedly hanged. He knows that he faces the son of Sir Marcus Medway. Grown from a small boy to a man who will ever be his most bitter enemy. David's hand touched the hilt of his sword and lingered there. His movement had been slow and deliberate, and he knew that Lorne's eyes had not missed it. Do your worst, Lorne, he thought. As God is my witness, I will be most happy to oblige you.

Polly's fixed gaze on David's face was suddenly distracted by a flicker of movement. Wraithlike, unexpected, a slight gray-cloaked figure had suddenly appeared at David's side. It was obviously a feminine figure, and Polly was frustrated because she could not see the face. The hood of the cloak was pulled well forward, seeming to indicate that the wearer had no wish to be recognized.

All about Polly, heads were bowing and eyes were closing as the Reverend Baxter's deep solemn voice began to intone the prayer for the dead. Polly did not close her eyes. Fascinated by the woman in gray, consumed with curiosity, she went on staring. She saw a pale hand appear from the recesses of the cloak and place itself upon David's arm. With a small pang of jealousy, quickly stifled, Polly noted that the hand was narrow and slender and smooth. The hand of a lady.

Startled out of his vengeful thoughts, David looked down at the small hand resting on his arm. "Yes," he said, "you wish to speak with me?"

"Obviously," an unmistakable voice answered. "I do not usually approach someone and touch them for the sheer thrill of it. And, if you please, will you be so obliging as to lower that cursed raucous voice of yours."

Annoyed by the thrill of excitement that the mere sound of her voice could produce, David waited until his leaping heart had settled to a steadier beat before answering her. "Ah, the gentle Shalada," he whispered mockingly. "Since my greatest enemy would hardly describe my voice as raucous, I can only assume that you have come here to resume the fight. Is it so, Mistress Lorne?"

Shalada's hand on his arm trembled. She was conscious of a tenderness, a warm melting feeling, an excitement that only his presence could bring to her. "No, it is not," she answered him, controlling herself, Her voice, covered by the mutterings of the others who had now joined in the prayer, was barely distinguishable.

Bending, he put his face close to hers. David asked, "What was that you said?"

Shalada drew back sharply. "No, I have not come her to fight with you." Then, more urgently: "Damn you for a great deaf giraffe. Do not put your face so close to mine, or you will attract attention. And do not call me Mistress Lorne, it is not my name."

David saw the dark glimmer of her eyes as she raised her head for a brief instant. "Do you expect me to believe that?"

"It's true."

"Damn that for a tale. Is this another trick to gain my confidence? Are you perchance planning another nice little murder in which you expect me to participate? Who is it to be this time, your father, your sister? It cannot be your brother, since he has already come to an untimely end. By the way, did you have a hand in that?"

"Shut up!" she whispered fiercely. She put her foot over his, grinding her heel into his instep.

"Curse you for a bad-tempered shrew," David said from between clenched teeth. He glanced down, and his frown faded. "One green shoe and one brown," he muttered, the mockery back in his voice. "An interesting combination, but one scarcely guaranteed to make you inconspicuous, which, from all the signs, I presume is your object."

David's voice had risen slightly on the last words. "Will you lower your voice," Shalada whispered. "Never mind my shoes. I have told you that my name is not Lorne. If you do not choose to believe me, you dumb ox, that is entirely up to you."

David's eyes smoldered with suppressed fury. "Never have I met a bitch like you before!" he said in a low dangerous voice. "If it were not for this audience about us, I would teach you a lesson you'd not forget in a hurry."

"Yes, I believe you would, for you're naught but a damned great bully. Now, then, will you listen to me?"

"If we may have done with the name-calling," David said coldly, "I might consent to do so. But do not bore my ears with some cock-and-bull story about not being a Lorne and expect me to swallow it. You must indeed take me for a fool."

"That is exactly what you are if you refuse to hear me out. And little though I relish the prospect, I am determined to speak, and equally determined to make you listen."

David glared at her lowered head. "Speak, then, you have my full attention."

"Not here, you dolt." Her fingers nipped at his arm. "I will wait for you in your room at the Goose and Grapes."

"You will do nothing of the sort."

"Yes I will. What is the number of your room?"

"So that's your little game, is it, you strumpet." David's whispering voice held the triumphant note of one who had just solved a puzzle. "Oh, yes, Mistress Lorne, of course you will wait in my room until I return. Then, after a suitable interval has gone by, you will begin screaming out that I have compromised you. What then, am I expected to marry you?"

"How dare you, you great conceited fool. I'd not marry you if you went down on your knees and begged me."

By Christ, but the bitch was trying him too high. David's brows drew together in an ominous line as he answered her. "Go down on my knees, eh," he said coldly. "Let me assure you that that particular situation will never arise." He considered her downbent head thoughtfully. "Then, if it is not that, maybe it is the opening gambit of some devil's plot you and your father have thought up. Am I nearer to the mark, Mistress Lorne?"

This time Shalada's fingers nipped David's arm so sharply that he was forced to bite back a cry. "Call me

Mistress Lorne once more, David Medway, and you'll be sorry. I have told you he is not my father."

Ridiculously, his emotions wildly out of control, David was divided by a longing to sweep back her hood and kiss her impudent mouth, and the impulse to throttle her for her cursed insolence. Unable to do either, he said in a low, even voice, "I am getting tired of this verbal sparring. Suppose you tell me exactly what it is you want of me."

"I will, when we are alone."

"But we are not going to be alone."

"Don't be ridiculous. Of course we are." Again Shalada raised her head, and in her fleeting glance he saw the anger sparkling in her big dark eyes.

Taken aback, swept by a fresh surge of outrage that she actually seemed to be trying to put him in the wrong, he said in a furious whisper, "How dare you glare at me like that! Why, I'd like to—"

Her quickly lowered head cut him off. "I know exactly what you'd like to do to me," she said in a muffled voice, "so there is no need to refine upon the point. Now, then, I want you to look across at that man and tell me what he is doing."

Confusion took the place of outrage. "What are you talking about now? What man?"

"Matthew Lorne, of course."

David's glare went to the stiff black-clad figure. Matthew Lorne's eyes were closed, his head bent over his clasped hands. "Your father appears to be praying, Mistress Lorne. Perhaps he is praying for the salvation of your soul, which appears to be even blacker than his own."

"I have told you that he is not my . . . that I am not Mistress Lorne. Oh, what's the use. You are too dense to see beyond your nose. Is he looking at me?"

"Not unless he has the ability to see through his eyelids."

"Then I am going now, Give me the number of your room and I will await you at the Goose and Grapes."

Curiosity, and a longing to be alone with this beautiful and infuriating girl who had managed to invade all his thoughts, overcame David's suspicion and anger. "Very well," he said curtly. "My room number is ten. I will slip away as soon as possible. And let me warn you once more. Try anything, and it will be the worse for you."

David heard the ghost of a laugh. "So you will slip away, will you?" Shalada's whispering voice mocked him. "I would tell you to do it as unobtrusively as possible, but I think you will find it a little difficult to accomplish, you dressed-up popinjay."

"Now, you look here. I've had quite enough . . ." David stopped short as he realized that he spoke to the empty air. As quietly as she had come, the gray-clad figure had just as quietly disappeared.

Fuming, and yet fighting an impulse to laugh, David turned his head and met Polly Carter's wide eyes. He wondered if she had heard any of the conversation. Uncertainly, he smiled at her.

Polly edged closed. "I seen the lady, sir," she said in hoarse whisper. "She wanting you to go with her?"

David hesitated, wondering how much to say. Deciding to be honest, he nodded. "Yes. She tells me she has something to say to me."

Polly shifted the child in her arms, automatically hushing the sleepy, protesting whimper he made. She looked up quickly at David. "It was Miss Shalada, wasn't it?"

Caught off guard, David said quickly, "Yes, it was. How did you know, did you see her face?"

"No, sir, I just guessed." Polly took a step nearer to him. "Likely you'll say it ain't my business, sir, and in a manner of speaking, it ain't. But I don't want nothing to happen to you. So don't you trust them Lornes, not a blamed one of 'em." She hesitated, then added, "Miss Shalada ain't so bad. Leastways, she wasn't when I worked up at the house, but for all that, she's a Lorne. So you listen to what she's got to say, if you're particu-

lar wanting to. But watch her close, sir. Don't you go
trusting her too much."

David thought of Shalada's angry voice saying, "Call
me Mistress Lorne once more, David Medway, and
you'll be sorry. I have told you he is not my father."

Staring at Polly, David felt confused.

"You mark what I've said, sir," Polly said in an urgent voice. "Miss Shalada's beautiful enough to turn
any man's head, but I'm begging you not to trust her
too much."

Unreasonable though he knew it to be, David was
forced to crush down a sudden surge of anger at what
he felt to be a slur on Shalada. Absurd, he chided himself, when only a few moments ago he had been thinking the very same things himself. Beautiful but
treacherous, that was Shalada, and he would be a fool
if he forgot that.

"I see that I have gone and made you angry," Polly
said in a mournful voice. "I never meant to."

"I know you didn't Polly, and I'm not in the least
angry." He laid his hand gently on her tumbled brown
hair. Why should he take out his anger on this worn-
faced girl who was so sincere that she could not keep
her anxiety for him from showing in her expressive
eyes? "I'll watch her," he added, "and I'll be very careful, so don't be troubling yourself about me." Smiling
at her, he took his hand away.

Polly looked up into his dark eyes, and a feeling she
had never known before moved inside her. It was a
feeling that was exquisitely sweet but at the same time
excruciatingly painful. She knew then that it wasn't just
gratitude she felt for David Medway, it was love. The
kind of love a woman gives to the one and only man,
the special man. Polly wanted to laugh at the absurdity
of her thoughts, but instead she found herself choking
on tears. She, a rough and uneducated girl, brought up
on a farm, whose only talents were the care and
feeding of animals, the killing of chickens when they
were needed for the table, and the mucking out of pig

sties. At sixteen years of age she had become pregnant
by one of the farm helpers, a man who was old enough
to be her father. And he, learning of her trouble, had
refused to marry her. Afterward, he was seen no more
about the farm. The farm was barely yielding enough
to make them a living, but the disgrace of her pregnancy had lost them even that. She and her widowed
mother had been turned out by their highly moral and
irate landlord. And yet she, that miserable girl, who
had known only two joyous moments in her life, the
first when Jamie had been placed in her arms, and the
second when David Medway had entered her life, was
actually in love with this grand lord. Sir David Medway, she had heard him called. Titled, handsome—
why, he could no doubt marry the finest lady in the
land. Were she Queen of England, Polly's fevered
thoughts roved on, Sir David Medway would only have
to beckon and she would leave everything to go wandering at his side. Queen, barefoot gypsy girl, what did
it matter as long as she could be with him?

David's anxious eyes scanned the tears rolling down
her cheeks. His voice came to her dimly. "Why are you
crying?" He looked at the sleeping child in her arms.
"Is it something to do with the babe, or with your
mother? Can I help?"

Polly sniffed back her tears. He mustn't guess. If he
could glimpse into her mind, she would die of the
shame of it. He wouldn't laugh, of course, for he was always kind, except, that was, when it came to Matthew
Lorne, whom he seemed to regard with such hard, bitter scorn and hatred. No, with her he would be tender
and understanding, but all the same she would see reflected in those dark eyes of his the hopelessness of her
love for him, and that she could not bear. So he must
not know. "No, sir." Polly gave him a wavering smile.
"Don't you go worrying yourself, for it ain't nothing at
all. I reckon I'm just being silly. I get sad thoughts
sometimes, that's all. As for me mum and the babe,
they're doing just fine, thanks to you."

"In that case, no more tears." He smiled. "I can't allow my favorite girl to cry."

His favorite girl. Once more Polly looked fully into those disturbing dark eyes of his. Eyes that made her feel like butter inside, butter that was fast melting beneath the heat of a fierce sun. His favorite girl. If only she could be.

"Polly," David's accusing voice said, "you're looking sad again."

"Am . . . am I, sir? Well, I ain't sad. Honest!"

"In that case, I wish your eyes would stop leaking." David took a handkerchief from the pocket of his tunic. Gently he dabbed at her wet face. "There, that's better, isn't it?"

"Much better, s-sir." Polly looked at the handkerchief clutched in his lean brown hand. "That's right pretty, ain't it, sir?"

"The handkerchief?" David looked at it. "Would you like to have it, Polly?"

Her face flaming, Polly stammered, "I . . . I would, sir. It'll be something to remember you by." Oh, dear Lord, why had she said that? He would guess.

But David, apparently unaware of her inner turmoil, put the handkerchief in her hand. "It's yours."

Polly stared at it through tear-blurred eyes. "It's got lace on it, and there's writing in the corner. What do the writing say, sir?"

"It's not writing, Polly. It's my initials. D.M. That stands for David Mewday."

The color in Polly's face deepened. "I'll always treasure it, sir. You been so kind and good, and I ain't likely to forget." She looked down at the baby. "Jamie, he's sleeping all snug and warm in your cloak. As soon as he's out of the wind, I'll let you have the cloak back."

"You'll do nothing of the sort," David answered her. "When the babe has no need of it, you can wear it yourself. It will keep you warm."

"Yes, sir. Thank you very much, sir."

David frowned. "For Christ's sake, don't keep thanking me, Polly." He hesitated, then said in a laughing voice, "Polly, I do believe you are thinking of me as some kind of a saint. It won't do, you know. For I am far from being that."

"You are to me, sir. And always will be!"

This was said so fervently that David's smile turned rueful. "Saint David," he murmured. "Somehow it does not seem to fit." He looked up. Then, touched by something he saw in her eyes, he wondered if she was still worried about his coming interview with Shalada. "I have asked you not to worry about me, Polly, and you are doing so, aren't you?"

"Yes, sir," Polly admitted. "I can't think what Miss Shalada can be wanting with you. It ain't my business, I know. But I can't feel she's up to any good."

"Well, don't worry. I will take care of Shalada in my own way. If there are any tricks up her sleeve—and it's possible there might be—she will find she is dealing with a man, not a green boy."

Polly's eyes sparkled. "Will you beat her, sir?"

"If necessary." David looked down at his scratched hands. "Though tangling with Shalada is somewhat like tangling with a tigress."

"You love her, sir, don't you?"

"Love her, love Shalada!" David looked at her in astonishment. "Why, Polly, what nonsense is this? In the first place, I hardly know her. And in the second place, I . . ." Frowning, he broke off. "The real truth is," he continued, "I don't know what I feel."

Polly stifled a pang of jealousy. "It don't take long to fall in love, sir. People can do it in a matter of minutes, if they recognize the person as being the right one for them." She drew in a deep breath, and then rushed on. "Anyway, you do love her, I seen it in your eyes and I hear it in your voice whenever you mention her name."

David hastened to change the subject. "Polly, listen to me carefully. Unless it is part of Lorne's plan that

Shalada should be found in my room, I would not like him to discover her there." He held up his hand as Polly opened her mouth to speak. "I know you have no cause to love the Lornes. If you should see Lorne looking my way, or attempting to follow, try to find some way to warn me."

Polly smiled, and though she was unaware of it, her love for him showed in her eyes as she answered him. "If Matthew Lorne should open them gooseberry eyes of his, or even take one step, I'll be across to the inn in a flash. I'll be watching, never you fear."

David's face clouded. "Perhaps I am asking too much of you. I would not have you put yourself in danger for me, Polly. If Lorne should see you and guess what you're up to, you could be in very serious trouble."

Polly's mouth set mutinously. "Don't care. I'd put me head under a chopping block if I thought it'd do you any good."

"Well, it wouldn't." David patted her hand. "You just be careful. I want that pretty head of yours to stay right where it is."

"Ain't pretty." Womanlike, Polly was caught by his last words. "Ain't never been pretty."

"You are mistaken. With some care, you could be very pretty indeed."

Flustered, Polly broke in, "Get along with you, sir. I'll have me eyes on old Devil Lorne, and what's more, he ain't going to catch me at it, nor see me if I got to slip away."

"What's that, Polly gal?" Jane Carter's lowered voice was quick and nervous. "What you muttering about?"

"Nothing, Mum. Don't fret yourself."

Half-opening her eyes, Jane Carter, said, "Why ain't you praying? Best not let Matthew Lorne see you with your eyes wide open. He might punish you."

"I been praying, Mum," Polly said sullenly.

"No you ain't. You been talking with that gentleman. Couldn't hear what you was saying, but I seen you. Where's he gone to?"

"Don't know. Why'd he tell the likes of me his comings and goings? Maybe he just got sick of all these long faces. Same like I am."

The gentleman, Polly thought, as her Mother's quavering voice resumed her prayers. Polly's eyes went to Matthew Lorne, hardening as they gazed. Don't you dare to open your eyes, you swine, she thought, her heart seething with hatred. Don't you dare to move one bloody muscle!

13

Striding into the inn parlor, empty at this moment, David was immediately conscious of the landlord's round curious eyes fixed upon him. The man's glance, it occurred to him, held a little more than curiosity in its pale gray depths. He hesitated, inclined to speak to him; then, changing his mind, he gave him a courteous nod and continued on his way.

The landlord's unctuous voice stopped him just as he was about to mount the stairs. "A good funeral, was it, sir?"

David turned slowly to face him. "A curious choice of words, landlord. However, if any funeral could be described as good, you might say that this one is passable."

The landlord drew away from the roaring fire in the big iron grate and drew nearer to David. Sweat gleamed on his florid face and his round bald head. Aware of the tinge of sarcasm in David's voice, he said quickly, "Didn't mean it like it sounded, sir. Never meant no offense."

"And none taken," David assured him, "especially in the case of this particular funeral." With an impatient movement he removed the ruby stickpin that held the lace at the collar of his high-necked shirt in position. Freed from the restraint, the extravagant lace spilled like a fountain over the front of his red velvet robe. "As usual, landlord," he remarked, "this place is abominably overheated. After the chill outside, it is like walking into a damned furnace."

The man inclined his head in an apologetic gesture. "I'm sure I'm very sorry, sir. It's just that I likes to be warm."

"So I've noticed. It's a wonder to me that your customers do not die of suffocation."

The landlord resented this remark. The man was a stranger to Waterford, and he had no right to complain if others liked to be comfortable. However, he was titled, and from his slightly autocratic manner, and the grand way he dressed, he was obviously a person of some importance. Also he might be other than he seemed, a king's spy, perhaps. Everyone knew that the king was parsimonious, and he might have sent out special agents to report on any unnecessary extravagance on the part of his people. Swallowing his indignation, the man scratched at his hairy arms. He was unaware that his feelings and a certain amount of disapproval showed in the light gray eyes that traveled slowly over David's colorful attire. "Couldn't attend the funeral myself," he said at last. "Had to get things ready for the crowd. After it's all over, they'll come flocking in here with their tongues hanging out."

"No doubt." David's smile was slow and cold as he added in a drawling voice, "I take it from your expression, landlord, that you not approve of my clothes?"

Startled, the man drew back, his florid face flushing to a deeper red. "I'm sure I don't know what you mean, sir," he said stiffly. "Them clothes what you got on is fitted for a gentleman in your position. And anyway, it ain't no business of mine what you choose to wear. For all I care, you could attend that there funeral in a jester's costume complete with cap and bells. Don't make a scrap of difference to me." Seeing the forbidding expression on David's face, he added hastily, "But there, sir, 'twas just my little joke. And like I said, it don't make no difference to me."

"But you think that it might to Matthew Lorne,"

David said. "Tell me, why is it that you are all so afraid of him?"

"Afraid?" The landlord's pale eyes opened to their fullest extent.

"Yes, landlord, afraid. Matthew Lorne must hold great sway over your minds."

"No he don't." The landlord glared at him. "Don't know about them others, but me, I ain't afraid of nobody."

David smiled. "Then I can only feel that your sense of propriety has been outraged because I did not attend the funeral garbed in black or some other sober color. Is it so?"

His eyes growing sullen before the sarcasm reflected in David's voice, the landlord shrugged his heavy shoulders. " 'Tain't as if you're related to the Lornes, sir," he muttered. "You can wear what you please, I suppose."

"So I can. But I will let you into a little secret, landlord. Were I related to the Lornes, I should not be standing here. I would long ago have cut my throat."

The man looked at him blankly. Questions trembled on his lips, but, judging rightly that they would not be answered, he suppressed them. Shrugging again, he said, "Just as you say, sir."

"Exactly." Putting his foot on the first stair, David was again arrested by the landlord's voice.

"But I was almost forgetting, sir," the man said. "I never stopped you to talk about funerals or clothes, it was to tell you that your two sisters have arrived. Waiting in your room for you, they are."

"My two sisters." David's head turned, a look of blank astonishment on his face. "Did I understand you to say two, my good man?"

"Aye, sir, that you did." Glad that the uncomfortable moments had passed, the landlord's red-jowled face split into a grin. "Nice surprise for you ain't it?"

" 'Extraordinary' would be more the word."

Seeing that the forbidding look was back on the

handsome face of his difficult lodger, the landlord permitted his grin to fade. Instead, he allowed his face to lengthen into an expression of prim disapproval. "I know exactly what you're thinking, sir," he gabbled, "and I agree with you."

David shook his head. "Landlord, it you knew exactly what I was thinking, I fear you would be greatly shocked."

The landlord seized eagerly upon the last word. "Shocked, sir, that's exactly what I was. It ain't at all the thing for young females to be going up to gentlemen's rooms, and so I told them. Gave 'em a proper piece of my mind, I did. Talked to 'em like a father, you might say."

"Like a father." A smile softened the severe lines of David's face. "And how was your fatherly advice received?"

The landlord's eyes lit with a faint wrath, and his heavy jowls quivered. "Well, sir, you'll find this hard to believe, but them gals never paid me no mind. Miss Fanny, her what's the timid one, was crying fit to bust, though I'd not be knowing why. But Miss Jane, her what's the haughty one, if you'll forgive me for saying so, insisted on going up to your room. Called me a dunderhead and an old fool, she did. Said she's have the law on me for watering my ale."

"She did?" David turned a laugh into a cough. "How like J-Jane."

"Proper cheek, I call it," the landlord rushed on, his barrel chest heaving, "and her not even coming from these parts. I ain't never cheated on my drinks, let me tell you. And even if I did, how's she to know?"

At the back of David's mind a questioned loomed large and disquieting. Who the devil was Miss Fanny? He had no difficulty at all in recognizing the identity of Miss Jane. But what was she up to now? He'd stand no nonsense from her, as she would very soon find out. Laughter overcoming his perplexity, he attempted to soothe the irate man. "Pay no attention to Jane," he said. "she was ever a determined minx and set on getting her own way. No doubt she simply tried a bluff on you."

"A bluff. Well, it didn't work, 'cause I don't water my ale. Why, if a thing like that got around, it'd take away my good name for sure."

"Never fear, your good name is safe. I will speak to Jane severely. I will . . . er . . . reprimand her."

"I hope so, sir. Could do with a talking to, that one. And anyway, I only let 'em go up because I didn't want no more trouble from that Miss Jane, for it was as plain as the nose on your face that she was all set to make some. Begging your pardon for saying so, sir, but that sister of yours has got quite a violent nature. She picked up one of me mugs and she threatened to smash it over me head if I didn't let 'em go up to your room. Them mugs is heavy, and they could make a nasty dent in a man's skull. So me being a peaceable man, sir, what else could I do?"

David tightened his quivering lips. "You may consider yourself pardoned," he said in a difficult voice. "You see, I am all too unfortunately aware of Jane's ability to make trouble."

The landlord looked at David suspiciously. "You ain't laughing, are you, sir?"

"No indeed."

"That's all right, then, I thought for a moment you was. The thing is, sir," the man went on, warming to his theme, "you having suffered her tantrums for a lifetime, so to speak, ought to think about giving her a lesson."

"I am thinking just that, landlord."

The landlord nodded. "That's good, sir, very good. The best thing you could do. I know it ain't my place to be telling you how to go about it, but if that Miss Jane was my sister, I'd have her over me knees in a trice, and no mistake about it. I'd lift up her skirts and I'd give her a paddling what she wouldn't be forgetting in a hurry."

A gleam lit David's eyes. "An admirable idea. Indeed, I may go even further and break her damned neck."

"Well, no, sir," the landlord said, looking somewhat taken aback. "I ain't saying I'd go as far as that, me being a peace-loving man. "It's just that if you let females have too much of their own way, they tend to get above themselves, and before you know it, they're making a man's life miserable. You got to prevent that, to my way of thinking. Got to give females a good lesson, I say."

"Certainly there are some females that need it," David agreed. "And Jane is one of them."

"That she is, sir. You never spoke a truer word."

David's dark brows rose in amusement at the man's vehemence. "And Miss Fanny?" he asked. "What did she have to say to all this?"

"Never a word, sir. Just stood there all huddled up, hiding her face in her hands and sobbing like her heart was broke. Cried even harder when Miss Jane give her a poke in the ribs. Hard was that poke, sir, and like to have broke her ribs. Poor little thing was quite overcome. Too overcome to stop Miss Jane if she'd gone and bashed me over the head like what she threatened. 'Sides, didn't look like she'd have the strength." He paused. "To tell you the truth, sir, I felt right sorry for that little Miss Fanny. Why'd you suppose she was crying like that?"

David shrugged. "I have no idea. Unless it was too close proximity with Sh . . . with Jane that caused her ditress of mind."

"But that ain't right, sir," the landlord said, looking shocked. "Sisters and brothers are supposed to love each other."

"It depends, I suppose, on the brother and the sisters. At this moment, I assure you, I can find no great love in my heart for Jane."

There was nothing of the haughty nobleman about Sir David Medway now, even though it was his own sisters who were under discussion. Emboldened by this unlooked-for leniency, the landlord went on eagerly, "Can't say as I blame you, sir, for that. Proper wildcat is that Miss Jane."

An odd look passed over David's face. "Yes," he agreed, "wildcat is one name that might describe her. Tigress is another."

Proper funny gent was Sir David, the landlord thought. That look in his eyes, for instance. You wouldn't think he was talking about his sister, but of somebody else. His lady love, perhaps. The landlord was startled out of his foolish fancies when David said in a cool, carefully casual voice, "People have often remarked on the resemblance between my sisters and myself. Did you note it?"

The landlord would have liked to answer in the affirmative, but the truth was that he hadn't seen their faces. "Don't know what they looked like, sir. They both of them had their hoods pulled too far forward." He pondered. "But there did seem something a little familiar about Miss Jane."

David's heart leaped. "What was that?"

"Can't rightly say, sir, though it's been worrying at me mind. It was maybe something about the way she spoke and acted."

"Like me, you mean," David prompted.

"Aye, sir, that must be it." Realizing what he had said, the landlord flushed. "Not that you carry on like that, if you know what I mean."

"I know exactly what you mean."

Fearing that he had offended, and not wishing to disturb the friendly basis which he felt he had now established between himself and the young nobleman, a friendship he fully intended to boast of to his cronies, the rotund landlord hastened to make amends. "I bet I know why them two sisters of yours have come," he said in a would-be-bright voice. "Somehow or other they got to hear about the witch Rebecca West, and they're wanting to see her take her walk." A note of pride crept into his voice. "Famous are them walks, and most everybody's heard of 'em. I'll bet that's it. Don't you think so, sir?"

"No I do not!" The cold hard glance that David turned on him caused the man to quail. "In believing that my sisters would be interested in watching such a disgusting spectacle, you are quite mistaken, landlord."

"I'm sure I'm very sorry if I've put you out, sir." The landlord frowned in puzzlement over Sir David's strange attitude. Then, thinking of the heartbroken sobbing that had shaken Miss Fanny's black-cloaked figure, he was ready to partially concede. "Well, perhaps not Miss Fanny, her striking me as being a fragile and tender-hearted little thing. But Miss Jane now, she's quite a different kettle of fish, ain't she, sir? I reckon she'd find the witch's walk a rare treat."

David's hands clenched. No doubt Shalada Lorne, wicked as she was, would enjoy it. The very thought gave him a surprisingly bitter and painful pang, but nothing of this showed in his face as he answered the man in a grim voice. "I hope you are wrong. For if I thought she would enjoy it, I really would break her neck."

Thoroughly alarmed at the expression on the dark, haughty face, the landlord retreated a few paces. Scratching at his arms again, he gave a nervous laugh. "Oh, come now, sir," he said hastily, "there ain't no need to take on so. I can't say I like it all that much meself, but for all that, a witch has got to be punished."

David thought of the hard stones and the great spiky cinders on the witch's trail when he had crossed it on his way back to the inn. Beneath the sturdy boots he was wearing he found them almost unbearably hard, and once or twice, before he had reached smooth ground, he had almost turned his ankle. If he, in his boots, had been forced to hobbled so painfully, what would be the effect on tender bare feet?

"You ain't looking so good, sir." The landlord's

voice broke in on his thoughts. "Would you be liking a drink of me good hearty ale?"

"No, thank you, I am perfectly well." David turned his bleak eyes on the landlord. "Tell me something," he said abruptly. "Do you not consider that life imprisonment, or burning at the stake, to be sufficient punishment for a witch?" he paused. "Must there be the added punishment of walking the trail?"

The landlord's ruddy cheeks paled as a memory he had tried hard to forget came back to him. "Only right they suffer the trail, sir," he said hoarsely, "considering the evil they do. And I do think they should go to prison for life." His eyes shifted, as though he were nervous of being overheard. "But to speak truth, sir, I ain't for the burning."

"I am glad to hear it." David considered him closely. "Will you tell me why?"

The landlord's eyes flared wide with alarm. "No, sir, I won't. I think I already said too much."

"I am not a spy or a bearer of tales, if that is what is worrying you," David pursued gently. "You may trust me. For the truth is that I have always believed that burning, stocking, and the various other forms of torture that men seem to delight in inflicting upon their fellowman are not only barbaric and unworthy of us but also an offense in God's eyes."

The landlord stared at him. "Be you a preacher, sir?"

Smiling, David shook his head. "No, I am far from that."

"Ain't you never injured anyone?"

"I fear so. No, I could never qualify for a religious calling, for despite all my grand words, there is one I would injure very severely, had I the chance."

"And who might that be?"

"It is best that you do not know."

The landlord continued to stare at him, his eyes growing rounder. "But all them other things you said. Don't you believe that witches should be punished?"

David looked back at him gravely. "Do you believe such beings really exist?"

At a loss, the landlord sputtered for a few moments before coming out with a shocked whisper. "But of course they exist, sir. Everybody knows that."

David shrugged. "I must confess that it is a matter that has often exercised my mind. However, if you are right, then of course they must be punished. But in the carrying out of that punishment, must we always be so inhumane?"

"I dunno, sir." He hesitated. "But I already told you I ain't for the burning." He gave David a long, frankly puzzled look. "You talk strange. Not like no one I ever heard before. Meaning no offense, I assure you, sir, but you sure that you ain't pulling my leg? I mean, it do seem to me like you might be a spy."

"But I am neither spy nor informer. I ask you to take my word for that."

Inclined to believe him, and yet still conscious of a small fear, the landlord went back to scratching his hairy arms. Then, almost as though the words were dragged from him against his will, he said slowly, "There's something what I've always had on me mind. I've often thought I'd like to tell someone about it. Ain't never dared, though. There's lots of loose tongues in this village, and if Matthew Lorne should get to hear, why, then, I daresay me life wouldn't be worth—"

"And especially am I not a spy for Matthew Lorne," David interrupted softly. David's dark eyes looked deeply into the landlord's. Yet he was not really seeing the man. In his imagination he heard the moaning of the wind in the trees, the groaning of the burdened branch that held the hanging figure of his father as it slowly turned in a grotesque dance of death. He blinked, firmly pushing the memory from him. "No, landlord," he repeated, "most especially not for Matthew Lorne."

There was hatred in Sir David's eyes. Implacable

hatred, and the landlord responded to this man whom he now knew to be an enemy of Matthew Lorne. After all, did not that expression in Sir David's eyes echo his own secret thoughts? Had he not in his heart always hated Matthew Lorne himself? Hated him for the fear he had put in everyone's heart, for the guard one must always place upon one's tongue, for the false accusations he brought, for his tyranny, for everything about him. Fear lay over the lives of the villagers like a thick, stifling blanket. "I believe you, sir." The words rushed from the landlord as he threw caution to the wind.

"This thing what I'm going to tell you about happened a long time ago. At that time, I wasn't no more'n a bit of a lad. Elizabeth Carter was accused of being a witch. Lizzie Loon, we lads used to call her, on account of her being feebleminded. We . . . we burned her, sir."

"You burned her, a feebleminded woman. Who accused her?"

" 'Twas Matthew Lorne's father who done that. Right good talker he was, could sort of sway you, if you know what I mean. Anyway, we listened and we all went along with him."

David felt suddenly cold with horror. A Lorne again. Another Lorne spreading terror and destruction. The bitterness that rose in him was like gall, invading every part of his body. "Go on," he said with some difficulty.

"Aye, God help us, sir, we listened to him and him not even a witch-finder like his son. He wasn't nothing much at all, just one of us, so to speak, a farmer. But by Christ, sir, he had a tongue on him, did that one. I reckon he must have put madness into us that night, for without his talking we'd not have thought of harming Lizzie Loon." Unexpected tears misted the landlord's eyes. "Why, sir," he went on with a slight break in his voice, "she was good to all us lads, was old Lizzie. Loved us too. Used to call us her 'childers.' "

David's hand clenched hard on the banister rail.

The man flushed darkly, and agony looked from his eyes. " 'Twas the madness that Matthew Lorne's father put into us. It was like we was all under some kind of a spell. I ain't excusing meself none. I helped the others drag poor Liz from her cottage. And I . . . and I even helped 'em lay the wood at her feet. 'Twas me and three other lads what set the fire." He shivered. "I ain't never been able to forget the way she screamed when the flames got to her. Reckon I'll be remembering that until the day I die. That's why I ain't for the burning, sir. Now you understand." He looked at David imploringly.

"I understand the guilt you feel, and it is right that you should," David answered him coldly. "But I cannot understand your lack of feeling in other directions."

The landlord looked at him blankly, "A witch has got to suffer something. Besides, it's Matthew Lorne's orders. The walk was his idea, and there ain't nothing we can do about it." He spread out appealing hands. "What can we do against Matthew Lorne?"

"Matthew Lorne is a disease." David spoke through gritted teeth. "You should get rid of him. Kill him!"

The landlord paled. "K-k-kill him? The soldiers would come swooping down on this village like a swarm of hornets. They'd hang the lot of us."

The red mist of hatred that had prompted David's words receded. The landlord was right, he thought. Matthew Lorne's power and prestige extended far and wide. His every action, however reprehensible, would be upheld and defended. He had heard that even the king was impressed by Lorne. Sufficiently so to call him into audience and personally congratulate him on his noble and zealous work in the hunting down of witches. Were Matthew Lorne to be harmed in any way, the king would certainly send his soldiers to punish those who had laid hands on the witch-finder's sacred person. So Lorne was, it would seem, invulnerable to all attack, and especially so from these cowed and frightened villagers.

Regretting his outburst, which had only succeeded in frightening, David gave the quaking landlord a curt nod. Turning, he made his way up the stairs, his mind a seething turmoil of mixed emotions. In his room Shalada awaited him. Dark and beautiful Shalada Lorne, whose very presence seemed to rob him of his cool reasoning powers. He imagined what it would be like to see her naked, willing, and himself thrusting hard inside that beautiful body. The answer came to him at once. To possess Shalada, he knew, would be a shattering experience such as he was unlikely to find in any other woman. Perhaps Matthew Lorne should look nearer to home in his search for witches. He might, unknowingly, be harboring one under his own roof.

David paused at the top of the stairs. Nonsense! He wiped his hand over his sweating forehead. What maggot had he got into his brain now? Shalada a witch. No, she was not that. She was temptress, a woman born to turn a man's wits to water. "If you think to bend David Medway to your will you have a shock coming!" With a militant light in his eyes, he marched on.

The landlord stood rooted to the spot, his eyes watching the staight velvet-clad figure out of sight. He was wishing now that he had never decided to ease his conscience. Sir David Medway was a strange man. In his short stay at the inn he had been in turns friendly and amiable, haughty, moody, and unapproachable, but he had certainly never seemed a dangerous character. Yet dangerous he was. That frightening blaze in his dark eyes, his violent words, had all combined to tell him this. The landlord shivered. Even when he had turned away and walked up the stairs, he had exuded a leashed-in violence.

Shaking his head, the man turned away. Walking over to his scarred counter, he picked up a clean rag and resumed his favorite task of polishing the pewter mugs. Generally he found the familiar actions soothing, but today it failed him. He felt jumpy and distinctly uneasy, and he found himself wishing quite fervently that Sir David would terminate his stay at the inn. If he did not, something terrible was bound to happen. He could feel it in his bones. Putting down one mug, he picked up another. Breathing on it, he began halfheartedly to polish it.

Entering his room, David closed the door behind him with a bang. For a moment he surveyed the two cloaked figures seated on his bed; then he said in a ironical voice, "Well, dear sisters, your brother is here. What is it you want of me?"

The black-cloaked figure did not move. She remained huddled on the bed, her back turned to him, tremors shaking her body. The gray-cloaked figure, however, did not hesitate; she was on her feet in an instant. "There is no need to employ sarcasm," she said sharply. "I certainly did not enjoy the deception. I had to tell that fool man downstairs that we were your sisters, or he would have refused to allow us to come up."

"I have heard the landlord's story, Shalada," David drawled. "And I feel quite sure that you would have overcome any resistance on his part."

"Oh, do be quiet, David Medway. I have not come here to bandy words with you. And I must say that you have taken your time in getting here. Do you realize how long we have been waiting here in this miserable room?"

David turned away. "I have no idea," he said. Taking off his hat and gloves, he tossed them carelessly onto an oaken chest. "And what's more," he went on, "I cannot say that I particularly care."

"I might have expected something like that from you." Shalada threw back her hood. "Anyway, never mind about that now."

"I won't, I assure you?" David did not look at her as he removed his cloak, folded it carefully, and placed it beside his hat and gloves. Fully aware of her impatience he was deliberately slow in his movements. "I repeat, what is it you want of me?"

"Help. That is what I want." Shalada's reply came promptly. "I am in trouble. You have to help me."

Still David did not turn. There was no appeal in her voice, not the slightest hint of pleading. She was in trouble, and he had to help her. The infernal impudence of her. Keeping his fury under control, he said in a cutting voice, "Why come to me, what gave you the idea that I would help you?"

"Because, despite your roughness and your bullying and your manhandling of me, I believe you to be a gentleman."

"I regret to disappoint you. I am no gentleman. I trust my refusal has made you realize the error of your conclusion."

"I told you, Shalada," the black-cloaked figure wailed. "I knew he wouldn't help us. Had you listened to me, we could have been far away from here. Why didn't you listen? What do I care for Rebecca West,"

"I care!" Shalada turned on her furiously. "I care, do you hear me, Tasmin."

Rebecca West, Tasmin Lorne. What was all this leading to? And what did Shalada mean by her furious words to Tasmin? Why should she care about Rebecca West? A possible solution came to him, and with it a growing anger. "I take it from Tasmin's words," he said, "that you were both in flight. From what, I am not interested in knowing. But you have, however, delayed your flight because you wished to see the witch take her walk. Am I correct in this assumption?"

"No, you are not. Turn round and face me, you great hulking dolt, or am I expected to address all my remarks to that foppishly clad back of yours?"

Ignoring the insult, David swung around quickly. "You do not wish to see the walk. Then why have you come here?" Could he possibly have been wrong about her? Urgency and hope were mingled in his voice as he said sharply, "Answer me at once!"

"Perhaps if you would stop talking and issuing your demands, I might have the opportunity."

The uncertain note in her voice, so uncharacteristic of her usual decisive way of speaking, brought David swiftly to her side. "God knows why I should do so," he said, "but if you are really in trouble, I will help you." His voice died in his throat as she lifted her head and looked at him fully. He saw the bruises on her face, her torn and bitten lips, and the thick crust of dried blood on her chin. He saw something else too, something he had not expected to see. She was frightened. It was evident in her eyes and in the trembling of her lips. So, he thought, her air of bravado and her crisp insulting words had been only a guise to hide this fear. Anger leaped as he touched her bruised face gently. "Who has done this to you?" he said harshly.

If she was surprised by his vehemence, she did not show it. "It doesn't matter," she answered him wearily.

In that moment David knew that his inner battle had been resolved. He knew with a clear quiet certainty that he loved her, and there was nothing he could do about it. She was the only woman for him, and the fact that she was a Lorne no longer seemed to have any significance. "But it does matter, Shalada," he answered her, "for I am going to seek him out and kill him."

An odd look flickered in Shalada's eyes for a moment. She seemed to hesitate. Then, when she answered him, the odd look was gone. "I am not going to tell you."

"You will tell me!" He gripped her shoulders fiercely. "I demand it!"

"No! Besides, why should you care so much? As I recall, you have put a few bruises on me yourself."

The mockery in her voice brought a flush to David's face, and he answered her heatedly. "That was quite different, and you know it, damned wildcat that you are! What was I supposed to do? Did you expect me to just stand there and let you claw me to pieces with those infernal nails of yours? I had to subdue you."

Tasmin looked around. Despite the harshness in David Medway's voice, there was tenderness in his dark eyes as he looked at Shalada. Her envious eyes took in the handsome face, the cleft chin, the way his thick black hair fell curling over his forehead. Jealousy rose up inside her in a black and bitter tide. "If Shalada won't tell you, I will," she cried, jumping to her feet. "My father did it, and she deserved it. I'm glad he hurt her."

David looked at Tasmin with contempt. Her eyes, two pale blue slits between puffs of swollen and discolored flesh, were directing such a look of malice at Shalada that he was sickened. Looking away, he touched Shalada's face again. "Is it true" he said incredulously, "did your father really do this to you?"

"He is not her father, he is mine!" Tasmin's voice rose high and shrill. In her desire to triumph over Shalada and to humble her in David Medway's eyes, her fear of discovery had fallen away from her at the moment. Forgotten was her mother's death, the horror of seeing her brother murdered before her very eyes. Their wild flight from that house of terror, her trembling hand clutched firmly in Shalada's. Shalada's voice urging her on, trying to instill courage in her, pushing her on when she would have faltered. Sneering, she continued to shout. "Nay, she is no Lorne, can't you see that for yourself? Look at that dark gypsy face of hers. I'll tell you who she is, she is Rebecca West's bastard! That is why she has dragged me here. It is why she has come to you. She wants you to save that witch!"

Whatever expression Tasmin had expected to see, it was certainly not the look of ineffable joy with which David Medway was regarding Shalada. "Shalada, you were telling me the truth."

"I was." Shalada answered him almost defiantly. "Tasmin, as you have just heard, has had her moment.

She has backed up my story with the ugliest words she could think of. Yes, I am the bastard daughter of Rebecca West. I do not know anything about my real father, except his name. I am not ashamed, so don't you think it. As for your feelings on the matter, I don't care about them either. You may make of it what you will."

David's finger lightly touched her trembling mouth. "And why so defiant, Shalada? Do you think it makes one scrap of difference to me? There is no shame in your birth. The only shame, in my opinion, was in being named Lorne." David heard Tasmin's gasp of fury, but he ignored it. "Don't you see," he said, tracing gently down Shalada's bruised cheek, "the fact that you are not Matthew Lorne's daughter is a cause for great rejoicing."

"How dare you say that?" Tasmin cried. Temporarily she had forgotten why she was running, and from whom. "My father took that little bastard in. He fed her and clothed her, educated her. She wanted for nothing. For years she bore the name of Lorne. And that name, despite your insults, sir, is a proud name."

David looked at Tasmin again. "You will be silent, Mistress Lorne. Say one more word, and you will regret it."

Always a coward at heart, Tasmin subsided at once. Throwing them both a look of hatred, she walked over to the bed and sat down.

As though she had not heard the exchange, Shalada took up the conversation from where it had left off. "I rejoice that I am not the daughter of Matthew Lorne, for I have always hated him. But the real issue is that I am the daughter of a so-called witch. Did . . . did you know that my grandmother Margaret West was likewise called witch? She went to the burning cross. I am the granddaughter and daughter of witches, so what does that make me?"

"I know not," David answered. "I only know what you are to me."

"And what is that?"

He laughed at the warning reflected in her eyes. "Nothing so very terrible. I have fallen in love with you."

Shalada ignored the excited thumping of her heart. For some purpose of his own, he was lying to her. She would not let him weaken her with words and make a fool of her. "Ridiculous!" Her answering voice was sharp.

"No, love, there is nothing ridiculous about my feelings for you."

Shalada was dazzled by the tenderness and the love in his expression. His dark eyes, soft and warm, were searching her face. There was a longing in her to respond. She wanted to say: And I love you, David, we were meant for each other, you and I. She closed her eyes, shutting out the sight of his face, afraid that he would see her foolish response to his words. No, she would not say it. She would not provide him with a laugh at her expense. He was trying to make a fool of her; she was certain of it. It was his revenge for the fight, for the insults she had heaped on him. "Do you think I am so easily fooled, David Medway?" Her voice came out hoarsely. "Love, is it? I admit that you make very pretty speeches, but the real truth is that you are wanting a wench to warm your bed. Why don't you admit it."

David smiled. "I do want a wench to warm my bed. But only if that wench is you."

"Liar!"

David saw the tears spangling her long lashes. "Shalada," he said very softly, "you are talking a great deal of nonsense, and you know it. So won't you please shut up."

Her eyes flew open, and the tears that had gathered there spilled down her cheeks. "Oh, damn!" she said crossly. "See what you have done to me. I despise a weeping woman, and it is all your fault."

"Of course," David agreed amiably, "everything that

will happen in our life from now on will always be my fault. Knowing my Shalada, I am quite prepared for that."

"I am not *your* Shalada," she flashed, "and I never will be."

"Shalada, I think you love me." His hands touched her breasts and lingered there. Then, feeling her stiff body relax, he drew her into his arms and closed his mouth over hers. After a long moment he raised his head and looked deeply into her eyes. "Admit that you love me."

Refusing to acknowledge the thrill that had shot through her at the touch of his lips on hers, despising the fire in her body, Shalada set her lips mutinously. "And if I say that I do love you," she said, hoping that he would not notice her trembling, "what then? Either you will laugh, or you will believe I have only said it because I want you to help me."

"Are you then so devious?"

Shalada's eyes flashed furiously. "I am not devious, and you have no right to call me so."

"But I did not," David answered mildly. "I merely asked a question." He paused. "You want my help, I know. Though you have not yet told me why. So tell me this. If you say you love me, would that be your reason for saying it?"

"No, but it is what you will think. Why not? You did not believe anything I said before. You called me bitch, cold-blooded little monster, murderess. So why should you believe me now?"

"I haven't the remotest idea." David's eyes smiled into hers. "Ah, no, Shalada," he went on hurriedly as she opened her mouth to make a furious reply, "I refuse to quarrel with you. It was a joke. A poor effort, I admit, but nevertheless a joke."

"Do you dare to deny that you called me those things?"

"Not at all. I said them, and I meant every one at the time. But that was then, and this is now. The mur-

deress and the cold-blooded little monster I take back,
with my sincere apologies."

"And the bitch, do you take that back too?"

David shook his head. "Never. For that is what you
are, Shalada, a hot-tempered, contrary, fighting, maddening bitch." His hands touched her breasts. "But
despite all of these drawbacks, I do love you. Do you
believe me?"

Quite suddenly Shalada found herself convinced.
Her eyes shone and her hands came up slowly and covered those on her breasts, pressing them firmly, silently
giving him the response he wanted.

Beneath his fingers David felt the tight swelling buds
of her breasts, and he was acutely conscious of his own
desire. "Do you love me?"

"You are an insufferable brute, but I do." She
looked at him, a promise in her eyes. "And when we
are well away from this place, I will prove it to you."

Afraid to linger over her lips, David kissed her
swiftly and then stepped back once again a teasing
smile on his face. "Now that we've got that established,
how may I help you?"

Before Shalada could answer, Tasmin's shrill voice
cut in. "I told you. She wants you to rescue the witch."

Ignoring her, David looked at Shalada. "And just
how do I accomplish that?"

For the first time Shalada looked at him with complete trust. "You will think of something."

"One man against my father and all those other
men," Tasmin said scornfully. "You are mad to even
think of it."

David thought once again of the great stones and the
spiky cinders on the trail. In his mind's eyes he pictured a woman walking that painful trail, a woman
who might vaguely resemble Shalada. Looking up, he
met Tasmin's eyes. "Nevertheless," he said grimly, "I
will think of something."

Shalada turned her head. "I hear the men crossing
over to the inn. The funeral is over. In a few minutes

Rebecca will be walking that trail." With an impetuous movement she flung her arms about David and held him close. "I would not have you put yourself in danger for my sake, darling. You must believe that. But if there is any way at all to save Rebecca, we must try."

David gently released himself from her clinging arms. Looking at her thoughtfully, he said, "Do you believe in witchcraft?"

Shalada looked back at him with a puzzled frown. "There may be witches, but if you want the truth, I have never really believed in them."

David laughed softly. "Neither have I."

"You are both mad," Tasmin cut in. "Of course there are witches!"

David took Shalada's hand and held it tightly. "So most people believe. There are very few like you and I, Shalada, we are the exceptions."

"Yes, yes, I know," Shalada said impatiently. "But what has that to do with anything?"

"Perhaps a great deal. I think I have a plan."

When he did not go on, she said abruptly, "Well, are you going to keep it all to yourself, or are you going to tell me about it?"

"I will tell you about it all in good time. If it is to succeed, we will need her." He nodded toward Tasmin. "But can we trust her?"

"Yes." Shalada spoke without hesitation. "When we run, she wishes to come with us." Seeing him frown, she added hastily, "We must take her, she is deathly afraid of her father. She knows what he will do to her if he catches her, and that is why I know she will not betray us." Seeing that he still looked doubtful, she turned her head and looked at the girl. "Well, Tasmin, am I right, can we trust you? It is your choice to make now. Come with us, or stay here. If you choose to stay, it will mean that your father will have complete domination over you. You know what will happen then, you might end up like Robert. Or if not, he will send you to that place."

At her words, the color fled Tasmin's face and the terror rushed back into her eyes. Cowering on the bed, she looked like a trapped animal. "Shalada, please, I swear I did not mean all those things I said about you. I r-really love you and think of you as my sister."

A small cynical smile played about Shalada's lips. "Yes, Tasmin, I am quite sure you adore me and that you will go on doing so until you know you are quite safe."

Tasmin wrung her hands together. "Shalada, you promised me. You would not turn me over to my father!"

"That depends entirely upon you," Shalada said in a hard voice. "Can we trust you? Answer yes or no."

"Yes, yes, you can trust me," Tasmin cried out desperately. "I will say nothing, I swear it! Y-you must look after me, Shalada."

"Shalada," David said in a quiet voice, "do you believe her?"

Shalada turned her threatening face from the girl. "Yes," she said, smiling at him, "I do believe her. Tasmin is treacherous and untruthful by nature, but in this instance she will be for us, and only for us. Her cowardice is greater than anything else."

Muffled sobbing came from the bed. "You say you have a plan," Tasmin gasped, "but what will happen to us if it fails?"

"Then we shall all be lost. Tell me, Tasmin, are you a good actress?"

"Tasmin blinked her tear-drowned eyes. "Why, I ... I don't know."

"I fear you will have to be."

"I can answer that, David," Shalada said. "Tasmin is an excellent actress. I have seen many instances of it in our happy home. Your acting and your ability to lie earned me many a beating, did they not, Tasmin?"

"Shalada, how can you be so unkind," Tasmin wailed. "Have I not told you that I love you?"

"Ah, yes," Shalada answered her sarcastically. "How

foolish of me to forget that." She looked at David. "Now, then, what is this plan of yours?"

Taking her hand, David led her over to the bed. "Sit down, Shalada, and we will discuss it." Seating himself beside her, he said earnestly, "There is not much time, so pay close attention. My plan, though admittedly flimsy, might just work."

He hesitated, his brows knitted in thought. Placing her hand over his, she asked him to go on.

Frowning, David spoke slowly. "It is a plan that hinges on boldness of action, acting ability, and the superstitious minds of the onlookers. Above all, on that. The boldness of action will be the part I will play. The acting ability will rest with you and Tasmin. As I have said, Shalada, there are few who share our enlightened views in regard to witches, and at this moment I am thanking God for that. So we will give them a display of witchcraft." He smiled. "Aye, Shalada, we will give it to them in full measure."

A spark glowed in Shalada's eyes, as though in some dim way she had caught his meaning. But, unsure, she said irritably, "I don't know what the devil you're talking about. And how can we pay close attention if you don't get on with it?"

"I am about to, my impatient wench. Now, then, listen carefully."

Tasmin's eyes widened as his deep, soft, slightly drawling voice outlined his plan, and she looked more than ever like a trapped animal. Shalada, on the other hand, was smiling. "It's good, David," she cried enthusiastically. "I know it will work."

Fresh tears began to roll down Tasmin's cheeks. "It won't," she said in a voice of despair. "We shall all be killed, my father will see to that. He will have no choice but to denouce us as witches after the exhibition you expect us to put on. We will be overpowered and flung in the prison. And later we will be taken from there and b-burned."

"Be quiet!" Shalada turned on her furiously and

seized a hank of her pale hair. "Don't you dare say one more word!"

"But it's true," Tasmin whimpered. "You know it is, Shalada."

"I know nothing of the sort. But I do know this. If you ruin the plan, I will kill you myself."

Tasmin howled as Shalada gave her hair a vicious twist. "Oh, don't, Shalada!, I . . . I will do my best."

"See that you do," Shalada snapped, releasing her.

"Perhaps we ask too much of her," David said, his eyes on the sobbing girl. "It might be best if we leave her here. Later, when it is dark, and the uproar has subsided, she might have a chance to get away."

Tasmin shrieked. Jumping from the bed, she flung herself at David's feet. "Don't leave me here, don't! I will do whatever you say."

David suppressed a pang of pity. If he spoke to her softly, she would no doubt break down completely. His voice hard, he said, "Then pull yourself together. The first sign of weakness I see, and you will most certainly be left behind."

Tasmin nodded. "I understand, Sir David. You will have no more trouble with me."

"I hope not."

Despite Tasmin's words, she gave a small shriek as a knock sounded on the door.

"Who is it?" David called.

"It's me, sir. Polly."

David let out his breath with a sighing sound. "Polly," he murmured, the missing factor. "I knew I had forgotten something." Raising his voice, he called, "Come in."

The door opened and Polly Carter sidled into the room. She closed it carefully behind her before turning. Her eyes widened slightly as she saw Shalada seated on the bed beside David, and, kneeling at his feet, the shuddering Tasmin. "A very good day to you, Miss Shalada, Miss Tasmin," she said in an uncertain voice. "I come to tell you, sir, that—"

Tasmin sprang to her feet, cutting off her words. "Why did you let her in?" she cried, her eyes wild. "What is she doing here?"

"Sit down, Tasmin," David said coldly. He waited until she had sullenly obeyed; then he beckoned the frightened Polly forward. "There is nothing to be afraid of, Polly," he said gently. "Mistress Lorne is a little overwrought, that is all. You came to tell me that Matthew Lorne is below, is that it?"

Keeping her eyes fixed on David, she said breathlessly, "Yes, sir. He never moved until the funeral was all over. But as soon as I saw him headed for the inn, I give the babe to me mum to hold, and then I ran as quick as I could. I seen to it that he never saw me, sir. I was up them stairs like a streak."

"Good girl, Polly." He paused, looking at her with thoughtful dark eyes. "Polly, would you and your mother and the babe like to get away from Waterford?"

"Yes, sir," Polly said without hesitation. A faint color stealing into her cheeks, she looked down at her feet. "But where would we go, sir?"

"You could come with me, Polly. I have an estate in Cornwall. You would live there in one of the cottages. There would be employment for you, plenty to eat, and fires to warm yourselves by when the days grow cold. Best of all, you would never again have to worry about your mother and the baby. Does that appeal to you?"

There was a complete silence in the room. Glancing quickly at Shalada, David saw that she was looking at Polly with warmth and compassion. Oh, my girl, he thought, my dear fiery fighting Shalada. How wrong I have been about you!

Polly cleared her throat and looked up slowly. There was such a look of shining wonder in her eyes that David felt a constriction in his throat. He spoke abruptly to cover his emotion. "There is one thing, though. I should warn you that I can be a very harsh landlord."

Polly's voice shook. "You couldn't be harsh if you tried." She shook her head as though to clear it. "But why would you d-do all that for me, sir? I ain't n-nothing to you."

"You are mistaken, Polly. I like you and I count you as a friend."

Without warning, Polly burst into tears. "Jamie'd grow right strong in that Cornish air. And . . . and, it do sound like h-heaven!"

"Polly, will you stop that infernal wailing!" David cast a laughing glance at Shalada. "I have been subjected to quite enough tears for one day."

Polly dried her eyes with a corner of her apron.

"Now, listen to me," David resumed. "There is something we must do before we can get away. I will explain what I have in mind. I—"

Tasmin cried out frantically, "You mustn't trust her. Tell her nothing."

David ignored her, but Shalada said in a warning voice, "If you don't keep that mouth of yours shut, Tasmin, I will shut it for you!"

"Miss Tasmin"—Polly turned to the girl and looked at her steadily—"Sir David could trust me with his very life. I'd never breathe a word about nothing he told me." Her expression grew fierce. "I'd do anything for him, do you understand me, Miss Tasmin?"

Shrugging, Tasmin threw her a sullen glance. "So you say, Polly Carter."

"And so I mean, Miss Tasmin." Polly turned to David. "Would you be wishful to go on, sir?"

Once again David outlined his plan.

Polly's eyes grew round with wonder when she learned that Rebecca West was Shalada's mother. Listening intently, only once did she interrupt in a shocked voice: "There do be witches. Real ones," she added, with an apologetic look at Shalada. "If we do like you say, ain't it likely that them witches might work us an evil?"

David reassured her. "There will be no evil. I don't happen to believe in witches."

Drawing herself up, Polly looked at David with shining eyes. "Then if you don't believe in 'em, I don't neither. And I . . . I ain't afraid."

"Good girl." David gave her an approving nod.

"Tell me what you want me to do for you, sir."

"It might be difficult," David warned.

"I don't care," Polly said. "It's for you, sir, and that's all that matters."

"You do get these females eating out of your hand, don't you, David?" Shalada whispered.

David shook his head. "No, not always. I know of one female who bit my hand. Scratched it, too."

"Oh, be quiet, dandy."

David grinned. "You'll answer for that later. In the meantime, kindly remain silent. I am speaking to Polly."

Polly, who had not heard the whispered exchange, was looking at him expectantly.

"Polly," David began, "do you think you could get hold of some horses?"

Polly's jaw dropped. "But you got a horse, ain't you, sir?"

Hiding his slight stir of impatience at Polly's slowness, David said, "My horse is stabled at Jeremiah Beasly's. But five of us, including one baby, can hardly ride on one horse."

Her face flushed with embarrassment at her own stupidity; her eyes flicked quickly from Shalada to Tasmin.

Understanding her thoughts, David said quickly, "Perhaps you did not quite understand me. We are all in this together."

"What, her an' all?" Polly nodded toward Tasmin's hunched form.

"We will need four extra horses, and I understand that Beasly has several for sale."

"Oh." Polly's troubled face cleared. "You mean you want me to go and buy them horses?"

There was the faintest twinkle in David's eyes. "I mean I want you to steal them."

Petrified, Polly stared at him.

"Yes, four horses. Understand me, Polly, in the ordinary way, I am no horse thief, but secrecy must be observed. It might give rise to suspicion if, in my name, I sent you to buy four horses. It would be a big sale for Beasly, I would imagine, and it might come to Matthew Lorne's ears. He might even begin asking questions."

Polly pleated and unpleated the corner of her apron with nervous fingers. She had heard that they hung horse thieves, sometimes even burned them. Looking up, she met Shalada's understanding eyes and Tasmin's sullen glare. Her chin squared pugnaciously. She had vowed that she would do anything, and she would. With the exception of her mother, he was the only one who had ever been kind to her.

Watching her, David said quietly, "You need not involve yourself if you would rather not. After all, you have your mother and the baby to think of."

Polly shook her head. "It is them I'm thinking of, and of you, sir. I can do it."

David's eyes were worried. What a fool he was. He had believed that his plan was so well worked out, but he had forgotten the essential thing, the horses. He would have thought of it sooner or later, of course, but by then it might have been too late to help. If Polly had not come along and jolted his memory, they might have fared very badly. Even now he could make the effort, and take the burden off this poor girl, but the time lapse might change everything. He, Shalada, and Tasmin had to be on the spot. "Polly," he said slowly, "are you quite sure you can do it? I have given you a very difficult task."

"No you ain,'t sir." Straightening her meager shoulders, Polly turned shining eyes on David. "You ain't to worry about nothing. Old Jerry, he ain't going to be there to watch me every movement with them watery suspicious eyes of his. He's not one for missing out on any excitement. He'll be out there with all them others to see the witch take her walk. Even the stable hands'll slip off. They always does when old Jerry's out of the way."

"Nevertheless, it won't be easy."

Seeing the doubt in his eyes, Polly was eager to convince. "It will, sir, easy as pie. You see, old Jerry always keeps them for-sale horses saddled and bridled. Only takes 'em off the poor creatures when he closes up for the night." She sniffed. "Tatty old saddles they are, too, and them bridles all but falling to pieces. Shame, I call it, but the customer'll generally buy 'em with the horse. And Jerry, old thief that he is, puts up the price real steep for them bits of rotting leather. Serve him right to have something stole off him for a change."

"That will certainly make it easier," David said, smiling at her vehemence.

"It will that, sir. And another thing," Polly added proudly, "I'm used to handling horses. Always did it when we had our farm, me dad being dead and me mum too feeble."

David nodded. "Polly, do you know my horse?"

" 'Course I do, sir. I seen him often enough. Heard you call him by name, too. Sam, ain't it?"

"That's right. Get hold of Sam first. Bring him to the front of the inn as soon as Rebecca West begins her walk. I doubt you'll be noticed."

"They'll all be too busy watching the witch hobble over them stones." Noticing Shalada's involuntary wince, she added quickly, "Sorry, Miss Shalada."

"The other four horses," David went on, "you will take to that grove of trees just behind the inn. They won't be noticed there."

"And after that?"

"You will wait there with the horses. Be sure that your mother and the baby are with you."

"They'll be there, don't you worry none."

David rose from the bed. Going to Polly, he placed both hands on her shoulders and looked deeply into her eyes. "You're a rare one, Polly Carter, and I'm proud to know you." Polly's gaunt face flushed pink with pleasure. "You are a fine and courageous girl." David's hands tightened on her shoulders. "There is something I want you to keep in mind, Polly. If we have not joined you within a certain time, you are to leave the horses standing and return at once to your home, you understand?"

"But what will it mean if you don't come?"

"It will mean that my plan has failed. That we are either dead or in prison. But you . . ." He broke off as Tasmin gave a stifled scream. "But you must protect yourself," he went on calmly. "You must not be connected in any way with us, or with the theft of the horses. So promise me that you will go home."

"Yes, I promise," Polly said in a choked voice. Tears glittered brightly in her eyes.

"We have no intention of being caught, if we can help it. So hold firmly to that thought, and don't be afraid, my little wench." David stooped, and kissed her wet cheek, and turned her gently to the door. "Go now, my dear. And be careful."

"That fool girl is in love with you," Tasmin said as the door closed behind her. "The way she was mooning at you with those eyes of hers made me sick."

David turned and came back to the bed. "You have confused gratitude with love, Tasmin," he said coldly.

Tasmin flushed, and tears of self-pity welled into her eyes. She had never been loved in her life. And it was likely, if this plan failed, that she never would be. "Polly Carter is a stupid, ignorant peasant girl. What right has she to fall in love with someone like you? Why, she has witch blood in her herself. A relative of hers, Elizabeth Carter, went to the burning cross."

"Lizzie Loon," David thought, remembering the landlord's story. He stared at Tasmin, his eyes glittering with anger. He disliked the girl intensely, and would have done so even had her name not been Lorne. "I care nothing about Polly's heritage," he said, managing to keep his voice even.

Shalada got up from the bed. Putting her arms about David, she said in a tense voice, "Pay no attention to Tasmin's nonsense. There are more important things. I think, from the increased activity I can hear below, that the walk is about to begin."

David held her away from him. Seeing the taut line of her jaw and the look in her eyes, he said in a gentle voice, "Are you very afraid, my love?"

Shalada's expression changed at once. "I'd be a fool not to be afraid," she said, holding her head high. "And so would you. But if you are thinking that I am some simpering miss who has to be coddled and protected, you may think again. I can take care of myself, and I have fully as much courage as you."

"By God, Shalada," David exclaimed furiously, "have I given you an argument on that? Don't try me too far!"

"Men!" Shalada, said scornfully. "Big brave omnipotent men. Why do they always have the idea that women are useless, just toys to be loved and cuddled when they are in the mood, and to be put to one side when they are not. Women are supposed to be not only their toys, but they must cook their food for them, clean the house, and make them as comfortable as possible, so that they can go on feeling like gods."

David glared at her. "And what has brought on this tirade?"

Shalada returned his glare. "I just wanted you to know that I will never be a toy. I will be an equal partner or nothing. I am a woman, and I will be treated as such."

"I know you're a woman." David spoke through gritted teeth. "Beneath that warriorlike exterior of yours, you are all woman. And before many more hours have gone by, I am going to make you prove that to me."

"Make? We will see about that."

"Aye, we will, on that I am determined. You yourself said you would prove it when we were well away from this place."

Shalada eyed him haughtily. "I have changed my mind."

"You're not getting away with that." Roughly, David pulled her closer. "If I have to force you, I will not let you go back on your word."

The smile that trembled on Shalada's lips was quickly suppressed. "Indeed," she answered, "do you think you're man enough?"

"Man enough for you, as you will find out."

David bent his head and fastened his mouth on hers. Almost instantly he felt her response. Laughing, his rage forgotten, he released her. "You see, I shall be the victor and you the vanquished."

"I said I would be equal," she flashed.

"You want to be equal," David said grimly. "Then by God, you shall be. I am not above helping my men to till the fields and to gather crops, and you shall labor by my side, Shalada. It is exhausting, back-breaking work, but you will not mind that, will you, for you will be equal."

"If you think I could not do it, David Medway, you are much mistaken."

"We will find out." She turned away from him, ignoring his last words.

Watching her, the stiffness of her shoulders, the tight set of her mouth, David felt unbounded admiration for Shalada. She was afraid, but damned if she'd show it. "Shalada," he said softly, "I love you."

She turned to him at once, the tightness of her mouth relaxing into a smile. "And I love you," she answered. "But if you try to take me against my will, I will still give you a fight."

"So it's going to be like that, is it?"

"Just like that."

14

Rebecca West presented an appearance that was strange enough to convince even the least superstitious among the gaping onlookers that they indeed gazed upon a witch. She was clad in a once-white shift that reached to just below her knees. The shift, torn at the hem, sent a tail of the material fluttering out behind her, giving the odd appearance of a tail. The bodice was ripped and afforded a partial glimpse of her small withered breasts. Her now completely gray hair was hopelessly tangled; it streamed in snarled confusion to her waist and surrounded a deeply lined yellowed and wizened face in which the muscles twitched uncontrollably. Her brown eyes were wild; they darted here and there, blindly fastening on this face or that, as though seeking compassion for her plight, some means of escape.

Strangely, despite the quick glancing of her eyes, Rebecca did not see the cold hard faces about her. Even if one among the crowd had had the courage to smile, step forward, and proclaim to be a friend of her youth, it would have meant nothing to her; she was beyond recognition, beyond feelings or thoughts of escape. She was numb, as though her body and her mind had been encased in ice, and through that screening of ice her eyes saw the hostile faces only as a blur, meaningless and unidentifiable. Her bare feet, already sore from her long trek from the cottage that had been her prison, to the marketplace that was to witness her torture and her final agonizing death, were torn and bloodied from the low-growing prickly vines through which she had been forced to tread, but she was not aware of the pain as she continued to move automatically along the uneven cobbled street which led to the witch's trail, where her ordeal was to begin. She was propelled by a rope about her neck, the other end of which was held in the beefy hands of John Avery, a burly local farmer who had applied for the job of leading the witch to her fate. Following behind Rebecca came a crowd of jeering children and young adults, themselves barely out of childhood. Many of the children were ignorant of the meaning of the epithets they called after the miserable woman; they only knew that in some way the ugliness that dribbled from their tongues helped to further degrade her, and, in addition, brought them the approval of the adults. Others in the crowd that lined the street hurled insults too. Some were silent. Fervently crossing themselves to ward off evil, they watched with wide frightened eyes as the woman who had been proclaimed a witch passed them by.

Still Rebecca felt nothing, saw nothing; the hate and fear of the people who watched her was like a great stifling cloak, but it did not touch her, it did not even flicker at the edge of her consciousness.

John Avery heard the sounds of Rebecca's distress, and he glanced at her quickly. There was no pity in his eyes as he tightened the end of the rope about his hand and continued to drag her along. His bitterness grew as he thought of the time when he had loved Rebecca West and had wanted to wed her. Margaret West, Rebecca's mother, had liked him, and she had been eager for a match between John Avery and her daughter. As for Rebecca herself, she had always been coy and flighty, but before Matthew Lorne had come upon the scene and dashed all his hopes, he could have sworn that Rebecca was beginning to return his love. Rebecca's mother, he knew, had hated and feared the witch-finder, but her mother's strong feelings had made no difference to the girl. It was as though she was hypnotized by Matthew Lorne, for once he began to woo her, she had had eyes for no other man.

Avery gave another savage tug on the rope as Rebecca moaned again. She was a witch, the daughter of a witch. Avery glanced at Rebecca again, and to his dismay he felt the hot tears pricking his eyes. Angrily he rubbed his free hand over his eyes, fearful that his sudden emotion might have been noted. There was nothing left, no trace at all of that fragile pretty girl whom he had loved so desperately. That Rebecca, her gleaming brown hair that sometimes sparked with unexpected red lights, her beautiful soft brown eyes, her full, luscious red mouth, and her tempting breasts, her skin always smelling faintly of apple blossoms. That Rebecca was gone forever, a fragrant page in memory. In her place was this gaunt, bent old woman with lined and yellowed skin and a face almost unrecognizable.

Trembling with the force of his unexpected emotion, Avery yanked on the rope again, almost causing her to fall. He had no mercy for her; any love he might have had for her was long since gone. It had been buried under a burden of troubles that grew more insupportable with every passing year. He had a wife who nagged at him ceaselessly, and a brood of grown-up children who had no respect for their father or for the old tried-and-true way of doing things. Feeling the tears rising in his eyes again, he bit deeply into his lower lip in an effort to repress them. Fool, he raged inwardly. More than a fool to have allowed his mind to dwell on that long-ago springtime of his youth.

A faint gasping sound came from Rebecca, and Avery tightened his hand on the rope. Life was strange, he thought. Now, because of his bitterness and the memory of the pain she had inflicted upon him, he was leading her to her death, this poor worn-out old woman who was all that remained of his sweet laughing girl.

Pain clawed at Avery, a pain so intense that it wrenched a harsh sob from his throat. Tears, hot and hurting, flooded his eyes and streamed unchecked down his brown seamed cheeks. Tears for himself, for Rebecca, for what might have been. So shaken was he by the bitterness of his grief that he did not notice the curious stares of the onlookers, and of one sharp-faced woman in particular. He was bound up within himself, consumed by remorse and agony. No matter what she was, no matter what she had become, she was still Rebecca and he loved her. Avery's nails dug deeply into the palm of his hand. He would soon watch her burn. His lips moved silently praying to God that he could remain unmoved by the sight and not feel her pain.

Suddenly frightened by the irreverence of his thoughts, he tasted the salt of his own blood as his teeth drove deeper into his lower lip. He thought he was going mad. His mind whirled and burned as he struggled with a desire to scream out.

From his place outside the inn, Matthew Lorne watched the distant figure of Rebecca West. He was frowning heavily, for he had seen a woman run from the crowd and halt the little procession. He would look into the matter later, he told himself grimly. John Avery had been given a job to do, and it was his duty to carry out that job, no matter who approached him. Discipline, order, obedience, these things must be observed when one worked for Matthew Lorne, as Avery would shortly find out. Lorne's frown lightened as he saw the procession start up again. Rebecca had a little way to go yet, but very soon she would be at the beginning of the witch's trail. His cold eyes fixed themselves on the tottering woman as he mentally willed her to hurry.

Matthew forgot Rebecca for a brief moment as the sounds about him, the pushing and the shoving of the spectators, recalled him to a sense of his own importance. Standing here, he was anonymous. It was beneath him to mingle with these people who crowded about him so eagerly. Inclining his head, Matthew moved forward. Reaching the witch's trail, he was satisfied for the moment to stand at the end of the line of drummers.

The drummers stood on either side of the trail. If they felt anything for the unfortunate prisoner, it did not show in their wooden expressions. They stood straight as soldiers, drums slung about their necks. The sticks, clutched tightly in work-calloused hands, were poised above the drums ready to begin the steady, monotonous beating when the witch set foot on the trail. But despite their stiff stance and the way their eyes stared steadily ahead, seeing and yet not seeing, they were not soldiers. They were men whom Matthew had recruited from the village for this special duty. This drumming of the witch to her doom prolonged the suffering, for the victim was not allowed to walk fast; she must keep pace with the drums. Should she attempt to hurry, she would be taken back to the beginning of the trail and forced to begin all over again.

Matthew's eyes returned to Rebecca. She was nearer now. Strangely, disconcertingly, he found his mind slipping back into time. He had known Rebecca West all his life, and yet it was not until he had returned from London, where the squire had sent him to complete his education, that he had seen her with his heart as well as his mind. Matthew's hands clenched as that long-ago picture presented itself clearly. Rebecca, skirts flying, running across a field studded with daisies. The sun had been gleaming on her lovely brown hair, and a little brown-and-white dog yapped at her heels. Rebecca, with the wild-rose color deepening in her cheeks when she had discovered him standing motionless by the gate. At first, Matthew knew, in his fine clothes and the wig he had affected for a short time, she had not recognized him. Her eyes had dropped, but not before he had seen in them an expression of shy admiration. "Afternoon, sir," she had said, curtsying.

Looking at the length of the dark lashes, the shadowed cleavage between the breasts that were partially revealed by the low-cut bodice of the yellow gown she was wearing, he was shaken by a strong and savage emotion such as he had never experienced before. To him, she was so lovely, so fresh, as fresh as the daisies beneath her small feet. It was in that moment that he had vowed she should be his alone.

The sharp hacking sound of a cough brought him back with a start to the present. His eyes narrowed vindictively as he continued to watch the prisoner's unsteady progress. Rebecca was old now, and worn-out. He put a hand to his quivering mouth, hoping to hide this weakness from the sharp eyes of those who might be watching him. An old woman, he repeated to himself, yet the ghost of that lovely young girl seemed to overshadow that old body, mocking him with memories. His ears were filled with the sound of her gay young laughter. No one had ever laughed as infectiously as Rebecca, as though she were overflowing with the sheer joy of living. Everything about her had seemed to be part of the joy that emanated from her. The sunlight that caressed her hair had been a part of her. The flowers too had been drawn into that aura of joy, painting her eyes the soft brown of pansies; the wild rose had tinted her lips and her cheeks. She had glowed, she had shimmered, and she had been his.

Matthew's hand dropped heavily to his side. Yes, his, until she had parted her legs for the Spaniard. His mouth tightened to a hard bitter line as he continued to watch her. Inside that apparent decrepitude, she was hiding from him, hating and defying him still. Inside, untouched by the years, she was as young and fresh as ever.

Matthew gasped as his head reeled and an intolerable pain shot through his head. He dug his fingers into his

291

temples as though by his actions he could pluck the pain from his head and throw it from him.

The drummer nearest to Matthew sent him a quick flinching glance. Instantly the drummer looked away, his hands clenching about the sticks he held. He tried to concentrate on the drama that was about to take place, but the memory of Matthew Lorne's contorted face and blazing eyes stayed with him. He's mad, the young drummer thought with a thrill of horror, Matthew Lorne is out of his mind!

Matthew shivered, his hands clawing at his cloak. The groan that burst from his lips caused the young drummer's shoulders to stiffen and his hands to tremble, but he did not turn his head for fear he might encounter those madly blazing eyes.

Matthew's fevered mind was reliving the sight of the cold stiff bodies of his wife and son as he called out Tasmin's and Shalada's names until his throat was hoarse. He was alone with his dead and Shalada was gone.

"Must find her," the young drummer heard Lorne mumble.

The drummer's shoulders quivered in a sudden spasm of nerves. He'd had enough of this duty. He wouldn't put anything past a madman. Lorne was still mumbling to himself, and the drummer strained his ears as he tried to distinguish words, but he could make out nothing intelligible. He wished Lorne would move away. Any sudden movement from him might cause him to go completely berserk.

"Shalada!" Lorne's sudden shout boomed into the drummer's ears, causing him to start violently and drop his sticks. "Shalada, where are you?"

15

Polly Carter had heard Lorne's sudden shouting of Shalada's name, and she grew cold with fear. She saw the people glancing uneasily at each other, the mumble of their voices as, no doubt, they speculated on Lorne's outburst. She did not trouble to speculate herself; she could only thank God that he had provided a diversion.

Above her head, Polly knew, Sir David and the others would be concealed behind the window curtains, watching her actions. Resisting the impulse to look upward, she wondered if they had heard Lorne's shout. Her fingers trembling, she tied the reins of the horse loosely about the rail in front of the inn. Sir David had been right after all, she thought gratefully; no one was displaying the least interest in her actions. Some were staring at Matthew Lorne, who, to her frightened eyes, looked like one demented. Others were watching Rebecca, who had almost reached the trail.

Sam nudged Polly's shoulder, snorted, and stamped an impatient hoof. Then, as though in inquiry, he rolled his large soft eyes in her direction.

"Hush up, Sam," Polly whispered, giving the horse a perfunctory pat on his quivering neck. "Master'll be with you right soon, so don't you start up with no noise." She patted his neck again. "I got to get back to Beasly's now, and right quick, 'cause me mum and the babe is already waiting behind the inn. I ain't got no more time for you just now, Sam, so you be a good quiet boy. You hear me?"

As if feeling himself admonished, Sam sighed and hung his head meekly. It was almost like he was human and understood every word she had said, Polly thought. Giving him a faint smile, she slipped quietly away.

Her heart jumped as she caught the turn of Matthew Lorne's head. Frozen, she stood still. She was sure his glassy eyes had seen her and he had wondered where she was going. Polly saw Lorne's head turn to the front again. After a moment of indecision she walked on, her hair fluttering in the wind of her swift progress. Safe inside the dim, acrid-smelling stable, Polly found herself chilled by the look she had seen on his face.

With the reins of the four horses bunched in her hand, she led the horses out, her heart jumping with panic at every ring of their iron-shod hooves on the cobbles. Taking them around the side of the stables, she expected a challenging voice to ring out at any moment. Convinced after a few shaken moments that she had not been seen, she led them down a small grassy incline and turned left toward the grove of trees that lay directly behind the inn. Her thoughts went to her mother. It had taken quite an argument on her part to get her mother to agree with the plan, for she had had a hard life both before and since she had been widowed, and for many years now she had lived under the shadows of hunger and fear and insecurity. "I can't do it," she had cried out in a shaking voice. "Suppose the babe cries out while we're hid among them trees and we're discovered. Think for a bit. We'd be brought before Matthew Lorne and he'd ask us questions. Once his suspicions were set on us, you know what would become of us."

Polly did know, and she felt an answering thrill of fear, but she would let nothing deter her now. The argument had seemed to her to go on forever, and all the while the precious time was slipping by. Moved by the haunted look in her mother's eyes, she had felt herself weakening, but she had forced herself to remain firm. "It's a good life Sir David is offering us," she had persisted, "a better one than we've ever known or are ever likely to know. I ain't throwing the chance of it away."

As though she were afraid to meet her daughter's fierce eyes, Jane Carter's head drooped. "And . . . and if I say I won't, Polly, what then?"

Hating herself for the new pain she must inflict upon her mother, Polly answered her in a hard voice. "If you won't, then you won't. But I'm going. I'll just put the babe in a box and hide him among the trees."

A gray tinge crept into Jane's face. "You'd leave me, lass?"

The pain stabbing deeper, Polly answered her in the same hard voice. "I don't want to leave you, Mum, and you must know that. Look here, I ain't never been much of a one for showing me feelings, but I love you. Still, I got to think of the baby, I got to give him a chance at a better life."

Jane raised her head and stared at her daughter. "You might be killed."

"So I might," Polly answered on a deep shaken breath. "But I'd rather be dead than live the way we been doing."

Jane was silent for a moment; then she rose from her chair and put her shaking arms about her daughter. "If you and the boy was to be killed, then there wouldn't be nothing left for me to live for. So I'll do it."

Polly hugged and kissed her thin tear-stained cheek. "You won't regret it. We ain't going to get caught 'cause I trust in Sir David to bring us through. And then there's Miss Shalada. A fighting fiery piece, she is, from what I hear. Why, I bet she'd be as good as a man if it came to a fight."

Jane's arms dropped and she shrank away. "What are you saying?" she said, horror in her eyes. "Miss Shalada's a Lorne."

"She ain't no Lorne. That man's not her father.

She's Rebecca West's daughter." Quickly Polly outlined the story she had heard at the inn.

When Polly's voice faded, Jane said in sorrowing tones, "Poor Rebecca. How she must have suffered at that man's hands. I remember her well, I do. So pretty and bright, always with a smile. She was like a butterfly, she was, or so she seemed to me. And then to be a prisoner in that cottage for all those years, her lass taken from her. It makes me heart break to think on it."

"She could have left that cottage anytime she pleased after Miss Shalada was born."

Jane shook her head. "She was as much a prisoner there as ever. How could she go away and never see her girl again? I couldn't have done it. A mother will endure anything for the sight of her child."

Polly thought of her own child, and she felt the welling of her love. "I guess I wouldn't have left that cottage either." She hesitated. "But look what she's come to now."

"It don't matter, she's seen her girl grow up. She'll suffer, all right, but at least she's had that." She held out her arms. "Get the babe and give him to me. It's like you said, there ain't much time, and if it's to be done, it's best done now."

Going out of the door with the child in her arms, Jane spoke only once more. "And Miss Tasmin, can she be trusted?"

Polly nodded. "She's scared out of her wits of her father, but at this moment I'll bet she's even more scared of Miss Shalada."

A sound caught Polly's ears. Pulling up abruptly, she stood motionless, her heart beating rapidly as the hot breath of the horses gusted against her neck. Hearing nothing more, she decided it must have been a rabbit or some small creature rustling among the undergrowth. It might even be a poacher. If so he wouldn't trouble her as long as she didn't trouble him.

Walking on again, Polly hastened her steps, the

brittle twigs cracking beneath her feet and the horses clopping patiently behind her. The twigs, in contrast to the new budding green of the trees, made her think of the death that awaited Rebecca West.

16

Rebecca's mind had swung from blankness to the painful reality of the moment that was almost upon her. Just a few more paces, and then she must set her feet upon the trail. If only her mind could have stayed blank, she thought despairingly, if only she could have remained unaware of the people and of what was going on around her. As though a blindfold had been removed, she saw the leering faces, the various colored gowns of the women, the drummers lined up stiffly on either side of the trail. And there was Matthew Lorne, tall, gaunt, black-clad, her nemesis. He was detaching himself from the line of drummers and moving to his place at the head of the trail. Waiting like a black vulture until she reached him. How he must be glorying in this moment.

Rebecca looked away from him, her eyes searching the crowd. Shalada! her heart cried out in agony. Where are you, my baby, my little girl? A silent prayer bubbled to her lips. God, in Your Mercy, let my child be safe. She looked at Matthew Lorne again, and she trembled with her hatred of him.

Somebody pushed against her, and was rebuked harshly. No, Rebecca thought, firming her trembling mouth, she was about to die, and it was wrong to hate. Matthew Lorne did not matter. However he chose to torture her body, he did not matter. Only her daughter was important, her beautiful, graceful, kind Shalada. She thought with a surge of pathetic hope, that if she concentrated all her thoughts upon Shalada she would not feel the great jagged cinders tearing at her feet, the broken glass, or the cruelly sharp cutting edges of the specially selected stones.

Rebecca drew in a deep shaken breath. Shalada! She could still remember that incredibly joyous moment when she had first looked upon her child's face. Almost as if it were happening now, she could remember all that had gone before. The kindly face of Tabitha Owens, the midwife, bending over her, the low soothing murmur of her voice as the birth pangs tore at her. She could feel the roughened texture of the skin on the small plump hands to which she had clung so desperately in her agony. Tabitha's voice encouraging her. She heard the thin wailing cry of her child as Tabitha placed the baby in her arms.

Pain clutched at Rebecca's heart. Never had she seen anything more perfect, more exquisite than the tiny babe nestled in her arms. This child, this miracle, was hers and Don Roberto's, for it had not needed more than that one glance to tell her who had fathered her child.

Tears burned in Rebecca's eyes and ran down her lined cheeks. How cruel when Matthew took her baby away from her. How great the agony of wondering if her child lived, if she was crying, hungry, abused—for how could she trust in Matthew's reports? Matthew, who hated her, who might well be lying when he said that the child did well. And then one day, as proof that he had not lied to her in this at least, he had brought Shalada to the cottage.

Rebecca lifted her hand and wiped away her trickling tears. Unaware of anything but her bittersweet memories, she let herself remember that day. Forming her trembling lips into a smile, she had gazed hungrily at the small delicate little creature who was confronting her, her soft baby mouth giving her back a shy answering smile. She had longed to gather Shalada into her arms; her hands had been hungry to stroke the cloud of shining black hair that fell from beneath a tiny white cap, but Matthew Lorne had stood beside the child like a grim threatening specter, and she did not dare. If she were to defy him, he might not bring the child again. His set expression had dared her to touch.

Shalada's great dark eyes had studied the strange woman, whom she did not know as her mother. Perhaps it was some deeply buried instinct that had guided the child's next action. Her smile widening to show perfect white teeth, she had put out her small hand and patted Rebecca's trembling one. "Nice lady," she had said in her piping voice. "I like you."

Rebecca's choked cry at this pronouncement had not appeared to startle Shalada. She had continued to smile and pat the strange woman's trembling hand as though she sought to impart comfort. Four years old Shalada had been then, and it had been Rebecca's first glimpse of her since she was born. Five minutes, that was all that Matthew Lorne had allowed her, five achingly sweet moments before he had taken the child away again. She could still hear Shalada's wailing cry as Matthew had seized her hand and hustled her roughly down the rutted lane. "Won't go, want to go back to nice lady."

In her despair, Rebecca had often thought of going away, but now she put those plans firmly from her. That one glimpse of her baby had defeated her. How could she ever have thought that a new life in different surroundings would take away the pain of her constant longing for her child? She could never leave this cottage, not while the chance existed to see her Shalada. At first, knowing Matthew, she had been puzzled that he had allowed her to see her child at all. Then, thinking it over, she knew why. It was to hurt her further, to turn the knife in the wound. To flaunt before her the knowledge of all that she had lost.

A sob escaped Rebecca's quivering lips. Sometimes months would go by before Matthew would come again, and he would never stay more than five minutes.

Unspeaking, his lips tight, he would study her as she gazed at the child. Then, still silent, he would take Shalada away. Rebecca had never been possessed of a great deal of courage, but longing fired her spirit. So there were times when she would leave the cottage. Taking a circuitous route, she would make her way to Matthew's great brooding house. Once there, her heart thumping painfully in case she should be discovered by her persecutor, she would carefully conceal herself and wait patiently for a glimpse of her child. Often she would be disappointed, and she would cry bitterly as she made her way back to the cottage. Other times she would be rewarded, and her watching eyes would grow bright with love. Shalada was different from his other children; she did not romp and laugh as they did. Shalada would sit apart from them, her somber dark eyes studying the exuberant Robert and the toddling Tasmin as though they were some curious species of animal, and her mouth would be set with some secret pain or anger. Rebecca wondered what this beautiful aloof little girl who sat so quietly with her small hands folded on her aproned lap thought of.

Quite suddenly a joy entered Rebecca's life, something she had never dared to hope for. Shalada, as she grew older, took to defying Matthew and secretly visiting the cottage. Although Rebecca could not talk, her happiness and her love had radiated from her. It had seemed to her that Shalada had returned her love, for often she would catch her watching her, and there would be a softness in her dark eyes. And then one day Shalada had uttered her love aloud. "I love you, you are like a mother to me." She had longed to cry out, "My darling, my Shalada, I am your mother!"

Rebecca stumbled, gagging a little as the rope bit into her neck. But Shalada knew the truth now, and knowing, she had run from her. She had fled in horror and fear, ashamed of this woman who was her mother.

"Look there!" A loud coarse voice jerked Rebecca

abruptly from her thoughts. "Now, ain't that a sight to see a witch crying?"

"Aye," a jeering feminine voice answered the masculine one. "It's a bit late for her to go crying now. I bet she didn't do no crying when she was working her evil." A sharp elbow dug into Rebecca's ribs. "See them stones and glass and things, witch? They ain't half going to hurt. Rip your feet to pieces, they will, and bleeding well serves you right."

Rebecca turned her head and looked at the woman who had accosted her. The woman, her florid face paling, shrank back, thrusting out two fingers in a sign to ward off evil.

"It ain't never too late for a witch, Mary," the coarse male voice said uneasily, "so don't you go getting too brave. Come away from her, lass, or she'll maybe do you in injury."

"Halt!" The cry of command was delivered in a voice so broken that Rebecca looked around in surprise. It had come from the man who had been leading her. He was staring at her so intently that she had the strange feeling that he was trying to see through her to the woman within. Her mind groped helplessly as she tried to fit a name to him. Her eyes took in his tear-ravaged face, the naked pain that looked from his eyes, and she was bewildered. For whom did that big man cry? Surely not for her. She was nothing to him.

The woman who taunted Rebecca elbowed her companion. "Look there at that John Avery. He's crying. Proper sight he's making of himself." A note of scorn entered her voice. She would never had thought Avery had it in him to cry. He was known to his neighbors as a hard, sour-natured man who had never been seen to crack his face into a smile, a man who never gave an inch. Heartless, her husband called him. Tough as nails, and tight-fisted with it. Dear Lord, her husband had good reason to know. On account of the money he owed the man, he had brushed up against Avery more than once in harsh encounters that had left him pale and shaken. It was true that he had owed the money for some time now, but he'd tried his best to pay it back. Her husband's best, however, was not good enough for Avery, for the man continued to hound him mercilessly.

Rebecca heard the woman's conversation and the name echoed deeply in her head. Her heart fluttered painfully. John Avery. How could she have forgotten him so completely? The years had brought changes in him. They had wrought deep lines in his face and grooved deeper ones beside his mouth. His thick crop of hair, once the color of ripe wheat, was now completely gray and receded slightly from his temples. But it was unmistakably the John Avery who had once loved her, and who cried for her now. "John" her trembling lips formed his name.

Her voice was only a whisper, but Avery heard. Staring at her, it was as though some miracle in time had taken place, for he did not see her as she was. Standing there, she was to him as young and as glowing as she had ever been. The smooth brown hair that tumbled over her slim shoulders glinted with red lights, and her narrow, tapering-fingered hands were held out to him as though in appeal.

"Rebecca," he said hoarsely. Heedless of the staring people and the shock that was evident in their faces, he walked toward her, the rope end dropping from his slack hand. He took both of her trembling hands in his and held them tightly. One part of his mind was aware of the deep network of wrinkled flesh that surrounded her eyes, but he rejected it. They were Rebecca's eyes, he thought, the blood rushing to his head. Brown, pansy-soft, eternally young, mirroring in their depths his youth and the intensity of his lost love. "Rebecca." His voice broke.

Rebecca withdrew her hands from his. "It's been a long time, John. When you came for me, I did not know you. I'm sorry for that."

Her words, the cracked tone, so different from the

lilting voice he remembered, was like a cruel blow over his heart. The young girl disappeared as reality came rushing back. It was all gone, his lovely dream, he could no longer hide in the long ago. His Rebecca had been dead a long time, and now he must let her go. Finally and forever he must relinquish her. Fresh tears gathered in his eyes as he looked at the old woman before him. "Rebecca"—he spoke to her gently, but with an underlying note of passionate regret—"I'm so sorry for my part in this!"

Rebecca turned her head and looked down at the trail that stretched before her. Glass glittered brightly among the great stones and the cinders. In a few moments, if God chose to disregard her prayer, she would feel that jagged ripping sharpness beneath her feet. Her heart beat sickeningly as wild terror washed over her. Pain spread outward from her left breast and ran agonizingly down her arm. Her fingertips were numb and she was finding it increasingly difficult to breathe.

"Rebecca, what is it?" John's voice came to her faintly.

She did not attempt to answer him. She stood there swaying, as though at any moment she might pitch forward on her face. She felt the comforting warmth of his arm about her bowed shoulders, and with the contact the pain receded. Her terror went with it, and she was filled with a sense of great peace. She knew then that God had heard her prayers and had answered them. She would be immune to this pain. She looked at John, her eyes shining. "Don't blame yourself," she said, looking into his stricken face.

He stared at her in disbelief. How could she, who stood in such need of comfort, now be attempting to console him? His guilt was a heavy burden upon him, so heavy that he feared that if he did not let it out, it would crush him. "You don't understand," he shouted.

The onlookers drew nearer until they formed a circle about him. In their eagerness to know the explanation of John Avery's strange behavior, they listened avidly, fearful of missing one word of the exchange between Avery and the witch. They need not have bothered to strain their ears. Avery's voice was pitched to such a height that it reached Matthew Lorne, standing grim and silent at the other end of the trail.

Avery's voice broke. Recovering himself, he began to shout again, "I volunteered for this duty, is that clear to you, I vowed to lead you here to this trail."

He could not disturb her newfound peace. There was nothing now that could do that.

A sob broke from Avery's lips. "I thought I hated you. I had convinced myself that I did."

Rebecca listened to his harsh sobbing for a moment, then laid her hand lightly upon his bowed head. "Hush! I do forgive you."

Avery lifted his head, his tear-swollen eyes looking into hers. "I know I'll never to able to forgive myself for what I have done to you this day."

Rebecca spoke to him gently. "Then I ask you to believe that I am innocent of witchcraft."

"I know that," Avery said simply. "Matthew Lorne has lied."

For the first time she looked apprehensive. With a painful tug at his heart, Avery knew that her anxiety was not for herself, but for him, who so little deserved it.

Avery started to say something, but stopped abruptly as the drums began. The beat was slow and steady and monotonous as it beckoned the so-called witch on to her fate. The drumming, starting up so suddenly, startled Rebecca. Her heart gave a frightened leap before settling back to its normal even pace. What had she to fear? She asked herself. God was with her. "It's time, John," she said softly.

"God help me!" Avery could not move for a moment. Then, as she smiled at him, he stretched out his trembling hands to the rope.

Rebecca stood very still. She felt a great pity for him as his work-calloused fingers made a fumbling attempt to remove the rope. His fingers stilled, burning against her flesh; his tortured mind magnified the sound of the drums. Unbearably loud, they pounded in his ears like thunder. He felt as though he were already dying as his hands fell away. "I can't, Rebecca. You are the only being I have ever loved. I can't be the one to send you on your way."

"Seize that man!" Matthew Lorne's voice rang out in sharp command.

Avery struggled desperately with the two men who, at Lorne's command, had flung themselves upon him. With the strength of temporary madness he managed to break their hold. Even as he did so, he knew that it was too late to save Rebecca. She was walking toward Matthew. In some way that he did not understand, she had already freed herself from the torture. She moved on slowly, keeping pace with the drums.

Panting, his eyes wild, his face glistening with sweat, Avery reached the comparative security of the grove of trees behind the inn. Flinging himself down on the damp earth, he closed his eyes and tried to will himself to die.

Peering from between the trees, Polly Carter turned startled eyes to her mother. "John Avery," she whispered. "I wonder what he's doing here?"

Jane Carter looked at the prone man. "Couldn't bear it, I expect," she answered. "He was in love with her. Everybody knew it."

Jane was silent for a moment. Then, placing a gentle hand on her daughter's shoulder, she said in a low voice, "The kind of love Avery had for her ain't the sort to die. I expect he sees her as she was, not like she is now."

Polly looked at John Avery with pity and understanding. He was lying on his back now. Tears ran from beneath his closed eyes, and there was a look of suffering on his face that made her heart ache. She had never cared much for Avery, but now she saw him as a poor suffering man. He must have believed, as most of them had done, that Rebecca West was dead. What must it have done to him to find that she lived, and that now, not far from the place he lay, she was walking to her death?

A thoughtful gleam entered her eyes. "There's only Sir David and them two girls to stand against Matthew Lorne and that lot out there," she murmured. "We could do with another man, at that."

Polly had sensed her mother's uneasiness even before she spoke, and she was ready for it. "What wild idea have you got in your head?"

"Don't you think he'd be willing to lend a hand now? If he loves her like you say, he'd do anything to save her."

Jane's hand tightened on Polly's shoulder. "He might be, if he wasn't so broke up with grief. But I'd leave it be, don't you go doing nothing foolish. Sir David won't like it."

Polly smiled. "I think he will." Her smile turned impish. "I think he'll like it just fine. I'm going to speak to Avery. You just keep watch over Jamie, and leave the rest to me."

John Avery started as a voice address him. He opened his eyes and looked dazedly into the thin face of the girl who had spoken. Polly Carter. What was she doing here, and why was she bothering him? "Go away," he said in a choked voice. "Leave me be."

She sank down beside him and rested her weight on her heels. Looking into his furious suffering face, she said gently, "Not until I've had my say."

17

"It will soon be time to go, sweetheart." David looked into Shalada's tear-streaked face. "Don't cry for your mother anymore. Soon she will be passing the inn, and win or lose, we are about to make the attempt to rescue her."

Shalada was silent for a moment, then said quietly, "I cried for her suffering, and yet the strange thing is that she seemed to feel nothing. Did you notice that?"

"I noticed." David spoke almost curtly. Annoyed with himself, he stifled the stab of superstitious fear that the sight of Rebecca West's serenity had caused. He lived in an age of superstition, but he had never subscribed to it. He refused to do so now. A possible explanation occurred to him. "It might be, Shalada, that she willed herself not to feel pain."

Shalada stared at him, her smooth brow wrinkling. "Can that be done?" she asked.

"I have heard of cases." David tilted her chin with a lean brown finger. "And now you must will yourself not to be afraid."

Instantly Shalada's expression changed. "I am not afraid," she flared.

David laughed. "Ah, that's more like my wildcat. I see that my innocent remark has unsheathed her claws."

"Innocent remark, bah! You meant it, David Medway. You think of me as a spineless creature like Tasmin. But I am not, and don't you forget it."

"I promise, love."

Shalada looked suspiciously into his dark eyes. Then, seeing the smile in them, she amended wryly, "Well, perhaps I am a little afraid. But only a little." She put her hand on his arm. "David, can we really do it?"

David was silent for a moment; then he said gravely, "I won't lie to you, Shalada. We are about to take a very big gamble, and it might cost us our lives." He touched his finger to the tears on her cheek. "But on the other hand, we could get clean away."

Shalada smiled. "Whatever the outcome, we'll be together, my bully boy."

"That matters to you, Shalada?"

"Yes, David, it matters. I love you."

David looked past her to where a scowling but determined John Avery stood beside the quietly weeping Tasmin. "And don't forget," he said, his eyes returning to Shalada, "there is a new addition to our little force, thanks to Polly." Seeing the doubt that clouded her face, he added quickly, "Don't underestimate Avery. He'd do anything to save your mother."

The doubt cleared. "Then if you say so, I believe you. But, David, what of Tasmin?"

David frowned. "She's the weak link. She's liable to do anything. But no matter, we'll pull through."

Shalada put her arms about his neck and clung to him fiercely. "You'll kill Lorne. Promise me!"

He felt the molding of her body against his, the heaving of her breasts as her breathing quickened, and the readiness of his own response angered him. Looking into her dark imploring eyes, he pulled down her arms and thrust her roughly from him. "You want Lorne dead, Shalada, and so do I," he said in a harsh voice, "but spare me your seductive little tricks, for they will accomplish nothing. I'll promise you this: I'll kill Lorne, but only if it is in self-defense."

Shalada spat the words out bitterly. "Damn your vow to your mother. He is dangerous, you know that. We'll never be safe while he's alive."

David's grim lips softened into a smile. "Anger does not always become you, Shalada," he drawled. "At this moment you remind me of a spitting cat. And for God's sake wipe your face. Whoever heard of a weeping witch."

She glared at him. "Curse you, then." She scrubbed roughly at her face. "You'll see no trace of tears when I go out there, so you need not worry."

"I'm sure of it." David took her stiff figure in his arms and kissed her lips until he felt them soften beneath his; then once more he held her away from him. "It might help you to know this, Shalada," he said in a quiet voice. "I think Lorne will attack. If fate is with me, I will kill him. Does that satisfy you?"

The last traces of her anger vanished. Suppose fate were not with him? She could not bear to lose him now. She put her hand to his face, her fingertips softly caressing. "Don't take any unnecessary chances."

He took the caressing hand and pressed a kiss on it. "No unnecessary chances," he promised. "I have too much to live for." His tone changed. "Now, then, is it all clear in your mind? You will go out first with Tasmin. You will distract the people from my actions. You're quite sure you know what to say and do?"

"Of course," she said impatiently. "But suppose the people are not awed and frightened?"

David shrugged. "That is the chance we must take. I think, however, that for a little while they will be."

Shalada glanced quickly over her shoulder. "And Avery?"

David smiled at the recollection of the way the big man had come bursting into the room with the announcement that Polly Carter had told him everything, and he was ready to do anything that needed to be done. David fingered the hilt of his sword. "I almost ran him through when he charged into the room like a mad bull, and that would have been a pity. Avery, my love, is an unexpected gift."

His smile widened. "Though he does not particularly

care for the part I have assigned him, he will be beside you while you go into your little act. He will help to hold back those in the crowd who might turn ugly. In other words, he is there to protect you. And, Shalada, if I don't kill Lorne, I feel sure that Avery will. He tells me that he is pretty good with a knife."

Shalada nodded. "Always provided that Avery himself is not killed."

"True. That would be a pity. But Avery, so he tells me, has little desire to live." He saw the shock in her eyes, and he said gently, "Someday I will tell you his story, then you will understand." He took her hand in his. "Time to go, Shalada. Let's get on with it."

Shalada's hand was cold in his as he led her from the room. Despite her proud boast that she was not afraid, he knew that she was. Her fear was there in her strained face and in the trembling fingers he clasped. But Shalada would not break under the strain. He could rely upon her. Wanting to comfort her, he whispered, "It will be all right. I'll make it all right."

"You will?" Her head tilted in the arrogant way he was learning to know. "You are not the only one concerned in this, in case you have forgotten," she said in a hard voice. "You just look to yourself, and don't worry your head about me. I can take care of myself."

Angered, he said sharply, "Damn you! Do you never bend? I swear you don't know how to be a woman."

"I can bend, David," Shalada said in a changed and softened voice that was charged with meaning. "And I can be a woman too, when the time comes."

Going down the stairs, David refused to let himself dwell on the implication in Shalada's reply. He must concentrate on the job at hand. He would be lost if he began thinking of Shalada's soft and pliant body beneath his. Her limbs tangled with his as he entered her. His lips against her breasts. He thrust the picture from him. Behind him, he could hear Tasmin's quick, shallow breathing that spoke of her terror. Unlike Shalada, she might break. He did not trust her.

They reached the taproom, only to find it empty. The fire, built up to an almost dangerous height, crackled merrily in the huge hearth, the flames sending flickering shadows over the walls and glancing on and off the line of pewter mugs ranged neatly along the length of the scarred bar. The landlord, it appeared, had made ready for the anticipated custom, but he had succumbed to the temptation to join the milling throng outside.

Releasing Shalada's hand, David walked over to the door. Opening it carefully, he peered outside.

Ignoring Tasmin's stifled shriek, Shalada asked in a voice that quavered slightly, "Is it time, David?"

David shook his head. "Wait until I raise my hand, then you will go outside."

Sobbing, Tasmin sank to the ground. "I can't do it," she wailed. "I'm afraid!"

Avery grasped her arm and pulled her roughly to her feet. "Do as you're told, missy, and no arguments." He shook her slightly. "And you stop that racket, 'less you want me to land you one across your face."

Shrinking away from Avery, Tasmin stared into his stony face. Avery too had become a part of her terror. Tasmin glared at him with weak defiance. Both he and Sir David wanted her father dead. But her father should not die, she thought, as an idea penetrated the whirling confusion in her head. No, he would not, because she was going to warn him of his danger. For a little while she must pretend to go along with Shalada, but only until Sir David mounted his horse. Then she would scream out her warning. Somehow she would tear herself free from Shalada and force her way to her father's side. She would tell him of the plan. She would say that she was innocent of plotting against him, because Shalada, being a witch like her mother, had put her under a spell. Her love for him, proving to be stronger than Shalada's witchcraft, had broken the spell, and here she was at his side, where she always wished to remain. Her father would believe her, she was sure. He would not send her away, as he had threatened to do.

Unaware of the two men watching her, and of Shalada's hard suspicious look, Tasmin smiled through her tears as she imagined her father, his harsh voice gentled, saying to her, "Tasmin, you are my good and dutiful daughter. Had it not been for you, I should be dead by now. No, of course I will not send you away, for I could not do without you. You will take your mother's place in the household. You will stay with me until you find a husband." Tasmin's stiff body relaxed. It would be all right. She had been a fool to run away. That too had been Shalada's doing. Her father would understand this when she explained. He would realize that you could not blame someone who, through no fault of her own, had been put under a spell.

"David," Shalada said in an urgent whisper, "I don't like the way Tasmin is looking. I think she's up to something."

David stroked her worried face gently. "If she is, it's too late to do anything about it now."

Matthew Lorne's eyes were hot as he watched Rebecca's slow approach. He saw the slight smile on her lips, and his heart felt as though it would burst with rage. There was a dizziness in his head. Colors seemed to be meeting and merging to obscure his vision of Rebecca. The misty greens of the trees, the various hues of the gowns, the more somber clothing of the men, and even the color of the buildings about him. He blinked hard, bringing back into focus the hard gray glitter of the witch's trail and the slight erect figure of Rebecca. For a terrible moment he had thought he was somewhere else and she had once more escaped him. Sweat trickled down his face, and he felt that he might choke from the restriction of his high collar. He put up a shaking hand and tried to loosen it. He could not bear her calm demeanor, her silence, her damnable smile. He looked at her torn and bleeding

313

feet. The bright patches of blood she left in her wake were instantly absorbed into the porous grayness of the path, vanishing, eluding his eyes, as she herself had always managed to elude him. His heart gave a hard thump as he thought he made out a figure walking behind her. He narrowed his eyes, staring hard. The figure was there. It was misty, but he could see it. A sound escaped his lips as he recognized the figure. It was the satanic power who protected Rebecca West. "I see you," he said in a dry feverish whisper. "You cannot hide from my eyes, evil one."

The drummers nearest to Matthew Lorne, forgetting the stiff stance required of them, glanced uneasily at one another. The look on his face, the glare of his eyes, sent a chill through them. He was muttering something about seeing an evil one, imagining that someone other than Rebecca West walked the trail.

A voice cut suddenly and startlingly through the heavy silence that had fallen over the spectators. Loud and clear and strong, it rose above the subdued mutter of the drums. "Observe me, good people," the voice commanded. "All of you here know me as Shalada Lorne, but that is a lie put out by Matthew Lorne. He has told you that he is my father, but he is not. I am the daughter of Rebecca West. He has kept my true identity a secret because he did not wish you to know that he harbored a witch beneath his roof. You call him a holy man, but he has deceived you all. He is an evil man, a liar, and a murderer."

The drums had stopped. Rebecca stood very still on the path. The people had all turned from her and were gazing at Shalada as if spellbound. Tears fell down Rebecca's sunken cheeks. Shalada was doing this for her. But didn't she know that she could never succeed? Matthew Lorne would manage to convince them that Shalada lied. The people were afraid of him, too afraid to go against him. Rebecca's eyes widened as she saw John Avery come out of the inn and range himself behind Shalada. So John was in this too. She stole a look at Matthew Lorne's livid hate-contorted face. The sight of it drained away the strange peace that held her, for now she felt the burning, searing pain of her torn feet. But far greater than her pain was her fear for Shalada. She screamed out in desperation, "Stop, my darling, it can serve no purpose. You cannot help me."

Some people turned to look at the weeping, trembling Rebecca, but their attention was soon distracted as Shalada addressed them again. "Why does Matthew Lorne torture one witch and yet continue to keep another beneath his roof? Because he is evil himself. It is because he desires to mate with a like evil."

Rebecca hid her face in her hands. How could Shalada hope to help her by branding herself as a witch? How could she stand there and call herself evil? She shuddered as Matthew Lorne's voice roared forth. "She lies. She is my daughter, and she is no witch. Her wits have been affected by the sight she has seen here this day. Do not listen to her demented babbling."

Shalada laughed scornfully. "My power is so great that you cannot touch me. Have you not seen my mother walk the witch's trail without a trace of pain? I did that; I took the pain from her. You don't know your own danger. If I desired, I could send you up in flames where you stand!"

Watching from the window, David saw the people falling back from her, fear written plainly on their faces. She had their attention. She was holding them through their own superstitious fear. Inside, she must be as trembling and as terrified as Tasmin looked, but she would allow no trace of that fear to show. He smiled to himself. Listening to the ring of conviction her voice carried, he could almost believe her a witch himself. Keeping behind the concealing curtains, he gently eased the window up, praying that it would not squeak. He felt a rush of cool air on his face, mingled with the odors of sweating humanity. Matthew Lorne, he saw, still had not moved. The malignant hatred David had glimpsed earlier in the man's face had vanished. His lips were moving, but he appeared almost dazed.

"I will give you a further demonstration of my powers." Shalada's voice rang out, filling the taproom. "Tasmin Lorne, come forth."

Tasmin's heart lurched at the harsh command, and her fear mounted almost to a frenzy. She wanted to run away and hide. Anything, rather than go out there and face all those staring people. She imagined her father's cold green gaze upon her, and she shuddered convulsively.

"Get out there, Tasmin." David Medway moved toward her.

"I can't!"

"You can and you will!"

Shrinking from David Medway's threatening gesture, Tasmin knew with a sense of utter despair that she must obey. It will be over soon, she told herself. I will play this game only for a little while. Like a sleepwalker, her eyes staring straight ahead, she moved across the room and stepped through the doorway.

"You will be still now, Tasmin Lorne," Shalada commanded. "You cannot move. You will never move again unless I give you leave to do so."

A concerted gasp came from the captive audience. With their own eyes they saw Tasmin Lorne's sudden immobility. She stood before them all like a small frozen statue. Her eyes were unblinking, and there was a look in them like that of a trapped rabbit. It was that look that convinced. That look that told them that Shalada was a true witch who did indeed have power over the mind of the girl.

"Now you feel pain, Tasmin," Shalada's voice went on. "You are burning up with unbearable pain. Show us how much pain you are feeling."

Tasmin's mouth opened wide in a piercing scream. All her terror was in the sound she made. She knew she was only playing a part while she sought her chance to get away, but now hysteria seized her, so that it suddenly became real to her. Her body writhed, her fingernails tore at her face, she clutched at herself in agony, and her face flushed to a dusky red as her screaming went on and on.

The people stared from the screaming Tasmin to Shalada, and the same frenzied thought was in all their minds. This was a real witch, a terribly powerful witch. If they did not get away from her, then perhaps she would do as she had threatened. She would burn them to ashes.

"I ain't staying here!" a woman screamed out, "I'm getting to my home. Christ help me! God protect me from the powers of evil!"

The woman's screeching words ignited the others and started a stampede. With one accord they turned about, their only thought to get away from the aura of evil that emanated from the self-declared witch, and away from the menace of her great blazing eyes.

Shalada hid her smile of satisfaction. The people were fleeing, but there was still danger. Still the chance that they might calm down and realize that a clever trick had been played upon them. Or worse still, at any moment Matthew Lorne might recover from his seemingly dazed state. If he opened his mouth and bade the people return, would they obey? She could not take the chance that the power he had always held over them was greater than the fear she had put into their minds. She must carry on. She must help David. From the corner of her eyes she saw David jump lightly from the window. Saw him untie the reins and vault on Sam's back. Shalada shouted after the feeling people, "I wish you all to bear witness to my powers!"

The witch was shouting after them, but the people did not heed her words. They only knew that they must get away before her witch's arms reached out and grabbed them back. Screaming, shouting curses, the women sobbing with terror, they pushed and shoved at each other, even knocking each other down in their anxiety to get to the safety of their homes. Some babbled prayers, but still they fought to clear a way through the press of their frantic neighbors.

Through the hysteria that gripped her, Tasmin became aware that something was happening. Her screams stopped abruptly as sanity returned to her. Tears streaming from her eyes, her mouth slightly agape, she watched the mad melee for a moment. A flicker of movement caught her eyes, and she turned quickly. David had mounted his horse forcing the animal through the crowd in an effort to reach Rebecca West. Pushing Shalada away, she sprang forward. "Father," she shrieked, "stop him. He is trying to rescue the witch and kill you."

Shalada shouted a warning as she saw the frantic girl plunge straight into the path of the snorting, rearing horse.

Tasmin's eyes were fixed on her father's face. Why did he stand there looking as though he was unaware of what was happening? The shadow of the rearing animal loomed over her, but she did not notice. She did not hear David cry out to her to move. She made only the faintest sound as one of Sam's iron-shod hooves lashed out and struck her head. Blood spilled from the gaping wound as she fell forward on her face. Her body quivered once, and then she was still.

Matthew Lorne stared about him with dazed green eyes. He had not heard Tasmin's warning cry, had not seen her fall. Wrapped in a sense of unreality, he could hear nothing, feel nothing. His lips moved silently as he told himself that none of this was real. He often had nightmares and he was merely experiencing another one. Pain was burrowing deeply in his head now.

The sense of living through a nightmare dropped away from Matthew as he turned his head and caught sight of David Medway. Seated astride his big horse, Medway was ruthlessly forging a way through to where Rebecca stood. Now sounds rushed in on Matthew, hurting his ears. He heard the sobbing of a woman who had fallen across the trail, the babble of voices all about him, interspersed with screaming, shouting, and cursing.

Snatching his knife from its embroidered sheath, Matthew started forward. The pain in his head had receded to a dull throbbing ache now, and his brain was working clearly. Sir Marcus Medway, the man whose hanging he had arranged all those years ago, had had a son named David. From the moment he had met the tall, dark, arrogant Sir David in the seamstress's shop, he had been disturbed by something that had hovered just beyond his memory. Something important that he felt he should remember. Deep down in his subconscious mind he had really known, he told himself. Yet it was not until the moment that he and Sir David had faced each other across those open graves that recognition had sprung into his mind. Sir David Medway! So that was why he had been haunted by pictures of a beautiful desperate woman, a woman who spoke with a strong foreign accent. The heady odor of the scented rushes that had crackled beneath his feet as he turned from the woman and strode from the room. The fleeting glimpse he had caught of a small black-haired boy with wide, terrified dark eyes. White sands silvered by moonlight. Waves that frothed at the feet of dark brooding cliffs and sent up torrents of crystal spray. Gulls that circled and screamed. The tall dignified man who had stood beside the beautiful woman had been faceless to him until that moment at the graveside, as faceless as he had endeavored to make all his victims of the past.

Matthew's hand tightened about the hilt of his knife. The small boy with the terrified eyes had grown up now. He had come back to claim revenge for his father's death. Already he had taken Shalada and spilled his seed into her. It was Medway and Shalada who had arranged this elaborate hoax, and its purpose was to rescue Rebecca.

"Why do you want to help me?" Matthew heard

Rebecca say. Her eyes wide with wonder, she stared up at her would-be rescuer. "Who are you?"

David did not answer her at once. Rebecca West seemed to be completely unaware of the heavily breathing Matthew Lorne standing a few paces from them, but he himself was acutely aware of him. He saw the knife in his hand, the rage that twisted his features into the semblance of a demon's mask. Lorne would not let him ride away with Rebecca, he was sure of that. Don't let me be wrong, David prayed. He must try to stop me; this is the chance I have been waiting for. Touching his sword hilt to challenge Lorne, he smiled into Rebecca's anxious face. He leaned from the saddle and held out his hand. "You need not fear, Mistress West," he said gently. "Shalada sent me to you. Your daughter loves you and wants you with her. Nothing can stop us now."

The dark handsome face above Rebecca blurred. Shalada had sent this man to rescue her. Her heart swelled with love and pride and gratitude. Her years of suffering were as nothing when compared to this one glorious moment. For her sake, her darling child had deliberately courted danger. Rebecca had not turned her head or glanced his way, but she knew that Mathew stood close to them, and she was deathly afraid. Her trembling mouth firmed. She would not let Shalada down now by showing that fear. She put out a shaking hand.

Her hand clutching tightly at Avery's shoulder, Shalada fought her way through to the side of the trail. "David," she screamed, as she saw Matthew's hand rise, "watch out for Lorne!"

David ducked as the knife flew from Matthew's hand. Missing its target, it fell at Rebecca's feet.

"No you don't," Avery roared as Matthew stepped forward to retrieve his weapon. He held up his own knife. "I've got something for you, Lorne. "I'm going to slit your gullet." He stared into Matthew's eyes. "But I ain't like you, I'll give you the chance you never gave others. Pick up your knife. Defend yourself against me, if you can." He bulled his way forward. "Go on, you bloody murdering swine, pick it up!"

David drew his sword. "Don't worry, Avery. He'll get what's coming to him."

Matthew heard the clang the weapon made as it was withdrawn. The sound sent the pain grinding deep into his head again. That sound, the words the two men were hurling at him. He did not understand what it all meant. Frowning, he dug the fingers of his left hand into his temples. If only the pain would stop. Something frightening was happening to him. He jumped as David Medway spoke again. "You have a sword, Lorne, use it!"

Matthew put a trembling hand on the hilt of his sword. There were eyes upon him, staring. He didn't know these people. Why didn't they go away and leave him in peace?

Rebecca looked at the tableau before her. Matthew Lorne motionless, a strange dazed look on his face. John Avery clutching his knife, his face red and belligerent, his eyes bloodshot and glaring with hatred. Her rescuer, the dark, powerfully built man with the handsome face, a face that reminded her vaguely of Don Roberto. The handsome man's face was set now. His sword was held upward as he waited for Matthew Lorne to draw his own weapon. Last of all her eyes turned to her daughter. She was looking at the dark man. There was terror in her eyes, but such a shining look of love on her face that Rebecca's breath caught in her throat. Her daughter loved this man whom John Avery had called Sir David. Shalada must have her chance. Stiffly, Rebecca stooped down and picked up the knife lying at her feet.

John Avery's arm dropped. He looked from Shalada to David. "What's the matter with him?" he said uneasily, nodding toward Matthew. "He looks like he doesn't know what's happening."

"He's insane," Shalada said in a low voice. "You're

321

right, Avery, he doesn't know what's happening. I don't believe he even recognizes us."

David gave Matthew a long penetrating look. He saw the vacant face and the expressionless eyes. With an exclamation of disgust, he thrust his sword back into the scabbard. "He is insane. To all intents and purposes, he's a dead man." He looked at Shalada. "I wanted revenge. I think I have it now."

Rebecca did not hear them. The only thought in her mind was to secure the happiness of her child before Matthew Lorne could destroy it. The knife at her side, hidden from the view of the others, she said in a clear voice, "Matthew Lorne, look at me!"

Matthew turned slowly and stiffly. A light came into his dull eyes as his disturbed mind took another turn. He was standing by a gate, and the smell of springtime was in his nostrils. Coming slowly toward him was the most beautiful girl he had ever seen. So lightly did she walk that her small feet seemed scarcely to touch the daisy-studded field. "Rebecca!" he said, willing her to remember him. He had been away for such a long time that he was suddenly afraid. "I am Matthew Lorne, Rebecca. I have been away in London. Do you remember me?" He saw the pansy-soft eyes widen at his question, and he wondered why she looked so startled. Had he changed so much, then?

Rebecca closed her eyes momentarily. What was wrong with him? It was going to be harder than she had thought. She had not expected to see such tenderness in his cold green eyes. But it was for Shalada; she must remember that. She must not allow herself to be moved by him. He was an evil man. He must pay for the suffering he had inflicted upon so many innocent people. He was smiling at her now. "Do you, Rebecca? Say that you remember me."

"Yes," she answered him. "I remember you. How could I ever forget you, Matthew Lorne!"

Matthew was taken aback by the cracked voice coming from such a lovely mouth, but he continued to smile. He was still smiling when Rebecca drove the knife deep into his stomach.

"Mother!" Shalada sprang forward and caught Rebecca to her. "Oh, Mother, what have you done?"

"I did it for you." Weeping, Rebecca turned in Shalada's arms and hid her face against her shoulder. "You would never have been safe while he lived," she said in a broken voice. "He would have ruined your life just as he ruined mine."

Shalada soothed her. "Hush, Mother, don't cry. It is all for the best. His mind had gone, you see."

Avery watched as Matthew Lorne staggered back a few paces, his hands clutching at the knife in his stomach. Finally he crashed to the ground.

Unsmiling, David went to kneel beside the prone man. Turning him over, he looked for a long moment at the wide, staring eyes and the fixed smile on the lips; then he laid his ear against his chest. "He's dead," he announced. He rose slowly to his feet.

"David," Shalada said sharply.

David swung around swiftly. Shalada was struggling to support the sagging figure of her mother. In two strides he was beside her. "I'll take her."

Shalada stared at the frail figure lying in David's arms. Alarmed by the waxen white of Rebecca's complexion, she said in a shaking voice, "She's not dead, is she?"

"No, darling." David gave her a reassuring smile. "See, she's breathing. It's just a faint. She'll come around."

Abruptly Shalada broke into tears. "She's had so little happiness in her life. I want to m-make up to her for all she has suffered."

Avery came close. "David"—he held out his arms— "let me carry Rebecca, please. It's sort of my final good-bye to her."

David hesitated. Then, moved by the look on the man's face, he placed her in Avery's arms. "You know where to go," he said. "The horses are waiting, and

Polly is no doubt becoming anxious. Go on. We'll follow."

David put his arm about Shalada. Most of the fighting had stopped, he noticed. In the miraculous way that news travels, the people had become aware of Lorne's death. David's arm tightened about Shalada's shoulders. Would they understand that a trick had been played on them and attempt to block their escape?

The staring people made no such attempt. Without a word they parted to let them through. Some who looked after Shalada's departing figure wondered if she were truly a witch. Others, gazing at the dead body of Lorne, believed it to be unimportant. Witch or not, the true evil that had darkened their lives had died with Matthew Lorne.

18

Shalada awakened with a start. Some alien noise had jerked her from sleep, and for a horrified moment she had the feeling that she was not alone in the room. Still heavy with sleep, unable to orient herself to her surroundings, she lay there rigidly, listening. Then, as memory swept back, she smiled at her own foolishness and allowed her stiff body to relax against the wide, soft mattress. Of course, she was at the Duke and Drake Inn, the last stop before reaching David's home. Her mother, sleeping further along the corridor, was safe now. They were all safe from the menace of Matthew Lorne. It was small wonder that her imagination was playing tricks on her. They had all been utterly exhausted when they had arrived at the inn, and the little boy, jostled by the long ride, had been wailing fretfully.

Shalada turned over on her side. She could scarcely remember saying goodnight. Stumbling with weariness, she had reached the haven of her room, pulled off her clothes, letting them drop haphazardly to the floor, and then tumbled into bed. Even David had failed to occupy her thoughts for more than a second before unconsciousness had claimed her. Now, trying to will herself back to a sense of peace, she concentrated on David's face, but almost immediately the picture wavered and broke, reforming into those last terrible moments at the witch's trail. The staring people, the look on Rebecca's face as she drove the knife deeply into Lorne. Lorne's own face, his set, almost pathetic smile, the blankness of his eyes, from which the light of reason had fled. That smile! When death had claimed him, he had still been wearing it.

The candle, which she had left burning, guttered in the wind that blew through the wide-open window. Shivering, Shalada rubbed her hand over her chilled arms. If she were at all superstitious, she might think it was the unrelenting wind of Matthew Lorne's malevolent spirit blowing on her now. Quickly, she put the uneasy thought from her. "Nonsense," she said aloud. "I am not in the least superstitious, and Matthew Lorne is gone forever. He will never trouble us again, thank God!" She glanced at the billowing white curtains. "The wind is only a reminder that summer will soon be on the wane," she added firmly.

A soft laugh sounded, bringing Shalada upright in the bed, her heart pounding furiously. "Who is there?" she cried, her eyes straining to penetrate the shadows beyond the candle's frail circle of light. "Answer me."

"Certainly not Matthew Lorne, my sweet," David's voice answered. "As you have just said, he is gone forever." David stepped forward into the light, and the agitated beating of Shalada's heart, instead of calming, accelerated. "What do you want?" she cried out. "How dare you come into my room?"

"Sheath those claws," he answered, a faint, amused smile curling his lips. "I feel sure you were expecting me."

"No. And I ask you again, what do you want?"

"Now, what do you think I want?"

"I—I have no idea." Angry at the tremble in her voice, Shalada grabbed for the sheet and attempted to cover her nakedness. She gave a cry of protest as he tore the sheet from her grasp and tossed it to one side. "Stop it! You have n-no right."

"Haven't I? I believe you gave me the right. Remember?"

She shook her head. "I don't know what you're talking about." Finding herself unable to sustain his gaze,

Shalada's eyes dropped. He was so tall and powerful, so vibrantly alive, and she loved him so much. Why keep up the pretense? Why fight him, when her every inclination was to throw herself into his arms.

"Liar." David's strong fingers were beneath her chin, forcing her head up. "You made me a certain promise, and I have come to ask you to redeem it."

Her thoughts chaotic, Shalada's heavy lashes lifted. His eyes were dark and tender, and yet with a gleam in them that spoke clearly of his hunger to possess her. Shocked and afraid, she felt a responsive surge of longing flush her body, driving away the chill of the wind. "Go away," she whispered weakly.

David shook his head. "I love you, Shalada, I believe you love me. Must I remind you of your own words?" He waited, and when she failed to answer, he went on softly, "You said you would show me how much of a woman you are."

Trying to hold on, she flashed, "Yes, yes, I remember. But I also said that I would fight you if you attempted to take me against my will."

"And will you, Shalada?" His hands touched her gently, caressingly.

"I—I—" Suddenly weak, she fell back against the soft pillows and closed her eyes tightly. "I'm afraid, David. I have never—" Her voice caught in her throat.

"There is nothing to be afraid of, my darling, I promise you," David said softly, his eyes filled with the sight of her. The dark, satiny spread of her hair against the white pillow, the agitated movements of her full, rounded, pink-tipped breasts, the gentle curving of her hips beneath an incredibly tiny waist, and the shadowed mystery of her womanhood. "Shalada"—he dropped down on the bed—"I love you, I would never hurt you."

Shalada tensed as his hands began a gentle exploring. Her eyes flew wide as his lips touched her breasts, his tongue flicking lightly over her stiffened nipples. "No, David," she ventured in half-hearted protest;

327

then, startled by the tremendous force of feeling sweeping through her, she added in a shaken voice, "You must not do this."

Ignoring her, his lips gently suckled, moved away to travel lower, burning, searing, driving away the last shreds of her resistance. Her veins seemed to be filled with fire, her body a stranger to her, so much did it long for him. "David!" His name was a choked sound in her throat. Her arms crept up, clinging, holding him close, her traitorous body jerked convulsively as she sought to get even nearer to him. "Oh, David!"

"Shalada"—David's emotion-roughened voice came to her dimly—"even now I would not force you. Say the word, and I will leave."

She was beyond thinking, beyond reasoning. He was here, she loved him, she wanted him desperately. She arched upward again, flesh meeting burning flesh, pressing herself hard against him as though seeking to absorb him into herself. "Stay, my darling," she panted, "stay."

For a moment David was still, and she trembled with the fear that he would leave her. Then his hands, firm and masterful, were thrusting her legs apart. "Shalada, you are quite sure?"

"Yes, yes." Her head turned wildly on the pillow. "David, what have you done to me? I have never felt like this before."

"Hush." He entered her quickly, with a hard, firm thrust that wrung a small scream from her lips. "David," she whimpered, resentful of the pain. "It hurts."

"Not for long, darling, you will see."

The sharp pain was dying, giving place to a smarting that she could endure. She lay quietly, feeling the urgent throbbing inside her, her excitement and longing building again, inciting her on to a feverish pitch of desire that must be satisfied. "Please"—her quivering fingers touched him. "Please, David."

His movements were gentle at first, a slow ecstasy,

and then, when she thought that there could be nothing more than this, he began to move faster and faster, shaking her body with savage force, carrying her with him to an almost unbearable threshold of delight. Her wide-flung legs clasped him tightly, moved upward to his waist, higher still to circle his neck. She was burning up, she could surely endure no more without screaming. She cried his name aloud as, in a white-hot explosion, a last spasm almost seemed to tear her apart, and then she was sliding down from those nerve-shattering heights as her release mingled with his.

"Shalada, beautiful, wonderful Shalada!"

She smiled at him, sleepily content, her body languid now. "My darling, my own darling."

David's eyes worshiped her. "I love you, Shalada." He pressed his damp face close to hers, and she could feel the rapid beating of his heart. "You were right, you are very much a woman." His fingers tangled in her hair. "My woman."

Her lips teased the side of his face, her arms strained his panting body close. "Yours, David," she whispered. "Only yours."

Dawn was tinting the sky when he rose reluctantly to leave her, and now she no longer had any wish to sleep. "David"—her voice stopped him at the door— "will it always be like this between us? Will you always love me?"

"Always." He moved away from the door, came back to the bed to gather her in his arms. "Never doubt it, Shalada." His lips touched hers in a lingering kiss.

Below her window she heard the ring of footsteps upon the uneven cobbles, a man's sleepy, grumbling voice, and the clank of a pail. The inn was awakening to the customary round. Afraid of the renewal of passion his lips were arousing, she pushed him quickly from her. "Go now. Remember that we still have a long ride before us."

"So we do." Smiling, he looked deeply into her eyes.

"And we have a lifetime of loving before us." His fingers stroked her quivering breasts, touching the aroused nipples gently. "We can afford to wait for a while."

"But not for too long." She blushed, horrified at her own brazenness. Her eyes implored him to understand.

Laughing, he stopped to kiss her hot cheek. "No, my fiery Shalada, not for too long."

19

Seated on the wide window seat, Shalada looked about her discontentedly. The cause of her discontent was not apparent, for the room with its red and gold furnishings, softened now by firelight, was luxurious, the huge bed in the center of the room, in which she had spent so many restless nights, was wide and soft and deep, a bed that invited sleep, except that her increased longing for David had managed to drive sleep away. Turning her head, she listened to the soughing of the waves along the shoreline. It was a melancholy sound, she thought, and well suited to her present mood. Thrusting at the window, she pushed it wide, breathing in the salt-laden air, hoping that this would drive some of her tension away. Finished with her deep breathing, she grimaced. Her limbs seemed to be stiffer than ever in their refusal to relax.

Turning her back on the window, Shalada flopped back against the cushioned seat and stared up at the ornate, flame-flickered ceiling, letting her thoughts drift back. The wild flight from Waterford was well behind them now, and in the month she had been in David's home, the terror of that time had faded like a bad dream. Lady Sybilla, David's mother, after taking one look at her unexpected guests, could not seem to do enough for them. She pampered and petted, and constantly thought up new ways to make them more comfortable. Under this treatment, Rebecca had blossomed. Her gaunt figure was already beginning to fill out, she looked younger, and the shadows of fear and suffering had vanished from her eyes. She was happy; for the first time in many weary years, she was truly happy. If she ever thought of those last horrifying moments before Matthew Lorne had died by her hand, it was not apparent in her quiet and contented demeanor. Perhaps, Shalada thought, for her mother, too, her dreadful experience had taken on the fleeting quality of a bad dream.

Shalada pushed back her heavy hair, her mouth softening. At first Rebecca had clung to her, afraid to let her out of her sight. It was almost as if she feared her daughter would vanish, never to be seen again. Then, gradually, under the influence of unremitting kindness and the serene hours, she lost even that fear. Now her time was divided between doing small things for her daughter, chatting happily with Lady Sybilla, sewing on a sampler, and visiting with Polly Carter and her mother.

Like Rebecca, Polly and Jane Carter had blossomed under the new and happy conditions. Jamie, Polly's son, had recuperated quickly. Sun-flushed and healthy, he was already beginning to toddle. David, solicitous of the Carters' comfort, often visited at their cottage. He had become the object of Jamie's adoration, and the little boy could often be seen clinging to David's hand, smiling up at him, and gabbling his unintelligible baby speech.

Frowning, Shalada moved restlessly. David, so solicitous of the comfort of others, seemed to have no time for her now. Angrily, she faced the unpleasant truth. His attitude was the reason for her frustration and discontent. It was true that he was always pleasant and smiling whenever he found himself in her company, but it was not enough, not nearly enough. Tears sprang into Shalada's eyes, and she brushed them angrily away. How could he forget what had passed between them? He had told her he loved her, and even if it had been with her consent, he had taken her body.

Shalada scowled up at the innocent ceiling, aware of the very real pain in her heart. She loved David, and if he did not return that feeling, she would want to die. Her lip curled bitterly as she thought of the sincerity in his dark, handsome face when he had spoken those words of love. Had it all been a game to him, then? For certainly he had made no move to return to her bed. Perhaps he thought her a cheap and shoddy thing, lightly to be discarded.

She jumped to her feet, unable to bear her thoughts, unable to bear the pressure of clothes on her heated body. Anyway, it was almost time for bed. Stripping to her shift, she threw her clothes to one side and sat down again. She touched her aroused nipples beneath the thin material and tears crowded her eyes again. "Damn you, David Medway," she exclaimed, clenching her hands together. "Damn you to hell!"

"Not to hell, Shalada," a deep, drawling voice said from the doorway. "It would be too uncomfortably warm."

Shalada turned her head stiffly. David, clad in a red brocade dressing-robe, regarded her with a slight smile on his lips. "You! I didn't hear you come in."

"You didn't hear me the last time, either."

Color surged into her face. "Please don't remind me of that time," she said haughtily. "Do you intend making a habit of entering my room unannounced? If so, I don't appreciate it. Now please get out of here."

David laughed, his dark eyes sparkling with teasing lights. "What a welcome to give the man you love. But why such a shrewish attitude? Did I not tell you that it would not be long before we were together again?"

"Fool!" She glared at him angrily, hating and loving him at the same time. "How can you say it has not been long, when it has been more than a month?"

"Ah, love, you have been counting."

Staring into his eyes, she felt the surging of her pride, her only defense against him. "Go away, curse you. Leave me alone. I don't want you here."

David moved nearer to her. "But you do, Shalada. And you want me as much as I want you."

"Absurd! Perhaps I wanted you for a time, but no longer." She turned her head to one side, afraid that he might read her longing in her eyes. "I thought I loved you, but I have found out my mistake."

"Have you, my darling?" Seated there, her cheeks brightly flushed, her black hair tumbling about her slim shoulders, her body clearly defined beneath the thin shift, David found her maddeningly lovely. "I think you are lying."

"Conceited swine! I don't love you. How many times must I say it?"

"A thousand times, and I'll not believe you," David said, forcing himself to speak calmly. "Have done with this nonsense, Shalada. I will have you, even if I have to force you."

"How dare you!" She jumped up to face him, her hands clenched, her eyes blazing defiance. "Do you think you can do as you will with me, David Medway? You have neglected me, treated me as though I did not exist, and now you have the infernal insolence to come to my room to claim what I suppose you think of as your rights." Shalada's trembling hand groped over the small table beside the window seat, seeking the candleholder. Her fingers curling about the handle, she raised it menacingly. "Get out of this room. Get out, I say!"

"Shalada, my love," David said mildly, "if you are thinking of hitting me with that candleholder, I really wouldn't advise it."

Shalada backed away as he took a step forward. "I'm warning you. If you don't leave at once, I will—"

"You will what, Shalada?" David grasped her wrist and twisted it. "What will you do?"

The candleholder clattered harmlessly to the ground,

and she stared at it with tear-filled eyes. "I will kill you," she said in a weak voice. She rubbed at her wrist. "You hurt me, damned bully that you are."

"A little twist like that," David said lightly. "Bah! It was nothing at all."

"It was. You all but broke my wrist."

"Nonsense." Smiling, David held out his arms. "Shalada, if you do not come to me this instant, I will really hurt you."

"I'll do nothing of the sort." Her eyes flew to his smiling face. "Is there no end to your arrogance?"

David shook his head ruefully. "No end at all, I fear. Come here, love."

"No!"

"I say yes." He put his arms about her stiff body and drew her close against him. "What is this talk of killing me, vixen?" David said softly. "It would be a sad thing to harm the man you love, wouldn't it?"

"You flatter yourself. I have no feeling for you at all."

"You love me," David answered firmly, "just as I love you."

"You have a strange way of showing it, then." Shalada tried to maintain her hard, defiant tone, but she was having difficulty with her breathing, and she was weakened by the feel of him against her, the hard bulge of his desire that told her plainly that he wanted her. For how long? she wondered. A night, a week, and when he had satisfied himself, would he leave her alone for another endless time? The thought was unbearable. "Let me go." She jerked out the words with difficulty. "Oh, why must you keep up this pretense?"

David kissed the top of her head. "My darling, don't be so foolish. It was not my intention to neglect or ignore you. I thought you would understand that I was trying to be considerate. I wanted to give you time to know your true feelings."

"Time?" She pulled away slightly and looked up at

him. "But you are so very sure of my feelings, so why would you do a thing like that?"

He laughed. "Always suspicious, that's my Shalada. And no, I was by no means sure."

"Indeed. You were when you came into this room, or so you said."

"True. Tonight, when we were dining, I was sure."

"I—I don't understand." Flushing, she bit her lip in vexation. Why didn't he take his arms away? It was impossible to think when he was holding her so closely.

"I looked up and saw you watching me," David explained. "The look in your eyes told me everything I needed to know."

The flush stained her creamy skin again. She too remembered that unguarded moment when he had looked straight into her eyes. Her feelings for him had been showing plainly, and she knew it. The next moment he had been smiling at some remark of his mother's, and she had been relieved that he had not noticed. Now she knew that those dark, penetrating eyes of his missed nothing. Rage and humiliation battled inside her. Was he laughing at her?

"Shalada." David's voice cut into her chaotic thoughts. "Have you nothing to say?"

"You—you misread my expression."

"Have done!" His arms tightened about her trembling form. "You must know that I love you, despite my apparent neglect. Now let me hear you say the same to me."

Abruptly, hearing the unmistakable note of sincerity in his voice, she surrendered. "Then I'll say it." Her words were choked and difficult. "I love you, David Medway. Are you satisfied now?"

"Abundantly." Shalada heard his soft, triumphant laughter as he swept her off her feet and carried her over to the bed. Dumping her down unceremoniously, he scowled. "Take off that thing you're wearing. I want to see all of you."

Happily, her heart beating fast at the look in his eyes, Shalada drew the shift over her head and threw it to the floor. Watching David, the bright firelight flickering over him as he divested himself of his own clothing, she wondered about herself. Was she entirely shameless that she should feel such joy? Finding no answer, she laughed aloud as he lay down beside her. Shameless or not, she didn't care. She loved him, she wanted the feel of him inside her. "David." She touched his lean brown body. "Oh, David!"

"My Shalada, so beautiful, so perfect."

She tried to answer him, but the words were stilled in her throat. His hands moved over her body, trailing a path of fire. His lips burned on her mouth, her throat, her breasts, traveled lower, as they had done before. She gave a choked cry as his lips touched her womanhood, and then she was urging him on, her fingers tangled in his thick hair, her voice crying out his name. Her own hands came down, touched, fondled. Only with him could she know this ecstasy, for there would never be another man for her. Her legs opened wide to receive him, and this time his penetration brought no pain, only a heady joy. She had been made for these moments, she thought, as her body jerked with his in a savage passion that met and matched his own. He stiffened, and then she felt his shuddering climax deep inside herself. "David, David! How did I ever live before I met you? You are so wonderful."

His eyes smiling into hers, David withdrew gently. "It is you who are wonderful." Bending his head, he kissed her breasts lingeringly. "I knew all that fire and fury would make for a wonderful and passionate woman," he said huskily. Pulling her upward, he crushed her in his arms. "Tell me again that you are mine, Shalada."

Against his shoulder, her head nodded. "You must know it, David. Did I not give you the answer to that question at the Duck and Drake Inn?"

"Nevertheless, my woman of fury, I would have you repeat it. I will never grow tired of hearing you say it."

"Darling fool. I am yours, only yours."

"That's much better." Laughing, he lowered her to the mattress and settled himself beside her. They lay quietly for a long time, with only their quickened breathing showing the effect of body burning against body. Then, startling her, David took his arms away and sat up. "Let's go outside, Shalada," he said eagerly. "We will walk on the sands for a while." Meaningly, his fingers caressed her thrusting nipples. "When I make love to you again, it will be with the moonlight silvering that lovely body. Will you come?"

Her limbs felt fluid, there was a throbbing inside her that must be assuaged. "Yes, David," she breathed. "Oh yes."

Lady Sybilla, who was about to enter her room, turned sharply as the pair emerged. She took one look at Shalada's tumbled hair, the bright glow in her cheeks, the robe bundled roughly about her, and she knew what had happened. *"Madre de Dios!"* She turned shocked eyes on David. "What have you done, my son. What does this mean?"

Smiling at her, David touched her shoulder. "It means that I have taken what belongs to me, Mother." He indicated the embarrassed Shalada. "It also means that this somewhat unkempt lady standing before you is to be my future wife."

Lady Sybilla drew herself to her full height. "So I should hope, my son."

Shalada took a step forward. "My lady, I—"

"My dear, there is no need for words." Shock and dignity dropping from her, Lady Sybilla patted Shalada's cheek. "I cannot approve of what my son has done, but I am overjoyed with his choice."

"Thank you, Lady Sybilla."

"No more talk." David grabbed Shalada's hand.

"You come with me. I will see you later, Mother."

Lady Sybilla watched as they ran laughing down the stairs. "Shocking," she murmured. A smile touched her lips. "Most shocking."

About the Author

Constance Gluyas was born in London, where she served in the Women's Royal Air Force during World War II. She started her writing career in 1972 and since then has had published several novels of historical fiction including *Savage Eden* and *Rogue's Mistress*, available in Signet. She presently lives in California, where she is at work on her new novel.

Have You Read These Bestsellers from SIGNET?

☐ **THE MESSENGER** by Mona Williams. (#J8012—$1.95)

☐ **LOVING SOMEONE GAY** by Don Clark.
(#J8013—$1.95)

☐ **FEAR OF FLYING** by Erica Jong. (#E7970—$2.25)

☐ **HOW TO SAVE YOUR OWN LIFE** by Erica Jong.
(#E7959—$2.50)*

☐ **WHITEY AND MICKEY** by Whitey Ford, Mickey Mantle, and Joseph Durso. (#J7963—$1.95)

☐ **HARVEST OF DESIRE** by Rochelle Larkin.
(#E8183—$2.25)

☐ **MISTRESS OF DESIRE** by Rochelle Larkin.
(#E7964—$2.25)*

☐ **THE FIRES OF GLENLOCHY** by Constance Heaven.
(#E7452—$1.75)

☐ **THE PLACE OF STONES** by Constance Heaven.
(#W7046—$1.50)

☐ **THE QUEEN AND THE GYPSY** by Constance Heaven.
(#J7965—$1.95)

☐ **TORCH SONG** by Anne Roiphe. (#J7901—$1.95)

☐ **OPERATION URANIUM SHIP** by Dennis Eisenberg, Eli Landau, and Menahem Portugali. (#E8001—$1.75)

☐ **NIXON VS. NIXON** by David Abrahamsen.
(#E7902—$2.25)

☐ **ISLAND OF THE WINDS** by Athena Dallas-Damis.
(#J7905—$1.95)

☐ **CARRIE** by Stephen King. (#J7280—$1.95)

☐ **'SALEM'S LOT** by Stephen King. (#E8000—$2.25)

☐ **THE SHINING** by Stephen King. (#E7872—$2.50)

☐ **OAKHURST** by Walter Reed Johnson. (#J7874—$1.95)

☐ **COMA** by Robin Cook. (#E8202—$2.50)

☐ **THE YEAR OF THE INTERN** by Robin Cook.
(#E7674—$1.75)

*Price slightly higher in Canada

More Big Bestsellers from SIGNET

NAL/ABRAMS' BOOKS
AN ART, CRAFT AND SPORTS
in beautiful, large format, special concise editions—lavishly illustrated with many full-color plates.

☐ **THE ART OF WALT DISNEY: From Mickey Mouse to the Magic Kingdoms** by Christopher Finch. (#G9982—$7.95)

☐ **DISNEY'S AMERICA ON PARADE: A History of the U.S.A. in a Dazzling, Fun-Filled Pageant,** text by David Jacobs. (#G9974—$7.95)

☐ **FREDERIC REMINGTON** by Peter Hassrick. (#G9980—$6.95)

☐ **GRANDMA MOSES** by Otto Kallir. (#G9981—$6.95)

☐ **THE POSTER IN HISTORY** by Max Gallo. (#G9976—$7.95)

☐ **THE SCIENCE FICTION BOOK: An Illustrated History** by Franz Rottensteiner. (#G9978—$6.95)

☐ **NORMAN ROCKWELL: A Sixty Year Retrospective** by Thomas S. Buechner. (#G9969—$7.95)

☐ **MUHAMMAD ALI** by Wilfrid Sheed. (#G9977—$7.95)

☐ **THE PRO FOOTBALL EXPERIENCE** edited by David Boss, with an introduction by Roger Kahn. (#G9984—$6.95)

☐ **THE DOLL** text by Carl Fox, photographs by H. Landshoff. (#G9987—$5.95)

☐ **AMERICAN INDIAN ART** by Norman Feder. (#G9988—$5.95)

☐ **DALI . . . DALI . . . DALI . . .** edited and arranged by Max Gérard. (#G9983—$6.95)

☐ **THOMAS HART BENTON** by Matthew Baigell. (#G9979—$6.95)

☐ **THE WORLD OF M. C. ESCHER** by M. C. Escher and J. L. Locher. (#G9970—$7.95)
